Vendetta

Dreda Say Mitchell

HODDER

First published in Great Britain in 2014 by Hodder & Stoughton
An Hachette UK company

2

Copyright © Dreda Say Mitchell 2014

A CIP catalogue record for this title is available from the British Library

ISBN 978 1 444 78943 0
Ebook 978 1 444 78944 7

Printed and bound by Clays Ltd, St Ives plc

Hodder & Stoughton policy is to use papers that are natural, renewable
and recyclable products and made from wood grown in sustainable forests.
The logging and manufacturing processes are expected to conform
to the environmental regulations of the country of origin.

Hodder & Stoughton Ltd
338 Euston Road
London NW1 3BH

www.hodder.co.uk

This one is for Uncle Moses. What an inspiration you are! Thank you for being such a calming and fiery presence, always making everything possible.

'If you seek revenge, dig two graves.'
Chinese proverb

one

Pain.

Darkness.

Mac woke up in a place he couldn't remember. Black surrounded him, hot pain danced in his body. The pain brutally cut away inside his brain. A nasty taste sat at the back of his throat, metallic mixed with the flavour of death. He was on his back, lying on what he didn't know. He was still in his clothes. Navy T-shirt, washed-out black jeans, military-style lace-ups. Laid out like a corpse ready to be put six feet under.

Where am I?

His gaze darted around. Abruptly his eyelids snapped down in a protective, reflex motion as something bright hit the room. Cautiously he reopened his eyes. Realised what the brightness was – light coming in from somewhere outside. Just a sliver creeping through a crack in a curtain that was dark with dirt rather than its natural colour.

Curtains meant a window.

A window meant a room.

But a room where?

There was softness under his head. The fingers of his right hand felt what lay beside him. Waves of material.

Softness.

Material.

Lying down.

He figured out what he was laid out on – a bed.

My bed?

Am I back home?

No, his bed was harder. The mattress he was on was soft, as if sagging with the memory of too many bodies. Mac tried to lift his head, but it wouldn't budge, glued to the pillow beneath it. He raised his hand. Felt the pillow. Something sticky. Something wet. That scared him. Shook him up. Something wasn't right here, just wasn't right. Had to get up. He counted in his head, pulling in shots of deep air at the same time.

One. Two. Three.

Tried to move his head again. It wouldn't budge. His mind went into an automatic three-count again.

One. Two. Three.

Teeth clenched tight, neck muscles straining, he ignored the pain as he finally heaved his head up. Swung his legs over the side. Dizziness blurred his vision. His fingers dug into the bed as he fought to see clearly again. The room came back into focus. He touched his fingers to the left side of his head. Felt the skin. Uneven layer on the outside, mushy crater on the inside. The crater didn't feel big. He pulled his fingers to his face and sucked in his breath. Reddish-brown, scabby blood.

Did I fall?

Hit my head?

The skin on his forehead screwed up as he fought hard to remember.

Where am I?

WHERE THE HELL AM I?

He eased up, the pain wrapping tight around his throat. He

stumbled over to the curtain. Pulled it back. Light flooded the room. Morning light? Afternoon? He checked his watch.

7:02 a.m.

11. The number flashed abruptly in his mind.

Was something happening at eleven tonight?

He turned back to the room and faced total chaos. Overturned chairs. A sideboard pulled away from the wall. A wardrobe with its doors hanging open, like gaping jaws trying to scream. And blood. Blood everywhere. On the 70s-style wallpaper. The shabby carpet. A scarlet smear, lipstick-style, across the cracked dressing table mirror.

What the hell happened here?

He spotted his rucksack and hooded denim jacket. Started moving, but did it too quickly and toppled straight over. Landed on his knees, the pain slashing every nerve end in his body. He stayed like that, winded, drawing the stale air into his lungs. Then he crawled over to a chair lying on its side. Set it on its legs. Used it to struggle to his feet. Mac took his time as he put one foot ahead of the other. Reached his bag and jacket. Started with the jacket. Checked the pockets.

Wallet with cards.

Mobile.

Passport.

Two e-tickets for a flight to Cambodia.

Cambodia? Why am I going there?

He looked at the name on the first ticket. His own, John MacDonagh.

Checked the other ticket. Woman's name. Elena Romanov.

Elena.

Like a slap to the face, Mac remembered what he was doing here. Where *here* was.

Hotel room.

Room 19.

He'd told Elena to meet him here at nine. But nine in the evening. So if it was light now, a whole night had come and gone. So where was Elena?

'Elena?' he yelled.

Images of what he could remember flashed through his head. Downing the dregs of a whiskey in the hole-in-the-wall bar downstairs; taking the stairs instead of the lift to the third floor; opening the door to the room. And . . . nothing. He couldn't remember anything after that.

'Elena,' he screamed out again, the same time he noticed her bag peeping out of the wardrobe. The contents of the bling, red fake Gucci handbag were scattered over the wardrobe floor. With his mobile in his hand, Mac staggered towards it.

Empty purse.

Make-up.

Keys.

No mobile.

No Elena.

The pain came roaring back, so hard he thought his head was being severed from the rest of his body. He needed to find out what damage had been done to his head, so he swayed towards the bathroom. Thrust back the partially opened door. Flinched as the light beaming from the bare electric bulb caught his bloodshot eyes. It didn't look like the other room. Tidy, ordered, except for the blue shower curtain that was pulled around the bathtub. He headed for the sink. Stared at the wound in his head in the cabinet mirror. It was crusted with blood that had leaked and matted against his hair and cheek.

He rested his mobile on the shelf above the sink, next to a discarded shower cap. The veins in his forearm bulged as he twisted the tap. Splashed cool water over his face. Pulled the towel from the rail. Tore off a strip. Wrapped it around the wound. Then he eased on the shower cap to keep his makeshift bandage in place. He went back to the main room as he rang Elena's number.

Waited.

The dialling tone echoed in his ears. It rang. And rang. Then voicemail:

'*I'm not around at the moment. But I'll get back to you as soon as I . . .*'

He clicked off. Tried again. This time he noticed something strange about the sound coming through the phone. It had an echo like it was . . . He pulled the phone back from his face. Listened. He was right, it was coming from somewhere in the hotel room. He moved towards the wardrobe where he'd found her bag but the ringing got fainter. He headed towards the bathroom. The sound got louder. He stepped back inside the chilled room as the ring bounced loud and clear against the walls. Mac rushed towards the shower curtain around the bath. Loud ring.

Reached the outside of the shower curtain as the call went to voicemail. As Elena's sweet voice pulsed in his ear.

'*I'm not around at the moment . . .*'

His hand reached for the curtain.

'*But I'll get back to you as soon as I can . . .*'

His palm caught the material.

'*Please leave a message.*'

Swept it back.

The mobile slipped from his fingers. Instinctively Mac recoiled. There was something in the bath that he wasn't expecting to see. A body. Slumped over at the waist. Head snapped forward. Dark, neck-length hair, toned even darker in patches by something matting it together. He knew what that something was. Blood. What kept him rooted still wasn't the body; wasn't the blood-gelled hair. It was the tiled walls. White

tiles coloured with the scattered debris of human offal. Brains.
There was no smell, but his nostrils twitched with an imagined
gut-churning stench.

His mind started spinning again. What the heck was he
doing in a dead-beat hotel with a dead body? Should only
have been him and Elena . . . Elena. Mac's gaze slammed
away from the tiles back to the body. The blood iced over in
his veins.

No.

No.

No.

Couldn't be . . . He wouldn't allow it to be . . . He reached
for the body . . . stopped before he touched it. He couldn't
leave any fingerprints. Instead he tucked one hand into the
bottom of his T-shirt. Reached over with his covered hand
and touched the shoulder of the body. Pushed back. The body
slammed backwards. Mac gagged at what he saw – a bloody
mess where a face had once been. No eyes, no nose, no
mouth, no . . . nothing. The hair was a woman's, the clothing
was a woman's. The trousers were . . . Mac reared back when
he saw the mobile phone lying between the legs. Elena's
mobile, in its distinctive lilac protective case with the bunny
ears, soaked in blood.

But that can't be Elena. He shook his head. It couldn't be . . .
But the body's left arm proved him wrong. Just above the left
wrist was a small red star tattoo that he'd only ever seen on
Elena. The left hand rested flat against the stomach. And at the
wrist was the bracelet she always wore, with its fine, delicate
gold links and tiny bunny-rabbit charm.

'No . . .' He let out an agonised whisper as he sagged to
his knees by the tub, crippled by the thought of another
death that had devastated his life. His right knee hit the
edge of something hard on the floor. Mac looked down. A

gun. *His* gun. His Luger P8. Mac picked it up. An automatic reflex, he sniffed the barrel, confirming what he already suspected, that it had recently been fired. Had he done this? Had he killed her?

The sound of sirens ripped up the air outside the hotel.

two

Mac rushed to the bedroom window. Peeped outside. Police were gathering on the pavement and more cars were pulling up. Men in uniform looking upwards. Whispering to each other. He had no idea why. But he knew he had to go. Now. Make it downstairs before the cops got inside the hotel. He glanced over at Elena's bloody body. God, he wanted to take her with him, but he couldn't. But he could take one thing. He ran back to her body. Tucked both hands under his T-shirt again. Unclipped the bracelet from her wrist. Dropped it into his pocket.

Ran into the main room. Scooped up Elena's handbag and belongings and dumped them into his rucksack. Shoved on his denim jacket and grabbed up his bag in one smooth move. Flicked the jacket's hood over his head to hide the shower cap. Breathing hard, he opened the door. Sweat pooled down his face as he checked the corridor. Not a soul in sight. He left the room. Made his way to the top of the stairwell. Peered over the rail. It was a dizzy, three-floor drop, but if he leaned over, he could just catch the goings-on at reception. Not a soul in sight again. Most importantly, no cops.

Mac began to walk downstairs as casually as he could. He hit the second floor. The first floor. Was halfway down the final set of stairs when he heard the doors to the hotel swing open and footsteps below. Mac twisted around. Crept back up the stairs. The voices could be heard clearly above.

'Good morning. We're the police . . .' There was a brief pause while ID was no doubt being shown. 'We've had a phone call this morning from one of your guests. She says she heard a commotion in a neighbouring room last night, room 19 . . .'

Mac could almost hear the shrug of shoulders from the receptionist. The cop went on. 'And when she left this morning, she found what she thought looked like a bloody footprint outside the room. She says she alerted you but you didn't seem very interested. We'd like to have a look at this room, please.'

Mac tensed. How the hell was he going to get out of this?

The receptionist asked, in a foreign accent, bored, as if she'd been asked this question too many times in the past, 'Commotion? Blood? This is just silliness. Have you got a warrant?'

'No, we haven't got a warrant – are you saying we need one? That you're not willing to help? Are you sure about that . . . ?'

Silence. Then the cop continued, 'OK – have you got a key for room 19?'

Mac thought fast. Safest thing to do was to carry on as if nothing was happening. Walk down the stairs, out through reception, past the cops all nice and innocent. He hitched the handle of his rucksack higher on his shoulder as he pulled himself off the wall. Took two steps to reach the top of the stairs. Stopped. Then he took the first stair; already he looked like a fugitive. He had a clear view of the people below. Three cops. All male. Two uniforms, the other plainclothes. Female receptionist next to them with a half-gone ciggie between her fingers. She moved, accompanied by two of the policemen.

They turned towards the stairs.

Mac took the next step.

They reached the bottom of the staircase.

Mac's foot hovered over the next step. He let it fall.

The receptionist climbed up ahead of the police, smoke drifting out of her mouth.

Mac watched the top of her bleached blonde hair as he took a step. Then another.

The tops of the cops' heads came into view. They were both looking down so they hadn't spotted him yet.

The cigarette smoke floated up towards Mac. Stung the inside of his nose.

Just one more step and the receptionist would definitely see him.

One of the policemen abruptly stopped. Crouched down to inspect something. 'This could be blood'. Turned his head and called out to the uniformed cop left in the reception, 'Make sure no one leaves the building . . .'

Mac rapidly retraced his steps towards the higher floors. Kept going. And going. Adrenalin and his head wound made him giddy. He reached the top floor. And froze. Waited to hear footsteps. Then he heard them, somewhere not too far below. Mac kicked back into gear. Knocked on the door of the first room he came to.

'Room service,' he said in a low voice.

No response. He tried the handle. *Shit.* Locked.

He kept up the pattern of 'room service', shoving down the handle of each room he came to. But they were all locked. It was going to be game over if he didn't get into one of these rooms soon.

There was one room left. Room 28. The door was flung open after he called out 'room service'. In the doorway stood a woman, middle-aged, with hair a sleek black that matched her spikey false eyelashes, body-hugging leather top and trousers, and hands jammed, fuck-you style, on her hips. Before he could speak she spat out, 'Room service? In this fleapit? Piss off mate, I've got work to do.'

She slammed the door in his face.

Below there was the sound of a key turning in a lock and the sound of heavy feet filing into room 19.

It was too late now for Mac to go downstairs; there was nowhere to hide upstairs. He looked upwards. Ran his gaze along the ceiling. There had to be an attic somewhere. Even a skylight. But where? Where?

He went to tap on the door of Room 28 again but thought better of it. Instead he tried the handle. In her eagerness to get back to work, the woman had left it unlocked. The woman looked round in shock when Mac entered. She opened her mouth but it snapped shut when Mac flipped his jacket back, displaying his Luger. She backed into the room while he clipped the door shut with the heel of his boot. 'I'll be in and out of here quickly so that you can get on with your business.'

Her business was an overweight man, spreadeagled and tied to the posts of the bed with a Union Jack-patterned hood over his head. He looked back at the woman and saw what he should have seen the first time he clapped eyes on her – the hard face of a woman who'd been turning tricks for a long time.

She hissed at him, 'What do you want?'

'I want to know how to get into the attic.'

'The *attic?* Look mate, if you're looking for money or drugs, I can't help.'

Mac walked towards her, but she stood her ground. But instead of stopping when he reached her he carried straight on past. Didn't stop until he reached the bed. She let out a gasp when he pulled out the gun and aimed it at the head of the hooded man.

'A dead punter is bad for your business. And your DNA will be all over the body, condoms or no condoms . . .' Mac shook slightly as his own words echoed around his head.

The man on the bed began bucking against his bonds, making muffled sounds.

'You know this hotel, so stop dicking me around and tell me where the attic is.'

She looked at the Luger. Looked at her customer. Back at Mac. 'There's a storeroom at the end of the corridor. You can get up to the attic through that. I've seen the owner doing it.'

'Get his wallet,' Mac said, gun still fixed on the other man.

The prostitute rushed over to the man's clothing on the seat of a chair and rifled through his jacket. She handed Mac a tan-coloured wallet.

Mac shoved the wallet into his pocket and said to the man, 'If the cops come knocking, you say nothing. You might think that you can make a deal with them so that nice wife of yours at home won't find out about your out-of-office-hours activities.' He didn't need to ask if the man had a woman waiting for him at home; his type always did. 'But I've got your wallet, which means I've got your name, which means I can find out where you live. If I get to hear you've been opening your mouth, one morning your wife's going to get a small package. Inside that package will be your wallet with a little note about what you've been doing when you said you were working hard to support your family.'

Without another word, Mac headed for the door. As he opened it, the woman called out, 'Hang on, you can't take his wallet, I haven't been paid yet . . .'

Mac put the gun away. Closed the door. The storeroom door was white and flush with the wall, explaining how Mac had missed it earlier. But now he had no problem prising it open and switching on the light. Small, littered with paint pots, old carpet and mattresses. And resting against the wall was a step-ladder, which led up to a trapdoor with access to the attic. He closed the door behind him. Climbed up the ladder, his bag bumping against his back. As he went up and opened the attic door, he heard voices and footsteps in the corridor outside.

'Get everyone out of these rooms and make them assemble downstairs.'

'Yes sir.'

'And you – are there any other rooms up here?'

The receptionist's voice told him, 'Yeah – there's a store-room and an attic upstairs, but we don't use them much.'

Mac scrambled up into the attic. Pushed inside. Caught the trapdoor and gently eased it back into place so it made no sound. The place was dark, so Mac used the torch on his mobile to check out the space. He found an old tea chest that he moved over the trapdoor so that it couldn't be opened from below and then he examined the roof. No skylight. He was trapped. And now he could hear voices below him in the storeroom.

Mac carefully examined the roof, through which he could see occasional chinks of sunlight. He reeled back in surprise when he kicked over a bucket that had been catching rainwater and sent a couple of gallons of water spilling out over the floor. Down below he could hear the voices of the police becoming more urgent. Standing on the sodden floorboards, with the silence of a thief, Mac began tearing away at the damp and moulding lining of the roof where the rotting wood strained under the weight of the slates above. Someone started pushing and then banging against the other side of the attic door.

three

It was only a matter of time before they got in. Mac kept tearing and pulling until he was through to the cracked and loose slates themselves. Pulled them off. Laid them to one side, one on top of the other. Flushes of fresh air blew into the musty attic and oblongs of daylight began to appear.

Behind Mac, the noise against the door stopped.

Silence.

Bang. The battering against the door started up again, stronger this time. A brief shaft of light from below appeared before the tea chest forced the door back down. Mac threw his bag out onto the roof. Gathered together the slates and put them on the roof, outside the hole he'd made. The attic shook as the police kept up the pressure, trying to force the trapdoor. Mac arranged paint pots on top of each other and used them as steps to climb up through his newly created exit.

Gusts of wind, after the rank air in the attic, caught Mac like a stiff drink. He gasped slightly as he carefully sat down on the unsteady roof. Then he put back the slates, using the sodden moss lying around to hold them steady and fill in the gaps through which daylight shone. As the last slate fell into place, the noise from the attempt to break into the attic below faded and became muffled. Mac crouched on the roof, which was littered with bits of pottery, weeds, old TV aerials and bird droppings. He clung to the hope that the frantic activity on the street below would mean no one would look up – in the same way he clung to the tiles.

He knew this street. He'd made it his business to check all streets and buildings before he used them, in case of an emergency, and this was just such an emergency. As carefully as he could, swaying sometimes in the wind, he began to thread his way over the roof. But should he look up or look down? He kept his head down, watching for loose or broken tiles, of which there were many. From time to time a piece of slate would come loose and tumble over the guttering before cracking in the courtyards below, but with the pulse of traffic, shouting and voices on the street where Elena's murder had taken place, the crashing slates went unnoticed. He was a good thirty-five to forty feet from ground level. He knew the rule. Don't look down. But he broke the rule, as people always do. He felt the long drop below deep in his stomach. Fall from this height and he was a dead man.

Mac stayed steady, keeping a sure foot, with only pigeons perched on chimney stacks to witness his escape. He crossed five roofs until he reached another building. No skylight, so he moved on to his next target. Two roofs further down the street. He kept moving until he finally saw the outline of a skylight.

And that's when Mac really should've been looking up, because two pigeons flew out of nowhere near his head. He arched back. Tried to control the wobble in his legs. His feet slipped away from under him. His body slid down the roof towards the concrete back yard below.

four

A nail tore through the flesh of his hand. Mac's head bent back at the pain. Desperately he tried to grab hold of anything that might break his fall, but it was like catching an eel. His head caught the metal guttering; with a supreme effort, he tried to jam his foot under the eaves while using a flailing arm to hook his elbow onto a rusty aerial that had fallen from a chimney and was hanging from black wiring looped over one of the stacks. Feet dangling, he broke his fall. He looked down at the dizzy drop to the bone-shatteringly hard ground below. He swung his legs up. Got back into position. With bloodied and bruised hands he crawled towards the skylight.

Peered in through the dirty, smeared and opaque glass – a landing with no one on it. He fished around in his bag and found a nail file among Elena's stash of make-up. Used it to scrape away the wood round the lock, which, like most of the fittings on this street's buildings, was rotten and decayed. He applied pressure. The skylight lifted up. Mac leaned in head first and listened. No one around. He dropped his bag onto the well-trodden carpet below. Lowered himself. He hung suspended, the tendons in his arms so stretched he thought they would snap. Let go. Dropped into a neat body roll. Wiped his hands and knew that his calculation had been correct. This was another one of the street's seedy hotels.

He picked himself and the bag up and walked smartly down

the stairs to reception. The area was empty. Mac banged the bell and two people emerged from the doorstep out front where they'd been watching the police at work and wondering what all the fuss was about.

One spun slowly round in a wheelchair. A bony, older woman, with the last remnants of beauty fading from her skin, her eyes hidden behind a pair of Catwoman-style sunglasses.

'Can I help you?' she asked, wheeling herself towards the back of the reception desk.

'I'd like a room please.'

He could see she was baffled as to how he'd appeared in her reception without her noticing, but she kept those types of questions to herself.

Instead she asked, 'How long for?'

'One night should be enough. And can I have a room facing the street?'

'Facing the street?'

Mac looked away from her face; even though he couldn't see her eyes, that stare of hers seemed to know too much.

'Yeah, I'm afraid it's a tic of mine. I have to be facing the street . . .'

The woman asked no more questions. Mac paid in cash. She made him sign the register. Passed him an old-style key. Room 26.

five

Door closed behind him, the first thing Mac did was to put the TV on. He wasn't even aware of doing it, just one of those automatic survival reflexes he had when entering a hotel room. One of the top ten rules of his job was to make sure the world never heard what you were doing by masking your activities with noise. He hiked the volume up slightly. The TV was showing a documentary, *It Happened in 1979,* and on the screen were Russian tanks grinding through mountains, unhappy soldiers mounted on the back as they invaded Afghanistan.

That's when Mac felt the tremors in his body. The blood and bones shaking in his legs. Suddenly the room around him hazed over. His vision blurred. He blinked. Blinked. But that made it worse as the room around him moved, swayed. Or was it him that was tilting?

Blink.

Blink.

He could barely see. Not now. He had too much of the present to torture him. He didn't need the past as well. No . . .

Flash.

The Luger was in his hand. Primed, loaded, his finger a hair's breadth from kicking back the trigger. And there she was, looking up at him from the bath. Elena. Her eyes, usually so soft, bulged with hard fear. Her mouth moved with words he couldn't hear. The air froze around him. He levelled the 9 mm at her face. Elena's mouth widened, stayed open, with the bellow of a scream he wouldn't let reach his ears. His finger jacked back . . .

Mac's mind came crashing back into the hotel room. He was no longer standing, but backed up against the wall, on his haunches, in the pose of a dog that had been beaten down. His breathing spurted out, echoes of the horror of the flashback. But was it a flashback? Could he believe what his mind was telling him? He'd suffered too many false flashbacks this past year to trust what his mind told him. Had he murdered Elena? That had been *his* gun near her body.

Elena's dead. Elena's dead. And you killed her.

six

Bile rose high into his throat. Gagging, Mac staggered up and bolted into the one place he didn't want to be, the bathroom. He heaved and heaved into the toilet bowl. Then wiped his lips as he slumped onto the cold tile floor. He didn't believe what the evidence was plainly telling him. Why would he do it? Why would he take the life of the one person he'd come to care for this last six months? The only answer he got was the ache and twitch of the wound in his head. A wound he suspected Elena had inflicted when she'd tried to defend herself. Shit, he couldn't blame her. If someone had attacked him, he'd have done everything and anything to rip them apart. But Mac still couldn't believe what his mind was telling him was true. No, he'd had flashbacks before, the type of flashbacks that were only reality in his head.

The ring of his mobile inside his jacket brought his thoughts to an end. He pulled out the phone. With it came the bracelet he'd taken from Elena's body. He fingered the tiny rabbit charm. One afternoon, after they'd made love, she told him it had been a gift from her father. The small rabbit in memory of her favourite Russian nursery rhyme her father would tell her as a child. A story about a hunter shooting a rabbit. He'd told her that didn't sound like the type of happy tale grown men told their daughters. She'd smiled, as she whispered, her heated breath brushing his lips, that it had a happy ending. But he never found out what that ending was because she'd kissed him.

Mac shook the memories back as he dropped the bracelet back in its hiding place. Stared back at the phone. He didn't answer it, just stared at the screen. It displayed 'Tom'. 'Tom' meant Phil Delaney. And what the hell was he going to tell him about this mess? Mac gave it a half-minute before he unlocked his phone and hit the Messages icon. Three unopened voicemails, two from last night, one from fifteen seconds ago, all from Phil. He listened:

'*Mac! Where are you? You missed our evening meeting.*'

'*Mac, where the fuck are you? Call me.*'

'*Listen – try and get me a message, any way you can. If I have to come looking for you . . . Well, you know what that might mean.*'

Yeah, he knew what that meant all right, but he couldn't think about Phil now. As he started to turn the mobile off, it pinged. Text message, but not Phil this time:

'*Friends. Please be reminded. My beloved son is six today. His celebration is at one p.m. Please be welcome and he looks forward to seeing our honoured friends.*'

Awkward English. Dangerous man. Reuben. The leader of the gang he'd been in for the last nine months. Both Phil and Reuben should have been history by now. Elena and he should have been long gone. And what were Reuben and Phil going to do when they found out about Elena?

Mac pulled himself up and walked over to the window to check out what was happening with the cops on the street. All the trappings of a murder investigation were falling into place. Police cars, some plain, some with their flashing blues-and-twos lights going, pulling up; blue and white tape across the street; uniformed officers standing guard. His fingers stilled as he saw a black woman getting out of a car. Tall, with quite a body on her, she was done up in the full regalia of a party girl. She seemed to get into a fast-paced verbal battle with the uniform behind the tape.

'I've already told you once to step back,' the uniformed police-man said as he shifted his body in front of the black woman to stop her getting past the 'Do not cross' crime-scene tape.

The woman was decked out in gold heels that matched her moon-shaped earrings, miniskirt, jeans jacket over a sparkling boob-tube top. Her glistening brown legs long in contrast to her mini finger-combed 'fro.

'I don't think you understand,' she threw back, shifting one hand onto her tilted hip. 'I'm . . .'

He cut her off as he pushed his face into her space. 'I under-stand all right. This is where you bring your customers . . .'

'Excuse me?' Her head reared back, making her earrings dance in the early-morning air.

'I said move it along before I arrest you for soliciting . . .'

'What the hell is going on?' Another voice joined them.

The uniformed policeman turned to find a young, plain-clothes detective behind him.

'Nothing sir. I'm taking care of this.' He waved his hand at the woman. 'I'm just informing this . . . uh . . . *woman* that the hotel is not open for *business* . . .'

The detective looked back at him, his mouth dropping open slightly, but before he could say anything, the woman got there first.

'I'm black, dressed like this, so I must be a working girl. Is that it?' Her blunt, dark gaze hit the uniformed cop straight in his face. She reached inside her jacket as she continued, 'I'm a working girl all right.' She flashed what looked like an open wallet in his face. 'And get an eyeful of my sexy bit of bling, which my punters just luurve.'

The uniformed cop swallowed as he read the name inside The Met Police badge in front of his face.

Detective Inspector Rio Wray.

seven

'Great . . .' Mac whispered bitterly.

The one cop he didn't need on his back was DI Rio Wray. If she was the woman in blue heading up Elena's murder, he was in big trouble. But the longer he sat here doing fuck-all, the more time Wray had to nail his arse. He needed to sort out his wound and then get the hell out. He strode to the mirror above the sink. Made himself stare at his reflection. Pale skin with a coat of grey, chestnut hair spiked in the middle with sweat-darkened strands stuck to his forehead and blue eyes deepened by a bleakness he found hard to comprehend. He gazed at the wound. It sat just over his left temple. And its shape . . . Mac's heartbeat clicked into a double beat of disbelief as he stared hard. Pushed his head closer to the mirror. If Elena had defended herself when he'd attacked her – if he'd attacked her – the wound should have been scratch marks, the remnants of bruising from repeated slaps and punches. But it wasn't. It was irregular, deep, more like a ditch, skin and some hair missing above the corner of his left temple. He'd seen that same wound once before, on a man he'd worked with one time. A bullet had whizzed across the skin of the lucky bastard's forehead, cutting deep but not penetrating. Mac knew what he was staring at – a gunshot. In his line of business he knew all about bullets and guns. No doubt about it – someone had tried to blow his brains out.

And that someone had murdered Elena, which meant that he hadn't killed her. Had he? No, he affirmed in his head. He hadn't done it. He had no reason to do it. But someone else obviously had.

Who?

The single question bounced around Mac's mind as he poured the bottle of miniature vodka from the minibar over his wound. He gritted his teeth, holding the burn of pain back in his throat. He needed to repair the damage done to his head, even though he wasn't sure how much damage had been done. If he went to an A&E he might as well walk into a police station holding a placard stating, in bold, black print, '*I was in room 19 at the Rose Hotel.*'

As Mac searched the shelves above the sink, he realised that he'd been the victim of a variation on a classic set-up. A deadly frame-up that starts out sounding like the beginning of a joke:

What happens to three men who walk into a room?

One gets bashed on the back of the head and wakes up hours later.

The second man is murdered.

And the third . . . well, who knows what happens to him because he's long gone after leaving a glaring piece of evidence that points to guy number one having murdered guy number two.

The variation, Mac suspected, in his case, was that he hadn't been bashed over the head but shot, left for dead. But with a bullet that had marked him but not lodged inside his body.

He kept searching through the contents of the shelf while trying to imagine who would want to set him up. But the list was too long. There were too many people. Body wash. Soap. Moisturiser. Shower cap. Another bar of soap. A small package. He picked the package up. Flipped the top up. Tiny needle and white thread. He pulled them out. Doused each with alcohol. His hand shook as he started to thread the needle. The eye was small. He couldn't get the thread through. He tried again. And again. Got it through on his fifth attempt.

He tilted his head. Jabbed it in. His body heated up as he tried to push into the flesh. But his fingers slipped and slid against the liquid inside the open wound. A tremor started at his wrist. Flew up his hand until his fingers shook like those of a seasoned drunk. He tried to catch the needle in the skin again, but his hand trembled with a mind of its own. Angrily Mac yanked the needle out. Threw it in the sink.

His rage boiled over. He picked up the stool near the sink and hurled it at the mirror. The glass cracked down the middle. The stool crashed to the floor, one of its legs breaking on impact. Violence pumping out of him, Mac marched into the main room, continuing his destructive rampage. He kicked the wardrobe door, toppled the bedside cabinet onto its side. Yanked the bedclothes in one vicious move from the bed. On and on he went, punching and kicking. He only stopped when his head was back, pounding in pain. He slumped to the bare mattress on the bed with his head cupped in his hands. He could deal with all the shit that had happened to him, but the one thing he couldn't live with was the guilt about Elena's death. If it weren't for him she'd be alive today. And if it weren't for the gunman who'd pulled the trigger. And whoever that bastard was, Mac was going to kill them. He was quite sure about that.

Who?

Mac came back to the single question again. There were plenty of people in his line of work who might want him dead, but why kill Elena? The more he thought about it, in as far as he was thinking at all, the more he felt that the only man who could have had a motive and could have tracked them down was Reuben.

Mac pushed his head up. Tried to calm down. Pulled oxygen into his bloodstream. His wound was going to have to wait. Now in control, he got up again and went back to the bathroom. Picked up the torn piece of towelling and wrapped it back round his head. Returned to the other room. Mac needed to find out as much as he could about what had happened to Elena before he went anywhere near Reuben. And he possessed the one thing that might give him the clues to find out more – Elena's phone.

Back inside the main room, he pulled out the lilac, bunny-backed mobile. Switched it on, but that was as far as he got. It was covered by a password that Mac didn't know. Elena had been the communication and techy person inside Reuben's gang, which probably meant she had one of those complicated sequences of four-digit numbers for a password. But that didn't faze Mac; he knew what most people didn't – digital gear was usually the easiest type of equipment to uncover a password from. There was nothing fancy to it, no clever hacking needed. What most people never realised was that their mobile phone screen clearly showed the pattern of their fingerprints where they tapped their password number on the screen.

Mac studied the black phone screen. Estimated where the numbers would be positioned. Then switched on the side light above the bed. Held the phone up to the artificial light. Fingerprints. They were smudged, but they were there. He estimated the unseen number they lay over.

1

2

3

4

7

0

Mac stopped, realising that there were six fingerprints in

total, two more than should've been there. He let out a low, irritated puff of air when he realised that his fingerprints were there on the screen along with Elena's. Why hadn't he picked up the phone with the edge of his T-shirt or the towel? No way did he have the time to find out a four-digit combination using six numbers.

But he gave it a try.

1708.

The phone remained locked into place.

1270.

2347.

7432.

His finger kept tapping away, but the phone wouldn't open. He kept tapping. And tapping. His head started screaming again. He almost threw the bunny-backed mobile across the room. But he didn't. He had to get access to Elena's phone. He didn't know how. But he knew a man who did.

A man who was either going to help him or slam the door right in his face.

eight

'OK, OK, calm down and tell me what the problem is,' Mac told Elena over his mobile.

But she didn't calm down. She got worse.

'It's happening tomorrow night.'

'What's happening tomorrow night?'

He heard her voice shaking with fear. 'At eleven . . .'

She was hysterical, her terror vibrating down the line.

'Deep breaths baby, deep breaths – that's it. Now tell me what's going on tomorrow at eleven?'

'I'll be killed, we all will . . .' She paused.

That stunned him like a power-punch to the throat.

'Who's going to kill you?' No response. 'Who, Elena? Who's he? Tell me.'

'You've got to get me –us – out of here before tomorrow night.'

'Us? Who else is involved in this?'

'Please.'

'Meet me now . . .'

'I can't. It's going to look strange if I just leave . . .'

'Fuck that . . .'

'No.' Her ragged breathing shook in his ear. 'Let's meet later. The hotel next to the one we usually go to . . .'

'No, Elena, I'm not dicking around with your life. Get here now.'

'I'll be there tonight. At nine. I'll text you the room number.'

'There's nothing to be scared of. I'll protect you . . .'

'You don't understand . . .' Her voice kicked higher. 'I'm not scared just for me . . .'

She bit her words back.

'Who else are you scared for Elena? Who are you talking about?'

'I'll tell you tonight. But Mac, we've got to get out of here. Book a flight anywhere. Brazil. Cambodia . . .'

'Stay calm. If anyone even looks at you the wrong way, I will . . .'

'Don't say it,' she pleaded.

'I'll kill them.'

nine

8 a.m.

'All right mate – where we off to?'

The sound of the cab driver's voice snapped Mac back to the present and away from the last conversation he'd had with Elena. He sat in the back of a cab, the line of his spine soaked with sweat. He couldn't get the sound of her voice out of his head; it was like she was whispering in his ear, right there now, next to him in the cab.

The cabbie half twisted in the front seat and asked, an echo of annoyance in his tone, 'Mate – are you all right?' He gave Mac one of those stares he no doubt used on many of the stoned-out kids he picked up from clubs in the early hours of the morning.

Mac set his features so his face gave nothing away. He told the other man what he needed to know, but as soon as the cab hit the streets, his mind stormed back into overdrive.

He.

Kill me.

Eleven tonight.

Elena had told him in their last frantic phone call about tomorrow night, which meant tonight. Eleven tonight. The words churned, their speed becoming hectic, frantic, as the cab zoomed by the gathering people on London's streets, getting ready for another groundhog day at work.

'Rough part of town you're off to mate,' the cabbie said conversationally.

Mac didn't answer. Instead he flicked his gaze up and noticed the older man stealing glances at him in the rear-view mirror. Stupid, stupid, stupid. He should never have got the cab so close to the scene of the murder. Should've walked a good ten minutes and then hailed one. Public transport hadn't been an option, that would take too long, and he didn't have time to burn if something was going down at eleven tonight. He'd really messed up. It wouldn't be long before the police were asking taxi drivers if they'd picked up any suspicious characters in the vicinity of a gruesome murder in a hotel. Maybe they'd talk to this cabbie? Maybe the cab driver would talk to them? Who'd ever heard of a cabbie that didn't talk? No way could that happen. Mac reached into his jacket and felt for his gun.

'Shed-load of coppers around today,' the man in the front seat continued.

Mac found his Luger. Touched the handle. 'I hadn't noticed.'

'They'll probably want to chat to you, won't they?'

Mac leaned forward, quietly pulling the gun out at the same time. He kept the conversation going. 'Why would they want to chat to me?'

On the other side of the road, a police car went by at full speed, lights blazing.

'You of all people must know what happened?'

You of all people . . . What did the cab driver mean by that? Did he know something about Mac? Know where he'd been? Who he was?

Mac started raising the gun.

'What makes you think that I know anything about anything?'

Mac curled a finger round the trigger.

The cabbie took a sharp right, the lumps and bumps in the road shaking the car slightly from side to side.

'I mean that you're in the hotel down the road with a great view of what was going on. You must've seen the cops arrive and all that. There's always some kind of argy-bargy going on around there. Probably a tart thing. That road's full of 'em.' As if realising his fare might be the customer of a 'tart', he began backtracking. 'Not that there's anything wrong with that, of course. I mean, we all like a bit of *fun* outside the home, don't we . . . ?'

Mac slumped back. What was happening to him? Had he really been about to brandish his gun at a cab driver? Steal his cab and drive off?

He caught the other man looking at him again in the mirror. Suddenly the driver's gaze shifted lower. Mac had forgotten he was still holding the Luger. Their gazes caught in the mirror again.

Silence.

Then the cabbie smacked his lips together and said, 'You're not lighting up in the back there, are you son?' The older man's eyes lowered back to the road.

Smoking? Smoking indeed . . . 'No, I've got filthy habits, but that isn't one of them.' Mac pushed his piece back into its hiding place.

'*Next, it's traffic news!*' The cabbie's radio became louder; pre-set to increase for traffic alerts. Mac realised he'd completely lost track of the journey and they were closing in on his destination. His fingers were white, as if he were still gripping the handle of the Luger.

'*M25 . . . Hangar Lane Gyratory . . . M4 into town . . . and we've got a police incident in Bayswater, where a number of roads are closed . . .*'

'You had a lucky break there, mate,' the cabbie cut over the radio. 'That was your road – another five minutes and you might have been trapped behind that tape they put up. Who needs that?'

Mac said nothing, only speaking again when he got the cab to drop him a couple of streets away from his destination. He got out and paid. As he disappeared, a newsreader on the radio announced in the background:

'*Police are appealing for witnesses after a murder in a Bayswater hotel last night . . .*'

Mac strode onto a run-down street in Brixton, South London. Among the betting shops, pawnbrokers and cheap loan operators stood an old-fashioned English butcher's. And next to that stood a blank door leading to offices above the butcher's. The door was reinforced, painted grey and would have needed a SWAT team with all its hardware to kick it in. Mac checked the door and then the entry phone. No name. No indication of a profession, just a number. Six. For a brief moment, Mac's finger hovered over the buzzer before he let it drop again. Ringing upstairs wasn't going to get him anywhere, and he knew it.

Instead he walked slowly down the street to see if there was access to the rear of the buildings. On the other side of the butcher's was a wooden gate that led to the rear where the bins that stored the waste were kept. It was a sound gate but easily climbable. Mac looked down the street in both directions but he knew this wasn't the kind of road where a man scaling a gate was going to attract much attention and, even if it did, he didn't care. He jumped up and grabbed the top with his fingers, kicking and scraping his way up the wooden panels. With a heave of his upper body and flick of his legs, he dropped down to the other side. Wiped the resin and creosote from his hands, made sure his Luger was easily accessible and then walked to the rear of the building.

The back door was open and he could hear music inside but there was no one around. He looked upwards. A net curtain flapped in the wind from an open sash window on the top floor. Next to that, a rusty Victorian drainpipe. Mac shook the pipe. It rattled and a small dusting of dislodged mortar carried on the wind from where the green metal pins held it loosely to the wall. After a quick look around, Mac reached up, dug his fingers behind the pipe, gripped it between his knees and began to carefully climb it, monkey style. Before he'd gone a few feet, the pins began to come away and the pipe swung and swayed.

He was still low enough to drop back down, but he didn't even consider it. He went on with patient speed and careful haste. Each time Mac hauled himself up another foot, he would pause while the pipe decided whether it had had enough yet and was going to come down. As the window sill of the open sash came within reach, he hesitated, as if in an attempt to dupe the pipe that the stress being imposed on its joints was finally over. As a final warning, a thick metal pin above him came away, bounced on his head and then fell with a clink onto the back yard below.

Deep breath.

He launched himself up, desperately grabbing at the sill. His fingers caught the mossy stone but he could feel himself slipping away. With a flailing leg he pushed his foot against the pipe, which finally came away from the wall and hung at an angle. But not before Mac had managed to get enough leverage to get an arm over the ledge and, gasping with pain and effort, his leg followed. Like a crab, he pulled himself in sideways and tumbled to the floor.

His grazed fingers and knee stung. Muscles battered and wrung, but he had no time to lose. He stumbled up and across the room, which had files, papers and books piled high, and opened the door onto the second floor's landing. Opened a second door and went into another room. An office of some kind. A large mahogany desk at one end with swivel chairs on either side of it. There was no sign of life, but Mac knew his quarry was around somewhere. He checked his watch.

A couple of minutes to nine.

Time was moving on way too quickly. Fourteen hours and two minutes to eleven tonight. The man who owned this office had to help him; it was his only shot at finding out what was on Elena's phone.

Abruptly Mac froze. Something cold was touching the side of his neck. Mac heard the distinctive sound of a gun's hammer being pulled back. That's when he realised what was touching the twitching vein in his neck – the twin rims of the muzzle of a shotgun.

A voice growled behind him, 'You're very sloppy for an undercover cop.'

ten

'The dead always speak,' the forensic investigator said to Detective Inspector Rio Wray, who stood in the bathroom doorway.

Rio was now kitted out in a white forensic suit and matching foot and headgear. Her nose twitched at the metallic residue of blood in the air.

'Looks like you've been out on the razzle,' the forensic expert continued, her gaze settling, with surprise, on Rio's lipstick. Rio wasn't a make-up girl – well, not at work, anyway; she only ever put on a bit of colour when she was stepping out somewhere special.

'A mate's hen night that went rocking into the morning. Got the call to come here on my way home. So what's the damage here, Charlie?'

'What you see is what you get, I'm afraid,' came the answer.

Rio stepped forward to join Charlie, who was already crouched down by the bath. The vic was female. Rio's mouth tightened as she took in the already decaying mush that had once been the woman's face. Blood, bone and brain splattered thick and high onto the wall. What a bloody mess.

'The injuries are typical of being shot in the back of the head,' Charlie continued. 'Probably a close-range shot just below the start of the crown at the back of the head. All it takes is the speed and impact of one bullet coming out of the other side to pull the face to shreds.'

'So the killer knew what he was doing?' Rio threw back, keeping her gaze on the massive injuries.

'That's your department. Mine is just to assess the forensics.'

Rio peered closer. Although much of the woman's hair was the colour of matted, drying blood, she could see it was dark, deep brown or dyed black. Without a face, it might take a while to verify who the victim was.

'If she was shot in the back of the head, wouldn't the body be lying forward or slumped to the side?' Rio asked.

'That's what you would expect . . .'

'Maybe the killer pushed her back?' Rio interrupted. 'Why would he do that?' Then she spoke directly to the corpse. 'We need to find out who you are.'

'Probably a prostitute,' another voice added. 'It's that kind of place.'

Both Charlie and Rio turned to find another officer standing in the doorway. Detective Jamie Martin. He was a good five years younger than Rio's thirty-three, with neat, formal sandy hair and grey eyes that darted around like he was trying to store every detail around him. He was also the newest member of her squad, one of those fast-trackers, which really pissed her off. But she couldn't show her irritation in public because she'd been tasked with 'easing him' into the team. He had just completed his first year and his performance review was due any day now.

'The hotel's a favourite haunt for ladies of the night to take their Johns,' Martin carried on, his voice fast with the eagerness of a young man wanting to do a good job. 'It's not the first time our lot have been called here.'

Rio swept her gaze over the victim again. The right arm rested at an angle across the woman's torso with the hand laid against the stomach. Had the murderer posed the victim like that? And that's when Rio noticed something else. Something on the right arm . . . She peered closer, just above the wrist. A tattoo. Small with a red star and yellow border. It wasn't a tattoo she recognised as a stamp of allegiance for any of the gangs she knew. Mind you, everyone and their dog was sporting tats these days. There was some type of lettering above and below it in a foreign script.

С волка́ми жить
по-во́лчьи выть.

'It's Russian,' Martin supplied. Rio hadn't even been aware he'd come to stand beside her. 'Cyrillic script.'

'Any idea what it says?' When Martin shook his head she added, 'Make sure someone takes close-up shots of the tattoo. Any witnesses?' She eased to her feet.

'Apart from the woman who flagged things up, guests in the neighbouring rooms are saying that they heard nothing and the hotel manager claims he 'can't remember' who he let the room to. There's nothing in the hotel register to say who booked the room – for which the manager is blaming the young kid who was on duty at reception last night who is "new" and "hasn't got the hang of things yet" . . .'

'Is the manager known to us?'

'Of course – he wouldn't be running a hotel round here if he wasn't. Nothing too serious, though – mostly handling and receiving stolen goods from years back. Claims he doesn't know a thing about last night.'

'Pick him up – run him in, and bring the other staff who were on duty with him. I'll talk to them later. Have you found out anything about the victim?'

'No ID around. Judging by her tattoo, she's East European. Russian, probably. Given this place's clientele, she was most likely a prostitute or petty criminal – maybe she got into a row with a punter about money?'

Rio shook her head. 'Not unless her John was a professional gunman, she didn't. Even your narkiest John doesn't normally resort to firearms. It's savage beatings usually. Perhaps it was something else. And, given the damage, he didn't want a quick identification either.'

'You think this was a hit?' Martin asked.

'Can't say that yet,' Rio answered. 'All we can say is that the killer is handy with a gun.'

They moved, with Charlie, to the other major scene of evidence – the bed in the main room. As they left the bathroom, Martin caught the arm of his superior, delaying her.

'Sorry about that business outside.'

Rio didn't respond. It wasn't the first time one of her own had fingered her for something else because of the colour of her skin. She'd known that being a black, female cop in The Met wouldn't always be easy, but she was a woman heading for the top and sticks and stones and racists weren't going to stand in her way.

'Go and chat some more to the manager,' Rio told him as she walked into the main room.

Rio followed Charlie to the bed and peered down at one of its pillows, which was stained a deep colour.

'I take it this is blood?' Rio asked.

'What we have is low-velocity blood splatter.' Charlie pointed to the different-sized circular drops of blood staining the blue duvet cover. 'It's almost as if whoever was on this bed was lying down with blood dripping from them. They were definitely injured when they were lying down.' Charlie pointed to the pillow and the pool of blood on it. 'Can you see how the bloodstain is on the side of the pillow; this would suggest they had a head injury—'

'But I thought you said that the victim was likely killed in the bath,' Rio cut in.

Charlie stared at her. 'I'm not sure this blood belongs to the victim.'

'You think this is the killer's blood?' Before Charlie could answer, Rio straightened and answered her own question. 'So we've got a killer out there who's in need of medical attention.' Rio swung to the door and shouted. 'Martin . . .'

As soon as an excited Jamie Martin appeared in the doorway, Rio fired out, 'We need to check hospitals. Walk-in clinics–'

But the younger officer didn't let her finish. 'DI, the manager has got something I think you'll want to see.'

eleven

The man got out of the Mercedes. Further down the street he could see the police coming and going behind their tape as they investigated the murder in the hotel that was all over the airwaves. He kept his head slightly down and to one side to shield his face and walked into the other hotel that Mac had left earlier. He ran his thumbs down the inside of the lapels of his jacket as he entered. The place was quiet except for a woman at reception. Her back was to him as she watched an old-style portable telly, her elbows pushing out to the side in a strange motion.

As if sensing his approach she swivelled round in her chair. That's when he saw the dark shades covering her eyes and the knitting in her hands.

'Can I help you?' she asked, placing her knitting in her lap.

'I'm looking for a man who registered here, maybe last night or in the last couple of hours.'

That bought a slight smile to her ageing face. 'We get lots of men coming in and out of here.'

'But you don't look overrun with customers to me, so you must remember him.'

She settled her hands over her knitting. 'You have the sound of someone on official business.'

'Don't worry about my business; just tell me what I need to know.'

Her head tilted to the side. 'But it is my business.'

His voice hardened. 'I could jump over the counter and find out for myself, but that wouldn't be very civilised, would it?'

Silence. Her head straightened as she pointed at the register. 'Last name in the book.'

He flipped the register to face him. Read: 'Room twenty-six. Mr Jones Smith.'

'Some people just don't want to be found,' she told him smoothly.

He looked back at her. 'What did he look like?'

'Well if I knew that, I would tell you.' She pulled off her sunglasses and revealed her cloudy, milky eyes. They stared straight through him. She was blind.

'How come you were watching the television?'

The smile pulled back onto her face. 'I do still have a pair of ears. I can hear the telly. I can also hear that you're a desperate man.'

He let her smart remark go over his head, instead saying, 'Can I check out room twenty-six?'

'No point, love, he's long gone. But if you see him, tell him he owes me for trashing the . . .'

He didn't hear her finish as he walked out of the hotel back into the morning light.

When he got back into his car, he took out his mobile.

'It looks like he was there this morning but he's left. Is his phone back on? . . . No, I didn't think it would be for now. Stick to that screen – I want to know the minute he resurfaces. We might have a problem.' He looked down the street at the taped-off police lines. 'A big, big problem.'

twelve

9 a.m.

The shotgun rested firmly against Mac's neck. The voice of the man holding it spoke in a flat monotone.

'Now, what would an undercover cop be doing breaking into my office? Apart from anything else, that's breaking the law, isn't it?'

'Calum, I need your help.'

A sour laugh erupted behind him. The shotgun jammed deeper into his skin. 'Help? If PC Mac thinks quipping is going to save him from a double barrel's worth of shot, he's lost his touch.'

Mac said nothing. A lifetime of seconds passed before he heard a grunt behind him. The cold steel slowly lifted from his skin. Click. The hammers slotted back into place. Calum Burns emerged from behind him. He was taller than Mac's five eleven, more toned than bulky muscle, with a face that could range from cheeky to marble cold in the beat of a second. He wore marble cold as he rested the shotgun upright against a wall. Without looking at Mac, he slowly walked towards the desk, his steps uneven, but careful. His movements surprised Mac because Calum was a man known to walk with a cocksure swagger. But Mac clamped down on asking about what was up with his leg, instead watched Calum settle in a chair.

Calum leaned idly back and stared at Mac with sharp green eyes. And spoke. 'The traditional way to ask someone for help is to call them, or press the entry phone to their office – not break in through their windows.'

'And what would you have said if I'd given you a bell?' Mac seated himself opposite.

'Fuck. Off.'

The charged atmosphere intensified. Sweat bubbled up from the pores on Mac's forehead. He flipped his hood back and peeled off the strip of towelling. Fished around in his pocket. Found Elena's phone and put it on the desk. Calum took no notice of the phone; instead he studied Mac's wound.

'Pistol shot?' Calum broke the silence.

Mac ignored the question and pushed the phone across the desk. 'I can't get into this phone and I need to know what was on it. Names, addresses, phone calls, texts – the lot.'

Calum twisted his mouth, but picked up the phone. 'And why would I do that? And please don't say "for old times' sake" or I really will blast you to kingdom come.'

'You're a security consultant-cum-fixer these days, aren't you? One of the best in the business – or so I've heard.'

Calum's face turned hard. 'You're not getting me, are you? The question is not "Can I help you?" It's "Why should I help you?"'

This wasn't going to be easy. Mac's head flopped back, his line of vision coming into contact with a framed document on the wall opposite. It was an enlarged copy of Calum's confidentiality agreement, which he'd signed, promising not to divulge any information about his 'resignation' from the police. It had formed part of his settlement when he'd left The Met for good. No one, not even Mac, had understood why Calum had been booted out of the Force. Of course there were rumours – a backhander, decked his superior, or been sharing whiskey shots with the wrong crowd. But no one really knew and Calum wasn't telling. He wasn't even telling why he wasn't telling. A confidentiality agreement meant nothing to him. None of it had made any sense. Sure Calum had been a bit fly, occasionally massaged the rules, but he'd been a good cop. No, he'd been great. Outstanding. Upstanding.

'This isn't police business if that makes a difference . . .' Mac started.

'A difference?' the other man slammed back, the muscles in his cheeks contorting madly. 'Do you know how many of my former *colleagues* shook my hand before I left? Zero. Do you know how many of my former *colleagues* rang me up to wish me luck for the future? Zero. Fuck-all.'

Calum didn't need to point out that Mac had been part of the 'fuck-all' crowd. Mac wasn't proud of not getting in touch with someone who'd been one of his closest friends, but Phil had warned him to stay well clear. If you breathe polluted air then everyone's going to think you're filled with poison, was the way his senior officer had put it to him. So he'd stayed away, tossed their friendship out of the window, blackballed him along with everyone else.

'I suppose it was too much to hope that anyone would stand up for me when I got kicked out. *That* I could take. The whole world is spineless, so I don't blame anyone for *that*. It's their idiocy I couldn't stand. Do you recall that nuclear shelter under HQ where the code for the door was so secret, it couldn't be written down? So they made it "9999" so the relevant people could remember it? Idiots, fucking idiots. No wonder there's so much demand for people like me.' Calum was seething but he added in an undertone. 'I could've used a few friends back then, you know . . .' His eyes were fierce, like green dynamite.

Mac leaned forward. 'Maybe some of those friends were waiting for you to tell your side of the story?'

For the first time Mac saw confidence replaced by uncertainty on the other man's face. 'Yeah . . . well . . . it was no one's bloody business.'

Mac slightly raised his hands. 'Yeah . . . well . . . I need to know if you're going to help me out with my bloody business?'

There was a long silence before Calum asked, 'Still playing naked cop?'

Most undercover cops were called UCs but a few called them naked because they were stripped of their former life in order to assume another ID.

'Who are you deep in with this time? Do I know them?' Calum persisted.

Mac didn't answer. An undercover cop, who answers questions like that, isn't an undercover cop any more. But he knew he had to say something.

Leaning back, Mac answered. 'I'm doing some work in the London end of an arms trafficking gang.'

That was vague enough.

'Let me guess?' Calum said with a gleam in his eyes. 'That'll be Russians, then. Must be a big mob to attract your superiors' interest. So that'll be AK Reuben's crew. If only because Reuben has put all the other gunrunners out of business . . .'

Mac kept his expression blank. 'How do you know all of this?'

'I'm a security consultant, it's my business to know that sort of thing.' Calum enjoyed the look on Mac's face. He looked at the phone. 'Why have you brought this to me? Any kid on the street could open that for you, never mind your techy colleagues. In some sort of trouble, are you?' He looked at Mac's exposed wound. 'Got into a gunfight with someone you shouldn't? No, it can't be that, your superiors would cover that up for you.' He sighed. 'Not that it matters, I'm not choosy about my customers. My fees are five hundred an hour plus expenses.'

Mac was overwhelmed with a strong urge to ram his fist into the other man's face. To see his jeering mouth shoved to the backside of his brain. How could he joke when Elena was dead? Dead . . . Dead.

He was back in the bathroom. Standing at the foot of the bath, facing Elena who was sitting inside it. Reuben stood behind her. And it was like Mac was chained to the floor because he couldn't move. Couldn't speak. Couldn't do anything as Reuben raised Mac's gun. Luger and hand moved almost in slo-mo towards the back of Elena's head. Her eyes caught Mac's. It gave him the time to see her terror. To hear her scream. To see the tattoo as she stretched her arm, in a pleading motion, towards him . . . Bang. A bullet tore into the back of her head. The richest red he'd ever seen splashed against the wall. Hit him in the face. A drop landed on his tongue . . .

'Mac? Mac?'

He came to with his forehead on the desk, with Calum's loud voice beating over his head. He couldn't catch his breath. Couldn't breathe . . . Mac knew he'd blacked out again.

'Easy, easy.' This time Calum's voice was in his ear. The other man circled his hands around Mac's upper arms and gently raised him.

'What's going on, Mac?' For the first time there was no mockery in Calum's words.

Mac stared back at him. 'I broke the cardinal rule. I fell for someone who was part of my investigation. Now she's dead.'

thirteen

Calum set a shot of Hennessey's in front of Mac. They were back on opposite sides of the desk. Almost like they were back in the old days, in a pub, chit-chatting like the best buddies they'd once been.

Seeing Mac's wary look Calum said, 'Forget I'm the cop who got booted out of The Met and think of me as Stevie's godfather. I've got nothing personal against you. It's the system I hate.'

That jolted Mac. Calum had been the best godfather a man's son could ask for – right up until the day Stevie was buried.

If it was one cardinal rule not to get involved with people you were investigating, it was another not to talk about your work. To anyone. Never mind a man of Calum's stripe. But Mac knew too many secrets; soaked in shock and with his head thumping, he was desperate to tell another human being. Someone. Anyone. Even a man like Calum. Perhaps especially a man like Calum. He would understand; he'd been there himself. Mac's story oozed out like a wound's poison and pus. He heard his own voice as if it belonged to someone else.

'I've been under for nine months in Reuben's crew. My brief was to find out who their major league supplier is. So I got myself introduced to Reuben as an independent armourer and we started doing business. Before I know it, I'm an honorary member of the gang.'

'Is that how you met her?' Calum took a gulp from his much larger cognac.

'Elena was their communications person; you know, the usual, dealing with messages and information.' Mac's face pulled into a lopsided, sad smile. 'That's how we met one day about six months back. I had to give her some info.' He shrugged. 'And that's how it started.'

What he kept to himself was that he'd also considered her for the role of the person he could get information from. Part of his job was looking for that one person on the inside who could keep him bang up to date with the information he needed; that vulnerable person who realised that the life they'd chosen wasn't the right way. And he'd found that person in Elena. Sweet Elena. So he'd cultivated her. Coaxed her. Eventually seduced her. But, before he even realised that it was happening, the tables had turned, until he'd broken rule number one – never, ever, get emotionally involved with a player in the game. But that human-to-human emotion had been locked down in him for such a long time that when she'd flooded him with it, it had gone straight to his soul. A soul he didn't think he possessed any more. He'd got in so deep with her that he'd started wanting to keep her safe. Shield her from the squalid and violent world she'd got involved in, the squalid and violent world of tackling it. So he didn't tell his superior he'd started screwing the enemy and didn't tell Elena that he wasn't the criminal she thought he was. Did he love her? He wasn't sure. But that didn't matter. What counted was the guilt. The guilt he felt about her death. And the only way to get rid of that guilt was to hunt down her killer.

'I woke up a few hours ago in a hotel room with a bullet wound to my head and Elena shot dead, minus her face, in the bath.' He pulled in a ragged breath. 'I didn't do it. It was a set-up.'

Calum sent him a confused stare. 'And you think AK Reuben is your guy?'

'It must have been Reuben's doing. There isn't anyone else. Is there?' He was almost begging for support.

Calum went into the detective mode he'd never forgotten. 'Of course it could be someone else. Say it was something to do with this Elena? Say it's someone from your past because, let's face it, you've put enough dirty faces behind bars. What if one of them is out now and managed to hunt you down? Shame you don't know who's running the investigation into the shooting, they might have been able to help you.'

'I do know actually. I saw her turn up. It's Rio Wray.'

Calum almost shook with hatred but said nothing. The hatred was enough.

Mac wasn't surprised at Calum's reaction. Once all three of them had been tight but, since Calum's dramatic exit from the Force, their bonds had frayed and broken. But something deeper had gone on between the other two and Mac didn't know what it was.

Calum folded his arms in disgust. 'Well, "Wray gun" won't put herself out for you; she'll be too busy polishing her commendations and making tea for her superiors to help an old friend.'

Mac slammed the glass on the table, sending some amber liquid bouncing in the air. 'I don't need Rio's help. I'll sort this out myself, I know what I'm doing . . .'

'Do you?' the other man asked sternly. 'You're not a well man, and I'm not just talking about the head wound. If you were thinking straight, you wouldn't have come here for a start. And as for that blackout you just had . . .'

That made Mac mad as hell. 'I did not . . .'

But Calum wouldn't let it go. 'You looked like you did after Stevie died – fucked up. You couldn't tell one day from the next and the only way you could get through the days was with a bellyful of meds from the quack. I'm not a shrink, but I know PTSD when I see it. You should be in hospital, not climbing up drainpipes.'

'Leave Stevie out of this,' Mac growled.

Calum stared back. 'I can't, because the only reason I'm going to help you now is because of him.'

Silence. Mac grabbed for the slice of towel and tied it back round his head. Flipped his hood back into place.

'Why don't you just got to this woman's home . . .' Calum continued, but Mac cut over him.

'The way I hear it, Reuben doesn't like any of his people associating out of business hours, so we always met in hotels. I never asked for her address and she never asked for mine.'

'Don't suppose you need to know where someone lives if all you're doing is getting your leg over,' Calum said. Mac sent him a deadly look, but it didn't shut Calum up. 'Well, I hope for your sake this has got zilch to do with Reuben. He's a big player. They don't call him AK for nothing. I hope they're paying you danger money. The streets are whispering that he's getting tooled up for some sort of gang war. A bloody one.'

'That's what people are saying. But I'll know for sure about Reuben later. I'm going over to his kid's birthday party . . .'

Mac didn't finish his plan because Calum broke in, horrified. 'Are you nuts? If Reuben was behind this and you go over there, you're dead before you get through the front door. And he'll probably get his kid to fire the fatal shot – he's that sort of guy. The very fact that you could consider doing that proves you've lost it.'

Mac's voice was weak. Almost lost. 'Perhaps. I'll take a gun. Maybe I'll get my shot in first. And if he takes me out . . . well, it doesn't matter anyway.' Mac could hardly believe what he was saying. Calum was right. It was insane. But he'd made promises to Elena. He whispered, 'But I need you to check her phone first.'

Calum sounded like a father talking to a troubled son. 'You're not well. You're not thinking straight. You're not thinking at all . . .' But realising Mac wasn't going to move from his position, he huffed noisily and picked up Elena's phone. Took a stray lead hanging from the back of his computer and plugged it into the back of the phone. He began tapping in commands on his keyboard. Mac noticed that, as Calum typed, his anger seemed to be draining away; he was watching the screen with growing interest. It was five minutes before Calum finally pulled the plug from the phone and spun it back across the desk.

'No can do, this phone's been wiped by someone who knows how to cover his tracks.'

'Are you sure?'

Calum pursed his lips together as his bitterness piled back in the room. 'You could check with your friends in the police and ask them to check it for you if you don't believe me. Oh – but you can't do that, can you . . . ?'

Mac thrust himself up. Picked up the phone. Pushed it into his pocket and turned at the same time.

'You're nuts, Mac,' Calum sighed. 'You go and get yourself shot at Reuben's – and use the stairs this time please, there's a good boy.'

As Mac opened the door to leave, Calum called him back. 'There are a couple of other things you don't seem to have considered.'

'Like what?'

'This body in the bath – how do you know it was Elena?'

Mac froze. 'Of course it was Elena.'

'The state you're in, you wouldn't recognise your own mother – face or no face.'

'Don't you think I want to believe that she's still alive?' Mac growled back. His palm shot into his pocket.

'This is hers.' He waved Elena's bracelet at Calum, the bunny rabbit swinging in the painful motion of a lynching. 'She never took it off. It was on the body. And she has a tattoo.'

Calum looked back at him before sighing with sarcasm. 'Bracelet and tattoo? Maybe . . . too bad you can't get in touch with Rio. She'll get an ID on the victim before too long. Of course, that's not the only ID she'll be getting. If your DNA is in the room, it won't be too long before she knows you were at the scene of the killing. Your DNA is on the database, isn't it? All undercover cops have their fingerprints logged. When she finds that out, you really will have a problem.'

Mac massaged his temples.

'Be honest Mac – how do you know it wasn't you who shot her?'

Mac's fingers dropped from his head. 'Me?'

'Yeah – after all, you don't remember anything, do you? Don't tell me it hasn't crossed your mind? Or what's left of it . . .'

The other man's words planted the seeds of doubt back in his throbbing head. In pursuing Elena's butcher, was he actually pursuing himself? Was it that, instead of not remembering the night before, he just didn't want to remember? He'd seen it before in his career plenty of times. The murderer of a loved one who couldn't accept what they had done and who then went into denial before finally that denial turned into insanity or suicide.

But he had had no reason to kill her. He opened his mouth and told Calum the biggest reason he couldn't have done it.

'You'll be telling me next that I shot myself in the head.' He shook his head. 'There was someone else in that hotel room. Whoever the fucker was took Elena's face off and thought they'd left me for dead. But you know what, I'm standing tall and alive and I'm going to make it my business to find her killer. And when I find him, that's when you can call me a murderer. In the meantime, don't stand in my way if Reuben is that man.'

Calum smiled at him and shrugged his shoulders.

Mac left, still clutching a dead woman's bracelet in his hand. The pain was back, see-sawing in his head, as he took his former friend's advice and used the stairs. He knew he had to get his wound sorted before he did anything else. And maybe Calum was right; he had no evidence that Reuben was behind the shooting. None at all. All the more reason to go to his kid's party. Even if Reuben hadn't killed Elena, maybe he could find out from the big Russian what mysterious event happening tonight at eleven had driven Elena into a blind panic.

How long did he have before his superiors came looking for him? They probably were already. How long before Rio discovered from the DNA match that he'd been in a hotel room with a murder victim? If he was lucky, the DNA match wouldn't come in until tomorrow. Odds against him, and Rio would be on his trail before eleven tonight.

He reached the downstairs door. Pushed it open. Dropped the bracelet back in his pocket. Stepped out into the street.

'Mac?'

He looked up to find Calum's head poking out of the window. His former colleague didn't look pissed any more, but Mac wouldn't put it past him to chuck a bucket of cold water on him.

'Still carry Lady L with you?'

Lady L was Calum's nickname for his Luger. Mac nodded, still suspicious.

'You might find this handy,' Calum said. 'Catch.'

He dropped a box down to Mac.

Mac caught it. Looked inside. A half-filled box of ammo and an EDC – everyday carry handgun. Exactly what he needed for what he had to do.

'I think I'm the one now who needs to get my head seen to,' Calum called out.

Mac didn't answer. Didn't tell him that he was on his way to see the 'house doctor'.

fourteen

10 a.m.

Mac was on the west side of London, a few streets down from Harley Street. He knew he was taking a risk here, going to see Reuben's 'house doctor'. But if he didn't get some medical attention soon it might slow him down, get in the way of finding out who'd popped Elena. And nothing was going to do that. Besides, a doctor topping up his wage packet providing under-the-counter care for criminal clients might have other information as well.

Mac found Harley Street. Stood on the opposite side of the road and studied the clinic he was after before carefully checking the cars that were parked up on the street. One caught his eye, a black Mercedes with windows tinted deep like the road to hell. It had a long, ridged, raised line just below the door handles that made the curve of the doors jut out like metal cheekbones. The driver's window was down so he was able to see the two men inside, both up front, decked out in suits and shades. One of the men looked across at Mac. He tensed. Were they waiting for him?

The driver of the Merc looked away. Leaned forward. Started the engine and then the car glided down the street and turned onto a main road. Mac didn't bother to wait and see if the car returned. He crossed the street again and walked up to a flat-fronted Georgian building with black railings that matched the style of the balcony on the fourth floor. *Sihaa Centre.* To cover itself for injuries and illness, the arms gang had provided itself with 'health cover' that left no trace behind for the law to follow. A contract had been agreed with the discreet clinic in Harley Street to make sure that, in the event of 'personal injuries', they would be taken care of, no questions asked.

Mac checked his watch.

10.03.

The place should be open but it looked locked up. He tried the handle of the main door. It opened. The reception area was all tanned floorboards, soft, lavender lighting and plump, cosy armchairs.

Mac took himself off down the corridor that led to the consulting rooms. Behind a half-open door he heard movement. He pushed the door wide to find Doctor Mo Masri, alone, cleaning instruments.

Startled, the doctor looked up and said, 'I'm sorry, can I help . . . ?'

The words died in his mouth as he recognised Mac. And Mac couldn't blame him. The last time he'd seen Doctor Mo hadn't been a feel-good moment. It had been in the summer when Mac had sustained a cracked rib after a particularly nasty incident at a lock-up down South London way. Word had reached a local gang that the illegal arms crew he'd infiltrated were on their patch and they'd tried to rip Reuben's people off. Bad move – the lightweights had bitten off more than they could chew and smashed ribs had ended up as the least of their problems. Doctor Masri had been called to treat his wound, and when Mac had undressed for the doctor to examine him, a sawn-off shotgun had tumbled out of his jacket.

The doctor now wore that same look of discomfort. He

swallowed. Tried to plaster on a professional smile. 'I'm sorry . . . this is a little irregular.'

'Most of your business is a little irregular, doc.' The other man's cheek was tinged with red. 'I've got a wound to the head . . .'

The doctor's discomfort increased as he forcefully interrupted, 'I'm afraid I'm going to have to ask you to wait in reception while I run our usual checks . . .'

But Mac wasn't in the mood to wait. 'I don't want to be rude, but you're a doctor and I'm a patient. You know who I work for and you've seen me before. Now make me all better again, doc.'

Deeply unhappy, Masri indicated to Mac that he should get on the deep-green leather examination table. 'Take a seat on the edge.'

As soon as Mac was seated, the doctor took off the strip of towel, placed it in the medical waste bin and then began his examination.

'You're a very lucky man. I suspect that if the angle of the gun that was aimed at you had been a fraction different, the bullet might have fractured your skull. Or maybe you wouldn't be sitting here now.' He said the last as if he wanted that to be the case. 'I'll need to shave some of your hair, clean up the wound and then put in some stitches or staples . . .'

'No staples,' Mac interrupted. 'I don't want to look like the son of Frankenstein.'

There were, of course, no questions about how Mac had been shot in the first place. Doctor Mo knew better than that. While the good doctor prepared to do his work, Mac hopped off the examination table and went back to the window. The black Merc was back. He said nothing as he resumed his seat. The doctor gave Mac some antibiotics and smiled at a job well done.

'Well,' the doctor started as he snapped his gloves off. 'If that's all . . . ?'

'Can you check me over and find out if I was drugged last night?' Mac interrupted.

'Drugged?'

'Yes. I've no recollection of what happened to me from yesterday evening until I woke up this morning with part of my head missing. I need you to check to see if someone slipped me a mickey.'

The doctor looked back at him as if he was seeing that shotgun again. 'The wound you've sustained might well have caused short-term amnesia. It's quite normal. It's also clear to me that you're going through some type of shock. Whether that was caused by the bullet or by the circumstances in which you sustained it, I can't say. If I were you, I'd just get back to . . . um . . . *work*. That's the best cure for shock.'

'Can you give me something for that, then? The "shock"?'

The doctor shook his head, 'If I'm going to test you for drugs or supply you with any sort of longer-term medication, I'm contractually obliged to seek authorisation from your employer.' Mac knew what that meant. Reuben didn't like his people using uppers and downers. 'Drugs make you an easy target for the cops and our rivals,' Reuben had told him.

'If you'd like me to request that,' the doctor carried on, 'I will happily do so. But experience suggests that you might have to wait some time for me to get an answer . . .'

'No,' Mac said. If the doctor talked to anyone in the gang then questions would start being asked. Plus, he didn't have time to rest up.

Mac gestured to the window. 'Can you think of any reason why two heavies in a Merc would be parked down the road from this clinic?'

The face of Mo Masri looked like he was seeing a fist coming straight at him. For more than half a minute he carefully watched the street. When he turned, Mac noticed how pale his skin looked, like he was now the one in shock. 'Can you excuse me a moment? I have to make some phone calls.'

Mac dropped one of his feet on the ground as he leaned forward. 'Is there a problem?'

From Mo's face it certainly appeared as if there was. 'No, I'm sure there isn't . . . I just have to make a call.'

Then he was gone. So the doc had his own problems to deal with, and so did Mac, one of which was dealing with this slipping in and out of reality – or shock, as the doctor called it. He refused to believe it was the same blackouts he'd suffered with a year back when Stevie had died, like Calum said. Mac jumped up and started searching for the pills that he needed to stay sane in the following hours. At first, he looked for the brand his therapist had prescribed him a year ago, but when he had no joy with that, he looked for anything that seemed right. He went through drawer after drawer, medicine cabinets and chests before rifling through the medical waste bin.

At the top of the bin was the strip of towelling that had once covered his wound, and below it piles of pill bottles – some empty, others not. He rummaged through, like a kid on a treasure hunt, until he came across three distinct purple bottles that contained what were known on the drugs circuit as 'steady pills'. Popular with soldiers, criminals and others facing battle stress or extreme pressure, steady pills made you calm but alert and ready for business. Illegal in most Western countries because of their unpredictable side effects, they were still produced in the Far East and South America, but you had to know where to go and who to ask in order to get some. And Dr Mo Masri was obviously one of those people. Only when Mac tried to read the writing on the label did he realise that they were in Chinese, which meant he couldn't be sure if they were 'steady pills' at all.

The door opened. Mac dropped two bottles and shoved one into his pocket. Casually he went back to the examination table as the doctor walked further into the room.

'The gentlemen in the Mercedes are here on official business. No need for concern,' the other man reassured him.

Instead of approaching Mac, the doctor moved to one of the filing cabinets. A slight creak sounded as he pulled open the second drawer. 'You might want to take this so your scalp doesn't attract any attention.'

He showed Mac a black baseball cap. Being a dedicated follower of Arsenal, Mac almost declined because it had 'Man U' scrawled on the front. But he took it. Settled it on his head. Pulled the peak low.

Then asked, 'Do you remember a girl in my outfit called Elena?'

'Do you mean Miss Romanov? I treated her for an injury she sustained at her gym once.'

'You wouldn't happen to have her address in your records?'

The skin around the doctor's mouth tightened. 'Even if I did, which I don't, I would not be able to give it to you, patient–doctor privilege . . .'

'Playing the good citizen all of a sudden doesn't become you, doc,' Mac sneered.

If the doctor didn't have her address, he was going to have to find it another way. But how?

Mac walked to the door. He turned to see the doctor studying the road from a window. He looked nervous. 'Expecting trouble?'

The doctor turned away hurriedly and pretended to inspect some files. 'No, why should there be any trouble?'

'I don't know – you tell me.'

The doctor whispered. 'There's no trouble.'

His words sounded like a prayer over a dead body.

'We've waited too long.'

One of the two men in the Merc was getting impatient. The driver lit a cigarette.

'It takes as long as it takes, you know that. We wait until the man in the hoodie comes outside.'

They waited five minutes more, but when Mac didn't reappear, the driver decided he couldn't wait any longer.

'It's time.'

They got out of the car, heads covered. Picked up speed as they approached the Sihaa Centre. Took the steps two at a time. Barged into the reception area, pulling snub-nosed .38 revolvers from their jackets.

Mac didn't leave by the front. He walked down a corridor. Pushed down the emergency bar on the back door and ran through the small, but ornate, back garden and scaled the wall. Dropped to the other side. That dodgy doc might be relaxed about the guys in the Merc, but Mac wasn't. As he hurried down the street he thought about ways of finding Elena's address. But nothing came to him.

His brain kept moving in pace with his feet. Then he slowly smiled as he realised that the good doctor had given him the clue he needed to find where Elena had lived. It might put him smack-bang in the firing line but he didn't care. All that mattered was avenging her death.

fifteen

10:34 a.m.

Mac walked into Work Dat Body Health Spa. He'd never have figured out to check out Elena's gym to find her address if doctor Mo hadn't inadvertently mentioned he'd treated an injury she'd sustained while working out. That's when Mac had recalled that she'd used it once a week and sometimes on Sundays. He'd even given her a lift there, a couple of weeks after they'd started sleeping together. She'd been running late so he'd offered to take her. Elena had made a bit of a fuss about not wanting him to go out of his way for her, but he'd subdued her reluctance with soft kisses and teased her about not telling anyone about her secret passion to become Miss Body Builder. Elena had playfully smacked him on the arm and they'd fallen about laughing. That was only five months ago, one month after he'd met her. Now she was dead.

Mac cruelly swiped the good times from his mind as he took in the reception area. He spotted the security camera pretty much straight away, perched just above a large framed shot of some guy with buff pecs. His gaze did another quick scan. No more lenses trailed him – well, not any he could see. Still he flipped his hood over the cap and kept his head low. The place was all chrome and spotless white. Chrome reception desk and light fittings and white walls and ceiling. Only the white tiled floor spoiled the look with a veined pattern that looked like it was leaking blue blood. The reception was empty, no one behind the desk. Good, that meant if the computer was on he could get on with his work without any interruptions. But he'd have to be quick.

He kept his stride easy, but long. As he got closer, quick, soft, techno-synth adrenalin music pumped from another room. He reached the half-moon desk. On top sat a flatscreen computer near a cash register. As he reached to spin the computer round, he heard a woman's giggle coming from somewhere in the back. He snapped his hand back as a young woman appeared from a door behind the reception desk.

Spotting him, she stopped. 'Can I help you?' she offered as she started towards him. She had that sprayed look – tan, the gleaming white teeth and fluffed-up hair.

He caught the name on her name badge as she took the chair on the other side of the desk. Trish.

Mac was all smiles. 'Yeah. I desperately need to contact a friend of mine, but I don't have her address. I know that she uses this gym and I wondered if you could just give me her address from your files.'

Trish raised a finely plucked eyebrow. 'I'm sorry sir, but that's against the gym's policy. All members' information is strictly confidential.'

Mac leaned forward, dropped his voice. 'It's urgent that I contact her. Something to do with her family.'

Trish shook her head. 'Sorry, sir. Maybe you can find a phone number? An email?'

Her email or phone number weren't going to help him locate her address. Mac felt the heat rising in his face. His next words were delivered with a snap and a bite. 'Can you help me or not?'

'Now there's no need for you to take that tone . . .'

Mac pulled his Luger and pushed it into her face, his anger darkening his skin. He needed that address; whatever he had to do to get it from this woman, he was going to do. Bang a gun in someone's face and one of two things can happen – the person freezes or screams. If Trish screamed, the game was up. She froze.

'Keep your mouth shut and nothing will happen to you,' he ground out. 'Get under the desk.'

But she didn't move, just gazed back at him, eyes wide with terror and shock.

'Now.'

She scrambled up and down, the harsh beat of her breathing filling the air. Mac vaulted the desk. Made sure that the receptionist couldn't see him put his piece away.

'Where do I find the members' details?' he growled down at her.

All he got back was a whimper.

'I'm not going to hurt you, just tell me what I want to know. But don't make a sound, not even a tear, or I'll really give you something to wail about.'

Her voice came back muffled, high and shaking. 'On the desktop there's a directory marked "Members". Go into it and click on a folder called "Details".'

Quickly Mac followed the instructions. Soon the list of members and their details came up on the screen. It was set out alphabetically, surnames first and personal details below. Rapidly he scrolled down the screen.

A. B. C. He kept going until he found R.

Raab.

Rabinovitch.

Rahman.

Romanov. He'd found her. But when he checked the first name it was someone called Katia.

He pushed the file up so he could read the name in the next entry.

Surname: Romanov.

First name: Elena

Address: 17 Fountain Road London SE15

No phone number. No email.

Suddenly voices hit the reception as two women carrying towels and talking came into view. Still chatting away, they walked towards the desk. Mac straightened up, but kept his hand on the computer.

'Hi,' one of the women said. 'We're looking for Trish.' Her gaze darted around.

He gave her a professional look when she caught his eye again. 'She's gone off somewhere while I sort this computer out.'

'But she said to renew my membership when I finished my session.'

He smiled. 'Best come back after you've had a shower and got dressed.'

For a second she hesitated. Then, 'OK, will do.'

As she turned away with her partner, Mac whispered, 'Take it easy, Trish, and everything's gonna be all right.'

No sound greeted his command, so he got back on with the job. Calmly closed the file. Head low, he vaulted the desk and headed for the door. Abruptly he stopped and swung back around. Headed back towards the desk. Jumped it again. This time he hit some buttons on the cash register. Ping. It opened. He grabbed all of the notes, mainly twenties and tens. Shoved them into his pocket. Then he was back on the other side of the desk. Hood swaying, head down, moving with speed to the door. As he opened it, Trish the freezer became Trish the screamer. The shrill noise she made followed him as he calmly walked down the street on his way to find out if Elena's home would yield any clues about her death.

sixteen

11 a.m.

Elena's home was in a bog-standard Victorian terrace divided into one-up, one-down apartments. On the doorframe were two buzzers. The one for the lower flat had the initials 'JB' on a card in a slot, while the other had no indication who the current occupant might be. Mac figured the apartment with no name must be Elena's. He stood back and looked up at the windows above. Curtains shut tight, no sign of life. No easy way of getting in either. The front door was solid and getting round the back would involve climbing through a whole series of back gardens, which would expose him to being clocked by some of the neighbours. And nosey neighbours usually called the cops.

So he went with the last alternative left to him, he rang JB's buzzer. A face appeared behind a bamboo blind on the downstairs bay window. Young woman who didn't look especially welcoming. Mac put on his best smile. She looked at him, hesitated for a few moments and then let the blind go. Seconds later, the door opened a fraction, guarded by a secure chain. The woman was pretty, with two blonde pigtails, which should've looked silly on someone her age but suited her small face.

'Yes?' she asked in a nervous, foreign accent.

'Hi. You don't know me but I'm Elena's boyfriend and I haven't been able to get in touch with her for the past few days. She hasn't been to work either. I'm desperately worried something's happened to her. She's not answering her phone or her mobile.' Mac looked upwards. 'And I'm afraid something's happened to her upstairs in her flat, that's she's had an accident or she's ill. I've called the police but they say they can't come for a couple of hours and I can't wait that long.'

Mac sounded desperate, panicky and strained. He didn't need to fake it; he was all those things anyway. But the girl looked unconvinced.

Mac pressed on. 'So I was wondering if you could let me in? Just to make sure she's not unconscious upstairs.'

The woman arched her eyebrow, so Mac pleaded, 'Please . . . I can't wait for the cops and I don't have a key.'

His hand drifted downwards and backwards towards his gun. He didn't want to have to wave his gun in front of anyone else, but he'd decided he was going into the flat by any means necessary. But as he did so the door was closed in his face before he had a chance to get his foot into the gap. He rested his forehead on the door in despair. Then he heard the clang of the chain being pulled on the other side. He lifted his head at the same time the door opened up. Ordinarily, he would have noticed the woman's beauty, but instead he looked down the hall to where another door blocked the entrance up to Elena's flat.

He looked back at the woman, 'Do you know Elena?'

'Only to say hello to. I haven't seen her for a couple of days.' She sounded deeply uncomfortable.

He walked past her to the door to Elena's home and tried to tug it, but it was locked. 'I'll have to force my way in.'

'There's no need – she keeps a spare on the ledge over the door.'

Mac reached up and felt along the ledge and found the key. Turned the lock and opened the door. Wooden stairs led upwards in front of him. When he looked back at the neighbour, she was staring intently at him, suspicion back on her face. He gave it less than ten minutes before she called the cops, so he needed to work fast. He took the stairs two at a time, leaving the door open behind him so he could hear anyone coming through the front door.

First thing he did when he got in the apartment was to check the escape routes. In the kitchen was a window that opened onto a lean-to, from which it was possible to jump into the garden. He opened it in case he needed to leave quickly. Then he walked back to the landing and looked around at the place where the woman he'd cared so much for had lived.

A standard operator's flat. Totally anonymous. Futon bed, chest of drawers with a few clothes, some bric-a-brac furniture, a few kitchen utensils and a half-used jar of expensive coffee. No pictures, no photos, none of the knick-knacks that usually clutter mantelpieces and shelves. It was almost as if Elena had never lived here but resided somewhere else. Then he saw that the two-piece cream sofa had a rumpled blanket on it, one of its cushions obviously used as a makeshift pillow. Had someone else been staying here as well?

He turned his attention back to the rest of the main room, but stopped at the sight of a mug with blackberry tone lipstick around the rim. Elena's colour of choice to grace her lips. He ran a fingertip around the mark, which ended halfway round the cup. It was like he could feel her. Like she was in the room. The sudden ache in his chest made him close his eyes. Mac still couldn't believe she was gone. They'd only been laughing together last week as they walked hand-in-hand to a café, her sleek, black bob gleaming in the unexpected sunshine.

He slipped his finger back as he reopened his eyes. Just as

he started to move his gaze on he noticed a small card by the mug. As soon as he picked it up, the scent that Elena wore rose up to him. He placed the card near his nose. Everything she touched seemed to carry a whiff of perfume. Inhaled deeply. Liquorice mixed with another fragrance that always reminded him of his grandmother baking cupcakes.

Thinking of yesterdays was going to get him no closer to finding her killer. He pulled the card back. Black writing against a simple white background:

Club Zee

No address, no email, no phone number.

He hadn't heard her mention the club before and it wasn't a place that had come up in any of his investigations. He started to toss it back on the table – then his hand froze. The scent made it feel like she was in his arms, and putting the card back was like he was losing her all over again. He shoved it into his pocket.

Scanned the room again. Only the tools of her trade, as the communication expert in the gang, were visible, including a shredder by the cast-iron Victorian fireplace. On a makeshift table was a high-end computer that had been handmade, together with an 'in and out' tray. Mac switched the computer on but the screen merely flickered and the machine refused to start. Next, he pulled off the lid of the shredder, but the machine was empty. Why put a shredder next to a fireplace? Unless you were burning something. He crouched down by the fire grate and emptied the remains of the last fire onto the carpet. The trouble with coal fires is that they don't burn evenly; as Mac knew from previous investigations, it was surprising what could survive them. He began to sift through the debris but, as he did so, he stopped, listened and realised there were the slow, quiet but definite sounds of footsteps on the stairs.

He pulled out his gun and took up position by the door to confront the intruder.

A voice called out, 'Have you found anything?'

It was Little Miss Blonde Pigtails, halfway up the stairs. He put the Luger away and walked onto the landing. Only when he saw her did he remember his hands were covered in coal dust and soot. He knew he looked more suspicious than ever.

He smiled. 'No, I'm trying to find anything that might help.'

She stood for a few moments before walking back down, but not before he saw the suspicion taking over her face again.

Mac knew he had to work fast. In the remains of the fire, he found a charred photo. It looked like a family snap, but only two faces were visible, both of them men, wearing what looked like military uniforms. They both wore wide smiles. But he soon forgot the photo when he saw a powder-blue Post-it that was charred at one end. There was writing on it. He flipped it the right way. Read:

'Get these documents to the big man in Hamburg. Don't fuck up. Fuck up = death.'

Death.

The word bounced in his head and his brain started to move quickly. Who would have had the nerve to threaten her? Could it be the person who'd been sleeping on her sofa? No, he dismissed that. It didn't make sense she'd offer shelter to someone who would kill her . . . unless Elena had done something to piss them off? His wound started pounding because he couldn't think of one enemy she had. He rubbed the spot between his eyebrows. Started thinking again, more slowly this time.

Fuck up = death.

Who would have the authority to talk to her like that? Reuben gave the orders. Mac had seen with his own eyes what happened to those who didn't obey orders. And sometimes to those who did. Mac considered the possibilities. Had Elena got something wrong? Or in her terror had she just abandoned her work? Not taken Reuben's messages? Or just bolted?

Mac slumped into the sofa. He did what Calum had told him to do. Sat down and considered the evidence. Motive?

If Elena had botched up something important of Reuben's then maybe he'd killed her and Mac was just meant to be collateral damage.

Or if Reuben had found out that Mac was a cop, he would have killed the pair of them, although Elena would have been the collateral damage in that case. Mac couldn't see how Reuben could have found out about his real role in the gang, unless he'd been careless somewhere down the line. It happened.

No. It was more likely that Elena had done something to put her brutal boss in a deadly mood.

Fuck up = death.

Fuck up = death.

Fuck up = death.

But what documents had Reuben – if this was Reuben – been referring to? Did they have something to do with what might be happening at eleven tonight? Maybe copies were in the remains of the fire as well. So Mac dived back into his search, but only found the remains of what he concluded was burnt paper. He rushed back to the kitchen to find a knife and used it to take out the screws on the computer so he could retrieve the motherboard and drives. But they were gone.

Next he was back in the kitchen emptying the bin. Peelings, wrappers, a discarded invitation to some event at the Russian embassy two days ago and a crushed box. He pulled it out and examined it. Froze. A home pregnancy testing kit. A chill swept through him. Had Elena been . . . ? He couldn't even think it. Was that why she was so hysterical when she called him?

'You've got to get me – us – out of here . . .'

Her words from their last conversation rang in his head. *Us.* Did she mean it wasn't only her life at stake but their unborn child's?

Please, please, not that. He couldn't live with the death of another child of his blood. Couldn't . . .

Quickly he checked inside the box. No pregnancy testing stick. His head snapped up when he heard footsteps again in the hall below. Heavier than the last time. No way it was the neighbour. He shoved the box in his pocket as he rushed to the bedroom. The footsteps came up the stairs. Like a disturbed lover, he hid in the wardrobe, but didn't close the door completely, leaving a small gap to spy. Whoever it was was now in the main room. He heard the continual hissing of what sounded like spray paint. Then silence. The footsteps retreated back across the room. Abruptly stopped. Mac slowly pressed open the wardrobe door. The air smelt different, as if tainted with some type of chemical. His gaze snapped towards the dressing table mirror, which reflected a bright burst of light being thrown into the main room. His mind thought quickly. Flame. The smell: accelerant. The fire started moving and licking a path straight towards the bedroom.

seventeen

Mac jumped into the sitting room, narrowly missing the line of the fire. He shot towards the landing but stopped short when confronted by a raging sea of flames; he knew there was no escape there. Palm over his mouth to guard against the rising smoke, he ran back to the bedroom and made straight for the window. He heaved at its edge. Shut tight. Swiftly he turned towards the chest of drawers and managed to manoeuvre it towards the window. Bent down and, with a groan that squeezed his chest muscles, lifted it by its bottom end. Tipped it against the pane. Crash. The chest of drawers did its job breaking the window. Chunks of glass and the chest of drawers toppled down to the back garden below. He kicked out the remaining glass. The opening sucked smoke outwards.

At training college he'd seen a reckoner that estimated how far a man could fall and what injuries he could expect from various heights. But those calculations didn't include having a fire at your back, singeing your clothes. He climbed backwards out of the window. Held onto the ledge with both hands and lowered himself so he was dangling by his fingertips. As he pushed against the wall to jump off, he remembered the jumping calculations as you often remember things in extreme stress. A man hanging from an upstairs window of a terraced house? About twelve to fifteen feet to fall. Injuries to be expected? It all depended, of course, but if you were lucky it might be bruises and strains. If you were unlucky, broken feet, ankles or legs. He remembered the last piece of theory – keep your legs together and knees slightly bent like a paratrooper. He jumped.

Hit the ground. Rolled over and over until he came to rest. He struggled to his feet. Sucked in his breath sharply as pain spun from one of his ankles. He tested it as he took a step. Nothing major, probably just some bruising. He threaded his way over the back garden. Already a few horrified and shocked onlookers were gathering at windows and in gardens, shouting at him and trying to help. He ignored them.

But he couldn't ignore the screams that were coming from inside the house. Little Miss Beautiful Pigtails downstairs. He doubled back, kicked and battered the door that led from the back garden to her kitchen with all the pent-up rage he felt inside. When he was in, he headed in the direction of the screams that rose with the hysteria of a siren in the smoke. As the building buckled, bent and blistered in the heat, he found her crouched in shock and stunned terror in her front room. Bending her double over his shoulder, he ran back the way he'd come, her screams muffled as she choked on the black fog that weaved a deadly cloak around them. Finally, he emerged into the daylight again, and dropped her on the grass at a distance. People were rushing towards them, which was his signal to be gone. He pulled his cap down low as he moved in the opposite direction, with the things he'd found in Elena's home secure in his pocket.

eighteen

Mac took five minutes to clean his face and hands in the Gents of the first McDonald's he came across. He inspected his ankle, which didn't hurt as much any more. It had a small purple bruise that would either fade away or start swelling. Either way he wasn't going to let it slow him down. He avoided looking at himself in the mirror – what was the point when he knew he looked like he'd invented the word crap? But his mind did turn to who had followed him to Elena's and tried to make him the guy on a non-November bonfire night. Maybe it was the two men in the Merc? Or Reuben? Or the Mr or Ms Nameless who'd been kipping on Elena's sofa, snug as a bug, last night? Too many maybes: what he had to deal with was the evidence he had at the moment. So he moved to a cubicle, locked the door, lowered the toilet seat and sat. Took each item he'd found at Elena's and laid them on the floor in front of him.

Post-it.

Charred photograph of two military men smiling.

Empty pregnancy testing box.

Small card with words *Club Zee* on it.

His gaze kept coming back to the Post-it. *Fuck up = death*. *Fuck up = death*. Yeah, that sounded like that madman Reuben. It must have been the Russian behind the fire at Elena's, wanting all evidence about her involvement with him gone. As a naked cop, Mac wasn't permitted to keep any kind of paperwork on him – too dangerous, it might compromise his position. But he kept a mental file of all the Intel he'd been given about the Russian before going into deep cover.

Name: Reuben Volk. Suspected alias. Birth name unknown.

Nationality: Russian. Region of birth unknown.

Age: Unknown.

Criminal activities: Arms dealer. Criminal activities outside the UK unknown. Russian authorities will not give access to any information about him.

Convictions: Unknown.

Family: Younger brother. Also criminal associate. Son.

Purpose of undercover op: No hard evidence but suspect that he's about to initiate a gang war to become London's foremost arms supplier.

Unknown, unknown, unknown. So much about the bastard was unknown, but what Mac needed now was a killer to take revenge on. Once he had his hands round his neck, he'd wring the truth out of him.

It had to be Reuben.

Reuben. Reuben. Reuben.

He couldn't stop the manic repetition of the Russian's name bouncing and bruising against the four walls of his mind. Without warning, the muscles in Mac's chest tightened. His breathing squeezed, felt like it was almost going to shut down. He knew what was coming next, so he fought it. Hard. But he knew he'd lost the battle when the green walls of the cubicle appeared to move, closing in on him. The ceiling started to drop. Blackness hovered over him, to the side of him, in front of him. Mac gasped for more oxygen. Gasped . . . his mind nose-dived.

He was back in the bathroom. This time, his back against the wall. As if he was shackled, couldn't move. Reuben stepped into the room, a picture of black in motion, from his gelled hair

*to the Luger in his hand. Mac called out his name, but the
other man walked past him like he wasn't even there. Reuben
kept moving. And moving. Until he reached it. The bath with
Elena inside it. Mac fought hard against the wall, but he
couldn't get free. Mac shouted out. Elena screamed. But there
was no noise, just a horrible, cold expectation of death. Mac
jerked and fought. Reuben smiled. Mac banged his fist against
the unbreakable wall. Reuben raised the Luger. Mac's hands
were broken and bleeding. Reuben aligned the gun with the
back of Elena's head. Mac and Elena cried out at the same
time. Finally sound came as the echo of a bullet shattered in
the room . . .*

Mac came to, shivering and sweating, slumped against a
pipe on the wall. He didn't know where he was. What was he
doing in this small space? Why was he sitting down? His
confused gaze flickered around. Tiles, door, kind of walls. Hard
seat. Toilet seat. He closed his eyes as he remembered where he
was. Placed his head in his hands. He couldn't go through all
this again, this mad 'one minute he was there and the next he
was not'. Just like what happened after Stevie was gone. It
terrified him, this lack of control. His hand groped inside his
pocket with desperation. Stilled when he found what he was
after. Elena's bracelet. He pulled it out and rubbed it flat
against his chest. It was almost like he could feel her. Like she
was there with him.

But she wasn't here. She was dead.

Dead.

There was a cold calmness about the single word that finally
helped him ease the air more freely into his body. He took
steady breaths in and out. In and out. Mac pulled the bracelet
away from his body and shoved it back into his pocket. Got
back on with the job he'd vowed to do.

He looked back at the items on the floor. Gathered the

pregnancy testing kit box, the photo and card and placed them inside his pocket as well. Which left only the Post-it note on the floor. He didn't put it away, instead stared hard at it.

Fuck up = death.

Of course he had no proof. But men had gone to the gallows for less evidence than Mac had. Reuben was going to the gallows. Even if it wasn't him, the killer might be at Reuben's son's party. He'd wipe out the entire gang if he had to . . . He'd made a promise to Elena to keep her safe. Now she was dead.

He snatched the Post-it off the floor. Shoved it into his pocket as he stood up. Checked his watch.

11:19.

Made eye contact with no one as he left the burger bar. Walked round the side of the building to the alleyway he'd noticed on the way in that contained three large dumpsters. He flipped back the lid of the first one he came to. Dropped his rucksack, containing Elena's bag, into it. All he needed was safely tucked away in his pocket. He flicked the lid back down as he made his decision about his next move.

He knew he was about to take a big risk. If it worked he'd have a clearer idea of what the fuck was going on. And if it didn't . . .

He'd either be behind bars.

Or dead.

nineteen

11:45 a.m.

The Munch Munch café. The one place Mac knew he shouldn't be found dead near. But he stood across the road from it, knowing that its biggest customers were the cops from the nearby police station, nicknamed The Fort.

He pulled his baseball cap lower. Stepped out into the quiet street. He was sure the light breeze carried fine flecks of rain, but the ground around him was dry, so maybe the rain wasn't there at all. He reached the café just as the door opened. He dipped his head sharply when he realised that he knew the people coming out. A young WPC he'd grown to like and an older male detective. From the smile glowing on her face, he knew that she didn't know the guy was married. When this was all over, he'd have a little whisper in her ear.

The couple were too engrossed with each other to pay him any attention, so he stepped back, head still down, to let them by.

He moved inside. A Euro-trash tune banged out from the plasma telly mounted on the wall, showcasing a video with a man jiving in close-ups with fluorescent green beams zip-zapping behind him. The place was almost empty, except for a solitary occupant. The person he was looking for. He walked through the aisle between the tables and the church-like mini-benches. He stopped at the table. Only when he rasped out her name did she look up.

'Mac, what the hell are you doing here?' asked Detective Inspector Rio Wray.

twenty

He took the seat across from her in the mottled-skin-coloured booth.

'Just like old times,' Mac finally said.

And it did feel like old times. This was their table. His, Rio's and Calum's. They'd started out together, three Bobbies on the beat, eager to uphold the law. At this table they'd compare notes on cases, put their heads together to make sure that those living on the wrong side of the street were brought to justice. As the years had passed, they'd still met at this table, but gone their separate ways. He'd gone under-cover; Rio had kept her eye on her career, moving on and up. And Calum? Thinking about Calum made him wonder where it had all gone wrong.

She didn't respond to his comment, instead asked, surprise in her voice, 'So what brings you down here? I thought you were on a job?'

There were a number of reasons why he was down there and one of them had already been settled. If Rio's team had already identified Mac's DNA in the hotel room, she would have arrested him on the spot. So that hadn't happened yet. But he also wanted to know what Rio's team had discovered.

As she spoke he could see her dark eyes checking him out – the baseball cap, the light bruises, the pale face. He needed to be very careful because the woman opposite him was no fool.

'I am. But just needed to come up for some air.'

She did that thing with her eyes that always made him feel uncomfortable – stared straight into his as if she were gazing deep into his mind.

'I'm glad you're here. I was worried about you being on your own today.'

He took a deep breath, knowing exactly what she was talking about. The one thing he didn't want to think about.

'Have you been to–'

'No,' he swiftly interrupted.

'I'll go to the grave later . . .'

'Just leave it alone, all right.' He knew his voice was hard but he couldn't stop it. The truth was if he had to think about *that* as well, he wasn't going to make it through the day.

'I can't do that,' she stubbornly went on. 'He was my godson. Today's the first anniversary of his death.'

Son. The word hovered over the table between them. Son. His son. His little boy. Stevie. Six years old and full of life. One day laughing his beautiful face off, the next day dead.

Suddenly Rio spun her mobile on the table to face him. He looked down and wished he hadn't. The screen showed a photo of Stevie taken last year, all honey-brown hair, Mac's blue eyes, with that grin that would've been complete when his two new front teeth came. But, of course, they never had. Sharply he turned his face away. He couldn't look at him. Couldn't. They stayed like that, his face turned to the wall while his dead son smiled up at him from the table.

Finally Rio inched the phone back to her. Once she put the mobile away, she almost put her hand over his, but she didn't. That type of emotional contact just wasn't her style.

'You look terrible.' Now that was the Rio he knew.

He turned back to her. 'Talking about terrible, I just wanted a bit of Intel that might be able to help with the job I'm on.' Rio took a slug from her coffee, so he carried on. 'I hear there was a body found at some hotel in Bayswater.'

Rio eased her cup down as suspicion clouded her eyes. 'Why come to me to find out about this case? All you've got to do is check in with your superior – what's his name, Phil? And I'm sure he'll get all the details you need.'

'I could do that, but it would take a while. If you could just tell me, I wouldn't have to jump through all those boring hoops.'

Rio slowly licked the moisture from her lips as she kept her gaze on him. He kept his eyes steady on her face, knowing if he looked away she'd know that something just wasn't right.

'Come on,' he coaxed softly. 'You might have info that can tip my case in my favour.' Then he said the one thing he knew would bring her round. 'The sooner I get my case finished, the sooner I can get home, close the door and think about . . .' His voice wavered. He couldn't say Stevie's name, just couldn't say it.

He saw the suspicion in her gaze give way to sympathy.

'The hotel murder? It was a pretty brutal and messy scene,' she finally said. 'A woman with her head blasted to pieces. No ID. So, genetics is all we've got to work with.' She reached for her coffee again. 'Pretty sleazy hotel, popular with prostitutes and petty criminals. Or undercover cops.' She laughed. He looked into her eyes to confirm she was joking. She was. Rio became serious again. 'So we're guessing she was a prostitute. Russian, by the look of it.'

'How do you know that?' Only after he'd cut in did Mac realise his question sounded too eager, too probing.

Rio did a sweep of his clothing again. Settled on his

baseball cap. 'Are you all right? You look mashed. Battered and bruised – are you in some sort of trouble?'

'I'm on a job,' he explained. 'Being battered and bruised comes with the territory. You know I can't talk about that. This girl?'

'You seem very interested Mac – may I ask why?'

'I told you I'm on a case. There's probably no connection but I need to cross-check.' But he didn't sound convincing.

Rio gave him a curious look before continuing. 'The victim had a strange red star tattoo on her left arm.' Mac eased back down. 'It had Russian writing around it. I've never seen one like it before. But, mind you, it could be a girl from Romford who saw it on the Net, so we're going to be asking around the parlours just in case it was done locally.'

'DNA?'

'The lab guys are still trying to find a match for our faceless lady on our system.'

'How long will that take?'

'I don't know – how long's a ball of string? If she's on the system, when I get back to the office probably. Lunchtime? This afternoon?'

'Any idea who pulled the trigger?'

'Hard to say at the moment. But we did find evidence there was someone else injured in the incident. We've got that DNA as well, so we're running it through the system. Maybe that'll help, maybe it won't. But, if you're asking me who I think it is, it's likely to be a John with a gun. But you know me, Mac. I always like to get my man, so we'll do a thorough job. Especially when it's a man who does something like that. If you could have seen what I saw, you'd know what I mean.'

Her gaze flicked back to him, her emotions firmly in place. 'It won't take us long to figure out who he is. If he's injured he'll turn up somewhere needing medical attention, although he hasn't popped up at any hospitals that we've checked so far. I think that the killer might be the kind of sicko who doesn't leave straight away but goes for a nap on the bed. But he was bleeding – how or why, I haven't figured out yet. So he has a snooze, and when he wakes up goes back into the bathroom to gaze lovingly at his handiwork. We found footprints that suggest he then moved across the bathroom to gaze at himself in the mirror. A man who adores the look of his face after he's murdered a woman. Nice type. The sort you could take home to your mum's.'

Mac felt sick. What if Rio and her team caught up with him and really thought that's what he'd done. Gloated in the mirror after . . . after . . .he'd pumped a shot into Elena. And possibly killed his own unborn child?

'Mac? Mac? Are you OK?'

He heard Rio's worried voice and looked up at her. Except it wasn't her he saw, but Elena. Elena as she'd looked the last time he'd ever seen her. Smiling down at him as she lay on top of him, naked in bed. Her head arched back, her hair flowing with the abandon of an ebony scarf drifting in the wind. And her face . . .Her face had been a rosy white, not a mash of twisted flesh as he'd seen it last.

'That's it.' The urgent tone of Rio's voice pulled him back to her. She leaned over the table. 'I'm going to contact this Phil . . .'

'I'm OK.'

'I don't know why you're undercover these days anyway. They should have given you a desk job after what happened to Stevie, and you being diagnosed with having PTSD . . .'

'I don't have post-traumatic anything,' he hissed. 'Phil needed me; there wasn't anyone else he could use . . .' He shoved up from his seat. 'I need to go.'

He started to twist round but was stopped by Rio's words. 'We do have another angle on the killer.'

He froze. Turned back. Let her finish. 'The hotel has got hidden security cameras in the reception. Not for customer protection, of course – the owner suspected his staff were stealing from him. We've got an image of a man, about your height . . .' Mac's breath stopped in his throat.

'But the image is hazy and the receptionist's description was crap. We're getting one of the techy guys to work on it and should have it back in a matter of hours . . .'

The ring of her mobile stopped her words. She took the call. Listened. Then said, 'I'll be there ASAP.'

She stood up as she cut the call. Walked towards Mac. 'I've got to go. Sounds like another murder. They're like buses, aren't they? – they come along in twos and threes. Let's talk later.' She started towards the door, but stopped as she pulled the handle. Turned back to him. 'If you don't ring Phil, I will.'

Then Mac found himself alone. He stood there for a while, sifting through the information Rio had given him. If Elena's DNA was on the system, it would be a few hours before they identified her for definite. Either way, it would be a few hours before his DNA was identified, as he was on the system. Then there was the security camera footage that he hadn't factored in. He needed time. But Rio wasn't giving him any. And as soon as Rio realised he had been in the hotel room with the body, he would be the hunted, not the hunter.

Mac left the café. Got ready to pop two pills . . . then he saw the car. Black Merc, just like the one he'd seen outside Mo Masri's clinic. He hadn't seen the car anywhere near Elena's flat, but maybe whoever was inside had been there as well, waiting to get him in a confined space so they could burn him alive? The heavily tinted windows were up so he couldn't see who was inside. It was parked up on the other side of the road. Mac kept his head down. Started walking. He heard the engine start. His feet beat against the street, taking longer strides. Tyres squealed behind him.

twenty-one

Noon

Mac ran. Eyes darting as he looked for an escape. A short Victorian lane, protected by two bollards, headed off down to his right. Turning into it, he chased over the cobbles, assuming the car would be too wide for pursuit. He heard the engine behind him ease up slightly and the scraping of plastic as the bumper tried to force its way past the bollards. He kept running. There was a pause, then the car reversed, accelerated, and then crashed its way through. Now it was hurtling down the lane at full speed.

For as long as he'd been a cop, Mac had enjoyed chasing and being chased; there was something primitive about it. Second-guessing the pursued or pursuing, jumping walls, weaving in between cars, disappearing into crowds or spotting the slightly out-of-breath pedestrian trying to blend in with the everyday. But not today. Someone had killed Elena and they were now on his tail trying to put him down permanently too, like they'd meant to in the hotel room.

At the end of the road, he reached out a hand and swung to the right on a lamppost, just before his pursuers could ram him. Although the brakes were applied, momentum carried the car out into the middle of the main road that lay in front of it. Mac turned and watched as passing traffic came screeching to a halt at angles to the Mercedes. Angry drivers sounded their horns. Yelled abuse at its driver. Mac kept running, looking and keeping a frantic eye open for any hiding place. For a few moments, the Merc sat motionless where it had come to rest, as if embarrassed at its mistake. Then it revved. Weaved its way past the angry drivers and began its pursuit again.

It soon pulled level with him and veered violently across the road, mounted the pavement and came to a halt, blocking the way. The driver's door began to open, but Mac leapt onto the bonnet and skidded down the other side. He stole half a glance as he went over but the black tint on the windows meant there was no identifying the men inside. He crossed the street to where a bus had been taking on passengers and was preparing to pull away. He hammered on the door but the driver merely shook his head and the bus set off. Mac kicked the bodywork of the bus as it went. The driver applied his brakes and sounded its horn. There was some shouting but it wasn't for him. The Mercedes had cut the bus up and was now thirty or forty yards down the road.

Mac seized his chance. He didn't run. He walked casually across the road and down another street. He put his head down, but now he wasn't being pursued, the energy in his legs started to slip away. He couldn't think straight and the blood vessels in his head throbbed. He walked a block. More sounds of an engine being pushed to the limit followed by brake pads being burned out on the road he'd just left. The car had doubled back and was now hesitating out at the junction of the street it was on, unsure where its prey was. Mac stopped and looked in a shop window. A pet shop. Rabbits were trying to jump around in the cramped pen behind the glass. He stole a glance down the street. His pursuers did a turn and came down the street but seemed unsure.

Mac walked down the street as calmly as he could. The car

went gently by while he went into the next shop. A mini-supermarket called Price Buster. The car came to a halt in the middle of the road, as if searching for a parking space. The shop was empty except for a teenage girl, wearing a sky-blue hijab with funky silver tassels hanging at one side, who stood behind the counter near a display of mobile phones. Seeing him, her hand fumbled under the counter. Panic button, he decided. Mac didn't blame her. Sweating, out of breath, panic-stricken and wearing a baseball cap, he could hardly have looked any more sinister.

He leaned into her face. 'Have you pressed an alarm?'

She gestured at the door. 'Get out.'

Mac panted, 'Is your alarm connected to the cops?'

But the girl was brave and she leaned towards Mac with attitude, until their noses were nearly touching. 'Get out – unless you want to get banged up.'

So her panic button was connected to the police – but in an area like this, it could be ten or fifteen minutes before they arrived, and Mac might be dead by then.

He leapfrogged the counter, the suddenness of his move making the girl stumble back. On a stand nearby was a plastic statue of Buddha, like the ones found in cheap tourist shops in the Far East. Mac grabbed the statue and pulled the painted figure from its base. It gave way to reveal a long metal spike.

He cornered the girl. Pressing the spike against her neck he warned, 'I'm not a criminal and you'll be all right as long as you do as you're told. I'm going to hide down under the counter, but you pull any shit and I'll run this through the femoral artery in your leg? You do know what will happen if I do that . . . ?'

'I'm not a dummy, mister; I've got a GCSE in biology. Probably bleed out and be dead in minutes if you cut me at an angle. But if it's a straight cut—'

'All right, enough with the mouth.' He crouched down. Pressed the makeshift weapon to her thigh.

'What do you want me to do?' she asked.

'Call the cops.'

twenty-two

'They said they'll be here in five minutes,' the girl said, reporting back her conversation with the police.

'What's your name?' Mac asked.

'What? So you can get the spelling right on my gravestone?'

The girl was full of sass; if this had been any other day, Mac would've admired that.

'Lean over to one of those throwaway mobiles and top it up,' he instructed.

He felt her move and without being asked she threw the mobile down to him. With one hand, Mac raised the bottom end of the right side of his trousers, then stuck his new phone into his sock. Once his trouser leg was back in place, he laid his other mobile on the floor.

'Nice and easy, I want you to pick up the mobile and take the SIM card out of it and pass it to me.'

She did what he asked. He tucked the card in one of the front pockets of his trousers, putting the phone that linked him to the outside world out of action for good.

Jingle. The door opened. Mac tensed. Someone was in the shop. Couldn't be the cops because five minutes wasn't up. He pushed the spike, just enough pressure for a warning.

Footsteps. Then a voice. Male.

'Twenty Benson, love.'

Mac relaxed. Just a customer. The girl leaned sideways and

pulled a pack of ciggies off the shelf. The transaction was done quickly. Footsteps faded towards the door. Jingle. The door opened as the man let himself out. Mac gently tapped the girl's leg with the spike as a mark of approval.

Abruptly, the girl started yelling, 'Behind the counter.' She kicked Mac in his arm. 'He's got a blade! He's got a blade! Behind the counter!'

The girl rushed to the side. Who the fuck was she talking to? Then he realised that the man with the cigarettes must have let someone else into the shop when he'd opened the door to leave.

Mac stormed up, spike raised. All he saw was a blurred, one-two, black movement of something coming straight at him. Bang, bang. Something hit his right arm, then his left. He grunted as the spike tumbled from his hand. He cried out as something hit him hard in the side of the neck. He went down. Stayed down as he lost consciousness.

twenty-three

The victim was tied to a chair. His eyes wide open. A hypodermic needle was sticking out of each eye. Rio Wray crouched down by the chair in the doctor's surgery as she stared at her second murder scene of the day. She winced. She'd had a thing about needles since she was a kid. Rio didn't wrinkle her nose at the stink coming off the body. She'd smelt that stench too many times before – the victim had lost the contents of his bowels and bladder as he'd died.

'Do we know who the vic is?' she asked the responding officer who had been first to attend the scene.

He stood behind her, next to Detective Martin. 'He's a Doctor Mohammed Masri. This is his clinic, a lucrative private practice by all accounts.'

Rio turned back to the unfortunate doctor. Looked over his body. Blood lay in dried stripes, layered on top of each other, beneath his eyes. The blood had a glaze to it; she presumed some type of clear liquid that had come from his eyes, but she wasn't sure. She'd get the forensic specialist to check it out when she arrived. The needles were stabbed into his eyes with little finesse, like someone aiming at the dartboard for the first time. The needle in the right eye was stuck just outside the pupil. What colour his eyes had been she couldn't tell because of the leakage of blood. From his name she guessed he must've been Asian, so his eyes were likely to have been some shade of brown. Rio switched her gaze to the other eye. Here the needle was almost dead centre in the pupil. Something to the side of the needle caught her eye. She leaned closer. Peered deeper. She couldn't be certain, but it looked like there was another tiny hole in the white of the eye, almost as if the murderer had stabbed the eye before and then thought better of it, taken the needle out and stuck it in the pupil. A murderer who thought they had time on their hands. A murderer who took pleasure in the pain they were inflicting. Most people would be shocked to hear that most of the murderers she'd caught hadn't thought about the pain they were causing. Most had been domestic situations; a husband angry at finding out his beloved was having an affair, a childish dispute between teenagers, a wife who just couldn't take the beatings her husband had been giving her for years any more.

The needles hadn't been the murder weapon. What had been inside them had been. Whatever had been pumped inside his eyes, travelling down through his body, had delivered the fatal blow. What that had been, she didn't know, but the autopsy would determine that. His mouth was open. The tongue hanging out like he'd been screaming until the very end. Froth and blood lay encrusted round his lips. She shifted away from his face and studied his tied arms. No, tied hands, she corrected herself. Each hand was secured to the thick black plastic arm of the large swing-back chair. The three middle fingers rested on the arm, while the thumb and small finger were tucked underneath. Tied with rope that was red and twisted like the twine of a washing line.

Rio stood up and spoke to one of the officers holding the security log. 'Make sure that forensics identify what type of rope was used to tie him. If it didn't come from here, we might be able to trace where it was purchased.'

'I didn't expect to see you again this morning,' a voice said.

She turned to find the forensic specialist, Charlie, and her team behind her.

'It's looking like one of those days for murder,' she answered.

The forensic expert stepped forward. Moved towards the victim. 'Interesting.'

'Like "your usual murder" interesting? "Serial killer" interesting? Or it just "gets your forensic blood flowing" interesting?' Rio asked as she moved to stand beside Charlie.

The other woman was grim as she peered closely at the victim. 'No, "I've seen something like this before" interesting.'

That got Rio's full attention. The other woman carried on. 'It was years back. I was doing some international work in Russia. Working on a joint op with the forensics team there. A small place, Vayasibirsk, not the type of place most people would have heard of. Quite pretty, really, except for the gang violence that was going on. A speciality of one of the gangs was sticking syringes full of bleach into the eyes of any witnesses they thought were going to inform on them to the police.'

Rio frowned. 'Why choose that method of murder?'

She kept her gaze fixed on the victim. 'It's like these Mafia killings in Sicily, message deaths. We found one victim, a young woman, dead beside her crying baby son. Next to her was a note: "The tongue speaks, but the head doesn't know."' She turned to look at Rio. 'Sometimes it's best to keep your mouth shut.'

Rio was about to tell the officer to take note of what the forensic expert was saying, but when she turned to her she was already writing the information down. So was this murder gang-related? A Russian gang who continued to use ways of murdering people from the old country in their new homeland? Maybe the doctor had patients he was seeing out of hours? The type of patients who didn't like going to hospitals?

'Who found the good doctor?' Rio asked the responding officer.

'His receptionist. She found him when she arrived at work after ten this morning. She was the last one here yesterday evening and locked up, so it sounds like he got here this morning. She said that he usually got here after eight.'

'Did she notice anything unusual?'

When he shook his head, Rio said, 'Which patients were booked to see him today?'

'None. The receptionist says that he always used Fridays to catch up on paperwork.'

Rio stared back at the forensic team at work, then at the body, and instructed Detective Martin, 'Ask around at the other practices. Find out if anyone saw anything or anyone this morning.' She called to another member of her team. 'Check the computer for medical records.'

Then Rio did a slow walk-through of the scene. The office looked tidy, nothing looked out of place. She opened drawers, went through bookshelves, inspected the floor. Nothing. She opened a filing cabinet, which sat next to a medical waste bin. Opened it. It contained the standard, manila-coloured patients' files. If the doctor had been treating someone off the books, she didn't expect to see their name inside, but you never knew. She took her time going through each folder. Names, ailments, treatments. She took out another folder. Most of the label on the front of it had been torn off, taking away the name of the patient. Rio opened it. Nothing inside, unlike the other files, which had listed patients' medical histories. A missing patient connected to the doctor's murder?

The urgent voice of the member of her team at the computer interrupted her thoughts. 'There's evidence that someone's been tampering with the database in the computer.'

Rio stared at the folder in her hand. Then back at the

computer. Who could the doctor have been treating that could lead to his death?

'I bet it's connected to this empty patient's file.' Rio waved the folder at him. 'Talk to the receptionist again about who the patients were. If we can find who the missing patient is, we get our first link to discovering whoever sent Doctor Mohammed Masri to an early grave.'

As her colleague left the room, she placed the empty folder in an evidence bag. As she passed the evidence to another member of her team, she noticed the medical waste bin again. Noticed something odd about it. The heaviness of the bin had left an imprint, a semicircle, on the carpet. An imprint would only be seen if the bin had been moved that morning.

Rio lifted the lid. Bent over and started looking inside. Bottles of out-of-date drugs. And something else. She stopped when she realised that she was looking at a strip of towelling covered in blood.

'Another evidence bag,' she called out quickly.

With her gloved fingers she slowly pulled out the towel. Held it up to the light. She looked away from the blood as something else caught her attention on the other side of the towel. Turned it around. There was some type of stamp on it. She brought it closer to her face. Black writing. Rio squinted, trying to read it:

The Rose Hotel.

The Rose . . . Rio froze. That was where they'd found the woman in the bath. So The Rose Hotel had once been an upmarket affair, with its name stitched in the linen, and now had fallen to become one that was used for turning tricks. Rio squeezed her eyes closed, blanking out the world around her. Instead she let her mind conjure up an image of the bloody bathroom she'd been in earlier. She took in the scene again.

Faceless body.

Bathtub.

Blood and bone splattered against the walls.

Sink.

Towel.

No, not towel. Torn towel.

Her eyes snapped open. Could this be the missing part of the towel? A jigsaw piece that linked the crime scene she was in with the one at the hotel?

The detective questioning the receptionist came back into the room.

'She says that she can't remember off the top of her head who all the patients are but, apparently, she kept backup paper copies of all the patients' files off-site for security.'

'Off-site? Is that allowed?'

'One of the advantages of going private, I would think.'

'Make a note of all the patients' names from the folders in the cabinet. Then get the receptionist to check the list against the files . . .'

'We can get one of the techy guys to have a look at the computer—'

The ripe curse word that Rio let loose cut the suggestion off. Rio didn't need reminding that getting any type of IT support quickly in The Met, with the cutbacks, seemed as likely as her hooking up with Denzel Washington and having beautiful, cry-free babies.

'No, our quickest option,' Rio continued, 'is to get the receptionist to ID the patient from the records she keeps off-site.'

Rio placed the bloody strip of towel in the evidence bag.

twenty-four

Mac thought he was back in the hotel room, except this time it was his arms and neck that were messed up. He opened his eyes, squinting with the pressure of pain. He faced a high, cream-coloured ceiling, with all the fancy work of an early Victorian house. He looked across the naked wooden floor and noticed a pair of legs in stormy-weather-grey-toned trousers, which ended in super-shiny polished black shoes.

He raised himself up, gritting his teeth to deal with the pain. Once he was sitting he gazed at the man, who sat in a chair with his arms folded. The man was in his mid-forties, with one of those ordinary faces that were invisible in a crowd.

'Did you have to whack me so bloody hard?' Mac grumbled at his superior officer, Phil Delaney.

'You're lucky I only hit you a couple of times with all the trouble you've caused me. Mac, what the hell has been going on? I've been looking for you everywhere. Why hasn't your phone been on? Why haven't you called in?'

As Phil blasted him with question after question, Mac eased his legs over the side of the couch. His movement was heavier near his ankle and he realised that Phil hadn't discovered his new mobile phone. He knew where he was – The Office Research Unit, which was the official name for Mac's undercover division. Instead of being based in a police station, the unit existed behind the anonymous walls of a four-storey Victorian house in North London. A house that looked like a wreck from the outside, which was a cover so that no one guessed what was going on inside.

Mac followed his boss's questions with one of his own. 'Were you following me earlier near Harley Street?'

'Harley Street?' Phil looked at him as if he'd gone crazy. 'Believe me, if I'd seen you there, you would've been back at base a lot sooner. The only place I tracked you to was some hotel with a blind woman manning the desk. So what's going on, Mac?'

So who was in the Merc at the doctor's? Clearly a black Merc like Phil's.

'Things happened,' Mac finally responded.

'What things? Like that cut in your head with the stitches?' Phil stabbed his finger at Mac. 'You'd better start talking or I might have to push this one upstairs.'

Mac contemplated the threat while he located his baseball cap. Shoved it on; winced as he walked over to a glass of water sitting on the large desk next to Phil's chair. He drank greedily, only realising then that it had been hours since he'd had any food.

Still holding the empty glass he said, 'Time just ran on, you know what it's like . . .'

Of course his superior did know what it was like. He'd become a legend as an operative in the field before taking over the head honcho's position in the unit five years ago. What had made Phil's major-league rep was his face – so unremarkable that people saw through him, past him. The ideal attribute for a naked cop to have. Phil had taken a personal interest in Mac and gone out of his way to share tips of the trade, which made Mac feel disloyal with the untruths he was about to tell.

'I was just doing my job,' Mac continued. 'If you want me to stay here and write a full report . . .'

Phil turned the intensity of his gaze onto him. 'Don't BS the man who taught you how to bullshit in the first place.' He sighed. 'We've been in trouble before, haven't we? Loads of times. We can sort things out – but I can't help unless you tell me what's wrong.'

Phil gave him a long stare, which seemed to include all the years they'd worked together and all the things they'd been through.

Mac looked away. 'I've already told you–'

But Phil interrupted again. 'Is someone after you? Are you being threatened? You've upset a lot of criminals and prevented a lot of crimes over the years – is one of those guys back on the outside and trying to get his revenge? If they are, I'll sort them out for you. Or is it something to do with your work in this gang?'

Mac placed the glass gently on the desk.

'This is all my fault, Mac,' Phil went on. 'I was advised to find you a desk job and not send you back into the field. After what happened, I should have–'

Mac snapped and shouted, 'This has got nothing to do with that and it's a bit cheap of you–'

But Phil slapped him down. 'You lose your son in tragic circumstances twelve months ago to the day. The only reason I took you back was because you reassured me you were ready to come back to work, that you were off the meds that were dealing with your PTSD . . .'

The strain pumped up through Mac's body as he screwed his hands into fists at his side. 'I'm not a fucking nut job . . .'

'I'm not saying that you are, but you know that stress can be a killer in our line of work. It's not easy pretending to be someone you're not, and also having to hold on to the baggage of the death of someone close to you. Everyone told me I was crazy to place you on a Level One assignment.' Mac's superior took a deep breath. 'So I've decided that you need to be placed on sick leave . . .'

'No fucking way.' Mac took a furious step towards the other man. 'I've got to get to Reuben . . .' Mac clammed up.

Phil remained seated. 'The Mac I know would never have threatened some defenceless teenage girl in a shop. The Mac I know is a clear thinker. Logical, cool, an assessor of facts and information. You're not that Mac any more. It's nothing to be ashamed of. We've all got our limits and you're well past yours. You're not well. You're not thinking straight.'

Not thinking straight? It was the same phrase Calum had used. And Mac resented it all the more because he knew it was true. And he was well past his limits. More than Phil realised. He played his last card.

'I can't leave the case now. There's something big going on tonight with Reuben Volk . . .'

'And what is it?' Phil now eased slowly to his feet.

'I don't know, but something is happening at eleven tonight . . .'

'Don't worry about tonight, I'll take care of things. You're done for now.'

'You can't do this to me. I've got to get to the Russian's—'

'Your gun, Mac. Then I'm taking you home. Let me deal with Reuben Volk.'

Mac knew there was no point arguing. He swore as he slammed the EDC handgun Calum had given him on to the desk.

twenty-five

Fifteen minutes later Phil Delaney closed the door of Mac's home, a flat that Mac had downsized to eighteen months ago when his wife had booted him out, divorced him and moved back to Hertfordshire. Phil stopped outside for a few seconds, just listening. When he heard Mac moving around, he headed downstairs for the exit. When he got back to his Merc, he stared at Mac's bedroom window. Then pulled out his phone.

'He knows about tonight.'

The curtains at the bedroom window snapped shut. Electric light came on.

'Well you'd better get him sorted out or else—' the person on the other end of the line came back furiously.

'Don't worry,' Phil cut in. 'He isn't going to be any more trouble. He understands it's over and that he's to stay well away from the Russian. Something's gone wrong, but he doesn't want to tell me what it is. It must have been serious, though. I did a trawl on the databases this morning and found he'd booked himself on a flight to Cambodia this morning, which he obviously didn't make for some reason.'

Phil took a steady breath as the light in the bedroom went off. 'We'd better hope he hasn't mentioned anything to anyone, or that's really going to mess things up.'

As soon as Phil disconnected the call, he made another one to his PA.

'Shazia, I need you to call Doctor Alicia Warren and tell her to meet me in the office ASAP.'

Phil kept his gaze pinned to Mac's home for another ten minutes. Only when the light came on again, behind the shadows of the curtains in the bedroom, did Phil leave the scene satisfied. A light that Phil didn't realise was programmed to go on and off and on again by an automatic timer.

twenty-six

1 p.m.

Insane. Insane. Insane.

The word battered the four corners of Mac's mind. The madness of revenge was the only explanation for why he was now standing in front of the barred iron gates that led up to Reuben's villa. The cop inside him ordered him to turn back; listen to Phil; to go home and mourn in the dark silence behind closed curtains. But then he felt *her* bracelet in his pocket. The madness deep in him grew.

He stared hard at the gang leader's home. A luxurious North London property of the type favoured by millionaire bankers, lawyers, media types. And arms traffickers. Standing behind the iron bars, dressed in Armani suits like rich zookeepers, two huge guards were keeping careful watch. They studied their new guest carefully and then one asked his name. When Mac gave it, the guard who'd remained silent pulled out his phone, eyes still on Mac, and verified who he was with someone inside the house. Reuben's other man flicked his gaze off Mac and got back to scanning the avenue and neighbouring properties for any sign of anything. In the distance, behind the house walls, Mac could hear children shouting and screaming. An image of young ones hyped high on happiness at another party swamped Mac's mind. Quickly he shoved the unwelcome memory away.

The guard finished his call and unlinked a rope chain from round the gate. He opened up, but only with enough space for Mac to pass through. Mac heard the crunch of gravel under his feet as he walked a few paces and then heard an angry call of 'Hey' behind him. One of the men took him by the arm and led him off to the portico.

The guard expertly patted him down, checking for hardware, a move Mac had only anticipated as he almost reached the house. He'd only remembered as he'd approached the gate that he still had his Luger stuck in his waistband. He'd backtracked and hidden it under a wheelie bin in front of a house further down the street and then returned. So Mac tried to remain relaxed, legs wide, arms spread. When the guard finished his search, he went through it again, more slowly this time, before finally, looking slightly disappointed, he motioned with his head that Mac was free to the join the kids' party.

Mac walked on, over the gravel, gunless and defenceless.

Insane, insane, insane.

He'd didn't even have a plan. Still wasn't a hundred per cent sure that Reuben was his man. But when he *was* sure, he'd need to choose Reuben's moment of death carefully. Of course a child's birthday bash was no place to commit a murder. But if this was his only chance, he had no alternative but to take it.

Click. Click. Click.

In the house opposite, from the master bedroom, a man took a few shots with a long-lens camera.

Click.

A picture of a man in a baseball cap approaching the main door.

Click.

A picture of the door opening.

Click.

A picture of one of the city's newest criminals, Reuben Volk, in the doorway.

twenty-seven

Mac looked into the eyes of a killer. But was it the right killer?

The man known as Reuben Volk on the passport he'd used to enter Britain, and AK Reuben to those in the underworld, had a face that was disciplined to show little emotion. He was an inch off Mac in height, had a body that stayed pumped up and tuned from the weights he used every day in his private gym, and wore his hair in the short-back-and-sides style of a soldier. The only jewellery he wore was a white-gold bracelet and a pair of shades parked on the top of his head like they were his most prized possession. But what Mac always remembered about his features were his eyes. So dark a brown that it felt like Mac was being drawn into the despair and dark of a never-ending tunnel. Were those brown eyes the last thing that Elena saw?

Mac checked him over for any signs that he was surprised that Mac was still among the living. A slight opening of the eyes? A red stain appearing beneath the skin of the face? A hand moving for a gun to put Mac down permanently this time?

Reuben's hand shot out. Instinctively, Mac reached for his gun, before remembering it was no longer there.

Reuben's hand clamped down on the edge of Mac's shoulder as he greeted him with a half-smile. 'So glad you could come.'

So glad he could come? He would indeed be glad if he wanted Mac dead. In that case his victim had made it too easy

for him. Mac searched the big man's frozen eyes for an answer.
But there wasn't one.

He felt the grip tighten on his shoulder as Reuben whispered. 'Have you got a problem . . . ?'

The way the question was posed didn't invite an answer.
Did he mean – have you got a problem? Or – you've got a big
problem.

Mac whispered. 'A problem?'

Reuben was looking him up and down. 'Yes. You seem to
have a few bumps and bruises. And you seem a little stressed.
Not your usual self . . .' Once again, Mac looked into the empty
eyes. A concerned gangster? Or Reuben's little joke? But he
got no answer.

'Daddy,' a high voice shrieked.

A small boy barrelled his way towards Reuben and wrapped
his arms lovingly round his leg. Reuben looked down at the boy
clinging to him and smiled. Mac realised that he'd never really
seen the other man's features transformed by a loving smile.

'This is my son, Milos.'

The boy turned his face towards him. Mac felt his belly rolling and his power of speech go. The boy's face was almost a
replica of Stevie's. The same gleam of curiosity in his blue
eyes; the tiny dimple in his right cheek; the two missing front
teeth. Abruptly the picture of that other birthday party flashed
through Mac's mind. Desperately he tried to push it back,
shove it away. But the image got brighter and clearer. Came
into full focus. Took over Mac's conscious mind . . .

twenty-eight

Stevie's eyes shone happy-blue as he stared at his banana-shaped birthday cake. He had been banana-mad since hearing the ditty 'Bananas in Pyjamas' on a kids' TV show six months back. The flames on the six candles matched the glow on his cheeks.

'Don't forget to make a wish,' Mac whispered, hunched down on the other side of the table, camera in hand, ready to snap that magic moment. 'And remember to close your eyes.'

The party was in full swing in the sitting room of the house he shared with his son and Donna. The place was decked out in streamers, balloons, party food and kids. And more kids. He didn't even know that Stevie had so many friends. A hush fell as everyone waited for the birthday boy to blow out the candles.

But instead of doing it, he looked up at his father, the happiness slipping slightly from his face. 'But what if it doesn't come true, Dad?'

The adults in the room, including Mac, chuckled. 'Believe me, son, it will.' He winked as he dropped his voice low. 'But only if you don't tell anyone.'

Stevie turned back to the cake. His eyes lit up. His little mouth moved as he gathered a deep breath. Then he leaned forward and blew. Click. Mac took the picture. All of the candle flames were gone except one. Stevie blew again. It wouldn't go out.

Blew.

It fluttered but bloomed back to full brightness.

Blew.

'Bananas,' Stevie let out crossly as the flame burned bright.

Mac pulled himself up and scooted to hunch down by his son. Put his arm round his shoulder.

'Let's make a wish together.'

Stevie grinned back at him and nodded. They both closed their eyes.

'Ready,' Mac said, a few seconds later.

Again Stevie nodded.

'After three,' Mac said, then chanted. 'One . . . two . . . three.'

They let out twin breaths of air across the cake.

The flame died.

twenty-nine

'Milos, say hello to my good friend Mac.'

Reuben's words slammed Mac back to the present. The air in his chest blew out of his nostrils. A film of sweat formed above his top lip. Blood pumped with such intensity around his head wound that he had a desperate need to hold his head in his hands. But he didn't. Instead he nervously looked at the kid and his father to see if they'd noticed his mood swing. But all he saw was the shy smile of a boy who held out his hand to him.

With a shaky smile in return, Mac shook his hand. The boy beamed with complete pleasure, as if shaking hands was the newest game he'd learnt. Reuben said something to Milos in Russian that had him skipping away. To Mac's shock and surprise, Reuben put his arm round his shoulder and led him into the party. Grim-faced members of the gang made jokes and horse-played with children, but Mac could see it was all faked. When the kids turned and ran, the same men who gave the youngsters rides on their backs were whispering to each other and scowling in turn.

Reuben was still playing the genial host. 'Today my son is six years old. Family is so important, don't you think? Do you have any children, my friend?'

Mac couldn't shake off Stevie's ghost; without realising what he was saying, the words formed like ash in his mouth. 'There was a boy. He died.'

Reuben said nothing but tightened his grip on Mac's shoulder. 'There will be other sons, my friend. Please treat my home as your own.' Reuben's hand fell away and the spark of emotion set off by his son left his face. 'Please understand I have things to do . . .'

Mac knew that Reuben hadn't been play-acting the doting daddy – but in reality he was a cold-blooded man dealing in death. Mac's brain shifted into gear and he began to plan. Priority number one was he needed a weapon. But what? As his gaze darted around, a woman approached him with a small plate of party cake. Impatiently he waved her away. He wasn't here to celebrate. Wasn't here to eat. Wasn't here . . . Sharply he looked across at the woman dishing out cake. Cake. Cake meant . . . Mac's gaze flew to the buffet table manned by two people from a catering company. With long strides he moved over to the table.

'What can I get you, sir?' one of the caterers asked with a professional smile.

'Just fill up a plate,' Mac answered, his gaze doing the rounds of the table. That's when he spotted the car-shaped cake with a serrated knife beside it.

'Will this do, sir?'

Mac jerked his eyes up at the plate being offered to him. 'Sure,' he let out. 'I think I'll just help myself to some of that yummy-looking cake.'

He took the plate and headed up to the end of the table. Picked up the black handle of the knife. Looked around. Shoved it into his inside pocket. The blade rested high against his chest. There were so many ways to kill a man with a knife. Slit his throat. Stab him deep in the eye. Plunge it into the heart, then, with the flick of a wrist . . . twist.

Mac dumped the food. The sound of male voices drew him out onto the patio. Reuben was standing a few yards away with his back turned, deep in conversation with his mad dog of a brother, Sergei. Sergei was the younger of the two – how much younger, Mac didn't know, but he guessed it was a big gap; one was maybe coming up to forty, the other in his mid-twenties. He wore a white vest, showing off his taut muscles, tats, and baggy, low-riding jeans. Sergei had a reckless streak that was reflected in the hard grooves around his mouth and eyes and in his feral, hand-raked bleached hair. Both men were dangerous, but Sergei was the one who'd never mastered the art of control.

'Uncle Mac . . .'

Mac felt a tug on the bottom end of his jacket and looked down to see the little figure of Milos below him.

Mac whispered, 'Careful,' afraid the knife might fall out.

Milos let go and sent him a brilliant smile of innocence. 'Do you want to see my new car? It's just like the real thing . . .'

Mac said nothing. He looked away from the boy, towards his father's back, and then out into the garden where a toy car was sitting. He also noticed that the members of the gang seemed to have thinned out. Mac looked at his target again while Milos tugged his trouser leg this time. 'Uncle Mac – are you all right? Your leg is shaking.'

Mac looked down at the kid's face and swallowed hard. What came first? The right of this boy not to see his father stabbed to death in front of him? Or the promise he'd made to Elena?

'Milos,' Sergei yelled. He gestured with his thumb. 'Hop it and play in the garden with the others.'

All the animation drained from the boy as his eyes grew wide with fear. He didn't leave with a happy skip this time, but ran as fast as his little legs could carry him. *So the kid's piss-scared of his uncle,* Mac observed. When Mac looked back across at the men, Reuben was gone. Bollocks, he couldn't find him. Sergei sauntered over to him, closely followed by his enforcer, Vladimir.

Sergei leaned close to Mac and whispered, in that fake American-ghetto accent he loved to use. 'My bro wants you. Now.'

Why would Reuben want him? Unless he wanted Mac in a place he could do what he liked to him without many witnesses.

The muscles in Sergei's neck visibly tightened and he hissed, 'That's not a request, that's an order.'

The enforcer took Mac's arm. Sergei was close by him on the other side. There was no way Mac was going to be able to grab the knife, with both men stuck to him like blowflies on a rotting corpse.

thirty

'Do you want the good news or the bad news and more bad news?' Detective Jamie Martin asked his superior as she walked into the office.

'I don't think there's any good news when you're dealing with murder,' Rio answered as she pulled off her jacket.

They were in the squad office at their HQ, nicknamed The Fort by those who worked inside it, because it was believed to be the site of a former Ancient Roman stronghold and had been used as a high-profile government building during the Cold War. The Fort was really three buildings: a middle section that was modern and transparent, reflecting what The Met proclaimed its relationship with the public was, and one block on either side, made of tough, acid-stained grey, 1950s brick. Rio's squad was stationed on the third floor of the new section. The place was brisk and busy.

DC Martin blushed at her remark and Rio reminded herself she was meant to be his personal supervisor. 'OK, let's do a sandwich approach – bad news, good news, bad news.'

She threw her jacket on the back of her chair at her desk and sat down.

Eagerly Martin got up and went over to her. He knew better than to perch on the edge, casualness just wasn't the DI's style, so he pulled up a chair instead. 'There's no match to the hotel victim's DNA in our system or dental records, which suggests she got into the country illegally and kept herself off the radar. So I've put in a call to Europol and Interpol to do a search.'

'Good news?'

'We've got a record of the DNA of the blood found on the bed in the hotel.'

Rio pulled herself straight. 'Good work, Martin. So what's the bad news?'

'When I tried to match the DNA to a face, the computer didn't want to cough up the info.'

'What do you mean it didn't want to play ball?'

He shrugged. 'Kept coming up as blocked with a code. I chatted to one of the lab guys who said it could be happening for lots of reasons, including the original information being put into the new system incorrectly.'

Fuck, fuck, fuck. Rio hated, totally hated, having to rely on machines. What she wouldn't admit to herself was that she didn't like not being in absolute control.

'We need that match . . .' she ground out.

'Yeah, I know boss, I'll keep on at the lab guys.'

'What about the image on the security camera from the hotel? Have we got a clearer image . . . ?'

Her words faded when she saw Martin look down, avoiding her gaze.

'Am I going to have to squeeze your balls to get the info out of you?'

That made the young man blush darker than before. She knew she could be blunt and vulgar, but that's just how she was. If Martin didn't like it, he could fast-track off out of her squad.

So Martin told her straight. 'The weather Up North has been shite, which means our expert has been delayed—'

'Get someone who works this side of the Watford Gap, for crying out loud.'

'Cutbacks. Apparently that department was slashed in the latest financial cull.' Rio threw out a noise of utter disgust. 'There isn't anyone else. He says he'll be here in a few hours. And there aren't any Russian translators working today, so we can't decipher the words on the tattoo.'

'Good job they're not invading then . . .' Rio blasted.

'They're on a three-day week–'

'Don't tell me,' Rio jumped in, her sarcasm hitting the ten button. 'Cutbacks.'

She almost turned the air blue. What the hell was The Met coming to when it was at the beck and call of bureaucrats who just didn't get the basics of police work? Might as well distribute leaflets in prisons saying there was going to be a crime festival in town every day and dick was going to be done about it.

'I could ask a friend of mine who works at the Russian embassy to translate the writing,' Martin tentatively threw out.

Rio shook her head. 'No can do. We're only permitted to use official personnel – using anyone else could contaminate our investigation. When we bring someone to trial for this murder, we don't need to give the prosecution any grounds to trip up our case.'

Rio slipped her thoughts back to the investigation. In all her years in the Force, she'd only known a few occasions where a DNA sample in the system hadn't come through with a name. Mind you, those IT idiots had changed the network last year, which had thrown a few spanners into the works, but that should all have settled down. She needed to get that DNA match.

Rio left Martin and moved out of The Fort towards the older building on the left side that housed the forensic team. This was one of the only police complexes that had an on-site forensic team. It was more an experiment, really, to see if, in the words of official policy, it would assist more 'joined-up thinking'. Joined-up thinking, my sweet black arse, Rio thought as she took the stairs to the third floor.

She saw Charlie as soon as she entered the front office of the lab.

'DI Wray,' the forensic specialist said as soon as she saw her. 'I'm glad you've come over. I've got two pieces of information that I think will help the investigation.' The other woman took Rio to her workspace and opened a file.

'I found something interesting from the scene. Blood on the wardrobe in the main room. It wasn't much, just a fine spray. From the direction of the blood, someone was hit by some-thing violent as he or she stood near the doorway.'

'Like a blunt instrument?'

'No, from the blood pattern, I think the person was shot.'

'Could the blood have belonged to the victim in the bath?'

'No. The blood matches the person who was lying on the bed. Maybe the victim shot him . . .'

'No.' Rio's spine stiffened. 'That doesn't make any sense. If the victim shot him, surely she would have managed to get away . . .' Her shoulders went back as another idea hit her. 'What if there was a third person there? Someone who shoots our dead woman, then shoots someone else as they come into the room. Leaves them on the bed to die. Except they don't die, they escape.'

Two victims, one murderer?

One victim, one murderer?

One victim, two murderers?

Rio's mind buzzed with possible scenarios.

'And the other piece of information,' Charlie shot over Rio's thoughts. 'You were right: the towel from the doctor's clinic matches the torn towel in the hotel room.'

At last, confirmation that the two murder scenes were

connected. Now all she had to do was figure out what that connection was. How the fuck was Doctor Mohammed Masri linked with the faceless woman in the bath? Had he treated the person who left the pool of blood on the bed? The murderer? She wasn't going to get any more answers until she found out whose medical record was missing from the doctor's.

Charlie carried on, 'And the blood on the towel at the doctor's matches the blood found on the bed in the hotel room.'

Two murders. Two different crime scenes. One killer connected to both crimes? And the only way of finding out was getting a DNA match on the blood. A match the computer system wasn't giving up. Dead end. Or was it?

'Detective Martin says that we can't get access to that information because of some code. Can you show me the information you found out about the blood?'

Charlie took a sip from her drink and grimaced at the heat it pushed into her mouth. 'I haven't been working on that aspect of the case, but sure it shouldn't be a problem.' She leaned over her desk and tapped away at her keyboard. The information for the DNA came up.

Match.

'This new system is bloody frustrating,' the forensic expert muttered under her breath as she pressed enter but nothing changed on the screen.

She looked up at Rio. 'You might have to find out who the match is by manually going through the files, which will probably take you ages . . .'

Her words dribbled away when she realised that Rio wasn't listening to her. Instead the younger woman's dark gaze was fixed firmly to the screen.

'What are you looking at?' she asked.

For a few seconds Rio didn't respond. Then she pushed herself straight. 'Nothing. Thanks Charlie.'

Rio strode away. Couldn't believe what she'd seen on the computer screen. A code in the top right-hand corner.

1402C.

The coding system she knew was used for undercover cops. But this one was different because it ended with the letter C.

thirty-one

Sergei led Mac towards the villa's garage like a condemned man. Most of the gang waited inside. The garage was a good size, free of clutter except for a monster 4x4 and bathtub that looked like it had seen some pretty damn good days inside a Victorian whorehouse. Reuben sat on the edge of the tub, one of his hands massaging the ornate tap mixer.

Reuben. Bath.

Mac wasn't prepared for this image because all he saw was Reuben in the bath standing over Elena.

'Ain't you hearing me, amigo?'

Sergei's irritated voice shook Mac up. His eyes darted around. Everyone was looking at him. Sergei's thug gently pushed Mac against a wall and then turned to face the front. Mac felt the knife pressing against his chest. All eyes were on him. Is this where he was going to take his final breath? Well, fuck, if it was, he wasn't going down without slicing up some criminal meat. His hand inched inside his jacket. Felt the top end of the handle. Then every eye snapped away from him and settled on their leader. Mac stayed like that for a few seconds, hand on the knife, back pressed against the wall until he was sure he wasn't the centre of attention any more. Sergei strode over to the bath and whispered something to his brother.

Finally Reuben got to his feet. His voice was low, but clear, with that edge of drama he always added at meetings to remind everyone he was Top Dog. 'We are looking at a war. Others are trying to take over our business. Men have already been killed; many more are going to die.' His gaze touched each man. 'And traitors have already been uncovered . . .'

Did he mean Elena? Him? Instinctively Mac's hand moved up, but stopped. A blade wasn't going to save him against a force of men this strong.

Reuben continued as if Mac was just another man in the room. 'And things are about to get very bad indeed. Of course I have already taken measures to ensure that the future of our company will be secure. It starts tonight with a delivery coming in at eleven.'

Mac heard the last words Elena had spoken to him:

'It's happening tomorrow night.'

'What's happening tomorrow tonight?'

'At eleven . . . He's going to kill me.'

Was this what she'd been so fearful of? A delivery coming into this country? But Mac had no time to think as he carefully tuned back in to Reuben's words.

'The delivery will solve all our problems. I'll be giving everyone information on their roles later on . . .'

'What's the delivery?' Sergei's enforcer, Vladimir, asked.

Reuben sucked the man into his deadly gaze. 'Why? Are you one of those traitors I talked about?' Reuben stormed over to him and got deep into his face. 'One of those giving information to our rivals?'

The man rapidly shook his head. 'No way, Mr Volk . . .'

'Because if you are,' Reuben spat into his face, 'I'm going to make you watch while I fuck your woman in the arse and then kill her. Then I'll do the same to your pretty teen daughter. After that you won't even have your teeth remaining so that someone can identify your stinking remains.'

Sergei placed his hand on his brother's arm. 'Hey, you know

Vlad didn't mean to diss you, bro. You know he's my boy, my NBK.' Mac knew that NBK meant Natural-Born Killer, an affectionate term Sergei often used to describe his enforcer, Vladimir, no doubt another phrase the young Russian had taken from his beloved rap music.

Reuben shook off his brother and faced the group again. The blood was strong in his face. Those tunnel eyes of his looking like they would take anyone who crossed him on a one-way trip to the pit of hell.

The muscle in his cheek moved with the wiggle of a worm under his skin as he fought for control. 'This delivery is going to be run on a strictly need-to-know basis.' A chilling menace crept into his tone. 'If any one of you fails, in any way, either by accident or for any other reason, your bloody body will be fished out of the Thames. Reluctant as I am to get involved in that sort of menial work, I will do it myself. With pleasure . . .'

Whatever was coming in tonight was important enough for Reuben to make sure its knowledge stayed in-house. Had to be arms coming in, Mac decided. But it couldn't be regular, run-of-the-mill hardware, or why would Elena think it would lead to her death?

'We have another problem,' Reuben carried on, his voice steadier now. 'The person responsible for our communications with abroad seems to have disappeared. Elena was meant to call me last night.' He looked around the gathering, searching everyone's face before finally his gaze came to rest on Mac. 'Has anyone seen Elena in the past twenty-four hours?'

Reuben caught Mac's eye for a brief moment before turning back to the rest of the crew. Mac's mind started reeling. Why would Reuben ask about Elena if he'd snuffed out her life?

'I saw her last night at an event at the embassy,' the gang leader continued. 'She was OK at first but looked upset by the end. She wouldn't tell me what the problem was, but I told her to ring me once she got home.'

This wasn't the first time that Reuben had mentioned shaking hands with the Russian embassy. He obviously had a contact there, which probably explained why the Russians wouldn't give out any information about him to the British authorities. Sometimes the line between politics and crime was almost invisible. *What had Elena been doing at the embassy?* Mind you, as Reuben's communications lady, she often went spinning around town with him.

Abruptly Sergei stepped forward. 'My girlfriend—'

But he was stopped short by Reuben yanking him backwards by his collar. 'What's the matter with you . . . ?'

Sergei lashed out at his brother's hand but, even as he did so, he recoiled in horror at what he'd done. No one, absolutely no one, put their hand on the boss and lived to tell the tale. Every man kept silent, waiting to see if Reuben was going to fuck his little brother up. But Reuben didn't speak, didn't move. Then he rubbed the back of his hand down the front of his trousers like he was removing dirt. His action gave his brother time to step back and hang his head like a whipped dog.

Reuben turned back to the gang. 'Our final item of business . . .' The rest of his sentence hung unsaid in the air as he nodded to one of his men, who set off towards the 4x4.

Reuben strode casually towards the vehicle. 'Gather around, my friends.' His tone made it sound like he was about to show them the greatest magic trick on earth.

Everyone, including Mac, shuffled forward. Reuben's next words stopped Mac dead.

'I'm afraid we have a traitor in our ranks.'

Mac reached for the knife the same time Reuben's henchman flipped up the boot of the BMW. The only traitor was

Mac, and he wasn't ending his life in the boot of some car like those bloated and discoloured Mafia double-crossers he'd seen in photos during his intense undercover training. He started pulling out the blade, but was stopped by muffled sounds coming from the boot. The men reached in and pulled out a tied-up sack that wriggled with a living person inside. They dumped the sack in the Victorian bathtub. Chokes, grunts and groans like a wounded animal filled the garage. It was Sergei who next took centre-stage. Calmly he moved to the back of the car and pulled out a beige overall and a large black holdall bag. He put the overall on. Zipped it up. Turned expectantly back to Reuben.

Reuben briefly announced the death sentence. 'This guy was approached by one of our rivals and offered a position. He turned them down but he forgot to report the approach to me . . .' He nodded at his younger brother.

Sergei smiled. Opened the bag. Took out a hatchet. Rubber handle, steel head. Then climbed up and balanced both feet on the rim of the bath. The sack was wriggling and bucking like a slug being toyed with by a bird. The victim's executioner took no notice as he swung the hatchet high. It sliced down through the air. Hit the body like a meat cleaver hacking its way through unripe fruit. Rich, red liquid squirted into the air and pooled in the bath. The hatchet went high. Sliced down. Blood. High. Sliced down. Blood shot back in the air the same time the garage door opened.

Two children appeared in the doorway. Milos and a little girl. Stunned, no one moved. Both the children gazed innocently at Sergei braced on the bath. And the blood. Reuben quickly moved to block their view.

'Daddy . . .' Milos started.

'Hey birthday boy.' Reuben smiled and ruffled his son's hair. 'Why don't you go back inside . . . ?'

'But we're playing hide and seek.'

'Ah, ah,' Reuben let out a mysterious giggle. 'I know where you can hide.'

He leaned down and whispered in Milos's ear. Obviously liking what his father told him, Milos squealed, caught his friend's hand and ran back into the garden.

Reuben turned back to Sergei. The smile vanished from his face. 'Finish it.'

The hatchet rose again. And again. Kept going until the sack was red and torn and the bath filled with severed limbs and body parts. The only sound that could now be heard was the puff and pant of Sergei delivering the blows. Satisfied with a job well done, the young Russian finally stopped.

Then he threw his head back and yelled with outrageous joy, 'Yee-har.'

Mac knew he should be shocked, but he wasn't. He'd seen and heard so many horror stories while undercover that some guy being hacked to death didn't move the needle on his shake-me-up radar any more. When he'd first started going undercover, he'd fretted about 'doing the right thing' when someone was attacked, but he'd soon learned that the only right thing was to keep his nose out unless it jeopardised his operation.

Mac pulled out of his thoughts as the garage door started opening again. Reuben shifted forward, naked emotion on his face; Mac suspected that came from the fear that it might be his son again. The fear that his boy might see him with bloody hands. Reuben's body blocked Mac's view of the person now standing in the doorway.

The Russian's shoulders visibly relaxed. 'Welcome to the party.'

The person stepped inside. Mac's heart rate shot up Calum.

thirty-two

1:20 p.m.

Phil Delaney closed the file on Reuben Volk on his desk. He pulled on his electronic cigarette, longing for more nicotine, but getting mainly mint vapour instead. He leaned back in his swing chair, thinking that the information on Volk was pretty thin. Those Russians were like vampires, reinventing themselves and drawing blood in every country they came to, leaving behind a trail that disappeared as quickly as the mock smoke he blew out from his make-believe cigarette. The only thing he knew was that *Volk* meant 'wolf' in Russian. The phone rang.

'Delaney,' he answered.

'I've just sent an up-to-date feed through to you.'

The line went dead almost at the same time as his metallic laptop pinged. He tapped a few buttons on the keyboard. Waited. Attachment. Download. Pressed download. The blood-red download bar went into action: 20% . . . 35% . . . 50% . . . 75% . . .

The door to his office bashed open, pulling Phil's attention away from the computer. A woman stood in the doorway.

'I want a word.'

His PA hovered behind her, looking as agitated as his surprise caller.

He stood up as he said, 'It's OK, Shazia, I'll sort this out.'

His PA looked from Phil to the woman, then she gave him a slight nod as she closed the door.

'Rio,' Phil started, as he moved to a very annoyed-looking DI Wray. 'I wasn't expecting to see you today.'

His laptop pinged. Download ready.

'I've got a few things I need to ask. First thing on my mind is Mac. I saw him earlier today and he looked like the dead walking. I thought people in your team in the field were meant to have close psychological supervision.'

He reached her. Hovered slightly too close to her, but Rio stood her ground.

'You know I can't discuss any operational details with you.'

Her chest rose as her breathing accelerated. 'I told you not to send him on another case; that if he came back to work he should be on strict desk duty. Tell me that he's got an Uncle in the field who's supporting him?'

Undercover cops usually had a key person nearby if they needed support quickly and, by the look on Phil's face, Rio knew there was no Uncle attached to this case.

'Are you just crazy?' she stormed. 'You do know what today is? That his son died today . . .'

Phil tilted his head and his gaze swept ever so slowly over her face. 'I know you're ambitious, but I don't think you're my superior officer quite yet.'

Her chest rose higher. 'You're meant to be looking out for him . . .'

'And I am.' Suddenly his hand came out and cupped her chin. 'He's not on any case. He was but I made him step down. He's at home taking life easy.'

Rio sighed, long and deep, throwing her head slightly back. 'Are you sure?'

'Would I lie to you?' Phil ran his thumb over her bottom lip.

Silence. They both looked at each other. Then moved at the same time. Their lips tangled in a hot kiss. Phil shoved his fingers into her mini-Afro. Rio twisted Phil round. Pushed his upper body flat against the desk. Started to unzip his trousers next to the laptop, which had downloaded a series of photographs. Photos that Phil didn't notice – from his surveillance team – of Mac going into Reuben Volk's house.

thirty-three

Mac was back in the garden, the faint sound of children's laughter coming from the house. He stood by a plum tree and watched Calum and Reuben talking in subdued, animated tones to each other, heads close, like old buddies. Calum wore anonymous black and blue clothes and had a baseball cap, similar to Mac's, pulled down over his forehead. It was the standard rig for people who went about their business to avoid looking memorable for witnesses and surveillance cameras.

They were back in the house in a room adjacent to the one where the kids were playing musical chairs to the accompaniment of a funky version of 'Humpty Dumpty'. Every type of curse word he knew attacked Mac's mind as he stared at Calum. What a class-A fool he'd been to even think about trusting Calum and not to guess that a character like Reuben was Calum's ideal client these days. Mac knew that Reuben didn't tell his gang everything; that he kept some things close to his chest – and Calum had obviously been one of them. But still, if he'd been thinking straight, he should have seen the possibility of Calum and Reuben hooking up. Mac ran over what he'd told his former colleague earlier.

That he was undercover in Reuben's gang.

That he'd been in the hotel room when Elena was murdered.

That he was hunting down her killer.

If the dodgy security consultant had passed on even a part

of it, he'd be in Reuben's gun line now, even if he hadn't been before. There was only one way he was going to find out.

Confidently he walked over to them. If things got hot, he convinced himself he could take them both down with the knife.

Reuben lifted his head away from Calum and gave Mac a long, cool stare. Confidently Mac eyeballed him back.

Finally the Russian spoke. 'Let me introduce—'

But Mac cut over him, tone cool and easy. 'We've met.'

He saw Calum slightly stiffen. Mac almost smiled with satisfaction at that. Yeah, now it was time to flip the table, to make the devious bastard feel like he was the one now shitting his pants.

Reuben leaned his head to the side, assessing both men. Then his gaze stayed on Calum. 'You never mentioned that you knew the independent armourer we were using.'

But Mac didn't give Calum a chance to respond, taking the high ground himself. 'Well, he wouldn't want you to know about that, would he? I mean, we've all got stuff in our backgrounds we don't want the whole world to know about.' Now it was Mac's turn to shift his gaze onto Calum. 'Isn't that right, Mr Burns?'

Now who might be ratting who out? Mac thought defiantly. He was enjoying seeing his one-time good friend squirm.

'Are you hiding secrets from me?' Reuben asked Calum as his fists clenched at his side.

Mac folded his arms. 'Go on,' he taunted Calum. 'Why don't you tell Reuben all about our *intimate* past,' he added, shovelling the shit of the whole situation into Calum's lap.

But the other man only smiled in that cool-customer fashion that had once made him so popular with the women in the Force. 'I wouldn't call it intimate. Not with Mac, anyway. We used to be real tight.' He shrugged. 'That was until Mac found out I was balling his missus.'

Mac's face tumbled. Calum and and his ex wife Donna? Was Calum the guy she'd been screwing after Stevie died? Calum just lifted his eyebrow and sent him a smug smile.

Reuben snorted in disgust, breaking through the tension, relaxing his hands. 'Don't let some whore get in the way of brotherhood. Only one way to deal with a woman who opens her legs for any man – shove a stick wrapped with barbed wire up her cunt and keep twisting and turning it until she isn't screaming any more. I made Sergei watch me do that to his first girlfriend who was fucking some meth addict on the side. He had to learn that a man never lets a woman come between business and friendship.'

Mac felt his stomach turn, but Calum appeared untouched by the sickening revelation.

'I was just telling Calum about Sergei,' Reuben continued, his voice dropping low. 'His girlfriend has gone missing. I don't know who the slut is and I don't want to know. I suspect she was one of those Club Zee bitches.' He made a sound deep in the back of his throat like he was about to spit. 'So if my brother gets out of hand today, just keep him in line.'

Club Zee. The name registered with Mac. The card he had in his pocket that he'd found at Elena's.

'Mac, I'll need you to have a clean place ready for me,' Reuben said, taking Mac's thoughts away from the card he'd found. 'A place that no one can connect to my organisation, where I can unload the delivery after we move it,' Reuben continued, switching the subject of the conversation.

Mac almost asked Calum how long he'd known about the delivery, but he didn't. No, he'd be talking to Calum all right. Soon. Real soon.

Instead he whispered to Reuben, 'I thought something big was happening so I took the precaution of getting a different phone. Here's the number.'

After he'd passed on the details to the Russian, Reuben abruptly raised his arms and shouted, 'Everyone, it's time to gather round.'

People started moving from the house into the garden. Some of the children ran, others held on to the hands of the adults they'd arrived with. Milos cuddled into his father's side. A table had been set centrally, with what looked like an enormous pie-cum-cake in the middle. There was a solitary candle and words iced on it: *Live long and free*.

Reuben gently pushed his son towards his birthday pie.

'Close your eyes. Make a wish,' Reuben whispered.

But Mac was long gone by the time Milos reopened his eyes. He was back on the street. The Luger and bullets were where he'd left them under the wheelie bin. Once he had them, Mac doubled back and hid in a front garden from where he could observe the gates to Reuben's house. Now all he had to do was to wait for that back-stabbing slime ball Calum to come out.

thirty-four

'I didn't come over for a shag,' Rio said, as she finished doing up the last button on her blouse while Phil buckled his belt.

They'd met at some tedious police conference, a weekender, where they'd spent their free time getting to know each other within the four walls of Rio's hotel room. Phil didn't feel guilty that he was betraying his wife; if he'd had a guilt complex, he'd never have gone into undercover work. And Rio – well, she wasn't looking for a long-term anything except for her career.

'We've talked about Mac . . .'

She took a step towards him. 'I'm working on this case. A murder in a hotel. A female found with her face shot off her in a bath. Not a pretty scene. But I'm working some DNA that was found there, not the victim's. The problem is there's a match on the computer, but I can't get access to it.'

'Now why do I feel that the remainder of your sentence has got something to do with me?' Phil moved away from her and sat down at his desk. He kept his gaze on her.

'The reason I can't get access is because there's a code. The one used for one of ours undercover.'

Phil's body tightened. 'And you want me to turn the code into a face? You know it's a general code, so I'd never be able to do that anyway – not that I would.'

'But there's something different about this. It's the usual 1402 code,' Rio hit back. 'But this one ends with a C.'

Phil went rigid and, for just a few seconds, emotion stood stark on his face. Shock? Confusion? Rio couldn't tell what it was, but he soon covered it over with the calm shadows that he usually wore.

He leaned back in the chair and laced his fingers in his lap. 'Even if I did know who it was—'

'Don't shit me around, Phil.' Her face glowed a hot brown with her fury. 'A young woman's time on this earth was brutally severed today. Tell me who it is.'

His tone remained calm. 'I don't know who every under-cover cop is. There are other undercover teams, as you well know. We use the same 1402 code like all the other units. We don't put letters, love hearts or smiley faces at the end of it.'

'Well, someone put a C there for a reason. So, who can I talk to and find out?'

Phil stood up again. Moved round the table. Took the few steps towards her. Ended up back in her space. 'No one's going to give you that information. If there was – and that's a big "if" – an operative in that hotel room, it will be case sensitive. My advice to you –' his hand touched her wrist near her pulse – 'is to leave it alone. Get on with your investigation and work around this DNA glitch.'

'Glitch?' she stormed in his face. 'You should've seen what was left of her. The inside of her head scattered all over the walls like she was nothing. Nothing.'

'Rio.' His palm swept up her arm. 'If you want to be in the type of places I think you want to get to in the police force, you've got to be able to leave the emotion behind.'

'Yeah, I'll think about leaving the emotion behind the next time you're screwing me.' She snatched her arm away. 'I'll find out who it is, Phil, with or without your—'

Her mobile went off. She slammed out of Phil's office, not

noticing the surprised expressions on the faces of Phil's team. She pulled out her mobile as she took the stairs.

Furiously, she answered the call.

'She was pregnant.'

Rio froze at the top of the stairs on hearing DC Martin's words.

'Two months gone,' he continued. 'The ME says that her system was filled with a sedative, something like Rohypnol . . .'

'So that's how the killer got her into the bath – he drugged her,' Rio uttered softly.

'There was no sign of a puncture wound on her skin, so it wasn't injected.'

'Were there any other marks or abrasions on her skin, like around her wrists?'

'None. No sign either that she put up a struggle.'

'Which means someone slipped the drug into her drink. And you know what that likely means . . . ?'

Silence on the other end of the line.

Rio answered her own question. 'Our vic probably knew her killer.'

She pulled the mobile from her face but didn't cut the call. Instead she stabbed a finger against the mobile's screen until she found the files containing her notes and information about the case. Stopped at the photo showing the close-up of the tattoo on the victim's arm.

Red star, yellow border.

С волка́ми жить

по-во́лчьи выть

'Martin?' she said into the phone. 'Let's see what we can find out about this tattoo.'

1402. C.

Phil ran his hand over his mouth. Damn. Mac. He'd

personally changed Mac's coding to distinguish him from the other members of his team in the field because he'd wanted to keep an eye on him after he'd returned to work following his son's death. Mac hadn't mentioned any hotel room to him when they'd met earlier. But then Mac hadn't been returning his calls. What the fuck was Mac involved in? A murder?

Phil quickly went back to his desk, ready to pick the phone up to give Mac a call. And that's when he saw the images on the laptop.

'Bastard.' He thumped the desk. 'Bastard.' He banged the desk again.

He shook his head, almost in disbelief, as he saw a still of Mac standing in front of Reuben Volk's door. He picked the phone up. Dialled.

'Why didn't you call me?' Phil spoke quickly to the same person he'd contacted outside Mac's home. 'Yes, I know what I said earlier, but things have obviously changed . . . There's no need to worry about Mac, he won't be on the street for long.'

He was already standing up when he ended the call. He pulled the door open and called to his PA.

'Give the surveillance team a call and tell them to send a live feed through to you. Then patch it through to me.'

He picked up his laptop. Didn't take his coat as he headed for the door. As soon as he got into his car, he used his laptop to patch into a live feed with his team watching Reuben Volk's house.

'Sir,' he was urgently told. 'He's left the house.'

Phil ignited the engine. Took the road. Said, 'Don't lose him.'

He looked ahead of him and cursed some more when he saw that he was caught up in roadworks. He thumped his horn three times, but nothing moved. He didn't have a choice now; he was going to have to use his blues and twos. He hit the button that activated the flashing siren. Wheels squealed as cars moved out of his way, some mounting the pavement. The twisting vehicles only made the already narrow gap even narrower. He flipped the steering wheel one way, then the other, as he moved through the space. Finally through, he belted forward. Checked the GPS. He'd be there in another five minutes if he kept this speed up. And then Mac would be off the case for good.

thirty-five

Calum was putting his mobile phone away as he finally left the Russian's home. Hunched in the front garden, Mac kept his eye on him all the way. As he strolled past the guards. As the remote-controlled gate opened for him. As he pulled the tip of his baseball cap low. As he walked unevenly down the street. Mac dipped lower as Calum walked past on the side opposite his hiding place. He twisted his body slightly to the rhythm of the other man's steps as Calum carried on down the street. Mac gave it five seconds, then stood. Didn't look left, didn't look right, as he quickly followed his target.

Seeing a gap in the road, to what looked like a side street, he made his move. He rushed Calum, grabbed him by the arm and jacked him sideways between a row of gardening sheds.

Calum was unresisting and didn't seem surprised. 'I thought you might be loitering around somewhere . . .'

Mac blocked the path back to the road. 'Why didn't you tell me that you knew Reuben and his travelling circus?'

Calum looked down to where Mac's hand was hovering by his waistband. 'You're not going to start waving Lady L around at me, are you? That would be really stupid, especially on a road like this. In fact, you might want to consider the possibility that Reuben's des res is almost certainly under surveillance by the law.'

But Mac wasn't listening, 'Why didn't you tell me you were

coming here? If you breathed fuck about what I told you this morning . . .'

Lost for words, the anger burst from Mac and he lunged at Calum. Grabbed the lapels of his coat and shook him violently.

Calum almost lost his footing as his weak leg slid to the side, but managed to stay upright. He made no attempt to resist, but he looked at his former friend with contempt and warned, 'Get your hands off me, mate, or there's going to be trouble. I'm serious – you've got enough enemies as it is, don't make another one out of me, because I'll be worse than the lot of them put together.'

They remained like that for a while, breathing heavily, the peaks of their twin baseball caps almost touching. Abruptly, Mac loosened his grip. Cursing, he let go. Calum looked up and down the road before saying, 'Look, it's none of your business, but Reuben just wanted a sit-down to offer me a job, which I've agreed to take on for a substantial fee.'

Mac scoffed. 'It's always money with you, isn't it? Is that why they booted your arse out of the door at The Met, because your paws came up dirty from the wrong cookie jar?'

Calum's green eyes glittered bright and hard. The blood rose in his face. 'Fuck you, Mac. If you'd really wanted to know what happened back then, you'd have given me a bell. But you didn't.' His finger stabbed out at his former friend. 'So you don't have the right to expect anything from me. I do what I need to do to put bread on the table. So I was at Casa Reuben for my business not yours, so there was no need for me to mention your name or what you told me this morning. I've got a whole new circle of friends now that don't include you.'

'And do you know what your *new best buddy* did before you arrived? He had a live human being chopped into pieces as a new party trick at his son's birthday.'

Calum gave a grim smile. 'I'm glad I turned down the hamburgers then.'

'Did you sleep with Donna?' Mac had been holding back on asking Calum about his ex-wife, but now it burst free.

Calum swore softly. 'If you think I'm the type of man who would've been carrying on with my best friend's old lady, you didn't know me at all.'

Mac's dimmed eyes came alive with hatred and suspicion, 'But that's the trouble, Calum, I don't know you. Not any more. So is the job you're doing for him connected to this delivery tonight?'

Calum sighed. 'Have you no idea what "commercial confidentiality" means? Now, if you'll excuse me.' He pulled the rim of his cap lower. 'I've got work to do. But let me give you a bit of advice that doesn't come with my usual consultation fee. Leave this one alone. What did you really know about this woman, Elena? Go home, get some rest. Look at the state of you, Mac – you're cracking up. If you carry on down this road, you'll either end up dead or on the funny farm.' His tone softened slightly. 'You're not the father my godson would've remembered.'

And leaving the memory of Mac's dead son between them, Calum walked in uneven steps away. Feeling like he'd been repeatedly hitting his head against a brick wall, Mac reached for the pill bottle he'd found at Doctor Mo's. All he needed was a hit, one hit to get his brain back into gear. He couldn't remember which pocket he'd placed them in, so shoved his hand into his inside pocket. That didn't contain the pill bottle, though, but the stuff he'd taken from Elena's place. He pulled the pieces out and looked at each one again.

Post-it note from Reuben.

Scorched photo of two men in military get-up.

Card for some club.

He rested them in his hand for a while, like he was hanging on to Elena's life. He was so weary, so bone-tired. But he had to keep going. He owed it to Elena like he'd owed it to Stevie to keep him safe. But he hadn't kept him safe. Determination flooded back into him. He started pushing the items back into his pocket. Suddenly his hand stopped around the club card. He raised it closer to his face. Read.

Club Zee.

What had Reuben called his brother's girlfriend? Oh yeah, one of those Club Zee bitches. Mac's mind shot into cop investigation mode. Two women. One dead, the other missing. And what connects them both? A place called Club Zee.

'Sir, he's on the move again . . .'

'Where?' Phil said, turning into a sharp right.

'He's turned a corner, boss – I've lost him.'

'Which corner?'

'End of the road – Willowfield Crescent.'

Phil hit Reuben's neighbourhood. All he wanted to do was to slam his foot to the pedal, but he couldn't afford to do that, not near the house under surveillance. So he eased back slightly. Cruised. Kept moving. And moving. Killed the engine just before hitting Willowfield Crescent. His phone pulsed on.

'Yes?'

'Sir.' Shazia, his PA. 'Doctor Warren says she can only meet you this evening . . .'

'I don't think I'll be needing her again,' Phil mumbled, almost to himself.

As soon as he cut the call, he pulled something out of his glove compartment. Jumped out of the car, not bothering to close the door. He ran forward. Stopped just before the entrance to the crescent. Took a breath, and then stepped into it. He saw a man up ahead straight away, sporting a baseball cap. Striding firmly, Phil took the pavement quickly, gaining on the figure with each step. His fingers tightened on what was in his hand as he extended his strides. Gained ground. Got closer. And closer. He reached him.

'Mac,' he called out.

Philip shoved the stun gun in his hand against the side of Mac's torso. Mac shook as the stun gun shot a thousand volts through his body, the force of it spinning him round. As he fell, Phil was finally able to see Mac's face. Phil swore viciously.

It wasn't Mac.

thirty-six

Stars, skulls, angels, wings ... more bloody wings. Rio was sick to the back teeth of seeing tattoos as she and Martin entered the umpteenth local tattoo parlour for the day. Why oh why hadn't she delegated the job to a couple of the other officers in her team? This tat house was unoriginally called The Needle, but it could've been named The Dark House because it was painted all over black. No colourful and fanciful designs. Just black.

'Been thinking about getting a warrant card tattoo after my performance review comes through – that's if it's good,' Martin suddenly said.

Rio heard the eagerness in his voice and sort of felt proud that she'd helped pull him from a shy rookie detective to the outstanding cop he was today. But she made no reply, just pushed into the shop. The inside was anything but dark. Powder-blue walls offset the many designs mounted on them. The sound of a needle hissed as a man with a sleek ponytail engraved what to Rio looked like a gargoyle on a woman's arm.

The man didn't look round as he said, 'Take a seat; I'll be with you in five.'

He had an accent – to Rio's ears it sounded Russian.

'We need to have a word,' Rio said as she moved forward, pulling out her badge.

The man finally looked round as she reached him and flashed her ID in his face.

He looked irritated as he cut off the needle, but there was the slight hum of another needle coming from somewhere in the back of the shop, behind the lilac beaded curtain. He briskly nodded at the woman in the chair, who got up and went to sit on one of the seats near the door.

'What do you want?' His tone was unfriendly.

Martin held out his mobile, which displayed a photo of the star tattoo on the arm of their victim.

'Have you done or seen this tattoo before?' Rio asked.

The man gave it a quick look, but he also flicked his gaze towards the back of the shop. 'No,' he uttered curtly.

'Look a bit harder this time,' Rio responded, grabbing the phone from Martin and shoving it into the man's face.

Reluctantly he looked more closely this time. 'No, no. And no.'

'I'm investigating the murder of a young woman . . .'

'And I've got a customer waiting.'

The humming in the back of the shop stopped, replaced by giggles. Without any warning, Rio marched towards the back.

'Hey, you can't just go in there . . .' the tattoo artist protested.

But Rio kept on going. Flipped her hand up to move the beaded curtain out of the way. Small corridor with two rooms to the side. The door to the room on the left was open. The sound of voices – excited, girlish voices – spilled out.

Rio reached it and stopped in the doorway. 'Well, well, well,' she said as she took in the scene. Two teenage girls, wearing school uniforms, were inside with an older woman. One girl was admiring a tattoo that had just been designed around her friend's belly button.

Hearing her voice, the people inside looked up. Rio eased into the room. Stopped when she reached the schoolgirl with the tattoo and looked down at the design on her body.

Love heart, with the words, 'Lisa and Scottie Forever'.

'Lisa,' Rio said to the girl. 'I'm sure you're meant to be in school or something, so why don't you and your mate hop on out of here.'

The schoolgirls looked nervously at each other, but recognised the voice of authority when they heard it.

'No need to pay, this one's on the house.'

The teens squealed with appreciation, one of them loudly saying the word, 'fresh', which Rio took to be the latest word for cool. The girls grabbed their bags and, chatting, left the shop.

Turned slowly to the male tattoo artist. 'You do know it's against the law to give a tattoo to someone under the age of eighteen.'

The woman and the man looked grimly at each other.

'Now I could run this in, but you know what that will mean: this shop will be shut down and you'll be facing a hefty fine . . .' She shoved the photo in his face again.

He swallowed. Spoke quickly to the other artist in Russian, who quickly exited the room.

He took the mobile and gazed at the photo intently. 'I've seen it before, but never done one.'

'Where?'

He swallowed again and Rio noticed that his hand was shaking slightly. 'It was a long time ago. I don't remember where.' He waved his hand dismissively. 'Some man came into a shop I worked in years back; he had one on his forearm. I've never seen it again. It's certainly not a design that I carry in my shop.'

'What about the writing?'

He moved the picture closer to his face.

С волка́ми жить

по-во́лчьи выть

'It's a Russian love saying. "Love is in the arms of the woman you love".'

'Are you sure, because doesn't the red star mean the Red Army?' Martin spoke for the first time.

'Stars are one of the most popular designs, including red ones, which will have nothing to do with any army,' the man responded sarcastically as he handed the phone back to Rio. 'Now, can I get back to work?' he added tartly.

'If you're lying to me . . .' Rio threatened.

'And why would I do that?' the man shot back. His tone shifted from hard to weary. 'I'm just a man, with a business, wanting to get on with his job.'

Back in the car, Rio leaned heavily back in her seat. 'Maybe our vic was just a prostitute and got turned over by a punter?'

'Boss, there's something about this tattoo . . .' Martin said.

'What you thinking?'

'I don't know yet.'

Rio sighed.

Love is in the arms of the woman you love.

Damn. She just couldn't figure out how the inscription was going to help with her investigation.

The sound of her mobile distracted her away from the tattoo. God, did her phone ever stop?

'DI Wray.'

It was the officer on the desk back at The Fort. 'There's a man here to see you. Says he has some information on your murder investigation at the hotel.'

thirty-seven

2 p.m.

Getting into Club Zee was a lot easier than Mac figured. He thought it would be all intercoms, heavy-duty doors and bull-neck bouncers. But all he had to do was push open the door. He'd forgotten that during daylight hours most clubs were empty, still clearing up from the night before, so security was usually lax, most times non-nexistent. Club Zee was one of those faded art-deco buildings that were dotted every now and again across London. Some of the walls were curved and twisted, while others were panelled with raised lines that stood out like ceramic prison bars. A car siren lit up the air somewhere behind him as he pushed against the smooth walnut door.

He squinted against the change of light, a soothing red that bathed a short, tight corridor leading to a jet-painted door. The lights put Mac in mind of a brothel, dimmed enough so the punters couldn't see the crap beneath the false glamour, and so the house girls wouldn't have to see the men in all their creepy glory. The thought of a brothel bothered him. He could deal with Elena dipping in and out of a place full of ravers high on hippy-crack laughing gas, but a house of pay-as-you-go fuck-ing . . . no, that would be the biggest betrayal of all.

The door at the end opened up under Mac's firm push and he entered a reception area. Wide, quite tastefully kitted out with a tanned wood reception desk, jungle green couch and accompanying single chair. There were pictures on the wall, framed prints, not of buck-naked chicks or Al Pacino doing Scarface, tooled up with that killer stare, but replicas of well-known paintings. Then he noticed that another framed picture wasn't a painting but photos, lots of photos mixed up together. But Mac wasn't paying attention to the walls; the only thing that got his attention was the fact that there was no one around. Good – gave him time to stick his snout where it didn't belong.

He started up a narrow flight of stairs that took him to the next floor. Black carpet, freshly vacuumed, over a space that was slightly bigger than downstairs. Another door at the end. He lengthened his stride, the sprayed air freshener stinging the insides of his nostrils as he neared the door. Pulled it open. Massive dance floor, its walls gleaming with the brightness of a metallic, silver shell. No one at the bar. No one anywhere. Mac rubbed his lips together in frustration. This was a large club, so how the heck was he going to find out about Elena's connection here? He didn't know the layout of the place. Which were the offices, the private rooms, or even those that might be reserved for one-on-one striptease?

'What are you doing there?' a voice called, taking Mac's decision from him.

He turned to find an older woman, maybe a few decades on him, with a green overall, the nozzle of a vacuum cleaner in her hand and skin around her mouth that was as tightly pulled back as her greying hair.

Mac stared back, letting his gaze drop directly into hers. He didn't blink as he answered. 'I'm looking for the manager?'

The woman scoffed. Twisted her thin lips. 'Manager? That's a laugh. But if you're looking for Jeff, the ponce who pays me a pittance, he's in the office in the back near the basement dance floor downstairs.'

And with that she turned her back on him and revved up the vacuum. Mac knew seeing the manager was taking a chance, but sometimes the best way to find out stuff was straight from the horse's big mouth. The sound of clinking glasses hit Mac as soon as he reached the dance floor downstairs. A man stood behind the slim bar, stocking up for the coming night, and a pole dancer, in an eye-hurting lemon crop top, did her thing upside down, her shock-blonde hair falling over her face. He passed her and approached the man at the bar.

'Looking for Jeff,' he threw out.

The man stopped. Gave him the quick once-over and then pointed his thumb at a door buried deep in another corridor past the Ladies and Gents. The door was slightly open, so Mac pushed and stepped inside. It wasn't big, but had enough space in which to fit the table that a young man sat behind. He was kitted out in a polo shirt and a sharp suit, his thumbs moving wildly as he played a computer game. In front of him were piles of papers, an open bottle of brown liquid that left a sweet odour floating in the air and a mirror with a single line of coke. No, Mac peered closer at the drugs; from the size of the grains, he bet it was Special K.

'Yesss,' Jeff let out in a gravelly London accent, and then made a loud whooping sound. 'Got you, sucker.'

Abruptly he flicked his head up, realising he wasn't alone. His skin was young but his eyes were red-rimmed and ancient. He threw the console on the table and leaned back. 'If you're looking for a job, we ain't hiring today. The only way we dish out work is on a strictly mouth-to-mouth basis, you get me?'

'The cleaner told me where to find you.'

Jeff smiled. 'Oh, you mean my mum.'

'I'm here on behalf of Reuben – Reuben Volk sent me.'

That got the effect that Mac was after. Jeff straightened up in the chair, running his palms down his polo shirt, as if trying to iron out any wrinkles. 'Tell Mr Volk that I'm looking after the place real well . . .'

So Reuben owned the place. He let Jeff prattle on as he made a real drama of shutting the door slowly and firmly. 'Reuben wants to know what's happened to his brother's lady friend. Seems she hasn't been seen for a while.'

Jeff ran his gaze nervously over Mac as he hitched himself onto the edge of the table. 'Grapevine is saying you were one of the last people to see her.'

Jeff rapidly shook his head, the ends of his sandy hair bouncing in the air. 'Well, that just ain't true; lots of other folk saw her at the club a few days back. I heard some of the other girls saying that she was up the duff . . .'

'Pregnant?'

The pregnancy testing kit Mac had found in Elena's flat, now tucked up in his pocket, flashed through his mind.

Jeff leaned forward and raised a palm in the air, as if that would add to the importance of his words. 'Look, I keep my fingernails clean and just get on with my job, that's all.'

Mac pushed up a semi-smile. 'There's no need to be nervous. All Mr Volk wants to know is where she is.'

The other man's eyes skated to the drugs laid out beside him. Flicked back to Mac. 'Do you mind?' His gaze went back to the white line. 'Haven't finished my lunch.'

Mac almost went into automatic sneer, he didn't have time for people who included drug taking in their leisure activities, but he relaxed his face and nodded. Jeff took the line with a noisy wheeze, pinched his nostrils and slumped, crooked, back in the chair.

His eyes blinked with the intent of the shutter of a camera as he looked back at Mac. 'That Katia was a real raver, although she never name-checked herself using that name here. She always called herself Annalisa or Anna . . .'

'So what does this real raver look like?'

Blink. Blink. Blink. 'Not my type, a bit bony for me . . .' He jackknifed to the front of his seat. 'Not that I'm saying I wanted to get down and dirty with her; I would never stare at Sergei's girl with the wrong expression in my eyes . . .'

Mac leaned his palms on the desk. Bent his body deep into the younger man's space. 'Mr Volk isn't interested in where your cock's been hanging out; all he wants to do is help his brother find his girl, so just tell me what she looks like.'

Mac guessed that Jeff was too far gone in ketamine heaven to suss out that surely Sergei would have given his brother a description of his girlfriend.

Jeff closed his eyes, deep thinking. Pushed them open again and went straight back into blink-blink mode. 'About five six or seven. Pretty snub nose with short-cut dyed-black hair. Well, it looked out of a bottle to me. And the tattoo . . .'

Mac froze. 'What tattoo?'

Sensing the change in the room, Jeff came over all nerves again, his hands jutting back in the air. 'Look, man, if I ain't meant to see no tat, I ain't . . .'

Mac jerked to his feet. 'What tattoo?'

'On her arm. A red star with some yellow and some fancy shit foreign writing?'

thirty-eight

'Did this Katia ever call herself Elena?'

Mac made himself ask the question. His mind was reeling with the information that he'd never prepared himself for. No, he wouldn't allow himself to entertain the idea. No way... No, it just couldn't be. But the stoned man in front of him was telling a different tale.

Five six or seven.

Snub nose.

Short-cut black hair.

Red star tattoo.

Elena. Was Sergei's missing girlfriend Elena? Elena wouldn't be screwing him and some other bloke at the same time. Would she? He tried to deny it but the description and the tattoo just kept hitting him back.

Jeff's voice tore over his twisting thoughts. 'I only ever heard her called Anna, Annalisa or Katia. Loads of the girls here have different names. I don't ask to see no birth certificates. Sergei must be keen on finding this girl because you're the second guy his brother has sent my way today.'

'Who else has been here?'

But Jeff didn't answer. Instead the corners of his eyes crinkled as he stared deeply at Mac, as if seeing him for the first time. 'How come you don't know Mr Volk sent someone else?'

Think quickly. Quickly. 'Because maybe this man was never

sent by Reuben.' Mac added with menace, 'If you've been flapping your lips about Mr Volk's business to—'

'Hold up. When the guy limped out of here, he only had the same information I've given you . . .'

'Limped?'

'Yeah. Well, sort of limped; took it slow each time he raised his right leg.'

Calum. What the fuck had he been doing here?

'Maybe Sergei's woman has gone off to get rid of the kid and don't want him to know.'

The baby. He couldn't ignore the presence of the pregnancy kit in his jacket any more. If this was Elena, had she been murdered while carrying his child?

Mac threw up in the sink as soon as he got into the toilet not far from Jeff's office. *Not my kid, not my kid. Please not my kid again.* And how was he going to deal with another child dying before its time? The feeling was crushing, overwhelming. Like a jackhammer brutalising him, over and over. He lifted his head as his hand wiped his mouth. Stared at his face in the mirror, but another scene reflected back at him.

'He's dead because of you,' Donna screamed at him. 'You were meant to be looking after him. How could you have taken Stevie away from me . . . ?'

Her face became Elena's, staring up at him in the bath in that ice-cold bathroom. Her hand was curved protectively across her tummy. 'What shall we call him? Stefan in honour of Stevie?'

Her image disappeared as the room began to close in on Mac. He started shaking. Stevie had died because of him. And now another one of his children was gone. The pressure pulled him under. He took out his Luger and shoved the barrel in his mouth.

thirty-nine

2:20 p.m.

'I understand that you've got some information about a crime that was committed at the Rose Hotel, Mister . . . ?'

Rio wasted no words with the cab driver who sat opposite her in Interview Room Number Four. The room was compact, square, with no window but a single table and three plain black chairs. The cabbie was somewhere between late fifties and sixty, with strands of grey hair peeping through a thin, dyed-black patch, and a belly that eased ever so slightly over his belted dark trousers, which had an immaculate crease down each leg.

'Miller. Lucas Miller.' He turned a saucy smile on her. 'Most just call me Lucky.'

Rio didn't smile back. Instead she said, 'I'll need to tape this conversation.'

She popped the tape on but also opened her notepad onto a clean page. 'So how can you help my investigation?'

'Well, he got into my cab . . .'

Rio quickly wrote.

Male.

'I've been driving a cab for the last twenty years, love,' the cabbie smiled slightly, displaying a gold tooth. 'Passed "The Knowledge" on my first go . . .'

'Where did you pick him up?' she cut in. She didn't have time for the cabbie to take her on a nostalgia ride through the streets of London. Over the years she'd learned that it was sometimes a good ploy to let those sitting on the other side of the table go off the beaten track. Made them more relaxed and the more loose they were, the more they started feeling they were your mate, which usually meant that they'd be more likely to give you the information you were after. But she didn't have time for that today, not with a faceless victim who still hadn't been identified.

Lucky Miller shifted forward as he sniffed through one nostril. 'On the same road that that murder happened. Picked him up on the street. He had a bag on his shoulder, a rucksack, so it looked like he'd come from one of the hotels.'

'How do you know he'd come from one of the hotels?'

'Well I sort of asked him, didn't I? I says to him, you gotta know something about what the Old Bill are doing all over the place, because you're a guest in one of the hotels. And he never denied it.'

Rio wrote:

Hotel on Crawley Street. Names of the other hotels?

She pressed on with her questions. 'What did this man look like? How tall was he? What age? Did he have any distinctive marks?'

The cabbie screwed his face up. Relaxed his facial muscles as he sniffed high up into his nose. 'Hard to say how old he was. I'd say maybe about the age of my Kevin, or a tad older.' Suddenly his face lit up. 'He's my firstborn. Had his thirty-second last week.' Rio almost jumped in, but let it go. 'Had a big birthday bash, which caused a bit of bother between the missus and his wife. Who was doing what; you know, power-play over who was going to make the cake.' He let out a small laugh mixed with the thickness of memories and phlegm.

Rio kept writing.

Thirty-two years old. Maybe older, mid-thirties?

'What about what he looked like?'

The cabbie closed his eyes and Rio knew he was trying to imagine the scene in his cab again. She was a visual learner as well, having a knack for going back to a scene inside her head without having to be there. A very handy tool for a detective. Snapped them open. 'Can't remember too much about his clothes, but he wore a hood . . .'

'Like he was trying to hide something on his head?'

'Dunno. I mean, all the young kids are decked out in those hoodies these days. If you ask me, I think they should be banned. Only one reason you'd want to keep your face hidden.' He pulled some air through his nose again. 'I think it was part of his jacket . . . Yeah that's right, a jeans jacket. Mind you, I couldn't see properly, what with him being in the back.'

Hoodie attached to jeans jacket. Maybe hiding something? A head injury?

'But he looked upset . . . ?'

Rio's head lifted up away from her notepad.

'How do you mean?'

'I couldn't say for sure, but his eyes were bloodshot, like he'd been crying, or at least going at it with a bottle of something strong.' He leaned back. 'There was something about him that put me in mind of my granddad when my Nan passed away. He looked kind of lost, like he's on the way to somewhere in my cab but don't really know where he's going.'

Upset? Or in pain from an injury? Head injury? Bullet wound?

He took in a long breath, not from his nose this time, but from deep within his mouth. 'Thought I'd have to tell him to get out when I thought he was smoking.'

'So he was a smoker?'

He leaned forward again. 'Well, he said that he didn't have a fag, but he definitely had something in his hand. Don't know what it was, but he pushed something back inside his jacket.'

Something inside his jacket. Gun? Knife? Or maybe just an everyday pen?

'How tall was he?'

'I'd say . . .' He twisted his lips. 'About five eleven, five ten; he didn't top six foot.'

Five ten or eleven.

'Do you remember anything else?'

He shook his head. 'When I heard the news report on the radio, I thought I should drop in and have a word. I mean, it might mean nothing, but no harm coming in. I mean he could've been anyone, just wanted dropping off in a rough part of town . . .'

'Where did you drop him off?'

He told her.

Brixton.

Rough end of town? Rio half smiled at that. She'd tried to buy a flat there a few years back and couldn't afford the three-hundred-G-plus price tag.

'I'm going to get one of my colleagues to get a police sketch artist to get your description computerised.'

A few minutes later, Rio was back on her own, leaning against the wall outside the interview room, staring at her notes.

Male.

Hotel on Crawley Street. Names of the other hotels?

Thirty-two years old. Maybe older, mid-thirties?

Hoodie attached to jeans jacket. Maybe hiding something? A head injury?

Upset? Or in pain from an injury? Head injury? Bullet wound?

Something inside his jacket. Gun? Knife? Or maybe just a freaking pen?

Five ten or eleven.

Brixton.

The cab driver's passenger might not have anything to do with the investigation. Might just be a guy taking a ride from A to B. Might be the client of a prostitute who just didn't want to be recognised? Or was this her naked cop?

forty

Mac's finger twitched against the trigger. *But what if it wasn't your kid? What if it was Sergei's?* The guilt was overpowering, but doubt was starting to creep through. Mac's inner cop kicked into gear, allowing his mind to take that step back and see all of the evidence:

Elena is murdered on the same day Sergei's girlfriend goes missing.

The description of this Katia-Anna-Annalisa fits Elena.

He'd only ever met one woman who showcased a red star tattoo.

His mind twisted back. *But if that was your child, are you really going to let some bastard get away with killing him? You owe it to Stevie, and maybe you owe this child too. Justice. Revenge.*

Slowly Mac eased the gun from his mouth. Put it away and took out the bottle of pills in two swift moves. He still wasn't sure if these were the same meds that Doctor Warren had doled out to him, but if he was going to find out the truth, he couldn't go around with the head that currently sat on his shoulders. As he popped two pills, the toilet door swung open. A woman with blonde pigtails. She became flustered when she saw him.

'This is the Ladies loo,' she said, her voice still clinging to its Russian roots.

Yellow crop top, blowsy blonde pigtails. The pole dancer

from the dance floor downstairs. Only when he caught her face did Mac realise that she was something else as well – the woman he'd rescued from Elena's burning building.

They both stared back, surprised. Hurriedly she twisted round, but Mac was on her in two steps. She gasped as he dragged her back inside and pushed her against the grass-green tiled wall. The tabs hit Mac's blood, heating him up. He looked her up and down, the same way he'd assess a suspect during an interrogation. Her eyes darted around, fingers resting on the strap of her bag curled, uncurled, curled.

The power of the drugs pushed his face a half-inch from her own. 'You claimed not to know Elena this morning. Said that you were just a neighbour.'

'I'll scream . . .' Her voice jerked, her accent stronger.

'Go ahead.' Mac's breath blew against her skin. 'But the boss of the club isn't going to be happy that you wouldn't tell me what you know about Elena's disappearance.'

At the mention of Reuben, her eyes widened. 'I don't know her really . . .'

'Then how come you work in the same club that she comes to?'

Her hand tightened against her bag. 'I just dance, that's all, keep the men happy and my eyes to myself.'

He shifted his body closer to her. The pattern of her breathing changed to a distressed and rapid in-and-out motion.

'I'm a man, so why don't you keep me happy by telling me the truth?'

She thought for a few seconds. 'All I know is she comes here with her friend. Another woman. Bit younger than her, I don't know her name. I don't ask questions.'

The last was said as if he should be doing the same.

A calmness came over him and a strength of mind that he hadn't felt in a long time. 'So who did you see come to her flat? Boyfriends?'

'She wasn't that type of girl,' she threw back vehemently.

'So you did know her?'

'All I know is, she had a few problems . . .'

'What problems?'

A whoosh of air left her throat. 'I don't know. Family stuff, I think. I could sometimes hear her arguing . . .' Her lips clamped together like she'd realised she'd said too much.

'Who with?'

'I don't know. Last night I saw her go out and only realised she was back when I heard the voices coming from her place upstairs . . .'

'What voices?'

She shrugged. 'Hers . . . I think another woman's. I think it was family stuff because they kept mentioning the word "papa" . . . you know, father. I don't want any trouble. I've got a family back home to think of . . . a little girl . . . I've told you what I know so leave me alone.'

It was the mention of her daughter that made him step back, give her enough space to rush out. He'd been a family man once, having to work all God's hours to provide for Stevie. Mac pulled out the remnants of the photo he'd found in Elena's fireplace. Two men, obviously pleased to be in each other's company. Maybe one was her father? So she was having family troubles – hey, didn't everyone? It probably had nothing to do with anything. But who was the woman she was arguing with? He thought back to the blanket and makeshift pillow on Elena's sofa. Probably this woman had been staying with her. The questions roamed his mind until he came to one conclusion – the only person who might have some answers was Sergei.

Mind clear, Mac left the Ladies and made his way to the exit upstairs. As he neared the door, a voice called out behind him.

Jeff.

'That's her in the photo. Sergei's lady.'

He pointed at one of the photographs in the frame hosting lots of other pictures; Mac realised they were showing off people having a good time at the club.

It was a party shot of about ten people gathered together. On the right, in the background, was a woman in a pink wig with her arm round a woman with chin-trimmed black hair.

Elena.

forty-one

2:35 p.m.

Rio stood in front of the whiteboard where Detective Martin had pinned and written all the information relating to the case.

Three photo shots of the gruesome remains of the victim.

Two shots of the bloodstained bed.

Rose Hotel.

Rohypnol.

Pregnant.

Photo of the towel found at Doctor Mohammed Masri's.

Hotel security film.

Doctor Mohammed Masri.

Cab driver.

Rio picked up a thick black marker and wrote: 1402c.

Just writing the undercover cop code made her fury at Phil increase. She was so fucked off with him. She almost laughed out loud at that. He's fucking her over while she's letting him fuck her. He knew who the naked cop was. Knew what he'd been doing in the hotel room. Just frigging-hell knew. She stared back at the board and the big, red question mark that James had placed in the middle showing they still didn't know who the vic was. Rio was going to find out who that under-cover bastard was, even if that meant she didn't sleep. She hadn't figured out yet how she was going to do it . . .

'What's the number mean?'

She turned to find Martin behind her, nursing a cup of coffee as he stared up at the board.

Rio didn't answer him. Should she tell him? Shouldn't she? Never hold out on your partner – that was one of the golden rules of teamwork, along with making sure you looked after your partner's back.

'I don't know yet,' she answered slowly with the half-truth.

James sipped, then asked, 'But where's it from?'

'When I've figured that out, you'll be the first to know. I take it our international friends still haven't come back with an ID?'

She didn't hang around to catch his answer because she already knew what it was. So with the anger towards Phil churning inside, she swiftly moved to her desk. Didn't sit down, but leaned over and picked up the telephone receiver. Punched in a number. Stood straight.

'This is Detective Inspector Rio Wray from Scotland Yard. I'm calling to find out if a DNA match has been secured on a murder I'm investigating . . . Yes, one of my detectives called through with a request earlier today . . . No problem, I'll wait.' She kept the phone to her face as Martin joined her.

The person on the other end of the line came back a few minutes later, obviously with news that made Rio twist her mouth. 'Well, tell Officer Branaski that when he gets back from his meeting he's to call me immediately.' Her voice softened. 'And please tell him that we really need to know who this young woman is because our priority is to let her family know what has happened to her as soon as possible, and that we're really grateful for his assistance in this. Thank you.'

Rio ended the call and turned back to the younger man; the expression on her face had moved from soft to steaming. 'Lazy bastard. If he doesn't pull his finger out, I'm catching a plane, and before he knows it he's going to have me and my shadow following him around until he comes up with the goods.' She finished with the rush of a train going helter-skelter off the tracks.

Martin gave her one of his 'What's up?' stares. 'Do you need a cup of something, DI?' His voice was as gentle as the way he placed his cup on the corner of her desk.

Agitated, Rio ran her fingers through her 'fro. 'What I need is to solve this case.'

'But what if they don't have a record that matches the DNA?'

It wasn't what she wanted or needed to hear. 'Then we're going to have to tear this town apart until somebody starts singing the words I need to hear. Somebody out there knows who she is. She's got to be somebody's daughter, lover, sister or friend.' Rio pressed two fingers against the bridge of her nose and closed her eyes.

'I'll get you that—'

Her eyes snapped back open. 'Some woman has been butchered on my watch and you think I'm going to be able to sit around here with my feet up taking afternoon fucking tea?' Rio ran a palm over her mouth. Let her shoulders drop. Got back in control. 'Right, what's happening with the techy guy for the security film?'

Martin just stared back.

'Find out where he is and how long it's going to take him to get here.'

Martin quickly moved, but Rio yelled at his back, 'And take *that* with you.' She pointed at the cup he'd left on the desk.

Alone again, Rio pulled off the top file in her in-tray. Flipped the cover back. Took out the top sheet of paper.

White.

Male.

Thirties.

Hoodie attached to jacket.

She stared at the e-photo of the cab driver's description of the passenger. Something familiar kept flitting across her mind, but she couldn't place it. Why did the drawing look so familiar?

She needed to find out who the cop was, but Phil was her only lead. Damn. Who else could she connect with on this? Who? Who? Her mind flicked through contacts in other departments. Vice? Drugs? Counter-terrorism? The list went on, but no one person jumped out at her. What she needed was another contact in The Office Research Unit, but that division kept itself to itself. Secrecy was what kept its wheels turning. There must be someone. Some . . . Her mind froze. Of course. Why hadn't she thought of him before?

Mac.

She threw the Photofit back in the file and pulled out her mobile. But before she could contact Mac, a voice near her desk said, 'DI Wray?'

A woman clutching a large bag stood by her desk. She was much smaller than Rio, her hair pulled back in a ponytail that stretched the already stressed skin of her face. Her eyes were bloodshot.

'I hope you don't mind me coming up? They said it was OK to do so downstairs.'

It took Rio a while to place her, but then she did. 'You're Doctor Masri's receptionist.' She pulled a nearby empty seat towards her desk. 'Please,' she offered.

'What's your name?' Rio asked gently once the woman was sitting down.

'Patricia.'

'I'm sorry about what happened to your employer and am grateful for any help you can give us in apprehending his murderer. But you didn't need to come, you could have just given the information to the officer I sent with you—'

'No,' the other woman cut in softly. 'I wanted to do this. I felt I owed it to Doctor Masri.'

She opened her bag. 'I found the missing patient . . . Doctor Mo's patient.' Her voice was thin and breathless with nerves.

The dead doctor's receptionist placed a manila folder on the desk. Rio used a finger to swivel it round towards her. Opened it. Read the name.

'DI?' Detective Martin shot out excitedly across the room. He practically ran towards his superior. 'Europol just came back with a DNA match to our vic in the hotel. We've got a name.'

'Elena Romanov?' Rio asked.

'How did you know that?'

Rio held up the missing patient file. A stunned Martin read out the name written in typed black ink inside. 'Elena Romanov.'

forty-two

'Do you think your feelings towards her have changed since she passed away?' Doctor Alicia Warren asked her two thirty appointment in her office.

The calmness of her consultation was disrupted by the sound of a commotion coming from outside. Raised voices, one of which was her receptionist's and the other she couldn't identify. Male voice. Low and urgent.

'Excuse me a moment . . .' she apologised to her patient as she started rising from the chair.

But before she could complete the action, the door burst open.

'I've told you that you can't go in there,' her receptionist shouted behind the man who stood in the doorway.

'We need to talk,' the man fired at the doctor, ignoring the receptionist.

Doctor Warren twisted her lips together as her fine-shaped eyebrows lifted in annoyance. 'I'm in the middle of a session and you should not be here—'

'Well, we're all in the middle of sessions, Doctor, so now, if you wouldn't mind . . .' the man cut in.

She should insist on him leaving, but he was her most valuable client, bringing in substantial levels of work that most therapists could only dream of.

Doctor Warren turned to her patient. 'I'm really sorry, but would you mind waiting outside for a few minutes?'

As soon as the patient was gone, she turned all her professional fury onto the intruder. 'Mr Delaney, I told your PA that I would see you this evening. Just because I've got a contract with your department does not give you the right to come here and behave like this.'

Phil Delaney took a seat. 'This can't wait.'

Resigned to the situation, the therapist said, voice cool and level, 'I can only give you a few minutes of my time.'

'John MacDonagh. Give me a window into his state of mind.'

The doctor leaned forward. 'John MacDonagh . . . ?' She stopped, her mind thinking back. 'The police officer whose son died?' At Phil's curt nod she continued. 'I can't talk about my sessions with him; you know that, it's confidential. I submitted a summary report a year ago . . .'

'I need more than a report filled with technical jargon.'

She leaned back, but a look of concern stretched her face. 'Has something happened to him?'

'Do you think that he's dangerous?'

Silence. Then she spoke again. 'In my report I made it very clear that he was suffering considerable trauma and shock over the death of his young son.' She neatly crossed her legs. 'What I didn't make so clear was that most of that trauma stems from the guilt and the blame he feels regarding his son's death. Do you know what it must feel like to lose a child?'

'This isn't about me, it's about him. If he was back at work, in the field . . . ?'

'Tell me you're joking.' For the first time, emotion came through her tone. 'Tell me that you did not allow him to come back to work. I made it clear, in my opinion, he was not ready to return to work.'

Phil didn't answer, just kept direct eye contact with her.

The therapist settled her voice back into an even tone. 'A man like John, in his line of work, carrying that type of grief, is vulnerable. He may think that he's in control, but he isn't. Well, not all of the time. So if he's put in a situation that heightens all those feelings of remorse, he's a human hand grenade ready to explode.'

'Is he dangerous?'

'Don't you understand what I've been telling you? His job is about righting the wrongs for the good of society, taking the bad guys off the street and making it safe for everyone else. The only wrong he's not been able to put right is his son's death. And who does he blame for that? Himself. He can't take vengeance against himself, so if he now finds himself in a situation where he thinks he can absolve his guilt and find redemption through another act, he'll do everything he can to make sure that happens.'

'Is he dangerous?' Phil repeated.

She paused. 'Dangerous? No. Potentially unstable? Yes. If he finds himself in the wrong situation, he could explode.'

forty-three

'Our victim is Russian. Thirty-two-year-old Yelena Romanov, but who more commonly used the name Elena. She also used the usual string of other aliases.'

Rio said, 'I'm surprised that the Russians came back this quickly; they usually drag their feet with us Brits.'

Detective Martin turned to look at her. 'It wasn't the Russians, it was the Germans.'

'Germany?'

'Five years ago, our victim was claiming to be a student studying for a communications degree in Munich. She was arrested by the police in a raid on a club in Berlin, which was believed to be a base for the Russian mob specialising in prostitution, drugs, the usual-usual. Here's her mug shot.'

Martin pressed an attachment at the bottom of the screen. A black-and-white photo came up. He clicked on it, enlarging it. The woman in the picture was more striking than pretty, with the type of bone structure that gave her a face that would be remembered. Her hair was dark, straight, with the ends just touching her slim shoulders. It was her eyes that caught Rio's attention – instead of being scared they reflected defiance.

'Was she arrested for tricking?' Rio asked.

'No. Being in the wrong place at the right time. Her mother was arrested too.'

'Her mother?'

'The mother claimed to be visiting her, so when the police went to the flat she was living in, they found the mother and pulled her in as well. They had the mother's DNA on file and that's how we've made the match to the victim.'

'Didn't they have the vic's DNA?'

James shook his head. 'They let her out on bail pending further inquiries and told her to stay put, but she skipped town before they could get a DNA sample. They didn't believe the mother had anything to do with the activities at the club so they let her go. But luckily the Germans were able to get some information out of the Russians at the time of her arrest.'

He minimised the photograph and clicked on another file. They both read the information.

'So,' Rio said. 'Our victim has a record in Russia as well. Arrests for drug possession, joy riding, being in nightspots that your mum wouldn't want you to be in.'

'But it says here that her father was a decorated war hero with a distinguished career in the Red Army. He was awarded the highest Soviet military medal after he was killed in the Afghan war back in the 1980s. So she came from a respectable, military family. Her lawyer managed to get her off the drugs possession charge, pleading that she was a kid who went off the rails after her father died. The family must've been connected because the charges were swiftly dropped.'

Rio said, 'It doesn't appear that she was ever arrested for prostitution . . .'

'But the evidence suggests that she may have been involved in it,' Martin interrupted. 'She was arrested in a club in Berlin that was known as a hooker hangout and was found dead in a hotel-cum-brothel in London.'

'Um,' Rio answered.

She eased back in her chair as her thoughts slipped into place. 'I think the thread here is gangs. Russian gangs. She was arrested at a club in Berlin that had the stamp of a Russian crew all over, and I'm betting that the nightclubs she was seen at in Moscow were also tied to the mob – or Brotherhood, as some call themselves. And the hit on her in London was a professional job. Yelena Romanov pissed off the wrong person, someone that she knew.' Rio flicked her gaze back to the computer. 'What's that?' she asked, pointing to the final attachment at the bottom of the screen.

James clicked on it. Another photo. A happy family shot of two dark-haired girls, one older than the other, locked in the embrace of an older woman. They smiled at the camera, just a normal family sharing their love with the lens.

'How does a young woman from a good family end up on the wrong side of the law and butchered in a bath?'

'How do any of us end up on the paths we do?' There was something about Rio's face that made Martin stare hard at her. He realised what it was. For the first time since he'd been working with the DI, he saw raw emotion on her face. A vulnerability that made him rethink his view of her as a hard-nosed professional.

Martin's phone went off, giving Rio some time to study the photos of Elena's family on her own. The girls were a dead ringer for each other, and had the features of the woman they posed with. Made Rio think of those times at her grandmother's house, back in the day. Sundays, usually, filled with the aroma of rice and peas, macaroni pie and sweet, sweet stewed chicken.

Rio reached for the dead doctor's patient file on Elena Romanov. Only a single sheet, no contact details. And the sheet was strange because it contained two blood test results, two different types of blood, one of which was AB – which, if Rio remembered her biology correctly, was a rare blood group. What the test was hadn't been recorded.

One victim, two different blood groups?

Before Rio could dig deeper, Martin yelled, 'Boss, he was lying.'

'Who?' Rio snapped her gaze away from Elena Romanov's medical file.

'I know you said that we couldn't use any unofficial translators, but I just knew something wasn't right . . .'

'Martin, just tell me.'

'The tattoo artist. I contacted a friend of mine who works at the Russian embassy. My friend couldn't come back to me straight away because—'

'Martin.' Rio cut the air with the power of a whiplash.

'The writing on the tattoo doesn't say, "Love is in the arms of the woman you love." It says, "To live with wolves, you have to learn to howl like a wolf." I trawled the Net – all I could find was that it's a Russian saying meaning if you want to be part of the crowd you have to act like the crowd. Couldn't find anything else.'

Rio was already standing up when she said, 'Let's go and find out why tattoo man is lying through his scumbag teeth.'

forty-four

3 p.m.

'What did you really know about this woman?'

Calum's words churned over in Mac's head as he reached
'Superb Car Washes & Valeting', the business that served as a
front for the gang's activity. Of course Calum was right; he
didn't know Elena at all. Didn't really know where she was
from, didn't know anything about her family. But what he did
know was she was dead and the man he was about to confront
was her lover along with him.

Thoughts still preoccupied with Elena, he walked across the
forecourt as two of the workers slapped their wet sponges
against a Mercedes. Three men, in dark blue overalls, some
working, some not, were next to a line of three cars waiting
for their shampoo and touch-up. There was no sign of Sergei,
so Mac figured that he'd be in the office, pretending to shuffle
papers that came from nowhere and meant nothing.

He reached the squat office building, the bottom of its
thick walls freckled in a black, nasty mould. He pushed the
door and entered a space that was more like the waiting room
in a cab office. The air was musty and the floor covered in a
carpet so thin and worn it wasn't clear what colour it was.
The door of the main office faced him a short distance away.
He felt for his gun. He'd give Sergei his chance to tell his side

of the story – then Mac was going to let his Luger do all the talking.

He pushed the door and nearly trod on a prone body, which made him stumble back. He looked down to find Reuben's son gazing back at him, a slick red toy Ferrari in his hand. Gazing at Mac with those blue eyes, so like those of his dead son.

'Milos, I've told you not to sit on the floor, little man, it's dirty,' yelled a male voice.

Sergei. He stood in the doorway of another room attached to the office, which looked like a tiny kitchen. He carried a half-glass of orange and a plate of chocolate, car-shaped biscuits. The child scrambled to his feet, his fingers went white as they gripped the car tightly. He stared at his uncle nervously. Sergei slapped the plate and glass on a table that sat just inside the room near the kitchen. He said something roughly to the boy in Russian that had the child running across the room to the table.

'Stupid kids,' he mumbled as he strode towards Mac. 'Wassup Mac, my man?' he continued in his fake ghetto-bro brogue.

He pushed his fist out to Mac in greeting, as if he was in a hip-hop video. Mac didn't want to touch any part of this man if he was Elena's killer . . . and lover. If . . . ? Mac pumped his fist with the younger man. Sergei moved back and threw himself like a sulky teenager, legs spread wide, into a wooden chair behind the desk. On the desk were scattered papers and three electronic gizmos. Although Sergei didn't indicate that Mac should take the chair opposite him, Mac did it anyway.

'Hello Uncle Mac,' Milos said quietly from the other side of the room.

Bright kid to remember his name, Mac thought.

Sergei picked up one of the gizmos and said in a pissed-off tone, 'Reuben told me to bring the kid.' His thumb hit a button on his hand-held digi-toy, making the screen come on. 'Like I ain't got enough to do today. Do I look like some babysitter? Eh?'

Like so many young people today, he didn't even look at Mac, but kept his eyes fixed on the screen as his thumb and now fingers moved. 'Thought the kid would be safer with me.'

'Safer?'

Sergei nodded but kept his head down, fingers and thumb moving. 'Word came through that the doctor we use, some Arab, got blasted this morning.'

Mac held back the surprise from his face. He remembered the black Merc outside the doctor's surgery.

'What happened?'

'Who the hell knows, man? All I know is, Reuben don't want the kid in any possible firing line.'

Elena was dead, now so was the doctor. The bodies were starting to pile up around him.

'*Vroom, vroom!*'

Distracted by the noise Milos was making, Mac looked over at him. The boy was back on the floor, under the table this time, playing with his car.

Mac switched his attention back to Sergei. 'I went down to Club Zee.'

Sergei's head flipped up. The gizmo clattered to the table. 'What were you doing there? I thought . . .'

'You thought what?'

The other man hesitated as he straightened slightly. Then said, 'Nothing.'

'Your brother told me to go down and check out whether anyone had seen your girlfriend,' Mac smoothly lied.

'Katia?' Sergei breathed the word slow and soft, like a teen in love for the first time. 'Did you find out anything?'

Mac pressed on with his lie. 'This and that. Of course it's difficult when you don't have a photograph, but I got one at the club.' Mac took the photo he'd taken from the picture frame and handed it to Sergei, 'Is that her?'

Sergei took the picture and stared. He didn't need to say anything for Mac to see the truth written all over his immature, lovesick face. The hate began to well inside him with the power of a fountain that needed to burst out. So Elena had betrayed him. The baby maybe hadn't been his. At least he might not have to live with another child's death on his conscience.

Sergei muttered, 'I knew I shouldn't have been seeing her because big brother hates any of us going out with anyone close to the crew. But I couldn't help it. First time I saw her, I just fell.' A sudden burst of fear crawled across his face. 'Don't tell Reuben about this . . .'

'Did you argue with her?' Mac knew he was taking a chance provoking Sergei, but all he wanted was the truth.

'*Vroom! Vroom!*'

'What?' Sergei half shouted across the table. 'Are you saying that I had something to do with her going walkabout?'

The last word was yelled as Sergei surged to his feet, fists balled at his side.

Mac raised his palms in a peace gesture. 'I'm not saying anything, just trying to get the full story for Reuben.'

'Well, fuck you. And fuck Reuben.' Sergei swiped up one of the gizmos on the table and threw it at the wall with all the fury he was feeling.

Mac's hand hovered near his hidden gun. 'Take it easy . . .'

'Don't tell me to take it fucking easy,' Sergei belted back.

'Do you want to find out what happened to her?'

Air puffed out of the younger man's chest for a few seconds. Then he answered. 'She was my girl, I was meant to be protecting her. How do you think I'm feeling now she's disappeared in a puff of smoke? I've got a reputation to uphold. If word gets around that I can't even look after my lady . . .'

Mac almost sneered. So that's what this was all about, Sergei's macho pride had been wounded and he wanted to know the collateral damage it might do to his rep on the street.

Sergei slumped back in his seat. Grabbed up the photo. 'No way would I touch her, no way. Why would I kill someone so beautiful?'

Sergei stabbed his finger again. At the woman . . . Mac hustled forward. Peered closer. That's when he realised that Sergei was pointing at the woman in the pink wig, not Elena.

'*Vroom! Vroom!*'

Mac's hand slipped off the end of the gun. 'So you weren't going out with Elena?'

'Elena?' Sergei said, wiggling his nose like a bad smell had entered the room. 'Elena's in the gang. You know what Reuben's rules are about that.'

'So what are your girl and Elena doing in the photo together?'

The younger man's face closed down. 'All I know is that they used to hang out together. Calum must've found Elena by now . . .'

Mac's surprise pushed him closer to Sergei. 'Calum?'

'Yeah, big brother sent him out to look for her and I know he told him to go down to the club. He takes care of all of Reuben's awkward jobs, so when there's anything unpleasant to take care of, our friend gets a call.'

'Do you mean like killing someone?'

Outside in the yard, a car horn sounded and there was some shouting.

'Dunno. I don't ask.'

Mac's mind spun with the new information. Had Reuben asked Calum to kill Elena? But before he could think through it further, there was more shouting from outside.

'Do you know if Elena had anyone staying with her?'

'*Vroom! Vroom!*'

'What the fuck . . . ?' Sergei growled, before he could answer Mac. He jumped up. Strode angrily over to the twin windows with a view of the forecourt outside. Looked out. Opened one of the windows and shouted, 'Hey, what's . . .'

But he never finished the sentence. Instead Mac heard the sound of glass breaking as an object came flying into the office. It spun like a mottled green ball on the wooden floor. For what seemed like minutes, but was only a split second, Mac watched the ball spin. When he realised what it was, he vaulted the desk at the same time as the room flashed in a white and blue sheet of lightning explosion.

forty-five

Mac didn't hear the hand grenade explode. But the shock-waves shattered his eardrums like a hammer blow and crumpled his body. The room shook from side to side. Furniture broke apart and erupted into the air. The windows burst outwards in a shower of glass. For a few seconds he lay winded. Then clawed desperately, coughing at the smoky air. Struggled to his feet, but collapsed backwards in a heap, gasping for breath in the acrid air.

Even the buzzing and humming in his ears couldn't shield him from the noise outside as more hand grenades went off. Then the steady thumping of a sub-machine gun. He heard the screams, yells and pleading of the wounded, crippled and dying. Mac grabbed a corner of the shattered desk, which was charred and smoking. Yelped with pain as the wood burned and came away in his fingers. He rolled onto his front, into a crawling position, and then rose upright like a dead man's ghost. There was silence, apart from the crackle of flames and the sound of water gushing from unattended hoses.

Mac found himself curiously calm, as if he were back on the meds he'd been given after Stevie's death that would take him in and out of the world. As the smoke swirled through the wreckage, he saw a masked figure appear outside. He looked through the empty space where the window had been and caught Mac's eye. The figure toyed with a sub-machine gun.

Raised and pointed it at Mac before hesitating. Suddenly a second, masked man appeared, a machine gun slung over his shoulder. He ran by, grabbed the first by the arm and shouted, 'Let's go, let's go!'

The gunmen took off towards a black Mercedes; soapy water was pumping over it in the car wash. Black Merc. Elongated, ridged line just below the door handles. Just like the one he'd seen outside the doctor's. Were these Doctor Mo Masri's killers? Mac wanted to chase after them, but his legs were too weak. He steadied himself and stumbled to the office entrance. His foot stuck. He looked down and realised that he'd trodden on Sergei's face. Or what was left of the other man's face. His body looked like it had been on a dissecting table, his liver and stomach, slopping and wet, strewn around him. Katia and Elena's happy-times photo lay in the muck of his exploded body.

Mac turned away from Sergei's dead body. The door had been blown into a wreckage of splintered pieces. Outside he saw a war zone.

'*We should warn you that some viewers may find the following pictures distressing . . .*' The warning from TV news flashed through his mind. Bits of human bodies were scattered around. Arms. Feet. A pair of boots stood in the road a good distance from two car-wash workers groaning on the ground. Blood spread in myriad, almost artistic patterns, across the paintwork. Across the body of a blue Ferrari.

Ferrari. Toy red Ferrari. The kid.

Mac jerked back to the office. Rushed inside the wreckage and began searching. And searching. Suddenly he stopped. In the back yard, by a door hanging from its hinges, he saw a small foot peeping from under a plank of wood that had once been the top of a table. He ran forward. Pulled the wood off. There, lying on his back amongst some weeds, was Milos. His body completely unmarked by the results of the attack, he seemed to be sleeping a child's sleep.

Live long and free. The words carved into Milos's birthday pie flashed through Mac's mind. But he could see that the child wasn't going to fulfil that dream because he wasn't breathing, just like another boy a year ago.

'I love you Daddy.'

The sing-song words, with the lisp from two missing front teeth, made Mac open his eyes. He lay on his back on a large turquoise towel, next to the one person he knew would never lie about loving him. Stevie. His son. He grinned as he slipped slowly onto his side. The six-year-old was facing him, his small body hitched up on his left elbow as he stared at his father. Apart from his honey hair, he was a little Mac all over. The blue eyes, the stubborn-set chin, the nose that was always going to be a dominant feature of his face.

They were at the beach. Southend. The day had started with a dawn that seemed unsure about whether the day was going to be hot or cold. And that uncertainty in the air had kept the people away from the beach. But not them, not Mac and son – oh no. They'd set off like it was going to be the best day of their lives. And if the sun didn't venture out, well hey, that wasn't going to get in their way. But it had come, bright and easy, just as they reached the beach.

They didn't get many times like this to be together. Well, not since Donna had given him his marching orders last summer, smacking the door shut on a decade of marriage. He'd been the one to make a dog's dinner of his marriage, not her, so he fully understood her hating his guts, but not once had she stopped him from seeing his boy. No, he'd been the problem. Never around when Stevie needed him. Months spent going underground, too busy being someone else rather than the father he should've been. The first chance he got after rinsing off the filth from his latest job, a kiddie-porn ring, was to have a special day with his little boy. Looking back, he should've realised that he was mentally and physically washed out and maybe he should've given it a day or two before he'd seen his son. But he hadn't. And it had changed his life for ever.

Mac made a mock-growl as he heaved Stevie sky-high. The child let out a giggle that rippled like the waves lapping against the shore. Mac settled the small body against his chest in a loving embrace. Closed his eyes. Soaked up the silence. The peace. The quiet. The twin breathing of his son and his own. The tiredness faded away and he drifted into the most comforting sleep . . .

He didn't know what woke him. A noise? The touch of the sea breeze against his skin? The dying warmth from the disappearing sun? He sat up. Looked around. Noticed the abandoned beach ball, bucket and spade that they'd taken with them. The deserted beach. Deserted . . . He shot to his feet. Frantically looked around. No Stevie.

'Stevie.'

No response.

'Stevie.'

He ran along the beach.

'Stevie.'

His shout became a roar. He swung his gaze around. Left. Right. Back. Forward. And that's when he saw it. Something bobbing in the water. A good distance away from the shore. He didn't stop to think. Just hurtled into the water. Started to swim. Long strokes painfully stretched his muscles. Water tumbled into his mouth, open with desperation. He got closer. Closer. He wanted to deny what his eyes were telling him he saw. A small body, lifeless, floating, head down, in the rough sea.

He reached it. Turned the body over. It wasn't true because it couldn't be true. Stevie.

The small body moved. Mac looked down at the young child in his arms. The tiny mouth sucked in a shuddering breath. Reuben's son was not dead.

forty-six

4 p.m.

Rio parked her beloved ebony BMW X5 outside the tattoo shop. When she'd first become a detective, a few people had pulled her aside and told her to get rid of the Beamer because, in their opinion, it would be too bling, too much of a reminder that she was 'black' – and she didn't want to keep pushing that in people's faces, now did she? She, in turn, told people to get out of her face and step back from her BMW, or Black Magic Woman, as she name-checked it. And she was the black magic woman that the police force was never going to be able to forget.

Rio got out the same time as Martin. Headed for the door. She noticed the Closed sign first of all. Tried to push the door open. Locked.

'Check round the back,' she ordered the younger detective.

She cupped her hands over a window and peered inside. No one. Nothing. Just a myriad of mounted designs like a junkie's psychedelic daze looking back at her.

'No one round the back.'

The tattoo artist was long gone. Was he running scared? And if so, why?

DI Rio Wray kicked the door in frustration.

* * *

Mac careered down the road in one of the half-washed cars from the car wash, mounting the pavement, overtaking, shooting lights and attracting obscene hand signals and shouts from other drivers. But none of that mattered. All he cared about was getting the unconscious child strapped in the passenger seat to the hospital. Abruptly the traffic came to a standstill.

'Come on, come on,' he growled. Then banged against the horn. Once. Twice. But the traffic was still going nowhere. He checked the kid. He seemed unnaturally still. Had he stopped breathing? Quickly Mac placed his palm against his small chest. He couldn't feel anything. But he kept it there, waiting. Waiting. Then he felt that slight rise in his hand from the oxygen still pumping in Milos's body. But if he didn't get out of this traffic jam, Reuben's son might not make it. The traffic started moving and Mac took no more chances. He mounted the pavement to the horror of pedestrians and kept going. And going. Then he hit the road again. Passed a side street with two cars in it. A black Merc, the other a metallic run-around. Two furtive men between the vehicles.

He skidded to a halt. No way. He couldn't be that lucky, could he? To stumble across the gunmen? But what about the boy? He looked down at him. Decision time. He made his decision in a few seconds. Jacked the car backwards until he was near the side street. Flew outside, gun by his side. He moved with the grace of an avenging angel towards the entrance to the side street. He didn't feel fear as he walked. The men were too busy, hurriedly transferring items from one car boot to another, to take note of his presence. As he got closer, Mac saw the holes in the black Merc. Bullet holes. He raised his gun at the same time as they saw him. One ran, while the other went for his pocket. Mac blasted a bullet in the ground near the man with his hand inside his coat. The warning shot made him pull his hand back. It came out empty.

Mac didn't say a word as he kept the gun trained right at his heart. The other man slowly raised his hands in the air. In the distance, Mac clocked the other gunman escaping over a wall and knew that there was no way he was going to be able to plug him from here. Mac lowered the angle of the gun. Pulled back the trigger. A slug slammed into the man's leg. With a groan the man dropped to his side. It felt good that afternoon to be finally shooting someone.

Mac finally spoke. 'You move and that will be the end.'

Mac kept his piece trained on the bleeding man as he moved towards the cars and inspected their boots. Sports holder packed with grenades and firearms, one of which was a high-end pistol with silencer. Mac shoved it in his pocket, along with a couple of hand grenades. He found a machine gun under a sheet. He pulled the sheet off and walked back to the man. Crammed the cloth deep down in his mouth. Then he smashed his Luger on the side of his head, sending the man into an oblivion as dark as the colour of the Mercedes.

forty-seven

Mac burst through the doors of the A&E department of Mission Hill Hospital, holding Milos tenderly in his arms. The boy looked broken. His arms flopped to the side, his legs shook with every step Mac took. Mac was scared. Really scared for the boy, because since taking that life-giving gasp of breath, his body hadn't moved again.

The place was packed. People standing. People sitting. People nursing their own wounds from life.

'Help me,' Mac shouted.

All eyes turned to him. Someone gasped. Then a nurse rushed towards him.

'This way,' she said urgently, already moving along the corridor.

He kept pace with her, until they reached a room. With one hand she pushed against some swing doors, making room for him to move inside. He entered a room with blue curtains surrounding three cubicles and the beep of machines pulsing in the air.

'Put him down, over there.' The nurse pointed to a fourth cubicle where a makeshift bed waited.

As Mac placed the boy down, the woman called out, 'Doctor.'

Female doctor, tall, looking professional but with tiredness lining the corners of her eyes, stepped out from one of the other cubicles. Her gaze went immediately to the Milos. She moved across and spoke to Mac at the same time.

'What happened?'

'He got caught up in an explosion.'

She looked at him quizzically, but he wouldn't say any more than that. The doctor started examining the injured child. Then threw some medical terms at the nurse. The nurse nodded and went into auto-action. Mac stepped back as she dragged a small trolley across the room. It rattled with the clang of medical instruments on it. Then she got an IV drip ready.

She turned to Mac. 'You need to wait outside. I'll get some-one to take details from you in a while.' She caught his eyes. 'We'll do everything we can for your son.'

Then she turned. Whipped the curtain round the cubicle. Mac didn't move straight away. All he could feel was the emptiness now in his arms. Finally he moved. Stepped outside the room. But he didn't leave. He stared through the door, with the chant of her words drumming in his head.

Your son.

Your son . . .

Mac stared at the medical team that worked furiously on Stevie. He'd tried everything he could to get his boy breathing once he'd got his body back to the shore. Nothing had worked. But he wasn't giving up, not on his Stevie. That's when every-thing he'd learned about how to deal with an emergency as a cop kicked in. He'd taken out his phone. Hit the Internet icon. Punched in details for the nearest hospital. Found it. A quarter of a mile away. Picked up his son. Placed him in the car.

He didn't remember the drive. Didn't remember entering the first building he'd got to. The café on the ground floor. Didn't remember the collective inhalation of surprise and shock that sounded from the people at the tables. From the man at the checkout till. Didn't remember the doctor arriving and taking Stevie from his arms. All he recalled was standing

*in the corridor and looking crazily through the glass-panelled
windows as they worked on Stevie. When the doctor checked
the clock on the wall, he knew it was too late. His blue, blue-
eyed Stevie was gone. Laid out, his lips a strange shade of
blue. And that's when he'd ended up on his knees. And cried.
Just cried.*

'We'll need to call the police immediately,' the doctor said to
the nurse.

The nurse nodded as she stared at the boy on the bed. They
still weren't sure about the extent of his injuries, but at least
they'd managed to get him breathing and stabilised.

'Find the father outside,' the doctor continued. 'Get as much
detail as you can from him. Reassure him. But don't mention
the police.'

She followed his instructions but when she checked the
corridor outside, there was no sign of the father.

forty-eight

Should he make the call? The question batted around Mac's brain as he sat tense in the driver's seat of the car outside the building that housed the butcher's and Calum's office. He pulled out his mobile. Toyed with it in his hand as he decided whether to contact Reuben. No doubt word had already reached the arms dealer about what had gone down at the car wash, but he wouldn't know what had happened to his son. Mac knew he shouldn't feel a fuck of emotion, not for a man who ran an illegal arms-trafficking outfit. But Reuben wasn't just a criminal; he was a father as well. A man who gave his kid a lavish birthday party. A man who would be devastated by what had happened to his boy, just like Mac had been twelve months ago.

He made his decision.

'It's me.'

'Sergei's dead . . .' There was control in the other man's voice, but Mac could also hear the spark of something else. Anger? Grief? He wasn't sure, but whichever it was, this man's world had been thrown down a path he wasn't expecting.

'I know . . . Listen . . .'

But Reuben ploughed on. 'I can't find Milos. No one can find—'

'I took him to the hospital . . .'

'Is he dead?' All the emotion dropped away from Reuben's tone.

'He's at Mission Hill. They're working on him. I think he'll
be fine . . .'

The line went dead. He stared at the butcher's shop below
Calum's office. The shop appeared shut up. He stayed put,
watching, double-checking that the workers inside the butcher's were indeed gone for the evening. When he was satisfied
that no one was around, he drove the car to the mouth of the
alleyway he'd used to get into Calum's office that morning. He
got out of the car. Moved to the boot. Opened it. Back at him
stared the bulging eyes of the gunman who was trussed up
inside. Mac popped a pill. Swallowed.

'Me and you need to have a little chat,' Mac said.

He dragged the man out of the car and reopened the butcher's for business.

A fist slammed into the man's jaw for a second time, spraying
a mist of blood into the air.

Mac flexed his aching fist as he yelled, 'You and I need to
sort a few things out. Let's start with an easy one – who
ordered the car-wash job?'

But the gunman tied down to the butcher's block only
glared back. They were inside a large room at the back of the
shop, which was well below room temperature and filled with
deadly implements laid out cleanly and tidily on shelves.
Mac's plan had been to use the deep freezer. Hoist the murdering bastard from a hook next to the carcases of dead animals,
but with the tips of his toes touching the floor so that he felt
the rage and pain from the bullet hole in his leg. But then he
decided that positioning the wounded man in such a way
maybe wouldn't give him access to what he needed to get the
truth. No, flat on his back was where he needed this killer.

'Can't remember? That's OK, we've got time. Let's try the
woman who was shot in the hotel, the gun and grenade play

at the car wash. Who ordered them? Same people?' Mac thought for a moment before adding, almost as if he was merely curious, 'And my miraculous escape at the car wash. How did that happen? Was that orders ... or was I just "lucky"?'

The last question had been plaguing Mac. The man had had a chance to take him out but hadn't taken it. Why? Was that what had happened at the hotel; he'd been deliberately shot, but in such a way that would've been no threat to his life? The chemicals from the pills rushed through his blood, building a power within. He sucked in a mammoth breath, the air in this death-house some of the sweetest oxygen he'd ever tasted.

'Come on – rack your brains. Try harder ...'

The man let out a sharp laugh that wasn't reflected in his eyes. Then he spat out a tooth from his bleeding mouth. Clamped his mouth defiantly tight. Furious, Mac raised his fist again, but froze with it in mid-air. Smashing this man's face into oblivion wasn't, he suspected, going to get him any nearer the truth. He needed to make this man feel pain, real pain. Mac dropped his hand as he twisted round. Walked over to a collection of aprons hanging from aluminium hooks. He pulled one off, surprised at its weight. Then he realised that this was no ordinary apron, but made of thin stainless steel, probably to protect a butcher from the impact of a slipping knife. He eased it on. Turned his attention to the shelves showcasing a butcher's tools of the trade.

Hammers.

Some kind of flat scraping instrument.

Wire brushes.

Long, thin, steel tool with a wicked point at one end.

Curved knives.

Butchers' knives in different sizes and blades.

Meat and bone saw.

Mac chose the long tool with the pointed end that reminded him of a screwdriver. He strode back to the man and stopped beside his legs. Located the bullet wound. He touched the outer edges of the hole with the steel in his hand. The man flinched, but didn't call out. Mac deliberately grazed the hard point around the mangled mix of flesh and blood in the top of the wound. Harsh, rapid breathing blew out from the other end of the butcher's block. Without warning, Mac forced down. Nice . . . and . . . slow. Maximum agony. A high scream bounced around the white tiled walls. Mac considered shoving the cloth back into his mouth, but decided against it. Sometimes the sound of your own scream intensified your feelings of terror.

'Hotels . . . the doctor's clinic . . . and of course we can't forget the car wash. Quite a little list. Go on – give us a hint. Why did the doctor have to go? Or are you the kind of hired gun who doesn't care about the details?' Mac finally demanded as the steel kept up its journey. 'But you know who hired your gun, don't you?'

Only screams answered him. Mac increased the pressure of his hand. Hit something hard. The bullet. His hand stopped.

'They might not have given you a name. But you know . . . people like you always do . . .'

Rapid breathing, no answer.

Mac pushed down. The man's body arched as high as the ropes around him would allow. There was no screaming this time, only the sound of a noise that Mac equated to the death cries of an animal. But still the man refused to talk. In frustration, Mac pulled the steel clear of the wound and threw it angrily to the floor. He stomped back to the shelves. Pulled off the saw and a knife with indented lines just above the edge of its blade.

Headed back, to his captive's head this time. The man's eyes were watery with pain, his facial muscles twitching and his lips moving like he was in the midst of a prayer. Mac placed the knife flat against the block. Kept the saw in his hand.

He stared his prisoner directly in the face. 'See my eyes? You know I'm going all the way with this. Now help yourself out by helping me out – name the person who's pulling your strings.'

The man gobbed pink spittle into Mac's face. Mac wiped it off with the back of his hand. Pulled the man's ear with the same hand and started sawing. A sharp spurt of blood hit Mac's apron. Then the blood oozed thickly down as the flesh tore.

'OK. OK,' the man yelled, the sound of his breathing noisy and nasty in the room. 'I'll tell you . . . tell you.'

Mac stopped. But didn't remove the saw.

'I'm listening.'

'We never touched any woman in a hotel.' Each word shook as the man grappled with the pain eating into him. His raging breathing pushed his chest high. 'We saw you for the first time when you went into the doctor's.'

Mac shook his head with mock disappointment. 'That's a shame.'

Mac inched down the saw. A full-throttle shrill tore up the room again.

'It's true,' he screamed, his head shifting from side to side, as if trying to wake up from a nightmare. 'We were only contracted to take care of the doctor and the young Russian.'

The saw froze. 'The doctor and Sergei?' Mac briefly floundered and wondered aloud in anguish, 'But what about the woman?'

No answer. Quickly Mac placed the saw on the block and replaced it with the knife in his hand. He put the tip of the knife against the man's throat. The air coming out of the man's nose and mouth was ragged and shallow.

'Keep talking.'

The man closed his eyes. Abruptly, with one swift move, he shoved his head up and forward, ramming the knife deep into his windpipe.

forty-nine

5 p.m.

The assassin was dead, but Mac still had one more card left to play.

'*He takes care of all of Reuben's awkward jobs.*'

Mac remembered Sergei's words about Calum as he hacked and crowbarred and finally shot off the chained doorway that divided the butcher's storeroom from a staircase that led up to Calum's office. The room upstairs was locked off too, but Mac fired two more shots into that. He'd lost patience with long methods that day. He walked into Calum's office determined to ransack, but without much idea of what he was looking for. But Calum had some answers, Mac was sure of that; he just didn't know what the questions were yet.

He strode past the shotgun that was still propped up against the wall, and headed straight for the desk. Jumbled papers, a couple of pens, paperclips and computer. Nothing of interest. That was typical of the security consultant; he might have been lower than a snake's belly, but he was still a professional. Never leave secrets lying around. His computer was on but Calum's main activity on it seemed to be playing solitaire. Mac went through the desk's drawers. Nothing. A filing cabinet with folders and three bogus cops' badges. But nothing else. Nothing. Nothing. Nothing.

He kicked the wall.

His rage hit the red zone and he started pulling books and files off the shelves and shaking them to see if anything fell out. When nothing did, he threw them on the wooden floor with increasing violence. Finally, he swept a row of books to the floor and watched them crash downwards. He stood, breathing heavily, and looked around the room. His gaze came to rest on the lead that hung from the back of the computer. Calum had used it that morning to plug into the back of Elena's phone before declaring it had been wiped.

Mac hunted around in his pocket and found Elena's phone. Plugged it in to the lead and took the seat in front of the screen. A few moments later a pop-up appeared announcing, 'New Hardware Detected . . .' It flashed a few times before giving way to a window as a program started up. The application had a title bar announcing it had been developed by 'Blank Frank' of Novosibirsk and there was a mobile phone number next to it. In brackets after that, Blank Frank had included the message, 'If you want support, you're out of luck!!! Ha ha!!!' Across the screen spread information about the make, the phone number and the network.

And he didn't need the phone's password any more, because its technical information was giving up access to all its hidden secrets.

Address book.

Texts.

Phone logs.

Voicemail.

He went through each one in turn. Most of the data on the phone had been deleted, except an option shaded eye-squinting green with the words:

'Four Texts Available'.

But Calum had claimed that all the data had been deleted.

Why had he done that? Mac pushed Calum from his mind – for now – as he clicked on the green box and watched as, scrolling down the screen, came the four texts. They were all timed and dated for the day on which Elena had become hysterical about Reuben's delivery. And they were all from one sender – Bolshoi.

You know how important that delivery is to me. You fucked up.

You bitch. You're a dead woman. So is your boyfriend. So long. Bolshoi.

I'll kill you myself if you're not dead already. Hope for your sake you are.

Are you dead yet Elena? Don't reply if you are. Bolshoi.

Mac read them over and over again and they merged into one.

Bitch . . . Boyfriend . . . Dead . . . Kill . . . Bolshoi . . .

Who the hell was Bolshoi? It wasn't a name he'd ever heard Reuben use before, but it must be connected to the gang because this Bolshoi talked about the delivery. And why was the delivery important to him? Elena had obviously done something to piss the guy off. But what? Mac stared hard at the screen. There it was in black and white, the evidence and the name of Elena's killer – Bolshoi. He searched frantically across Blank Frank's application in an effort to find more information, but there was none. Calum shifted back centre-stage in his thoughts. His so-called *friend* had been holding out on him. But why? What was Calum not telling him about his involvement with Reuben?

'Bastard,' Mac shot out as he dug back into his pocket and laid out on the desk all the items he'd found at Elena's flat.

There were the charred remains of the photo of the two men in uniforms. Reuben's Post-it note: *Get these documents to the big man in Hamburg. Don't fuck up. Fuck up = death.*

Get these documents to the big man in Hamburg . . .

Mac realised that earlier he'd been so intent on linking Reuben to Elena's murder, he had only taken account of one part of the message.

Was the big man in Hamburg the mysterious Bolshoi? He knew Reuben's crew brought in their deadly gear from the continent and it was reasonable to assume someone was in control over there. Hamburg was an obvious place, too: a big port city with easy access to all points westward and a big and varied population. But 'big man' suggested someone important, and Mac had never heard Reuben describe anyone like that. But why would Bolshoi want Elena dead? What had she done? How had the big man in Hamburg known about Elena's boyfriend? And what was going down tonight with this delivery?

Had the big man from Hamburg turned up yet in Rio's investigation? What if Phil Delaney's intelligence network had picked him up? If he had, Phil hadn't mentioned it. Mac looked over Calum's computer applications once more. It was too bad he couldn't hack into Rio and Phil's files, and it wouldn't have surprised Mac to learn that Calum had a program supplied by the likes of 'Blank Frank' that allowed him to do it. But in the absence of that, Mac decided he'd have to find out another way.

Mac stood up. But when he heard a noise on the floor below, he drew his gun and hurried to the window. The street was clear. But he heard the heavy, uneven sound of footsteps as someone came up the stairs towards the office. Mac sat back down, covering the door with his Luger. The person paused outside the door. The handle turned. The door pushed open. Calmly Calum walked in. He didn't seem surprised to find Mac in his chair, pointing Lady L at him.

fifty

'Who's Bolshoi?'

Calum remained casual, not breaking his slow, measured stride as he moved towards the desk. 'You're gonna hurt someone if you keep waving . . .'

But Mac wasn't in the mood for the other man's sidetracking games, so he shoved out the question again. 'Who's Bolshoi?' His grip round the gun tightened.

Calum sighed, his eyelids half cloaking his intense green gaze as he took the seat on the other side of the desk. 'I see you found your way into your girlfriend's phone then?' One of his hands rubbed absently at the side of his neck. 'Seriously, Mac, you're losing your touch. A fourteen-year-old kid could have opened that for you . . .'

'Who. Is. He?' Mac's finger tensed round the trigger. 'Just because you stood up for Stevie doesn't mean I won't take you down. There's a corpse in the butcher's that knows I'm way, way beyond caring what I do now.'

Calum's face didn't shift from deadpan at the mention of the body downstairs. Then he shrugged. 'He's just a guy. Works out of Hamburg. Arms, drugs, the usual . . .'

Abruptly, Calum hitched himself out of the chair.

'Stay down,' Mac stormed.

But Calum turned and kept walking, his limp more pronounced. Mac pumped the trigger twice. Two shots banged into the ground near the other man's feet. But Calum kept walking. He stopped at the shelves on the other side of the room, near the shotgun against the wall. Took down a bottle of Hennessey's and a couple of shot glasses. Made his way back to the desk, face still emotion-free, and placed the glasses on the table. Poured. Picked up one of the drinks and retook his seat. This time his pose was tight; his body didn't touch the back of the chair.

He savoured a mouthful of cognac, and then spoke. 'I warned you to stay out of this . . .' He slammed back the remainder of his drink. 'Bolshoi is the boss guy for Reuben's gang. He runs the operation from Hamburg – amongst his other activities, which are many.'

'And why did he have Elena killed?'

Calum cocked his head to the side, the lines at the corners of his eyes deepening slightly. 'Are you sure . . . ?'

Mac's impatience increased. 'Stop dicking me around, you saw the messages on her phone. You saw those texts this morning, but you never said a word. Why is that, Calum?'

Calum jerked forward, his annoyance blatant and in the open for the first time. 'You're not listening to me, Mac. Like I said, you need to leave this one alone. Take a train to the seaside, get on a plane, take a sleeping tab and snuggle down in bed; do whatever you need to do to stay out of this.'

'You're Reuben's bitch, aren't you?'

Calum's skin darkened. 'Yeah, sure I am, that's why I didn't tell him what had happened to Elena when he sent me over to that crap club to ask tom-fool questions about her. I've been covering for you . . .'

'I don't need someone like you to watch my back.'

'Not even if I decided to call Rio and tell her all about what I know?'

'Do what you've got to do, but you ain't leaving this room till I know the truth.'

'What, you mean like the truth that it was you who killed her?'

That stunned Mac, like a punch out of the blue.

'I've told you what happened, I didn't murder her.'

'I've been covering your arse, keeping everyone off your scent. But don't keep lying to yourself and me about what happened . . .'

'You're wrong . . .'

But Calum wouldn't stop. 'Look at the facts. You're a cop. Get all the evidence together and what does it say? Only one person could've killed her . . .'

Mac lunged across the desk, the gun dropping from his hand. Calum leapt out of his reach. Mac rushed round the table and took a swing at his opponent. But it didn't connect because the other man backed off as quickly as his bad leg would allow him.

Calum shoved his hands up. 'Pack it in. Don't make me kick your behind. You don't need it and neither do I.'

'You back-stabbing, betraying . . .'

With rage, hatred and a chemical rush from the pills welling up inside him, he landed a full-frontal punch on Calum's face. His opponent reeled back against the wall. Mac moved in for the kill. Swung his foot but, in his blind fury, missed. His whole body jarred, vibrating with pain, as he connected with the wall. Calum picked up the shotgun. Mac kicked out again. Calum tipped up the shotgun and swung it at Mac's calf. Mac flipped up and tumbled to the side, banging his head against the edge of the desk. Crashed to the floor.

It took a few seconds before Mac could refocus; he saw an anxious Calum standing him over him, and noticed what appeared to be a misshapen red kiss on the side of the other man's neck. On the top of his head, Mac felt Doctor Mo's stitches oozing sticky red blood again. But he ignored the head wound or any pain and he stumbled up again.

'Mac, that's enough.'

But it wasn't enough. It was never going to be enough. The room swaying in his vision, Mac charged. Another wild punch that a weave and bob avoided. A second punch, right hook this time. When he lashed out, the room blurred around him. He couldn't see but just kept hitting out. Lashing out . . . Something hard struck him across the back of the head. He went down. The room was still moving as he looked up, but the light began to change colour, with black circles dotted around.

'Mac? Mac? Can you hear me? If you can, I'm giving you a final warning. Stay out of it. Stay out. Because next time this happens, you'll wind up dead.'

The dizzy light changed to total black.

fifty-one

Calum was long gone when Mac came to in the office. Wincing from the headband of pain wrapped round his skull, he rolled gingerly to his side. His ab muscles tightened as bile threatened to bale out of his body. He locked his throat muscles as he fought it back. Closed his eyes as he gulped in air. Then he remembered the time. Fuck, how long had he been out? Urgently he checked his watch.

Twenty minutes until six.

Just over five hours before the delivery. But he didn't get up, instead started to plot his next move. Calum was a dead end by now, long gone and swallowed up by the streets. That left the man in the frame – Bolshoi. He needed more Intel on him. But where could he get that from? Maybe go back to Reuben and play a smart game of cat-and-mouse chat, where the Russian would naturally let the information flow? No. That might just put him in the firing line if Reuben got suspicious. That left only one other source – Phil. His superior was bound to have information on a known international criminal. Somehow he was going to have to hack into Phil's computer files, which was no easy task. In an ideal world he could've just asked Phil, but this was no ideal day. Phil had ordered him off the case, so going back to HQ was a dead man's game.

Yeah, but what if . . . the power of Mac's thought made him sit up. What if he could access Phil's files from another police source, another police building? Somewhere like The Fort? It was a risky move if the security camera footage from the hotel was already in. But he knew he didn't have any choice.

He stood. Ran his fingers over his scalp and found the bullet wound had opened slightly. His fingers came away smeared with dirty, burgundy-scabby blood. On the floor was his cap, which he eased gently back on. He checked his pockets to see if Calum had taken anything off him but he hadn't. Even his Luger was still lying on the desk where he'd dropped it.

He walked over to the filing cabinet and opened the third drawer and there, sitting pretty, were the bogus cop badges he'd seen earlier. Three, all for different departments. Vice, Serious Crime Squad and Fraud. Mac chose Serious Crime. He pulled out the pills and popped a single one into his mouth. Whatever the meds were that he'd found at Doctor's Mo's, they were like magic because, despite the shit stacking up around him, he felt the power within him start to grow. He took out Elena's bracelet. Unclasped the chain link. Then retied it round his right wrist with the rabbit charm touching his thumping pulse.

fifty-two

6 p.m.

You can get into anything if you've got enough front. That was Mac's game plan for gaining access to The Fort. He couldn't enter using his own ID because, for all he knew, Rio might have seen his image on the CCTV footage from the hotel. He entered the building just as a suited man, sporting shades and a briefcase, was leaving. There were a few people around, but no one Mac recognised. He carried on walking towards reception where a young woman sat behind the front desk. She looked up at him, her teak-toned skin relaxed, but there was no accompanying smile.

'Detective Brand,' Mac said confidently. Then he flashed the false Serious Crime Squad ID.

'Have you got an appointment with someone?' Her gaze was keen as she took in his baseball cap.

He let his lips stretch out into a slow smile. Leaned over. Whispered, 'I'm with the LYZ team. On a job – you know what I mean . . .' He waved his fingers at his cap. 'We've got clearance to use the computer terminals upstairs. I understand that there are computers set aside for our people to use. Check with Phil Delaney if there's a problem'

A woman in a suit walked by and Mac beamed at her and said, 'Good to see you again. How are the kids?'

Baffled, but unwilling to embarrass herself by admitting she didn't know who Mac was, the woman smiled back and answered, 'I'm good and the boys are fine, thank you.'

As she went by, Mac gestured with his thumb at the woman and said to the receptionist, 'She's great, isn't she?'

Mac didn't know the woman from Adam, but it was worth a shot.

The girl on the desk seemed half convinced but still unsure. 'What did you say your name was again?'

Mac decided to clear away any remaining doubts. 'Brand – known to the LYZ boys as "Fire" Brand.' He flicked his wrist up to check the time on his watch. 'Look sweetheart, I don't want to be rude, but time is money and I'm on the police dollar here. If you've got any doubts about me, call Phil Delaney – or get security down here, they'll sort me out.'

She checked him out on her computer system, discovering there was indeed a DI Brand – Mac was always careful to use real names. So she buzzed him through the security doors and into a smaller space with twin lifts. Mac punched the up button on the first lift. The lift made a whooing sound from somewhere above. A few seconds later, its metal doors opened in front of him. Mac stepped inside. Pressed 2. He dropped his head as he leaned against the coolness of the back of the lift as the doors started to close.

Abruptly a hand thrust between the doors. The lift made a juddering sound. The doors froze. Pulled back. The person on the other side walked into the lift.

'Mac?'

He looked up into the face of DI Rio Wray.

Rio held on tightly to the e-Photofit of the cab driver's passenger as she looked at Mac.

'Surprised to see you here,' she said as she pressed 3. 'Heard on the grapevine that you were off your case and told to take some quality time at home.'

The doors closed as she moved to stand beside him. She looked at his face and battered clothes. Whatever he'd been up to, it certainly hadn't been quality time. And the baseball cap made him look like a street hood.

Mac said nothing for a few moments. Then, 'Office gossip Rio. I'm very much on the case.' He noticed she was looking at his face and added, 'Hence the injuries . . .'

She believed that. Knew he'd want to be working on the anniversary of his son's death. It was better than the alternative.

Her hand tightened on the Photofit. 'If you want me to come with you at some stage to Stevie's . . . ?'

Her question fizzled out and the stubborn tilt of his face told her his dead son was still off limits.

'How are you getting on with that case? The tart in the bath?' he asked lightly.

Rio opened her mouth. Almost told him what the Germans had come back with, but she shut the words back behind her lips. Phil was hiding something and blabbing to Mac, one of his men, was not a smart move. No, it was time to play the game her way.

So she innocently asked, 'Do you know which one of your team uses a C in their 1402 code?'

Rio wasn't expecting the surprised look on Mac's face. 'Never heard of anyone having a letter attached to their code . . .'

'But why give someone a different code?'

This time he shrugged. 'Come on Rio, you know better than that. Even if I knew, I couldn't give you that kind of Intel.'

'Hmmm, that's what Philip Delaney . . .'

He gazed deeply at her. 'You've been talking to Phil?'

She blushed, which she was thankful her dark skin didn't

reveal. No one knew about her *special* connection to Philip Delaney. 'You know who it is, don't you? You can tell me, Mac, I'll be finding out in a little while anyway. Go on – give me a hint.' She finished with a cocky smile.

'I thought you were one of those by-the-book detectives. Now you're asking police officers to reveal confidential information without authorisation? You'll end up like Calum if you're not careful.'

'Like Calum?' Her smile vanished. She shoved the Photofit in front of him. 'That's someone in your team, isn't it? Do you know who it is?'

Mac looked down. Kept his eyes on the computer-generated image. 'Could be anyone. There are dozens of people on my team and all the other UC units.'

The lift doors opened. Mac moved ahead of her. Stepped out onto the second floor.

Rio watched him go. 'I admire the way you stick to the rules, but it doesn't matter. I'll have my answers pretty soon . . .'

He stopped. Twisted his head to the side and caught her with the corner of his eye. He didn't speak, waiting for her to finish her sentence.

The doors started closing. 'I've got an expert working on the security camera footage from the hotel right now. I'll have a face in less than twenty minutes.'

The doors slid shut.

fifty-three

He had twenty minutes. No, fifteen, if he was lucky. He couldn't run – that would only draw attention to him. He couldn't believe that Rio had thrust a Photofit of him right in front of his eyes. Was she blind? He power-walked down the narrow, light corridor. Didn't make eye contact with any of the people who passed by. He entered Room F4:8, a large, open-plan office, which was buzzing with activity. People talking. Phones ringing. The tap-tap of someone at a keyboard near the entrance.

He swung his gaze to the left wall, where the hot-desk computers were located. Six of them, on a narrow counter that ran underneath the length of the window sill. Only one other person was at a terminal, on the far right-hand side. Mac knew her. Melody Strauss, a woman who ran a team similar to Phil's, but one which specialised in hunting down people traffickers. Mac averted his face as he walked by in case she recognised him, but she was engrossed in her work and didn't look up.

Mac took the high-backed stool in front of the one on the far left. Firstly, he logged into the computer as Rio Wray to see if she'd updated her notes. Several years earlier he'd sat beside her as she'd done some work on a case. They'd shared a little joke about her inability to remember PIN and phone numbers and how she'd been repeatedly unable to access her satellite TV service because she couldn't remember her password. So she'd chosen her birthplace 'Plaistow' as her password for nearly everything. Only it was 'Plaistow1'. Of course she was supposed to change her password every couple of months and choose something unguessable. But Mac knew Rio better than that. He also knew that the system was only going to give him three goes at using a password and then it would log him out for good.

He tried Plaistow1. Rejected.

Plaistow2. Rejected.

One chance left.

Plaistow3.

Like getting a row of bells on a fruit machine, he'd hit the jackpot. He smiled to himself and accessed the 'Homicide: Rose Hotel' in the Murder Squad's files. There, neatly organised, was the information that had been collected to date. That was the great thing about Rio; she always did a job properly. He didn't look at the photos of Elena's body, but he was unable to resist the temptation to run the CCTV clip that showed the footage of him that morning. How could Rio not have realised that was him? Or perhaps she had and their little chat in the lift had all been a performance. She knew he was in the building. He wasn't going anywhere.

Mac's fingers turned to ash when he read the initial inspection report on the body. 'Victim was pregnant.'

That punched him in the gut. He ran off as much information as he could on the printer. Looked around. Checked the clock on the wall.

Ten minutes gone.

He logged out of Rio's account and tried to enter his own. Up came the message 'Access Denied'. Whatever else Phil had managed to get up to during the day, he'd found time to do that. Helpless, Mac looked around the office until his gaze found Melody Strauss.

It was a long shot but it was all he had, and he was too desperate to assess the risks.

He got out of his chair and left the office. He made a mental note of the number on the door and then walked down the corridor. Taking out his mobile he called The Fort's reception and asked to be connected to the extension in room F4:8. A woman answered.

'F4:8 . . .'

Mac kept his tone smooth. 'Reception here. I'm trying to track down Melody Strauss and someone thought she might be in this office. Is she there?'

The line went dead for half a minute before another woman picked up the phone. 'Hello – this is Melody Strauss.'

Mac turned the pitch of his voice higher. 'Ms Strauss, this is reception. I've got a man at the desk who says he needs to speak to you urgently on a police matter.'

Melody sounded baffled. 'Well, who is he?'

'I don't know, ma'am. He won't give a name. But he says it's very important. Information on the case you're currently working on.'

There was an agonising wait before Melody sighed, 'OK. I'll come down.'

Mac stood against the corridor wall, playing with his phone, stealing glances at the door to room F4:8. Sure enough, a few moments later Melody emerged and walked towards the lifts. Mac walked back and went through the door. Made a beeline for the computer that Melody had been sitting at and where she'd left various files and notes lying around. He smiled in triumph when he realised that she hadn't logged herself out. He was in, on a superior's level of access.

Mac began a search for any mention of Bolshoi. It came up blank. No mention of him anywhere. But in the list of personnel associated with Reuben's crew, Calum's name appeared. There were details on his role as a freelance associate of the gang. Mac attempted to view Calum's individual file.

'Access Restricted'.

That meant information about Calum was only available when you had the highest level of clearance, and neither Rio nor Melody had it.

The trouble was, it could be for an infinite number of possibilities. But one thing was certain. Calum's role in the whole affair was far bigger than either the man himself had admitted or Mac had yet guessed. And the police were aware of Calum's involvement.

In the links to the operation against Reuben, Mac discovered something else that interested him. It was a connection to another set of files associated with the case. The final extension on the folder name showed that it had been compiled at the highest levels of the Home Office. Mac pressed the cursor against the file to get into it.

'Access Denied'.

Shit, shit, shit.

Mac had one last card to play in his hunt for Intel on Bolshoi. The previous month he had been liaising with the German police on an arms case possibly connected to Reuben's gang, and had been given temporary access to their intelligence files. Bolshoi was in Hamburg and it was possible that he might turn up on them.

Mac checked the clock. Eighteen minutes gone. It was possible – indeed it was likely – that Rio was already searching the building to arrest him for the murder of Elena. Melody would be back shortly. Now was the time to seize his slim chance to escape.

But he had to chance it.

Mac turned back to the computer, even though time was running out.

fifty-four

6:23 p.m.

Tap, tap, tap.

Rio's foot beat impatiently against the ground as she sat in the chair. The techy was doing as techys do and proudly explaining the myriad ways in which software was aiding police work, instead of swiftly attending to the business at hand.

Rio cut him short. 'Yeah, it's a wonderful world. Now what have you got for me?'

Hurt, her guy ran the footage and stopped it at the appropriate moment. He began to click his mouse and draw lines.

'So, as you can see, if we define this more closely here . . . cut out the light and shade . . . ask the computer to refine and coordinate the colouring at that stage . . . slow down the glare here and use the background image to fill in the gaps . . . eliminate the judder there . . . we can get what I think is more than a passable image of your suspect. Here you go, detective. There's your man.'

Rio leaned in close. 'You are shitting me . . .'

But she didn't finish her sentence as she leapt out of her chair and ran for the door.

fifty-five

6:25 p.m.

Mac accessed the German files and pressed the button that translated them into English. If the British reports were a bit short of information on Bolshoi, these ones didn't seem to know where to start because of their volume of information. There was no first name, just Bolshoi. He was mentioned in arms, drugs and corruption cases all over Europe. And murder. But whenever Mac tried to access the details, it was the same story as in England.

'*Zugriff abgelehnt*'. Access denied.

Mac narrowed his search down to references to England. The machine seemed to be taking its time but Mac hardly dared look at the clock.

'Come on, come on . . .'

But, once again, everything seemed to be '*Zugriff abgelehnt*'.

Except for an innocent notice to a surveillance team that was watching Bolshoi at his apartment in Hamburg:

'*Urgent Notification: Bolshoi will be travelling to London. British Police advised (Liaison: Philip Delaney X2245X). Date of Return: To Be Advised by the British. Surveillance Suspended.*'

There was a case file associated with Bolshoi's trip. As he tried to access it, Mac whispered, '*Zugriff abgelehnt*' under his breath. And he was right.

So Phil did know about Bolshoi; not only that, he knew the man was coming to London. But Phil had never mentioned it to him once during his investigation. Why? He suspected Calum knew too. But how and why? And he was still no closer to working out why Bolshoi had had Elena killed, or how he was going to kill Bolshoi in turn.

Mac looked up at the clock.

6:27.

He needed to get out of here now. He left the terminal and went to the office door and checked the corridor. Clear. He strolled as casually as he could towards the lifts. As he did so, his new phone pinged. Text message. Reuben.

We need to make arrangements for your role tonight. Call.

He couldn't contact him now; he'd do it as soon as he got out of The Fort. Mac looked up and froze. Standing in front of him were Rio Wray and two police officers.

fifty-six

6:28 p.m.

For Mac, running into Rio in the corridor felt somewhat like bumping into a former lover where things had ended badly.

'1402c, we need to have a chat about things,' Rio said calmly. 'I'm sure we can sort everything out . . .'

The statement hung in the air, but Mac's mind was already on other things. He'd have rated his chances against Rio and her two boys on the street, but in a corridor at The Fort . . . with dozens of officers milling around . . .

He forced a smile right back. 'A chat? Sure – why not?'

All the time, his gaze was over her shoulder, casing the corridor. At the end, by a door that led to a stairwell, two burly detectives were sharing a joke. Mac checked over Rio's two guys. There was no escape that way. He knew that behind him was a lift to the upper floors. No escape that way either.

Rio never took her eyes off him as she said to the men with her, 'Why don't you assist Mr MacDonagh to my office?'

They got in position on either side of Mac. The three men set off towards the stairs with Rio bringing up the rear. They walked down the corridor, past the joking detectives, through the doors. Past the lift. Down the stairs.

As they descended, Rio's voice said behind him, 'Mac, whatever's happened . . .'

So sudden, no one saw it coming; Mac shoved both palms against the backs of the policemen and pushed them violently forwards. They stumbled and fell like broken puppets down the stairs. As they landed in a heap at the bottom, he twisted round. Grabbed Rio by the front of her blouse and threw her to the ground. He bolted up the stairs as Rio screamed, 'Don't be a fucking fool, Mac; you can't get out of here . . .'

But he was gone. Through the doors and back into the corridor. The two joking detectives were still there. He bombed it to the lift. Pressed. It opened. Mac heard the commotion behind him. He jumped inside the lift. The doors slid shut just as his pursuers arrived at the lift with their hands outstretched. The lift hummed upwards and when the doors slid open he pressed one floor down again. When it opened this time, he slid out into an empty corridor.

A loud, blaring noise shattered the air. Fire alarm . . . no, the intruder-detection warning and he was the intruder. The building would shortly be going into lockdown, exits sealed, and an armed security team in flak jackets would be tearing the place apart looking for him.

Mac rushed down the corridor, peering through the glass windows of each office he came to. In one, he noticed three women on computers busily working away, apparently unfazed by the alarm. He took a few deep breaths to steady himself, so that he appeared as normal as possible. Then he opened the door to the office and smiled at one of the women. 'What's going on? Is there a fire?'

She smiled back, one of her palms resting behind a love-heart photo frame of two cute boys. 'No, it's the intruder alarm. Don't worry; it's always going off . . .' Then she added without being asked, 'I'm Linda . . .'

Mac smile broadened. 'But that'll mean a lockdown, won't

it? I'm only visiting but I've got an appointment somewhere else and I need to leave.'

Linda warned him, 'You're not going anywhere, I'm afraid. But don't worry about it. In five minutes' time they'll realise the intruder is the milkman and you'll be able to get out. You might as well pull up a chair in the meantime.'

'Have you got a piece of paper and a pen?' Mac calmly asked.

She smiled and found what he wanted on her desk. He wrote quickly and then passed the paper to her. Linda read it and laughed. But when she caught his eye, her laughter died. The note read:

'I've got a gun. You're going to get up and come with me to reception, making it look like we're two colleagues having a laugh and a chat. If we get stopped, I'll do the talking. If you do as you're told, you'll be fine. If you don't, those pretty little boys of yours won't see Mummy ever again.'

Mac gestured with his head for Linda to follow him. But she stayed frozen in her chair. He tapped his pocket and extended his two fingers to indicate a gun and, slowly, she got up out of her chair. They left the office with him walking jam-tight by her side. Outside, the corridor was clear, and so they carried on walking. Above and below them on other floors, they could hear the sound of running feet and shouting. The lift doors were open but above them a notice flashed: 'Out of service'.

Mac whispered, 'Stairwell . . . You're doing good, just stay calm and no one's going to get hurt.'

They went down the stairs. As they did so, two armed men came running up from the other way. One yelled at them, 'What are you doing? Everyone's confined to their offices.'

Mac realised he'd grabbed Linda's arm for support and he whimpered, 'But that's where we're going, our office is on the bottom floor.'

The man waved his gun at them, 'Well, move it.' And with that they were gone. Mac and Linda kept walking until they reached a mezzanine balcony just above the ground floor. Mac locked an arm round Linda's waist and jammed her so close to his body he felt her erratic breathing vibrating against his skin. He peeped down at the reception area. Armed police everywhere and, by the security gates, Mac could see Rio Wray and a couple of her sidekicks, positioned like spiders in the middle of a web.

Linda twisted her head slightly and whispered, 'You're stuffed. You might as well go down and turn yourself in. You can't get out of here.'

'Shut up.'

But she was right. There was no way out through the exit.

'You're coming with me to the basement.'

Linda stiffened. 'Please, don't rape me . . .'

He knew he was wrong to terrorise this ordinary mum, but the only way to make sure she stayed in line was to get her to think of the worst. The basement was his only option if what Calum had reminded him of this morning was true.

'Do you recall that nuclear shelter under HQ where the code for the door was so secret, it couldn't be written down? So they made it "9999" so the relevant people could remember it? Idiots, fucking idiots . . .'

He marched Linda towards the rear of the building, down a dimly remembered flight of stairs until they reached a solid steel door. The door had a sign attached; it was stencilled in the font used by the Civil Service: *In The Event of a Nuclear Attack, This Door Will Be Sealed.*

fifty-seven

6:35 p.m.

The sign was rusting slightly round the edge and the door hadn't been used in a very long time. Not since the days when the prospect of a nuclear attack had meant every official building in London had had a bunker installed under it, so that important people wouldn't get fried by radiation. Deep underground, they could carry on with the administration of the blackened and blasted city above. As if anyone would have cared. When Mac had first joined The Force, the Cold War paranoia of the 1980s had lingered on, and so, in a drill once a year, everyone had donned radiation suits and trooped down to the bunker. They were given offices to ensure that the corpses above would still be able to rely on the forces of law and order. It was regarded pretty much by the staff as a day off. And, of course, it wasn't without its comical side. In the confused and confusing tunnels and passageways that spaghettied under The Fort, staff used to get lost and no one really knew where the bunker began and ended.

'Do you recall that nuclear shelter under HQ where the code for the door was so secret, it couldn't be written down? So they made it "9999" so the relevant people could remember it? Idiots, fucking idiots . . .'

But had the fucking idiots changed the code since the end of the Cold War?

'Stay put,' Mac ordered Linda.

She just nodded, wrapping her arms round her trembling body as soon as he let her go. Mac opened the metal panel to the code box. The crusty keypad was stiff under his nervous fingers. He stabbed his finger at a single key.

9999.

Pulled the handle to the door. It remained defiantly shut. Not such fucking idiots after all, then. He examined the pad. It hadn't been cleaned in decades. He turned in desperation to Linda. 'Have you got a hairpin?'

She rapidly shook her head. Mac began hurriedly thumbing through his wallet. He took out a credit card and used the corner to scrape away at the edges of the key. When he'd done, he tried again.

9999.

Bollocks, same response. He tried again, his anger mounting. He sawed away with his card so violently that there was a click, followed by the sound of a small object falling to the floor. Mac looked down. The number nine key had come away. Disbelieving and dazed, he picked it up.

Linda begged, 'My boys are too young to lose their mum.'

Mac threw the nine back on the floor and examined the broken keypad. Where the nine had been was a small metal button caked in dust and grease. Using his fingernails he tried to clean it up, and then tugged it backwards and forwards. Behind him, at the top of the stairs, he could hear shouting behind the door. He pulled the button towards him and pressed it in.

Pulled and pressed.

Pulled and pressed.

Pulled and pressed.

There was a brief pause before the heavy lock groaned and dropped. He yanked on the door handle and it gave slightly but refused to open. He grabbed it with both hands, put his foot on the wall. And heaved. Slowly, and with much creaking and wailing of the hinges, the door opened to the bunker beyond. He peered inside.

That's when there was a scream behind him, 'He's down here! He's down here!' He turned to see Linda fleeing up the stairs.

He didn't have time to go after her, even though he knew she would lead Rio straight to him.

fifty-eight

6:40 p.m.

Cursing, he slipped into the bunker. Slammed the door. Turned the lock.

Darkness.

He searched along the chilled wall, hands weaving like a man reading Braille. There had to be a light switch somewhere. The air was dank, unpleasant in his lungs, as he kept moving sideways. His right hand hit something. He stopped moving. Let his fingers feel. Round outline. Size of an egg. He felt over it. Stopped when he encountered something jutting out of it. Slim, cold, hard metal. Switch. He flicked it on.

Blue fluorescent light.

The first thing he noticed was a corridor in front of him. Mac ran along the corridor, past the offices marked clearly for various individual posts in the new blasted Britain, past conference rooms, past rooms with iron bedsteads for the survivors. But no sign of another exit. He choked on the concrete dust particles floating in the air. He doubled over, coughing hard. Wearily, Mac rested on a wall, trying to suck oxygen into lungs. But, as he did so, echoing through the blue-lit corridors, he heard banging and deeply muffled shouting. The enemy were at the gates. He ran on.

Another junction. One sign pointed to 'Executive Committee

Rooms', whatever that was. Another unhelpfully suggested that if you wanted 'Ministry of Defence liaison' you should turn left. Mac stopped again. He knew there would be an exit point somewhere into another building. The distance he had already run and the necessity for interconnection between government departments meant there had to be. He began running again, but then brought himself up short. He could hear the echo of voices and movement. No doubt about it now, they were in the bunker.

He fled in what he hoped was the opposite direction to his pursuers, ducking and diving although he could see no one. And still the endless rows of blue lights and the endless offices and empty rooms and official signs. He reached another junction. One sign again pointed to 'Executive Committee Rooms'. Another if you wanted 'Ministry of Defence liaison' . . . Bollocks, he'd run in a circle.

Behind him, he heard a shout of: 'Don't just run around – find the access points and seal them off.'

Mac looked around on the wall at the end of the passageway and saw the dark shadows of figures against a background of blue light. He pulled out his gun and darted off towards MOD liaison. But as he turned a corner, at the other end of a passageway, he saw two cops, dressed to kill. For a few seconds they stood looking at each other before one of the officers raised his gun and shouted, 'Stop or I'll shoot . . .'

Mac ducked. Twisted back round the corner. The sound of the gunshot that followed pulsed like thunder up and down the enclosed space until it faded and died. From another direction, he heard a shout of, 'He's shooting, he's shooting, take cover . . .'

Mac ran wildly, without any sense of direction. Down another passageway. Past endless rows of more lights, like in a bad dream. As he ran he noticed another route off to his left.

This one seemed to run in a straight line and was unlit. In the distance, he heard the sound of running water. Occasionally there was a blur of murky yellow light shining up from the floor. A stench in the air turned his stomach. He ran down the path; the sound of water became louder before fading again. The smell became a stench, with sulphur its main fragrance. Suddenly the ground beneath him wobbled. He stepped back. Looked down. A large, square, iron grille. And underneath it was a stream of dark, running water. A sewer.

He almost gagged at the stink as he got down on his knees. Wrapped his fingers around the grille. Pulled as hard as he could.

No movement.

He ran on in the blackness, until he came to another grille. Tried to tug it free. No movement.

He did the same to the next grille.

No movement.

Beams of torchlight suddenly shone down the tunnel. Shouts. Mac jumped to his feet. Began motoring forward. Stopped dead in his tracks when more torchlight shone up ahead of him. He was caught like a rat in a trap, but he didn't even have a rat's sewer to escape down.

He crawled backwards, keeping low, to the grille he'd just left. Felt the hinges with his fingers. Placed the barrel of the Luger between them and began trying to shoot the hinges off in turn. In front and behind, the torches were switched off as the shots echoed. He stood up and back to the wall, firing his remaining bullets at the grille. When he put his hands out in one last desperate attempt to pull away the metal bars that were keeping him imprisoned, he found the grille had plunged into the water below. He followed it, squeezing through the space and dropping ten feet into the freezing stream.

Following the flow, he waded forwards. The smell was

overwhelming as he ploughed on through the murky water, searching for the telltale signs of a manhole cover. Fifty yards on, like the trail of a descending angel, a shaft of light came into view. An iron ladder led up to the surface, and Mac used his shoulders to dislodge the cover at the top, emerging blinking into the daylight, in the middle of a road. A car was coming straight at him. He managed to duck as the driver let loose with his horn. The sound of the vehicle shooting over the opened manhole blasted overhead. Mac took a breath. Listened. No noise overhead. He shoved his head above ground level again. Empty road. Climbed out.

Mac pulled his cap low and walked to the pavement, his wet trousers flapping against his legs. Soon he disappeared into the thick stream of passers-by.

fifty-nine

7 p.m.

Phil Delaney puffed hard on a real cigarette as he looked at his computer screen for the umpteenth time, seeing if Mac had been detected through his mobile. He knew it was useless because Mac would've dumped the phone by now, or got rid of the SIM card. But you never knew . . . But he did know, as the info on the computer screen came up blank again. When he got his hands on him . . .

The hard knock at the door cut through his vengeful thoughts. Before he could respond, the door thrust open to reveal his PA. She closed the door with quick efficiency and said, 'Someone's been trying to access our security files.'

Phil straightened up as he abandoned his smoke in the ashtray beside him on the desk. 'Where from?'

'The Fort.'

Phil's mind swirled. Came back with a name – Rio Wray. No, he shook her name back: even Rio understood not to go that far. She might be an eager beaver, but she wasn't going to commit career hara-kiri. She was a by-the-book cop every step of the way. So if it wasn't her, who else could it be?

He leaned back in his chair with the appearance of being relaxed. 'Thank you, Shazia.'

But instead of leaving, she hesitated.

'Is there something else?' he asked.

She shook her shoulders back like she was about to make an important announcement to an audience. 'Just to remind you, sir, that smoking in public buildings is strictly prohibited.'

And with that she was gone. Trust him to have a personal assistant who also doubled up as the health and safety rep of the building. He picked his cigarette back up. Pulled in some much-needed nicotine, and then took out his mobile.

'I've found Mac,' he said as soon as he connected.

'Good.'

'I said I'd found him, not that I've got him.'

Phil eased up as he continued. 'We need to shut Mac down. Permanently. So this is what I want you to do . . .'

Rio began shouting orders as soon as she got back to the squad room.

'Check out the CCTV.'

'I want patrols on the roads and underground.'

'I want that bastard found.'

The atmosphere inside the squad room was explosive and loaded with disbelief. That someone would have the brass balls to come into their law-abiding house and run rings around them, take potshots at them . . . and yeah, get away from them. It was the last one that stuck in all of their throats most of all; shit, if it got out that they couldn't even apprehend someone inside the walls of The Fort, their reputation would take yet another nosedive in the public confidence stakes. Rio still couldn't believe it.

Mac.

Mac, for crying out loud. But then all the pieces had been staring her straight in the eye – the baseball cap he wore to cover his head injury, the description from the cabbie, the code for the undercover cop. And his enhanced face on the security footage. But Mac a killer? That was one leap she still couldn't make. But she had to deal with that possibility. Personal feelings didn't have a place in this.

'We're nearly there,' Martin let out close to her. She was so caught up in her manic thoughts, she hadn't even heard him approach her. 'We've got his image, so it shouldn't be too hard to find out who he is,' Martin carried on.

No one in this room, other than Rio herself, knew who Mac was, especially with his baseball cap hiding most of his face. Should she tell her team that they were hunting one of their own? This was a sensitive situation, and she knew that the top brass would want to spin this one. The press were bound to find out what had happened – that's if they hadn't already – and no doubt the PR team from the commissioner's office would be handling that.

'Just carry on coordinating the search for now,' Rio finally said to Martin. 'Leave all the ID stuff to me.'

Her mobile rang. She pulled it out.

'DI Wray.'

The top brass were already in play. 'Yes, sir?' she answered her senior officer, Detective Chief Inspector Newman.

'I need you to come upstairs.'

Rio got her story straight as she headed for the top floor. Her superior's suite of offices was decorated with the feel and quiet of a library. DCI Newman's PA looked grim-faced at her desk as she nodded her head towards his door. Rio took a breath. Knocked once. Opened the door. The adrenalin pumped back into her body when she saw who waited inside. Not her superior, but Phil Delaney.

sixty

'You lying piece of filth.'

Rio's harsh words blasted inside the room as she stared at her lover and Mac's boss. He sat at DCI Newman's desk, while she stood in front of it.

'Sit down.' The calmness of his voice was in stark contrast to the heat of her own.

But, instead of following his instruction, she leaned her palms against the desk, the veins in her forearms coming to the surface, bunching and throbbing. She thrust her head forward. 'You've had me running around in crazy circles from the get-go. You knew all along that the code number for one of your people belonged to Mac. Didn't you?' Her voice rose. 'Didn't you?'

'Sit. Down.'

She stared him out, the rage inside her making her nostrils flare. Didn't move. Her bottom lip trembled, as though the words inside her mouth would come bursting out any second. But she held them back. Hitched herself off the desk. Took the chair, but arranged her body on the edge of the seat.

'You and I both know that Mac's a pro. No way would he have murdered that girl in the hotel.'

'Then why is his face plastered over the security film from the hotel's reception? And his blood in the room? What the fuck was he doing there in the first place?'

Phil leaned slightly back in the chair. 'You know I can't tell you the ins and outs of an operation. It's—'

'Yeah, I know, confidential. But let me tell you what isn't so top secret is Mac running around this building like some kind of Looney Tune. One of *our* people could've been murdered – doesn't that bother you?' Rio wiped her hand across her face like she still couldn't believe what Mac had done.

Her words didn't move him. 'What bothers me at the moment is that you stop pursuing Mac. I've already had a word with your DCI and a number of other people. Leave this one alone, Rio.'

She twisted her mouth in bitterness and threw her words out with a bite that would terrify most people. 'I'm not surprised that it doesn't bother you that someone in this building might have been killed—'

'I didn't say that it didn't . . .'

But Rio was having none of his explanation. 'But then that's how you've always run your people – that cowboy Research Unit you head up: get the job done by any means necessary. Don't let anyone, even your fellow cop, stand in your way.' She shook her head. 'After Stevie died, I told Mac he shouldn't go back to your team. That what he needed was some downtime. Time to get his life back together. Time to be a real person again, not the make-believe man he became every time you shoved him undercover.'

For the first time she saw irritation sweep across Phil's face, an expression that wasn't so unlike the one he made when he came inside her. 'You don't need to tell me how devastated he was at the death of his son . . .'

'Then why did you make him take this job, whatever this job is? You knew he wasn't emotionally or mentally ready. I don't know if you've noticed, but the guy looks like utter crap.' She took a deep breath and then let out the words that had been beating at the back of her mind since she'd seen Mac's face become clearer and clearer on the security footage. 'What if he went over the edge? Lost himself and killed that girl? He's probably suffering from PTSD again.'

'He didn't touch her. My people are going to be taking over the whole case . . .'

'You know that I should remain as the IO on this . . .'

'Rio, I'm concerned for you.' Phil's voice softened. 'I don't want anything else to happen to you.' He stretched his palm out towards her. Laid it on the desk.

She gazed at it. Then the corners of her mouth turned down like she was observing a rattlesnake. She looked back up at him in disgust. 'Is that why you're here, Phil? To sweeten me up?'

Abruptly she shoved out of the chair. And before Phil could say anything, she raised her skirt, displaying her knickers and stockings to him for the second time that day.

'Rio . . .' he growled.

But she kept her skirt up. 'Come on,' she taunted. 'Is that what you were going to do? Bang me on Newman's desk? Twist and turn my pussy so I'd do whatever you wanted?' She let her skirt fall. 'Well, fuck you.'

She turned towards the door and kept moving.

'You won't find him.'

His words stopped her. She hesitated. Then turned her head to look at him over her shoulder.

'He's off the street. I've got him in custody.'

sixty-one

Rio leaned hard against the wall of the fourth-floor stairwell.
A wave of relief swept inside her. At least Mac was off the
street. She didn't know whether to believe Phil about Mac not
doing the murder. Murders? Maybe he'd killed the doctor as
well, let Masri treat him and then silenced him for good? How
could Mac have gone from the idealist cop she'd met at
Hendon, pumped high on upholding justice, to a killer of a
woman and an unborn child? No, there had to be an explanation for all this fucked-up shit.

'Boss?'

She found Detective Martin at the bottom of the stairs. He
took the steps two at a time to reach her.

'You OK?'

That almost made her smile. She was meant to be looking
after him, not the other way round. She nodded.

'Word is that you're not heading the case any more. You're
going to let them tip you off it?'

'First rule of a detective is to follow the rule book.'

'But what if I told you I found out a few other things?'

She pulled herself off the wall. 'What are you talking
about?'

'I contacted my translator friend at the Russian embassy
again . . .'

There was something in his voice that made Rio step

forward. 'You don't happen to be seeing this *friend* of yours in an intimate capacity?'

Seeing the blush stain his face, Rio groaned. 'We can't use this information because you're personally . . .'

Martin waved his hands and crowded in on her slightly. 'No, let me finish, DI, and then make your decision.' He took a hard breath. Waited. Finally she nodded. 'When I asked my friend to translate the writing on the tattoo, what I didn't tell you was he informed—'

'He?' Rio cut in sharply. She hadn't figured the newest member of her team was gay.

Martin cleared his throat. 'He told me that, a few nights back, the embassy hosted a party for former Russian officers who had fought in the Afghan–Russian conflict back in the 1980s, who are now resident in London.' Rio opened her mouth to interrupt him, but he held up his palm. 'Our victim's father was in the Red Army and got that medal of honour, so I got to thinking that maybe my friend might know something about him. Strange thing was, he didn't really want to speak at first. Then he told me that Gregory Romanov had been part of an elite unit and had been killed in an ambush.'

'Nothing strange about that,' Rio finally said.

'No. But he said that there were rumours that Romanov died suspiciously.'

'What does that mean?'

'I don't know, my friend sort of clammed up. I know it probably doesn't mean anything, but it gives us a deeper insight into our victim. But he did tell me something else.'

Rio raised her eyebrows expectantly.

'Elena Romanov came to the veterans' bash at the embassy. But she didn't come alone.'

'Who was with her?'

'She was accompanied by her sister. She's living here in London. I don't have an address yet . . .'

'Have we got a name?'

Martin nodded once. 'Katia.'

sixty-two

7:35 p.m.

The gunman in the hotel room stared at the four passports laid out on the bed. After making his escape from the man who'd followed him, and his associate from the car wash, he needed to get out of the country now. Just needed to decide which ID to assume to make it happen. He chose the US one.

Name: Felix Bloom

Occupation: Businessman

Well, the last accurately fitted in with what his job really was, except he was in the business of murder. He'd taken his time getting back to the hotel as a precaution in case he was being followed. As soon as he realised he was in the clear, he'd backtracked to the hotel. A real shame about Peter, though, but that was the way the game panned out sometimes. He packed his carry-on pack and a suitcase that was filled with clothing he'd never had any intention of wearing. He zipped up the case. Then he wiped the place clean. Now he had only one more task left to do.

He took out his mobile. 'The samples have been taken care of.'

'And everything went well?'

He hesitated. Confessing that you'd messed up was never a smart move.

'What happened?' the other person asked, making him realise that he should never have paused.

'We had one problem along the way.'

'What problem?'

'All you need to hear is that our business transaction has been successfully completed. Now all I need is the remainder of the fee.'

'I'll come and meet you . . .'

'No, I will come to you.'

'No, I can't afford for you to be tracked back to me. So just tell me where you are and we can both be on our way.'

So he reluctantly told the contractor. It was never good for anyone to know exactly your location in this business.

Katia.

The name marched inside her mind as Rio walked towards her BMW. Martin was still trying to find an address for her, and Rio knew she had to get to her before someone else did. Mac? She still didn't want to believe that Mac was the man with his finger on the trigger, but the evidence said different.

Mac's blood in the hotel room.

Mac's face on the hotel's CCTV footage.

The e-Photofit that was a dead ringer for him.

As she pulled open the passenger door, her mobile started going. 'DI Wray,' she answered.

'Rio.'

Her body tensed. 'Sir?' she said, addressing DCI Newman. 'I've got everything under control. I've identified the prime suspect and believe that he may already be in custody. Phil Delaney told me I was off the case—'

He cut over her. 'Don't tread on any toes. Just be careful.'

'Why would I need to be careful?'

Long pause. Then he spoke again. 'Just don't tangle with

Philip Delaney. He might be able to wreck your career – or worse, put you in the firing line.'

The line went dead. Wreck her career? Phil? Firing line? Was she in some type of danger?

With question after question bouncing against the four walls of her mind, she jumped into the driver's seat. Shoved the key into the ignition. Checked the rear-view mirror. Froze. In the back seat sat a hooded figure. The light danced shadows across the face, making it hard for her to see the features. But she saw the gun.

Recognised the voice of the man who said, 'Don't do anything stupid, Rio. We just need to clear the air. Now drive.'

She didn't need to see his face to know it was Mac.

sixty-three

8 p.m.

'I didn't kill her.'

Rio said nothing as she stared at Mac in the back seat of her car. Stared at the Luger on the seat beside him. He'd made her drive to the roof of a car park where the darkness of the sky appeared heavy and deep. Rain was gushing over the car.

Mac looked like a desperate man. Unshaven, hollow-eyed, with an expression that Rio had seen many times on the faces of murderers – grief. A wave of pity came over her, just for a pinch of a second. Then she hardened her heart. Reminded herself that it was her duty to uphold the law.

'If you turn yourself in now, I'll do everything I can to make sure things go better for you.'

'You're not hearing me, Rio.'

'You can give your side of the story once you're in custody.'

'I would never have killed her.'

'Let's drive back together. Now.'

'I loved her.'

That stopped their quick exchange. Their eyes caught and held. He needed to know she wasn't backing down, so she kept her gaze steady. Finally he looked away.

'So you did know her? Elena Romanov?'

Rio got her answer as Mac winced and wiped his hand over his mouth.

'She was a member of the illegal arms gang I've infiltrated.'

'How well did you know her?'

'If you're asking if the baby she was carrying was mine, then the answer is yes . . . Well I think so.'

Rio knew he was hurting; she could see it stamped all over his face. She also felt the pain of her friend losing another child, but she shoved it away. Pain or no pain, Mac was a fugitive from the law and her job was to bring him in.

'How did your relationship with her start?'

His gaze shifted out of the window. His distraction made Rio eye the gun. She recognised the moment. The moment to do something to get out of this twist. She switched back to his averted face. Back to the gun. *Do it now.*

But her chance disappeared when he turned back to her. And she wished he hadn't – not because her chance was gone, but because of the pain in his face. A pain that softened the edges of her determination to do what was right.

Finally he answered her question. 'It was a straightforward op. Deep cover as an independent armourer; gather as much info on the gang to put them away for ever. So I looked for the weakest link. You know, the person who isn't sure whether they've made the right choice in their life. And that was Elena. Young, beautiful . . .' There was a hitch in his voice. 'So unsure. She was their communications person – almost invisible, really . . .'

'She was working for a criminal gang, not giving out parcels to the poor on behalf of the Red Cross.' Rio drew in a weary breath. 'It sounds like she came from a troubled background and possibly her father had enemies . . .' Rio clammed up.

'Enemies? What enemies? What do you know about her father?'

'Look, all I know is that her father died in a war, years ago.' Rio deftly switched their conversation. 'Now you, on the other hand . . .'

Mac's face screwed up. 'Don't you think I feel shit about what I did?'

'You might feel like crap, but Elena Romanov can't feel a thing because she's dead.'

He leaned forward. 'I never meant to sleep with her; she was just so easy to talk to.' A faraway expression settled in his eyes. 'She made me laugh. Do you know how long it had been since I've done that? You know, a "shout out to the world that I'm still living" laugh. It started out with me milking her for information and ended up with me not being able to go to sleep without her breath against my neck.'

'How did you end up in the hotel room with her?'

'I don't know.'

'Stop fucking me around . . .'

'I don't know,' he repeated forcefully. 'I got a call from her late last night. She said she was scared, that someone was going to kill her. That's when she told me about . . .'

He swallowed the next word. *So you are hiding something,* Rio thought. But she let him carry on.

'I just knew I had to keep her safe. So I told her to meet me at the hotel room. The last thing I remember is opening the room door. Then waking up with a bullet wound in my head.'

He pulled off his cap. Rio drew in a breath when she saw the wound.

Rio remembered Charlie's assessment that the person on the bed had been shot by someone behind him, standing in the doorway. The wound on his head seemed to verify that Mac had been shot.

His words kept coming. 'Someone set me up. Shot me and then murdered Elena. When I woke up, I found her dead in the bath. Whoever did it used my gun.'

Rio's gaze skidded to the Luger. 'Then let me take you in. Tell your story and we can investigate . . .'

'Only problem is, you don't believe me.'

'Why would someone shoot you and not make sure you were dead? Why leave you alive to tell the tale?'

He shook his head. 'I don't know. All I know is that I need you to give me time . . .'

'No way . . .'

'I've got to find out who killed her and I know it's got some- thing to do with . . .' He stopped talking.

'Something to do with what? Has this got anything to do with Phil Delaney?'

'You've seen Phil?'

'Did you escape from him?'

'Escape?'

'He said that he had you in custody?'

Mac leaned back. 'What else did he say?'

Rio looked him over. 'He never had you in custody, did he?' She twisted her mouth. 'That rotten, lying . . . what game are you and Phil playing? What else is going on here, Mac?'

He said nothing.

'I can't help you if you don't tell me everything.'

Mac fingered his gun. 'I need you to tell me everything that you've found out through the investigation.'

'And if I don't? You planning to add me to the pile of bodies you've left behind?'

'I'd never hurt you, you know that. But . . .'

A phone pinged. Rio knew it wasn't hers, but Mac ignored the noise. Instead he said, 'Don't stand in my way.'

And before she could say anything else, he rushed out of the car and into the rain towards the exit.

Rio revved the engine. Put her foot to the pedal. Come hell or high water, she was taking Mac in.

sixty-four

Rio slammed the car backwards. Swung into a one-eighty. Motored around the parked cars. The front of the car bumped up as it hit the concrete slope leading to the next level at speed.

Level Four.

Rio twisted the wheel. Tipped the car into a tight angle. Carried on down the sloping path.

Level Three.

She kept twisting and tipping.

Level Two.

Level One.

Twist. She slammed the car back as another vehicle got in front of her. A monster SUV.

She wound the window down. Yelled, 'Get out of the fucking way.'

Two small faces looked at her from the back seats of the SUV. Cursing at kids wasn't going to help her promotion prospects. But there was nothing she could do but trail behind the front vehicle.

Ground level.

Rio swung her car round the SUV and shot towards the barrier. Crashed through it. Gazed ahead, but all she saw was a rush of late-night shoppers going into the shopping centre opposite. If Mac was in the crowd, she couldn't make him out.

But then Mac might not have gone into the mall; he might have exited on another level. Slowing down, she cruised the perimeter of the car park, taking her time looking for him. Finally, when it was clear he was probably long gone, she stopped the car beside a row of large steel, blue-lidded dumpsters. As the car came to a halt, a rattling noise sounded from the back seat. Rio rolled her eyes. Not the car going on the blink again – she'd only had it serviced and sorted last week. She turned around and immediately saw a small cylinder-shaped object, tan-coloured with a white flip cap.

A pill bottle. It rattled with the jangle of tablets inside when she picked it up. She couldn't decipher the writing on the label because it was in another language. It must've fallen out of Mac's pocket.

She took out her mobile and called Martin.

'I want you to check out something for me.'

'I found the address of our vic's sister. Tracked it down to a gym she used.' He paused as if thinking. 'Strange thing, some thug held up the receptionist at the gym this morning. Do you think that's our man?'

Bollocks. Rio squeezed her eyes tight. Odds on that was Mac as well. Was Mac out gunning for the vic's sister now?

'Give me the address,' Rio ordered as she reopened her eyes.

He told her where it was.

'Meet me at The Fort and we'll drive over there together. But before that I want you to ID some medication. The label is in Chinese, I think–'

'Ma'am . . . ?' Martin gently cut in.

Rio could tell something official was coming because he rarely called her 'ma'am'.

'What's on your mind?'

'My performance review came in. Just wanted to say thanks

for giving me an outstanding rating.' He coughed awkwardly at the end.

'You're a good cop.'

She cut the call because she couldn't allow emotion into her life at the moment. She still had a job to do. Rio held the mobile up and over the bottle. Pressed camera. Emailed the picture to Martin. Then Rio drove off past the rubbish dumpsters.

Mac lifted the lid of the middle dumpster. Peered outside. There were rows of cars parked nearby but not Rio's. Outsmarting his colleague was a lot easier than he'd thought it would be. He'd expected her at least to get out of her car and search in the nooks and crannies of the car park – stair-wells, between vehicles . . . the dumpster. Rio must be losing her street smarts. Either that or she had another lead on Elena's murder.

The lid creaked as Mac pushed it fully back. He tried to vault out, but a wave of tiredness hit him, almost making him rock back against the black bags below. He took a minute. Tried to control the drooping of his eyelids. Weariness, that seemed to go beyond the physical. Abruptly alertness made his eyelids flash back into gear and straightened his spine. He stretched an arm outside and leaned it against the dumpster. Then did a smooth lift with his legs and sailed outside, the same way he'd learned to do as a child playing in the park near his grandparents' house. He leaned up against the wall. Pulled out his phone and read the text. Reuben:

8.30 at the Town House.

Mac counted the time left before the delivery at eleven.

Nine thirty.

Ten thirty.

Thirty minutes.

Two and a half hours left.

Mac's face set into a grim expression. Reuben was the only link left to Bolshoi.

sixty-five

'You were right, the writing on the pill bottle is Chinese,' Martin told Rio as they cruised through the streets of Camden towards Elena Romanov's sister's home.

The roads on the fringes of Camden Market were unusually dead. The place was a Mecca for young people hanging out at the bars, clubs and eating holes. But tonight it looked like the place had packed up early for the night. Must be the rain or the recession keeping people at home, Rio thought, as she drove through the tired-looking streets. She checked her GPS again. Ten more minutes max to reach the home of Katia Romanov.

'And it's in Chinese for a reason,' the younger detective continued. 'It's banned over here. The only way you can get it is through the wrong type of hands.'

'Why isn't it available?' Rio asked as she eased the car into a different lane.

'Suicide bombers . . .'

'You *what?*' What the hell had Mac got himself involved in?

'They've been known to take it before heading off to a target. It's got various names, but its street name is HPS, which is short for happiness because it initially gives the user an intense feeling of well-being and immense power. You know, danger doesn't mean a thing.'

Is that what had happened to Mac? He was on an intoxicating power trip?

'Sounds like an alternative to Prozac,' Rio said. 'Why ban it if it makes people feel on top of the world?'

'But that's the problem,' Martin explained. 'The good times don't stay with you for long. After a while, the user finds that they're see-sawing between wanting to sleep and a raging alertness. Starts to really mess up the mind. Can tip people over the edge.'

Fuck. Mac was already way out of control and, if he was doing this shit, God alone knew what he might do next.

'Boss, does this drug have anything to with the murders?'

Rio knew she should tell him. Mac was their primary suspect and Martin should be told the full details of the investigation. She twisted her mouth at that, because she'd been the one to tell him that information-sharing on a team was crucial to solving a case. But if she told him about Mac, she'd have to tell him the rest. *Can't do that. Not an option.* Well, at least not until she'd spoken with this Katia character.

So Rio changed the subject. 'You planning on staying in the squad now your PR has come through?' Rio asked, using the slang term for probation period.

'Of course ... that's if you want me to stay?' There was doubt in his voice.

Rio took the car into a right turn. 'I'll be upfront with you: I was a bit narked when I found out you were one of those fast-trackers. I thought you were going to be a know-it-all about the job on the first day. But you weren't. You've really put your head down and learned the trade.'

'If I can turn into a cop like you, ma'am, then I've done my job well.'

Rio almost laughed at the ma'am; it reminded her of when he'd first started, sticking rigidly to the rules.

'I'll be proud to have you stay . . .'

Abruptly her words fell back as she caught sight of a couple walking arm-in-arm on the opposite side of the street.

The car screeched as she brought it to a shuddering halt. Rio jumped out and rushed across the road towards the couple. The man swore when he saw her, the woman looked confused.

'Fuck. Off,' Rio told the woman.

Sensing trouble, the woman moved quickly away, but not before Rio heard what she muttered under her breath in Russian, an insult that someone had translated years back for Rio when a suspect was mouthing off at her – 'Black monkey.'

'This time I want the truth,' Rio said to the tattoo artist.

She backed him into the doorway of a closed shoe shop.

'I told you what I know–' he started.

She cut him off. '"To live with wolves you have to howl like a wolf." If you don't tell me what the fuck it means, I'm going to pin every violation I can think on you and the next time you come into contact with tattoos is when your cell mate is carving the words *my bitch* on your arse.'

He sneered, 'You think I'm frightened of your English prisons? They're a holiday camp compared to what we have back home.'

Without warning, Rio grabbed his arm, startling both him and Martin. She frog-marched him to the side street that was more like an alley.

'Stand at the entrance with your face towards the road,' she instructed Martin as she took the man deeper into the darkness.

She stopped in the middle. Thrust him up against the wall.

'You'd better start talking or–'

'Or what?' he sneered. 'You're going to close my business down? So fucking what?'

'No,' Rio said calmly. 'I'm going to make sure you never do business again.'

She landed a right to his jaw that had him howling out in pain. Delivered two quick, solid punches to his belly. Groaning and holding his midriff, he sank to his knees. She kicked him in the groin, which had him vomiting into the gutter.

'Boss?'

Rio looked sideways to see Martin gazing at her. 'I told you to keep facing the street. Do. It. Now.'

He did it quickly. She didn't need to be dragging him into this. If this backfired and tat man here made a fuss with his brief, she didn't want Martin to be anywhere near the action. If he didn't see anything, there would be nothing for him to tell. She was shaken up herself. She had never, ever, beaten on a suspect before, despite the advice from one of their training tutors at Hendon that a clip round the earhole was as good an interrogation method as any. No, she'd always played it by the book . . .

Rio stamped on the man's right hand. His scream of rage tore up the air. She crouched down and gripped the front of his hair, snapping his head up to her. He gasped for air as she ground out, 'I'm going to keep stamping on your hand until every one of your fingers is shattered. Try being a tattoo *artist* –' the last word wrung out from her with full-blown sarcasm – 'with a hand that doesn't work any more. So I'll ask one more time, "To live with wolves you have to howl like a wolf." What does it mean?'

'It's the Red Army,' he finally said, his features twisted in pain.

'What about the army?'

'All I know is that some people in the army wear that tattoo. I told you the truth when I said that I saw it on a man many years ago. People looked scared of him . . .'

'Because he was a criminal? A gang leader?'

'All I know is that some of these army men are . . . how do

you say . . . ?' He waved his hand. 'Psycho. Mad. Nutcases. It's as if death means nothing to them. That's all I know.'

'Then why take off earlier?'

'Because I don't want anything to do with this. If this involves one of those Red Army headcases, count me out. I don't want to end up dead, lady, because they find out I've been talking. So lying about the tattoo's meaning means I'd escape . . . How do you say . . . ?' His eyes rolled back as he fought to find the English word. 'Retribution.'

Rio kept her gaze directly on his, trying to suss out if he was telling the truth. But all she could see was a man who looked terrified for his life.

She stood up. 'Piss off,' she told him, and he needed no further prompting to hit the street again.

'Red Army?' Martin questioned behind her. Rio turned.

'Elena Romanov's father was in the army, and your man at the embassy said he possibly died in suspicious circumstances,' Rio said.

'And the murders all have a Russian angle – Elena Romanov was Russian, Doctor Masri was killed in an execution style known to be used by Russian gangs. But the victim having a tattoo that was obviously worn by a unit in the Red Army doesn't make any sense, unless she was a member.'

'Let's hope Katia Romanov can fill in the gaps.'

sixty-six

8:31 p.m.

'What were you doing at that police station?'

Reuben's question took Mac by surprise. They were both seated in a room that was expensively decorated, with a deep carpet on the floor, an antique bureau, a cosy fireplace with a large portrait of Peter the Great over it and sweeping red curtains over the large window. The Town House masqueraded as a members' drinking club but was in fact a slightly upmarket whorehouse.

Before Mac could answer, a young woman entered, who was wearing a short pink dressing gown and stared at them with autopilot happy eyes. She carried a tray with two glasses on it and what looked like a bottle of vodka. Laid it down on a glass table and then left them alone.

Mac countered with his own question. 'How did you know I was there?'

Reuben reached for the bottle and poured them both a shot. As he handed Mac a glass he said, 'My lawyer was down there in connection with the car wash. He was looking after the interests of the wounded car-wash workers the police picked up. He passed you as he was leaving.'

Mac calmly picked up a glass. Sipped. Yep, vodka, but with a splash of a sweet liqueur; he hated the stuff. But he took a bigger mouthful, his jaw clenching as it burned a path down his throat.

He kept the glass in his hand as he finally answered, 'It was only a matter of time before the cops came looking for me, so I went in for a little chat. I didn't need them turning up just before the delivery, because that could've really messed things up.'

Reuben crossed his long legs, keeping his cold gaze on Mac. 'Didn't it occur to you that I might have a set of eyes there? My work is always eased by the cooperation of those in important places.'

'Like Calum?' Mac threw back. 'You do know that he was once a cop?'

That drew a rusty laugh from the other man. 'I know everything there is to know about Calum. Just like I know everything about you, Mac.'

Mac froze. Had Reuben found out who he really was? He carefully checked the other man's face, but it was expressionless.

'Oh, you mean that I was screwing Elena?' He tossed her name out like a bone to a dangerous dog and shrugged his shoulders to suggest it was a small matter.

And it seemed Reuben agreed with him. 'Why didn't you say anything when I asked if anyone had seen her?'

'I haven't seen her for a while.'

Reuben assessed him. Took a drink. Spoke. 'You know she's dead?'

'What?' Mac let out, with all the shock of someone finding out the news for the first time. His glass smacked against the glass of the table as he settled it back down. 'What the hell happened?'

'She was found in some nasty hotel room with her face shot off. Did she tell you about having to meet someone?'

Mac shook his head, keeping up the dazed routine. 'Do you

think her murder is connected to what happened at the car wash?'

Reuben twisted the side of his mouth. 'I don't believe in coincidences. Someone, somewhere, is snuffing the life out of my people one by one.'

Mac let the harshness of his words grind in the room before saying, 'What are you planning to do about it?'

'Nothing. Not yet, anyway. But once the delivery has arrived . . .'

'But what if someone is making sure you never make the delivery? Half your guys went down at the car wash. It could be another gang . . . ?'

'Don't you think I've considered that,' Reuben snarled, turning the atmosphere in the room ugly.

Mac sensed this was his moment and took it. 'But what about Bolshoi . . . ?'

Reuben's gaze became fierce. 'Who told you about Mister Bolshoi?'

'Look, I don't like to speak ill of the dead, but it wasn't only her lips between her legs that kept opening up when we were getting it on.'

Reuben flung the glass at the wall with such force it shattered into tiny pieces before it hit the carpet. 'That . . .' The rest of his words were a stream of furious Russian that Mac didn't need to understand to know they weren't complimentary about Elena. 'I told Mister Bolshoi we shouldn't have her in the crew, but he insisted . . .'

Mac straightened his spine. 'So Elena knew him?'

Reuben stopped pacing and turned to Mac. 'The only way he was going to let me set up in London was to take her on as my communications person.' He sneered. 'I hate working with bitches. They only bring trouble.'

Mac leaned over and picked his glass off the table. Held it

out to Reuben. The other man just stared at it. Then moved forward and snatched it. Drained the remainder of the liquid deep into his body.

'So who is Bolshoi?' Mac asked. He knew he had to tread really carefully here.

'Mister Bolshoi,' Reuben threw back as he slammed the glass onto the table. He pushed down into his seat. 'Call him Bolshoi and you'll be lucky to still have your balls left. He's "Mister" to everyone. I wouldn't be the man I am today if it wasn't for him.'

Mac kept his tone light. 'You sound like you know him well.'

Reuben crossed his legs again, his breathing easing back into a regular rhythm. 'I got myself into the army young. No one cared. There wasn't exactly a queue of kids volunteering to play soldiers in the mountains of Afghani—'

'You were in the Afghanistan war? But that was back in '79 . . .'

'I joined right near the end in '87. I thought I was going to be some kind of hero like my grandfather who fought the Nazis. Instead I was fucked up and scared – it was like Vietnam had been for the Americans. I got into drinking. I was swigging medical alcohol, anti freeze – anything I could get my hands on. I was going off the rails, but luckily one of the officers took pity on me . . .' Reuben tailed off, his eyes heavy with sadness. Then he seemed to notice what he'd been saying and stiffened. 'Don't worry about Mister Bolshoi, my friend. It's safer.'

Silence surrounded them. Mac knew his line of questioning was at a dead end.

'How's Milos doing?'

Some of the strain left Reuben's face. 'He's out of danger and I've got you to thank for that. And I won't forget it. I'm in your debt now. For this is all about my son. The world is in a permanent state of war these days, and now I'm fighting for him rather than my country.' He straightened his legs and leaned forward, his tone reverting to that of Reuben the arms dealer. 'Later I'll need you to meet me at Club Zee and we'll go to the delivery together.'

'But where is the delivery happening?'

Reuben laughed, not a lick of humour in the deep sound he made. 'When we meet, you'll know where we're going.'

Mac's mind quickly shifted through the information he now had about Bolshoi. *Mister* Bolshoi.

He was the real face behind Reuben's operation, just as Calum had confirmed.

He'd been an officer in the Red Army.

He'd known Elena before she came to England.

Reuben, Elena, Mister Bolshoi. The only thing that tied them together was this delivery.

He was just going to have to sit it out for now, until the delivery arrived, before making his next move. Then Reuben dropped a bombshell into the room.

'I hope Katia went the same way as her bitch-sister.'

Mac looked confused. Whoever the other man was talking about was bringing the heat of anger back to his face.

Reuben saw the expression on Mac's face. 'Elena's sister, Katia. I just found out that the whore was screwing Sergei. I told Elena to keep her sister well away from him . . .'

Mac didn't hear the rest. Elena had a sister? Here in London? Then he remembered the gym membership database and the name Katia Romanov. What a fool to dismiss the name and not realise she was connected to Elena. Double fool, because the database would have given him her address as well.

'Did her sister stay with her?' Mac asked, remembering the makeshift bed on the sofa at Elena's home.

'I think she stayed there sometimes, but she had her own place.'

So her sister had probably spent the night with her. And now she was missing. Maybe even dead?

'Does she know about Elena and Sergei?'

Reuben snarled. 'I don't care if she does or not . . .'

Mac leaned urgently forward. 'But what would Sergei care about? I know you loved your brother, and surely he would've wanted her to know what had happened to him?'

Mac watched as the emotions on Reuben's face changed from fury to simple grief. 'There's no point going to her home. Remember Sergei couldn't find her anywhere.'

'I've got some time to kill before the delivery – let me go and see if she's back at her place.'

Reuben said, 'She lives in north London. Camden. Eight Calvin Street.'

sixty-seven

8:55 p.m.

Rio's Black Magic Woman hit the street where Katia lived. Stopped outside the address she'd been given and was surprised. She'd been expecting some type of tatty hostel or block of flats. Number Eight Calvin Street was a house. Four storeys. Plain-bricked Georgian. And worth well over a couple of mill, if Rio's guess was right. So Elena Romanov's sister was either a woman with money to burn, or knew where to get her hands on a hot stash of cash?

The front yard had been replaced by a carport; sitting there was a red Mini. Rio turned to Detective Martin. 'Make a note of the plates and we'll phone them in after.'

The street was empty as Rio pulled back the solid knocker on the front door of the house. The door shook. The rain eased up slightly as she waited with Martin for someone to answer. No one came. Rio tried again.

'Doesn't look like anyone's in. We'll have to come back.'

Instead of answering him, Rio moved towards the large front window. The Roman blind was up. She cupped her hand around her face and peered inside. No sign of anyone. Rio took two steps back and stared up at the twin windows on the next floor. Curtains drawn. Her gaze skated to the top floor. Curtains closed.

She moved back to stand with Martin in front of the door and said, 'Give me your jacket.'

'What?' came his startled response.

She held out her hand. He shrugged out of his deep blue jacket in an awkward set of movements. Handed it to her.

'Step back,' Rio ordered.

She wrapped the jacket round her right hand and wrist. Stepped close to the door. Turned her face away as she punched her material-protected hand against the door's glass panel. The glass shattered, with a few shards falling onto the street but the majority of it dropping inside.

'Boss, I don't think we should be doing this,' Martin said, nervously looking at Rio, but also casting his gaze along the street.

'This case is going to be solved today,' was all she said as she unwrapped the jacket from her hand.

'But don't we need a search warrant?'

She handed him back his jacket. 'Wait in my car.'

'What?'

'You've just got an outstanding performance review, which means you can't afford to have any red strikes against your name. So wait in the car.'

Without waiting for his response, Rio shoved her arm through the broken door panel and stretched it out along the inside of the door until she found the lock. Turned. Opened.

She stepped inside. The hall was narrow, with lemon painted walls and a white carpet. Despite its colour, the carpet was stain-free. The staircase was tight and wound upwards and down to a floor below street level. Rio stopped at the first room she came across, the same one she'd peered into from outside. The door was already open. Three-piece suite. Low-level round table. Old-style jet-black fireplace. Bare floorboards. No photos, no ornaments, no sign that someone

had put their own brand of love in this place. More a show-
room than somewhere lived in and ... Rio jerked round when
she heard a noise behind her.

'Crap,' she let out, seeing Martin standing there. 'I told you
not to come in here.'

He gave her a lopsided smile. 'Sorry – but you know I'm
always going to cover your back.'

Rio wasn't sure whether to cuff him round the ear or be
grateful for his loyalty.

'Check through all this stuff here and the floor below.'

'And what am I looking for?'

'Anything.' She wasn't sure herself. 'Just anything.'

As soon as Rio took the stairs up, the quiet intensified. A
sweet fragrance drifted to meet her as she neared the first
landing. At the top of the stairs was a small table on long legs,
with a vase of flowers. Lilies. Oriental, if she had the scent
right. A few of the off-white buds had yet to bloom, but most
of the flowers were open. Rio noticed small, drying drops of
water. Someone had been in this house not that long ago.

She made her way along the landing and opened up the
first room. A bed and a built-in wardrobe. Nothing else. Then
she noticed the cream cross above the bed on the wall. The
same type of cross her grandmother would make with the palm
she got from church on Palm Sunday. So Katia was a Catholic.
She checked the wardrobe. Nothing inside. Not even hangers.

Abruptly Rio turned when she heard what she was sure
were footsteps outside on the landing.

'Martin?' she called, as she moved towards the door. Stepped
outside. No one. Must be the old house talking, Rio decided,
with its unexpected creaks and groans. She checked the second
room. The same as the one before; nothing in the wardrobe,
but a palm cross above a bed.

The third room was different. On the bed lay an open

rucksack. Squirrel grey. The type with a pull-out handle in the top and mini wheels at the bottom for easier transportation. Clothes were stuffed inside. Not too many, just enough for a weekend away. Was that why the rooms were so empty? Elena's sister going out of town? Rio sorted through the clothes, but found nothing else. She needed to get a search warrant ASAP to do a thorough search of the house.

She took the shorter section of stairs to the next floor. Only one room there. This was empty except for the steam iron in the corner with its cord wrapped neatly around it and the palm cross on the wall. She left the room and walked back to the stairs, but stopped when she felt the carpet dip slightly beneath her shoes. Rio wriggled her toes and the balls of her feet against the carpet. Yeah, the ground was moving. The carpet was a neat fit with the edge of the wall, but was it properly nailed down? She moved towards the edge and dropped to her knees. Started tugging at the carpet, but it wouldn't budge.

'Martin,' she yelled as she kept pulling.

No answer. *He must be on the lower floor.* She used both hands this time, the muscles in her arms burning as she kept the pressure up. The carpet gave way. In one fluid move, Rio dragged the carpet across until the ground where she'd been standing was bare. Floorboards like downstairs. She took out her keys from her bag. Used one to try to prise a floorboard up, but it wouldn't move. She did the same to the one next to it. And the next. The fourth board rose up. She pulled it clear and threw it to the side.

Rio looked down into the hole. And smiled. Inside was a frame lying face down, a folded piece of paper and a small plastic bag. Rio started with the picture frame. A photo, almost a replica of the one Europol had sent over with Elena Romanov's file. Still the two girls, but this time they posed with a man. She figured it was their father. The smallest girl was in his lap, while he had his arm slung around his eldest daughter's shoulder. Something on his arm caught her eye. She dragged the picture closer. A tattoo. Red star with a yellow border. The tattoo artist said it had something to do with the Red Army. Maybe all new recruits in the army had to have it done? Then why did this man's murdered daughter have one as well? She decided to leave the questions for now and pick Martin's brain when she got back downstairs

Placing the photo to the side, Rio opened the sheet of paper. A4-sized street map, the type downloaded from the Internet. She couldn't make out what it was at first. Carefully she looked it over, trying to identify names written in bolder black writing.

Tower of London.

Royal Mint.

Tower Bridge.

Then she figured out what she was looking at – a map of St Katharine Docks. Why would someone have hidden a map of the area? Maybe they were planning on stealing the Crown Jewels from The Tower? Yeah, right, Rio told herself sarcastically as she stood up. Next she opened the small plastic bag. Whistled when she saw what was inside – several passports with various names and nationalities. So she'd been right, Katia Romanov was getting ready to leave the country, but as someone else. No one was leaving this city, not on her watch.

She left the evidence scattered on the floor and took the stairs two at a time.

'Martin? Martin?' she called out as she reached the ground floor.

No response.

She searched the main room. No one there.

Checked the next room, a morning room that was bare except for the fireplace. No Martin.

She called his name again as she made her way into the long kitchen. She found him with his back to her, sitting at the wooden table.

'Martin?' she said as she moved round to face him.

His head was down, his chin brushing his chest.

'Detective.' She pushed his head up and stumbled back in shock.

Blood gushed from a deep, thin line around the front of his neck. She swivelled round, but only had time to take one step as she saw a hooded figure standing behind her.

Flash.

Something moved towards her. An arm. Holding something. She tried to move. Too late. Something hard smashed against the side of her head.

As Rio fell into deep blackness she didn't remember the arm or what hit her. But she did remember what she saw on the arm. A red star tattoo.

sixty-eight

9:05 p.m.

The hit man, now calling himself Felix Bloom, heard the knock on the door just as he'd decided to leave. The contractor had kept him waiting too long, way too long. With or without the money, it was time to get out of town. So the knock at the door – just as he was placing his silencer in his pocket – took him by surprise. Probably the contractor, but he wasn't taking any chances.

He pulled his gun out. Approached the door.

'Who is it?'

'Room service.'

He recognised the squeaky voice of the young man who'd brought him a late lunch forty-five minutes earlier. But still . . . He kept the silencer primed behind his back as he slowly opened the door. The young man grinned at him; he held something in his hand.

'There was a delivery for you, sir.'

The hotel employee held out a mobile phone.

But Felix didn't touch it; instead asked, 'Who left it?'

'I don't know, sir, I wasn't there when it arrived, I was just told to bring it up to you.'

Probably the contractor's way of ensuring they were communicating on a clean channel.

He took the phone. Gave the boy a crisp note. Closed the door. The phone rang almost immediately. He looked at the screen. Number blocked. It rang a second time. He placed the phone to his face. Took the call.

The phone exploded in a shock of light, blowing half his head away.

sixty-nine

Rio woke to a screaming pain in the side of her head and face. Nasty. Deep. Like glass shards digging away at the right side of her brain. Where had the pain come from? She tried to pull herself up, but couldn't. Tried to scream, but couldn't. Tried to see, but the world was a desolate black. Something covered her face. No, not just her face, but her whole head, like another layer of unwanted skin. And her lips were stretched wide around something rammed inside her mouth. Her teeth dug into it, her dry tongue curved below it. It was soft and rough but she couldn't push it out.

Can't breathe, can't breathe, can't breathe.

Yes you can, yes you can, YES YOU CAN.

Deep breaths. Deep breaths.

Innnnn. Ouuuut. Innnnn. Ouuuut.

She tried moving again. Her arms. But they were stretched away from her body. Held fast by bindings round her wrists that kept her locked to something hard and cold. Her fingers moved, though, but with a stiffness that made them feel like they would snap and break off. She tried moving her legs, but they were tied too. Wide apart.

Flash.

An image shot through her mind.

Her looking down on a dead woman.

Bath.

Elena.

Murder.

All of Rio's senses kicked in as she finally figured out where she was. Tied spreadeagled to the bed in a house in Camden.

Flash.

She saw the arm moving towards her.

Flash.

Saw the tattoo.

Oh God.

Martin with a mini-waterfall of blood gushing from his throat.

Desperately, Rio arched. Tugged at her arms. Her legs. They wouldn't move. She tried again, the tendons in her muscles extending to breaking point. She arched the middle of her body up. Struggled in the air as the breath inside her tangled inside her throat. Puke rose from her belly to the back of her mouth. Bitterness soaked her tongue.

Choking. Choking. Choking.

She swallowed the vomit.

Breathe. Breathe. Breathe.

What was that? A noise. A single tap against the floorboards. A light rush of air. A footstep. Breathing.

Oh God. Someone else was in the room.

She collapsed back against the bed. Cringed back into the softness of the mattress beneath her. Tap. Tap. Tap. The footsteps got closer. Then quiet. The type of quiet that only ever bears bad things. The heat of a shadow fell over the bed. Fell over Rio. The mattress dipped near Rio's left side.

Deep breaths. Deep breaths.

Fucking innnnn. Fucking ouuuut.

She jumped when something touched the skin below her neck. Hard. Cold. Sharp. The pinpoint of a giant needle? Then it moved downwards, towards her blouse. Snapped into the material.

Oh God.

A knife. It moved back up. Dug into the centre of her bra. Slashed her bra wide open. Made quick work of splitting her skirt. Moved down. The blade cut into the elastic of her panties and scraped against the hair and skin underneath them. Rio fought back when she felt the cold air touch her naked vagina. She arched up, twisting frantically from side to side. No fucker was going to put their dirty dick inside her. The knife moved away from her body. She waited for the feel of the hands forcing her legs apart. The body. The stabbing inside her.

Waited.

Tap. Tap. The person stood somewhere near her head. She felt the dreaded other person for the first time as fingers held her left arm, just below where they were bound at the wrist. Rio screamed soundlessly as the knife stabbed into the skin below her wrist and ripped down, slashing skin and veins. Blood pumped out, shooting pain all over her body. Then more pain as the same was done to her other wrist. Dizziness and confusion settled over her as the blood leaked out of her body.

Tap. Tap. Tap. Footsteps. No more sound. No more light breathing. Her attacker was gone. Blood pumping out of her wrists, Rio knew she didn't have long to live.

seventy

The first thing Mac saw when he reached Katia's home was Rio's BMW. Bollocks, that's all he needed – another confrontation. He needed to think what he was going to do about Rio before he went into the house. He could wait, keep himself low in the car until she left. But he didn't have time for that. The clock was ticking away towards the delivery. No, somehow, some way, he was going to have to get into that house. Only thing he could do was to hold Rio at gunpoint and spirit Katia away – that's if Elena's sister was there, of course. He didn't like the idea of putting a piece in Rio's face, but what alternative did he have?

He reached inside his pocket for the pill bottle. Nothing. Frantically he searched his other pockets. Nothing. Bollocks, bollocks, where was the stuff? He needed to be hyped up when he did this. His head was already feeling like it was on a one-way journey of departing his body for good. He checked his watch. No, he didn't have time to lose.

He eased out of the car and closed the driver's door as quietly as he could. On his toes, he approached the house, keeping his footsteps slow and even. When he reached the front door he realised that it was open. He frowned; it wasn't like Rio to give a person an opportunity to slip in and out or out and in. He remained silent, listening. Nothing. No voice, no telly, no radio. Just an unsettling quiet. He pulled his gun the same time he pushed the door. No one. Crept inside. Silence. Still on the tips of his toes he stepped inside, hiking the gun higher. He stretched out his arms and moved. Darted his gaze around, trying desperately to gather an alertness that his body was fighting hard against him feeling. Long slim passageway, mirror, coat rail, but nothing else. He tipped open the first door he came to. Sitting room, no one inside. Kept moving until he found the open door of the kitchen. There was someone at the table, head snapped over.

'Don't move,' he whispered behind the seated figure.

No response. Not even an automatic reflex. Quickly he stepped round. Faced the person. Couldn't help the sound that left his mouth when he saw the pool of thick blood dripping over the edges He tipped up the head of the person who he already suspected was dead.

Tipped up the chin. 'Jee-sus,' Mac let out when he realised he was staring into the sightless eyes of Rio's right-hand man, Detective Jamie Martin.

Immediately he swung round and started yelling, 'Rio. Rio.'

Mac kept the gun high as he shot out of the room. Took the stairs two at a time.

Paused at the top of the landing. No one. He kicked open the first door he came to.

No one.

'Rio,' he bellowed again as he shot back onto the landing.

He crashed into the second room and stopped dead. Someone tied to a bed. Blood around them. Clothes ripped down the middle exposing breasts, vagina and skin. Dark brown skin. God, Rio.

He dropped to his knees. Yanked off the pillowcase covering her head. Her head lolled to the side, eyes closed.

'Fuck,' he said as he pulled the gag – an orange flannel – from her mouth.

He laid two fingers against the pulse in her neck. Couldn't find one.

No. No.

He wasn't going to believe that she was gone. She couldn't be . . . He felt a pulse, but it was weak. Quickly he looked over Rio's body. Saw the damage done to her wrists. Saw that the cuts were vertical. Whoever had done this knew that the quickest route to death from a slit in the wrists was not horizontal but ripped straight up or down. He needed to stop the bleeding or she wasn't going to make it. Quickly he grabbed up the flannel and wrapped it round one of her wrists. But he needed something to do the same to the other wrist, so he bolted out of the room and found the bathroom. Seconds later he was back with a white towel. He tied it tightly round her wrist. Placed a finger to a point inside Rio's elbow and pressed. Did the same with her other arm. Now all he could do was pray that the force he was applying to her pressure points combined with the makeshift tourniquets around her wrists would stop the flow of blood.

His phone went, but he ignored it. Just kept up the pressure. If anything happened to Rio . . .

'If you think you're going to die on me, think again you stubborn, big-mouth cop,' he let out, staring at the sick brown tone of her face.

He kept the pressure up.

One minute.

Two.

Three.

His phone went again. He ignored it.

Four.

Nearly at five, the blood slowed down. Eased back. Disappeared. He gazed down at her spread legs. Had the bastard raped her as well? Gently he pushed her legs together. He took out his phone. Voicemail from Reuben. He listened.

Delivery coming in early. 10.30.

Shit. He needed to get across to Reuben's now, at Club Zee. He checked his watch.

9:12.

One hour and eighteen minutes.

That didn't give him a heck of a lot of time to make it to Reuben before the new delivery time. But what about Rio? He couldn't just leave her. But if he didn't, he'd never make it. He rubbed the inside of his nose with the tips of two fingers. What was he going to do? A wave of weariness coursed through him. He was so tired, so tired. He searched for the pills. Empty pocket. Then he remembered they were long gone. No chemicals to help him make his decision. Rio or Elena's killer? Bolshoi. Rio.

He punched in a number.

'Bartholomew Station . . .'

'Listen. You need to send an ambulance to Eight Calvin Street . . . Just bloody listen, it's Detective Inspector Rio Wray and Detective Martin. They're both down . . .'

He snapped off the connection. Gave Rio one last look before rushing for the stairs.

seventy-one

9:40 p.m.

Mac made it to Club Zee fifty minutes before the new time of the delivery. The security on the front door was heavy, a total contrast to the easy in-and-out access Mac had experienced earlier in the day. The same two men who'd been on guard duty at Reuben's house stood with menace and an air of steel as they checked out the street. Mac got straight into the frisk pose when he reached the door but – obviously remembering him from earlier – one of the men nodded and let him through.

The only person in the reception was Jeff, the manager, who appeared only interested in the phone in his hand as his fingers and thumb beat against it. He looked up when Mac came in.

'Las Vegas Bar, second floor,' was all he said, but Mac felt his gaze burning into his back as he took the stairs.

The bar was at the rear of the building and its interior lived up to its name. OTT glitz, electric mauve and blue strobe lighting and a miniature Statue of Liberty ice bucket lit up in puke yellow on the bar. All of Reuben's gang were sitting, while he stood like a lion presiding over his pride up front. The mood in the room was expectant and taut.

'You're late,' Reuben called out as soon as Mac stepped in the room.

'Yeah, I had a few things left to do.' He gestured to the cuts
and bruises on his face. 'I had to dole out some justice to
someone who thought he could get away without paying me
my dues.'

'And Sergei's bitch? How did she take the news?'

'She wasn't at home.'

'Don't worry, I'll find and take care of her tomorrow.' And
from the sound of his tone, he wasn't talking about wrapping
her in his loving embrace.

Mac moved loosely across the room and leaned against the
bar as Reuben started to speak.

'This is what's happening with the delivery tonight.'

Every muscle in Mac tightened, his heart rate kicking up a
gear as Reuben finally got down to telling him all he needed
to know about the delivery. Well, he hoped that was what he
was going to do.

'I know you were all expecting to meet slightly later, but my
contact in Hamburg has moved the transaction thirty minutes
earlier, so we'll need to be in place by ten thirty.'

Bolshoi, Mac thought. Why would he move the delivery
time? Something must've happened? Or maybe Bolshoi was
just keeping everyone on their toes, which meant that this was
an important delivery.

'The delivery will take place in St Katharine Docks.' He
nodded to one of his men, who went behind the bar and came
back holding a large map with key places circled in red.

'We'll be assembling in a warehouse near the quayside. We
don't need to worry about anyone appearing, because the
place is empty and has been earmarked for redevelopment . . .'
As Reuben continued to talk, he indicated the places marked
on the map.

St Katharine Docks.

Empty warehouse.

Mac stored the information away.

'The delivery will be arriving by boat. I need some of you inside the warehouse with me and the rest of you to be lookouts on the outside.' His voice hardened. 'All of you have seen today's bloodshed, which means that someone out there doesn't want us around. Probably one of our rivals.' An evil smile creased his lips. 'But believe me, after this delivery, there will only be one king in this town.'

Sounded like Reuben was gearing up for a full-on battle to eliminate his rivals. Mac's cop persona slipped back into place. He didn't want any more blood spilled on the streets of the capital. He should contact Phil . . . No he couldn't do that while Elena's killer still breathed air.

Reuben snapped his gaze onto Mac. 'After the delivery is unloaded, I'll need you to check it over and make sure it matches the manifest.'

The Russian's gaze swung back across the gathering. 'Anyone messes up . . .' The menace coating his tone meant he didn't need to finish the sentence. 'We leave in five minutes.'

He took a step back, signalling the end of the pre-meeting. But Reuben wasn't finished with Mac. He beckoned him over. Pulled him to a quiet spot at the end of the bar.

'I was only partly telling the truth in my little speech. I do want you in the warehouse to check the delivery. But I also need you around. I need someone I can trust. These people . . .' He gestured with contempt at the men who were leaving, 'As soon as the bullets start flying, some of them will run away like little girls.'

'Is there going to be gunplay then?'

'After what's happened today,' The Russian shook his head. 'Who knows what might happen?' His voice dipped to a deep growl. 'But if anyone comes looking for me, I'll be ready. You need to be ready as well, so whatever you're packing, make sure it's fully loaded.'

They were both distracted by a newcomer entering the room. Mac had been expecting this. The appearance of Calum. In fact, he'd been surprised that his former friend wasn't already in attendance. Calum spotted Mac and Reuben, but he didn't move from his position just inside the door. A terrible feeling swept over Mac like he knew that something bad, really bad was about to happen.

'What are you doing here?' Reuben asked Calum.

He didn't answer, instead let his gaze swing around the men in the room. Then he took two halting steps inside. Pushed closed the door. The bang as the door connected with its frame echoed throughout the room.

Then he spoke, his eyes on Reuben only. 'I know I said I wouldn't—'

The gang leader cut over him. 'If this is about the money we talked about—'

It was Calum's turn to interrupt. 'No, this isn't about my fee.'

Silence. Calum walked slowly towards the Russian and Mac. This time his gaze screwed into Mac.

'Some information has just come into my possession that you all need to know about,' Calum called out dramatically.

Every man stared intently at him.

Calum kept moving forward, his gaze never leaving Mac.

'Reuben, I'm sorry to do this so close to the delivery.'

Mac sensed what was coming. The blood receded from his face.

Don't do this.

'It had better be good, Calum, because we're getting ready to head out.'

Don't do this.

Calum smiled. 'There's an undercover cop in this room.'

The oxygen was sucked from the room as a collective intake of breath.

Don't do this.

Reuben pushed up off the bar. 'What are you talking about?'

Calum moved slowly, but surely, to Mac. Got into his space. 'I'll let Detective John MacDonagh tell you all about it.'

seventy-two

'He's talking bullshit,' Mac said calmly.

He knew he was backed into a tightening corner, but that didn't mean he couldn't get out of it. Reuben swung his gaze urgently from Mac to Calum.

'The only person we know for definite who's been a cop in this room is Calum,' Mac carried on.

Reuben pinned his attention on Calum, which gave Mac the time he needed to turn the tables on his former best friend. 'The way I hear it, no one really knows why he got tossed out of the cop shop. What if he didn't get slung out? What if it was all a screen for making him undercover?'

Mac's nerves only got tighter when he realised that the man he was accusing was saying nothing. Worse than that, Calum had that smug, 'gotcha' expression smoothed over his face.

Finally Calum spoke. 'You tell me, Reuben. What do you think?'

Then his hand snaked inside his jacket. Pulled something out. Looked like a wallet. Mac's face screwed up. A wallet? That didn't make any sense. A wallet . . . ? As Calum passed it to Reuben, Mac's mind ticked away.

'Open it up,' Calum instructed the Russian.

As the gang leader flipped the wallet open, Mac realised what it was. Shit, his game was up. Mac went straight for his Luger, but Calum already had his Glock 19 in his face, his thumb pressed into the thumb rest. Mac froze, the sweat matting against his forehead as the mutterings of the men filled up the room like a mob just getting started at a lynching.

Reuben moved towards him and slapped the opened wallet in front of his face. His warrant card.

Name.

Rank.

Number.

Most damning of all, a photo.

Mac always left it in Phil's safe hands when he went on an op, so how traitor Calum had got it he didn't know. But Mac didn't have time to figure that out as a hand reached into his jacket. Someone else wrenched both his arms behind his back, making him clench his teeth. One of the other men jammed a hand into his jacket and pulled out his Luger. It was the first time that Mac saw confusion and shock stamped across Reuben's face. Mac knew there was no point denying it, so he stared defiantly back at the Russian.

He knew his man well enough to know that when he was angry he was bad, but when he was quiet he was worse. Reuben looked at Mac like a disappointed father. 'You know what really pains me about this, my friend, is that I took you into my confidence. Treated you like a friend, even a member of the family. Of course the greater the betrayal, the greater the . . .'

Reuben found a bottle of spirits on a table. Gripped it tightly and then crashed it against the wall in a move that seemed to cost him no effort, but showered his audience in brandy and shattered fragments. He examined the jagged edges of the cut glass, then threw the broken bottle down where it crashed against the floor.

Mac almost let out a huge puff of relief, until he saw the Russian pick up a second bottle. Champagne this time. Smashed it against the wall. Then scored the wall with it. Only after he saw Reuben run his fingertips along the bottle's edge did Mac figure out that he hadn't thought the edges of the first bottle were vicious enough. The edges scored deep but uneven gouges out of the wall. 'That's better,' Reuben let out softly. 'A fit weapon for a family traitor . . .'

He was in the mood for sadistic violence now, and Mac knew he had little time. 'Your slimy little sidekick here is right – I'm an undercover cop, and you know how that works, don't you? I can alert my controller and have half The Met here in ten minutes, armed and ready for action. I'm telling you now that I've already done it.'

It was pathetic and Mac knew it. But it was all he had. He stole a glance at Calum, who turned away in embarrassment. The big bear of a man in front of him pulled himself close and said with contempt. 'Is that so . . . ?' Bottle in hand, he took a swing at Mac, who saw the glass glittering in the lights as it came towards him. But there were no cuts, just a reinforced fist in the face, which threw Mac backwards. He crashed into a table, scattering its contents over the floor. He rolled across the floor, groaning and moaning, coming to rest face down on carpet that sweated alcohol and dirt. He managed to heave himself onto his back and found Reuben standing over him. His steely face staring down at him, broken bottle in hand.

'Where are your police? Eh? Where are they now . . . ?'

He slashed the jagged edges of the bottle towards Mac. But it never reached him, because Calum grabbed the Russian's arm.

'You're getting very upset, boss. That's not a good idea, not with the delivery round the corner. Why don't you let me take care of this? You head on – I'll do a good job here. You can rely on me. I've got my own reasons.'

But Reuben didn't move.

Calum leaned in close to him. 'Think. You can't be late for Mister Bolshoi. No one is late for Mister Bolshoi.'

The gangster hesitated for a moment before he straightened up. Chucked the bottle away. Calum aimed his gun at Mac. 'I'll take care of it.' Calum pushed his gun closer to Mac's bleeding face. 'I'll take him downstairs . . .'

'No, shooting him won't be good enough.'

But Calum had that covered. 'I'm a professional. I know where to shoot a man to ensure a long, lingering and painful death. It's not your usual MO, but needs must. I'll take him down the drinks cellar; you can get your boys to clear up the mess tomorrow.' Seeing the doubt on Reuben's face, Calum added, 'I might've been a cop once in my lifetime but, believe me, my blood runs cold for them now.'

Silence.

Reuben slowly checked his watch. Then gazed long at Calum. Back at Mac. His lower lip rippled with the deadly ease of a reptile's skin. He looked back at Calum. Nodded. Looked at his two heavies who had secured Mac's gun and arms. 'Go with him. Make sure the job gets done properly.'

Calum nodded.

Reuben wiped some of the alcohol from his face as Calum and the two men bent Mac's upper body forward in a painful stress position. Then they manhandled him out of the room. Once outside, Calum tapped his gun lightly across Mac's temple. The impact wasn't great, but it made his legs collapse beneath him. The two men dragged a dazed Mac along the corridor and down three flights of stairs. They didn't care that his body twisted and bumped on its descent. They hit a dimly lit corridor. Reached the cellar, which had a heavy oak door.

He was yanked into the cellar, where rack after rack of bootleg booze was stored. Calum ordered the two men, 'Stand him up straight.'

Before turning to Mac and saying, his green eyes sparkling as if he was high on good shit, 'Before we get down to business, this one isn't from Reuben, this is gratis for attacking me this afternoon, you little bastard.'

A fist to the face sent Mac crashing backwards into metal shelving. He slumped downwards to the floor while bottles crashed around him. Amid the acrid fumes of spilled alcohol and damp wood, he was dimly aware that Calum had his Glock ready and primed back on him.

Reuben hadn't left, but stood at the end of the corridor leading to the basement. He was never a man who liked loose ends and Mac might become a loose end if this job wasn't done properly. So he waited. Waited.

Bang.

Pause.

Bang. Bang.

Satisfied, he turned back to the stairs to get on with the job of meeting the delivery.

seventy-three

Mac couldn't understand why he was still alive. Calum had punched him out ... he didn't remember a thing after that. Almost darkness surrounded him. He reached out for something to help him stand. His hand searched through the air until he found what felt like a length of metal. Pulled himself up, but the metal shook and bottles tumbled and crashed around him, making his body curl inwards to protect himself.

Mac tried again, letting his eyes adjust to the gloom. Then straightened up, feeling along the wall for the light switch. He found it. Flicked it. Nothing happened. He moved over to the door and tried to pull it open, but it wouldn't budge.

No answer. If he started yelling for help that might alert the wrong type of people. Instead he headed back across the room to see if there was any other way out, and tripped headfirst over something lying on the floor. Winded, he lay for a while. Having settled his breathing into an even beat, he got to his knees. He reached over to feel what had taken him down. Large, bulky, cloth, like a sack of old clothes left outside a charity shop. He slowed the movements of his hands as he moved upwards. Felt something lukewarm. Couldn't place what the material was. Moved up. A ridge poking out of whatever he touched. Funny shape, with one hole ... no, two ... Mac's hand jerked back when he realised what he was touching. A nose on a face. And from the temperature of the skin, a face attached to the body of someone who was dead. He hoped it was that bastard Calum. But was Calum such a bastard if he'd left him alive? He didn't know what the other man's agenda was, but he wasn't ready to put his name back in his mobile's contact list under 'favourites.' Beside, he didn't have time to think about Calum Burns, he needed to get out of here. Now.

Mac heaved the body towards the light coming from under the door. Peered at the face, and realised it was one of the two heavies that Reuben had ordered downstairs to make sure Calum carried out the execution properly. Mac ran through his pockets, hoping to find a gun of some sort, but he drew a blank. He did find something useful, though – a packet of cigarettes and a Zippo. He struck the light, increased the flame and could now see his way more clearly. Over by the wall, in a sitting position, head slumped to one side, was Reuben's other thug. Stone-cold dead too – bullet neatly between the eyes.

Mac searched the second body, more carefully than the first. Pockets. Under the shirt. Trouser leg . . . Froze when he felt two straps attached to the right leg. His hand moved up slightly. A handle. Not a gun, but something else. He slid the handle out. Ignited the lighter again. Held the object up to the flame. An automatic flick knife.

He extended the blade. Sharp, Teflon steel. Walked back to the door. Using the lighter, he examined the door looking for joins in the wood. They were tightly fitted together and lacquered over, but just visible. Mac plunged the knife into the wood. Started to dig away, using one of the broken bottles as a lever when enough was chipped away. The timber varied in strength – some was quite soft, other bits more resistant, so he focused on the areas that were easier to make holes in.

He soon got a rhythm going, until the bottle went clean

through the door. The gap was wide enough to get his arm through and he felt his way along to the lock on the outside in the forlorn hope that the key might have been left in it. But it wasn't there. He listened for footsteps or voices in the corridor outside, but there was none. Mac went back to chipping away with a renewed zeal. His arm ached like crazy but he kept going. Finally stood back and admired his handiwork – an arm-sized hole. His fingers were stiff and cracking under the strain. That he could live with, but he reckoned at the current rate of progress it would be an hour before he could get out and he didn't have an hour to spare.

He went to the racks. Grabbed bottles of booze and soaked the wood around the hole he'd made inside and out. Flicked the Zippo on. Touched the flame to the alcohol-soaked wood. The wood burned slowly with a blue flame, like a Christmas pudding.

The fire on the wood was slow moving but it was producing a lot of smoke. That was actually an added advantage. If an alarm went off, there was a good chance someone, perhaps even the fire brigade itself, would turn up and set him free. He used the jacket of one of the dead men to fan the flames and send the smoke outwards. The fire seemed to burn more easily for a moment or two, but then began to gutter and die. He tried again, more alcohol this time, hacking away at the charred wood when it became soft and blowing and fanning the flames. He lined up one bottle after another and poured on more spirits whenever the flame seemed to be dying away. Finally, it seemed to be working. But it worked too well.

The fire began to spread to the doorframe and up and down the door. Mac began to choke as the air from the cellar was sucked out and smoke was sucked in to replace it. He ripped a piece of the shirt from one of the corpses and tied it round the lower half of his face. He carried on, coughing in the face of the smoke, hacking at the wood with his knife and broken bottle. The flames were licking upwards towards the ceiling. He stood back, closed the blade and began to kick at the burning door. It stood fast, tight in its frame. Cinders and sparks were falling around. After another futile kick, the problem became clear. He was kicking outwards but the door opened inwards.

Mac used the jacket again, this time wrapping it round his hands like oven gloves, and began to tug on the hole with all his might. Bits of charred wood came away, scorching his fingers and landing smuts on his clothes. Parts of the door came inwards while the rest remained solid. He high-kicked the weakened structure with his foot again. It splintered, cracked and fell into the corridor.

Followed by clouds of smoke Mac emerged, straining for any gasp of oxygen that the corridor might provide. The fire had spread outside, fitfully and unevenly, but it was still spreading. He ran into the room opposite, a storeroom – no use. Into the room next door. Cloakroom – no use. It was only when he managed to find a kitchen that he found what he was looking for. He knew Calum wouldn't have taken his and the heavies' guns far. A rubbish bin was the usual place to dump unwanted weapons, and in the kitchen he found not only his Luger but three other guns, poorly hidden, under some peelings and wrappings. Stuffing the weapons into his pockets, he fled up the stairs and opened a door.

A woman, dolled up in party clothes and thick make-up, stood outside looking worried.

She shrieked, 'I smelled smoke, what's happening?'

'There's a fire, call nine-nine-nine.'

He ran down the corridor; more people were emerging to see what was happening. Mac ran on but he stopped when he realised one of the people was Jeff, the manager. He pulled out one of his collection of guns and pressed it against Jeff's forehead. 'What kind of car do you drive?'

Jeff instantly raised his hands, his eyes going wide. 'Take it easy, let's stay calm.'

'Car?'

'It's a Bob Marley, sports version.'

'The keys,' Mac demanded.

'Don't take my motor, it's new,' the younger man pleaded. 'We've got a Honda. Pretty nippy. It's painted to look like an emergency paramedic's bike with blue sirens, the lot. One of those kidney transplant delivery ones. We use it here when we need some speed. It's in the garage.'

'Paramedic's bike?'

'Sure. Have you ever seen the cops pull over one of th—'

'What's the time?' he cut over Jeff.

Jeff hesitated as if he dared not lower his hands. But at Mac's brisk nod he checked his watch.

10:11.

That meant the delivery was going down in nineteen minutes' time.

seventy-four

10 p.m.

I'm not going to make it. Not going to make it.

Mac carved up the tarmac. He wore the high-vis jacket and crash helmet that had been stored with the bike. The motorbike raced through the streets, blowing its siren, lights flashing electric blue. Shot traffic lights, ignored bus lanes and didn't give a damn about speed cameras that clicked as it zoomed past. All that mattered was getting to the delivery. He cranked the speed up. Took Tower Bridge at 60 mph, the wind propelling him, making it feel like he was flying in the air. Weaved his way through the lines of traffic and did an illegal turn on the other side. Headed south back towards the river, leaping the traffic humps. The bike did a strange up-and-down dance as tarmac gave way to Victorian cobbles. Mac began urgently searching for a place to park.

The dock was surrounded by walls on three sides that had once – in another lifetime – been warehouses teeming with imported and exotic goods. Now they housed shops, restaurants, bars and pubs. The lights from the buildings were low, as if trying to give privacy to the patrons in and outside. Despite its old walls, St Katharine Docks had the newness of a place that had been built the day before. And the stench of money blew from the mile-high apartment prices, via the upmarket cuisine, to the yachts and boats that were like sleek playthings on the water. This was a part of East London that had managed to successfully bury its history of crime and grime. The delivery was about to change that.

He checked out the masts and the soft glow of red and white lights on yachts and pleasure craft, trying to ID one that could be used for a delivery. But it was hard to figure out which size boat could be used since he still didn't know what the delivery was. Pulling up between two cars, leaving the engine running, he checked his watch.

10:28.

The delivery would be about now, but it would take time for contact to be made between shore and boat, establish the good faith of the crew and shore party and, of course, make sure no one was going to be ripped off. It didn't give him a big window of time to find the abandoned warehouse, but it was all he had.

Mac turned off the engine, flicked down the rest and eased off the bike. On the back of the vehicle was a carrier in which Mac had put his guns and cap, in the spot where the transplant kidneys were supposed to be kept chilled. He kept his yellow jacket and helmet with its insignia on, put the carrier over his shoulder and moved off to inspect the area. At an access point to the docks, he noticed a telephone van illegally parked. Exactly as it had been indicated on Reuben's map back at Club Zee. There would be two gunmen inside, protecting the gang's flanks and providing support if there was any trouble.

Casually he walked past the van, snatching a quick look inside when he got near the window. Two men, dressed as telephone engineers. Seeing him, one of the men slipped his hand inside his jacket. *Take it easy, Mac, stay calm.*

Then the man's hand came back out, empty. The last

thing Mac saw as he passed the van was the tense way both men's eyes darted around. He still didn't know which warehouse he was after, but from the position of the men it couldn't be far. Mac walked down to the waterfront. Across the black, inky water and its shimmering, reflected multi-coloured lights, he could see a row of warehouses. But which one? He scanned them. His gaze skidded to a stop when he saw a redevelopment sign on one; well, it looked like a sign to him.

He sat on a bench, took off his crash helmet, tied it to his belt and put his cap on. But he left the jacket on for now. No one would suspect a man in a high-vis jacket. Gangsters and cops preferred more low-key disguises. A man in a suit came sauntering along the waterfront, talking into a mobile phone. Mac recognised him straight off as one of Reuben's men, so dipped his head slightly, taking advantage of the shadow. He felt the man's eyes on him, but soon he drifted off, keeping up his pretend chat on the phone. The Russian probably had more people out and about in the harbour than he had in the warehouse.

Mac couldn't take the chance that one of them might recognise him; he needed to step up his game and that meant only one thing – heading off to the warehouse. He reached into his carrier. Took out one of the guns. Star Megastar, heavy-duty, double-action trigger, fourteen-rounds capacity. *Impressive*. He checked the magazine. Fully loaded. Tucked it into the front of his trousers and then pulled the front of the jacket over it. With an urgent intake of chilled air, he set off to the warehouse.

Out on the water, there was laughter coming from a yacht looking for a docking place. The fact that a family was on deck with a cute dog didn't mean this wasn't the boat carrying the delivery. In fact, it was more likely to mean that it was.

Respectability was always good cover. As Mac turned ninety degrees to follow the waterfront, he noticed a council street-sweeping vehicle working the cobbles, long after it should have been returned to its depot. Another nervous man at the wheel with his equally nervous colleague, looking the area up and down.

As he closed in on the warehouse, Mac spotted a group of youths in hoodies, wheeling and circling on bikes. They took a keen interest in him as he got closer to them.

A mixed-race youth rolled up and parked his bike directly in front of Mac. 'Where you think you're going?' He had that accent so many young people now used which, as far as Mac was concerned, made him sound like a Neanderthal.

Mac didn't show his irritation. Instead he tapped his carrier and explained carefully, 'Paramedic. I'm on duty.'

'This is our patch. You can't walk around here, bruv, without paying a toll.'

'I help sick people.'

The youth looked at his comrades, who seemed doubtful. But finally one of them said, 'OK, let him go.'

Outside a shuttered entrance to the warehouse, two men in official-looking uniforms were watching the confrontation carefully. The youth slowly wheeled his bike backwards and Mac walked on while one of the youths sneered, 'Support the NHS.' Mac heard their immature giggles fading as he moved on.

He avoided walking directly past the men in uniform at the shutter, but instead did a circuit of the building. The broken windows and hoist points were all covered by corrugated iron and were too high to get access to anyway. Again, at strategic points, cars and vans were parked as indicated on Reuben's map. He had everything covered. Mac walked on and found another bench out of reach of the watching squads and sat down. He checked his watch. The delivery should have been well under way, but nothing was happening. Not in the harbour, not around the warehouse, not among the various boats that were tied up. Something had gone wrong.

seventy-five

10:35 p.m.

Rio's eyes snapped open, pain still with her. And the fear. She remembered the room, the bed, the knife, a tattoo . . .

Beep. Beep. Her head turned slightly to find she was hooked up to a machine; its light, pulsating strong and bright, had the intensity of a lifeline. Lifeline. Hospital. She was in hospital. The rest came back to her – some bastard had tried to kill her. And Martin . . . ?

She squeezed her eyes with emotional agony. *How could I have let that happen to him? I was meant to be looking out for him! Should've insisted he keep his arse in the car!*

She tried to lift herself up, at the same time noticing the bandages on her lower arms, but a voice somewhere in the room stopped her.

'Don't move.'

She slumped back as footsteps padded across the floor. A nurse looked down at her and smiled.

'How are you feeling?'

Rio opened her mouth to speak, but coughed instead.

'Drink this.' A hand cupped the back of her hair and raised her head. Eagerly Rio tipped her chin to touch her lips to the side of a blue plastic cup that the nurse held. The liquid tasted like a chemical wash, leaving a nasty aftertaste on her blistered tongue, but she sucked and swallowed. Sucked and swallowed.

'Easy.' The cup was pulled back. Rio's head hit the pillow again.

Only then did she realise that her superior officer was in the room too, sitting in the armchair by the bed.

DCI Newman stood up. 'So how are you feeling?'

She gulped in air, which scraped against her dry throat. 'How did you find me?'

'Someone called it in.'

'Who?'

He shook his head. 'We don't know . . . A man. But don't worry about any of that, you need to rest up.'

Her features became stark. 'Detective Martin . . .' She couldn't manage the rest of the words, but that had nothing to do with the state of her throat.

DCI Newman gave her a grave look. 'I know. There was nothing anyone could do for him.' He shifted his shoulders back. 'You don't need to worry about informing his family, I've done it . . .'

'But I should've been the person doing that . . .'

'They understand. I'll come back and see you tomorrow, so get a good night's sleep.'

Rio shuffled, trying to sit up. She slumped back down, but that didn't stop her from speaking. 'Sir, we found a map of St Katharine Docks in Katia Romanov's house. Something is going down . . .'

'Rio. I told you earlier that this investigation is over for you.' His hand fell against her shoulder, but strangely it didn't feel comforting. He squeezed ever so slightly.

'Time for your medication,' the nurse gently interrupted. 'This will ease the pain and help you sleep.'

She passed Rio a white paper cup with two blue pills in it.

Rio placed them in her mouth and then her throat worked with the water she took.

Newman smiled at her. She closed her eyes, but her eyeballs twitched under the orange-black haze of her eyelid. Less than a minute later, the door closed.

Rio sprang into action. Spat out the tabs hidden under her tongue. Pulled herself up. Ignored the dizziness as she tugged the tubes from her body. Shoved off the bed and, with painful arms, picked up her neatly stacked clothes on the nearby chair. Awkwardly dressed. She checked the corridor. No one around. Head down, she briskly walked and vowed that she was still going to solve this case. And now DC Martin's murder.

seventy-six

Mac stared hard at a yacht as his brain ticked away. It wasn't one of those flash, racy vessels, but of a much more modest style. Behind its wheelhouse a man's head occasionally bobbed up and down, surveying the area. From time to time he would appear and take a longer look before disappearing below. Mac looked at his watch.

10:40.

Then back over at the warehouse, where nothing was happening. When he looked back again, Mac saw the man on the yacht had emerged and was standing on the prow, from where he had a commanding view of the scene. He was dressed in a smart suit, a cravat, and wearing a peaked cap like a Sunday afternoon sailor. Mac started to look away, but something about the man drew his attention. That something was the way the man carried himself: the ramrod straightness of a soldier.

The man turned slightly, giving Mac a better, but still half-shadowed view of his face. Mac squinted his eyes. There was something familiar about that face . . . but he couldn't place it. Where had he seen it before? Where . . . ? Mac quickly dug into his inside pocket. Pulled out the charred remains of the photo he'd recovered from the fireplace in Elena's home. Studied the photo. Studied the man. He couldn't be sure, but the man looked like a dead ringer for one of the military men in the photograph. The one on the left with the crooked front tooth in his smile. Sure, the man on the boat was older, but the line of his nose, jaw, even forehead all looked the same. The man flicked up his wrist and checked his watch. Then, before Mac could investigate him further, pulled out his mobile as he disappeared into a cabin below. Mac still couldn't be sure, but hey, what did he have to lose?

He walked out of the shadow and approached the yacht. Took light steps along the gangplank. The boat swayed ever so slightly as Mac took two easy steps onto the deck. He remained still for a few seconds. Listened as the night breeze kicked up around him. Moved towards the opening leading to the cabin below. Mac peered down. Short, single flight of wooden stairs. Once again listened as he pulled out the Megastar. He could hear a voice, but couldn't make out the words. Either the man was talking on his phone or had company. The slight motion of the vessel rippled through his body as he took the stairs. Carefully. Slowly. One at a time. When he reached the bottom, the view of the cabin was laid bare to him. The yacht might not have looked expensive up top, but this cabin was a mariner's dream. Smooth cream ceiling with spotlights, all-round windows instead of walls, and walnut furniture, including the impressive bed where the man sat, with his body half turned away from Mac.

'Can I help you?' the man said, obviously sensing he was no longer alone. No panic in his voice, no worry.

Slowly he turned round, punching off the phone as Mac entered the room, gun raised. He looked surprised, but unworried, that he had a visitor pointing a double action at his chest.

'Can I help you ... Mister ... ?' he repeated, showing his crooked front tooth.

seventy-seven

Definitely a dead ringer for one of the men in Elena's photo. The soft spotlight on the man's face smoothed out the wrinkles around his eyes and the deep grooves bracketing his mouth. But it sharpened the silver hair that had once been completely nut brown.

Mac spread his legs, keeping his stance evenly grounded. 'Who are you and what are you doing here?'

'Of course,' the man said calmly, as if he were beginning a presentation in front of an audience. One of his hands leaned into the black and red luxury blanket as he crossed his legs. 'My name is Andreas Schmidt and I'm a businessman from Germany. I've been in London securing a contract and now I'm enjoying a sailing trip around your beautiful English coastline. I've travelled up from Ramsgate today and I'm planning to sail around Essex tomorrow.'

Mac reached into his pocket and put the charred photo on the foldaway table by Schmidt's bed. 'I've had a long day and it's not over yet. And if you think I'm going to put up with you screwing me in the rear, think again, Herr Schmidt. I'm guessing that one of the two men in this photo is you, and the other the father of a friend of mine. But I don't have to guess, because you're going to tell me which one you are.'

Schmidt picked the photo up. He didn't falter but lingered over it a little too long before putting it back down. 'I don't know what you're talking about. Now, if you don't mind, you must leave my yacht or I'll be forced to call your famous English Bobbies . . .'

Mac's boiling rage took him across the room. Without hesitation he pressed the gun against the man's forehead. 'There've been a lot of men – and women – already killed today, so if you don't want to be the next, you need to get your memory back – fast.'

The man uncrossed his legs and laid his palms flat on the blanket. 'OK, I'm the man in the photo. And you're right: the other man is Elena and Katia's father. My name is Andrei Popov. Satisfied?'

'Satisfied?' Mac increased the pressure of the gun. 'I haven't even started yet. Like your name, sounds like you've got a whole string of them to tap into and I'm betting I know one of them – Mister Bolshoi.'

Popov laughed – a strange, muffled sound that seemed half caught in his nose. 'The very real Mister Bolshoi would take strong exception to his name being used by someone else.' His laughter stopped dead. 'And I can assure you that Mister Bolshoi doesn't take kindly to impersonations of himself.'

'You know him, then?'

'I've never met him. What's your interest in him?'

Mac's finger tensed around the trigger. 'I'm asking the fucking question—'

'I'm here on a job for Mister Bolshoi,' the other man abruptly cut in. 'He asked me to bring over a delivery for a business associate of his, a Mr Volk. But there seems to be some sort of problem.'

Mac looked up and down the cramped space inside the yacht. 'Did you leave the delivery behind? Only there doesn't seem to be one.'

A shout sounded from outside, sharply drawing Popov's

attention away from Mac. There was another shout. Startling him, Popov pushed Mac's gun away and said, 'I need to deal with this, Mac.'

But Mac pushed the gun back in place. 'How do you know what my name is?'

The older man got up, as if the gun wasn't there. 'Mister Bolshoi takes a keen interest in all of the people in his organisations.' Popov started walking towards the stairs. 'I can't stop you from shooting me in the back, but remember that I'm merely here to do a job.'

Tension flooding his whole body, Mac kept the weapon on the other man, but he didn't pull the trigger. He'd never shot anyone in the back before. And the man was unarmed. Instead Mac lowered the gun as he followed Popov up the stairs. More shouting greeted Popov's emergence onto the deck. Mac couldn't make out the words, but he raised his gun and levelled it with the older man's head. Mac's gaze adjusted to the darkness. Further down the harbour wall, some of Reuben's men were walking along examining vessels. It would only be a matter of time before they reached the boat.

Popov twisted to Mac and barked, 'There are assault rifles and magazines under the bed in the cabin. Bring back two—'

'Guns? Is that what this delivery is?'

Popov savagely hissed, 'We don't have time to talk about what I might and might not be delivering. If you don't get those guns, we're dead men.'

Reuben's men were getting closer.

'Reuben changed the time of the delivery,' Popov threw out quickly.

That made the heat in Mac's gun hand intensify. 'But Reuben said that Bolshoi changed the meet time . . .'

Mac felt like he was being sucked into a rat hole. Why would Reuben lie about Bolshoi?

'Mister Bolshoi doesn't work with people who suddenly think they are the boss,' the other man said, supplying the answer for Mac.

But was it the right answer? Is that what this was all about? Reuben trying to take over Bolshoi's operation?

Mac hitched the gun up a quarter of an inch. 'I'd better get on with killing you then . . .'

Popov's gaze drilled into him. 'Are you sure you're going to have time to shoot me and get off this boat before Reuben's men reach us, Detective John MacDonagh?'

The chill of being totally engulfed in the rat hole spread through every nerve ending Mac had; he felt stunned that Popov knew who he was. But before he could deny it, the other man rapidly continued.

'Mister Bolshoi knows everything and, from what he hears, Reuben thinks you're dead. If Reuben comes on board, you're a dead man; I'm a dead man. So get the guns now.'

seventy-eight

10:53 p.m.

The sound of the men on the dock was getting closer, their voices getting louder.

Mac remained frozen until Popov yelled, like an officer in combat, 'Do as you're told.'

Without warning, he leapt forward and snatched the automatic from Mac. Mac jumped forward, but Popov stepped out of reach. Swivelled round and, holding the gun with both hands, pumped the air full of lead as he fired at Reuben's men. One toppled headlong into the water, while the others broke for cover.

'Mac, the guns,' Popov yelled, not turning to him, but keeping his finger pulling back against the trigger.

Mac ran back down to the cabin. Under Popov's bed was an arsenal of assault rifles – AK47s, M16s, T65s and a deadly accurate-looking Bakalov. Mac grabbed two AKs and as many magazines as he could carry and hit the stairs again. He crouched low as he reached the top, hearing the high-pressure crack and pop of bullets echoing in the air. He kept up his bent position as he ran to Popov, who snatched one of the rifles and threw Mac's piece away with contempt.

'Get to the front end of the boat.' Popov shot out commands like he was back as a soldier on the battlefield. 'Lie down like me – hug the deck like a lover, keep narrow . . .'

Mac ran, head down, to the bow of the boat, hiding behind the anchor housing. Reuben's men were keeping up a steady roll of shooting, and parts of the yacht were flying off into the water. The men were shouting insults as they fired. Mac shook as the deck vibrated with the return fire from Popov, who was now shouting insults back. 'Come on, you sons of whores! There's only two of us! Why are you hiding like old women?'

Popov let loose another round of bullets while two of the gang, who'd been goaded into the open, fell dead. He cackled with laughter.

Mac was stunned at the transformation of Popov from calm businessman to maniac soldier who obviously didn't fear death.

Mac kept his rifle trained on the buildings in front of him but could see no one. The silence wasn't really silence at all; he knew there was something happening, but he just couldn't hear it. Two heads popped out, Jack-in-the-box-style, from round the corner of a building. Mac took aim. Squeezed the trigger. Shit, nothing happened.

Mac hunted around for the safety catch. Found it. Released it. Two men ran along the shadow of the wall. His body and the boat vibrated as he fired at the enemy. They fell into the dark of the night.

Popov taunted, 'Come on, girls! Stop wetting your trousers and come out and fight like men!'

In front of him, Mac saw two more men, their heads bobbing over a car bonnet they were sheltering behind. He took aim and sprayed the car. The men fired back, pushing Mac deeper behind the anchor housing. They exchanged fire until one of the men emerged dragging his wounded partner with him. Mac was momentarily distracted by another sound. Sounded like a splash, but he didn't have time to check out what it was as bullets tore up the deck near him. A bullet went over his head and Mac fell back, slamming flat against the deck. Parts of the mast were splintered by gunfire and lumps of painted wood scattered around him.

'Mister Bolshoi sends his greetings from Hamburg!!!'

Mac turned round and to his horror saw that Popov was no longer lying down but was standing up on the deck in full view of the enemy, loosing off bursts of fire. 'My daughter shoots better than these plastic gangsters! Come on, here I am! Where are you?'

Crazy fucking man. Mac watched in disbelief as Popov walked down the gangplank onto dry land, training his AK on the scene, advancing towards Reuben's gang. 'The Afghans were real fighters, but these schoolgirls . . .'

But there was no more shooting. The enemy was dead, wounded or had fled. The scene was silent. Popov fired a volley of shots in the air to mark his victory and then walked back, gripping the handle of his gun and letting it rest on his shoulder like a duke returning from grouse shooting.

Popov puffed his chest out and inhaled through his nose. 'Don't you just love a good fight? The music of ammunition playing in the air.'

Definitely nuts, Mac concluded.

'Why did you do this?' a voice interrupted.

They both turned to find a man with soaking clothes coming up the last stairs from the cabin.

Reuben.

And in his hand he held an Uzi, pointed straight at Popov. Mac realised that the splash he'd heard must have been Reuben diving into the water, going under, and bashing his way onto the boat by breaking one of the cabin windows below.

'Reuben,' Popov said, and for the first time Mac saw him lose his calm. Shock glazed his face like a coating of unwelcome sweat.

Mac's finger got ready to jerk back on the trigger, but

Reuben sprayed a wave of bullets at his feet and swiftly turned the sub-machine gun back on Popov. 'Don't try it, Mac, or you'll be a dead man – like you should already be.' He switched his attention to the older man. 'Why are you shooting at me?'

Popov looked at him for a few moments before answering, 'Word came through that another gang were here, so I assumed it was them who were shooting at me . . .'

Reuben savagely shook his head. 'Stop bullshitting me. You're not even meant to be here. Where's the delivery?'

Defiance broke into the older man's eyes. '*I'm* the delivery.'

'What?' Reuben couldn't help but take a shocked half-step back. 'I don't understand . . .'

'That's what always worried me about you, Reuben, you never . . .'

Popov's hand moved like lightning and he threw a knife straight at Reuben's gut. He dived to the side as the knife hit and Reuben's Uzi went off involuntarily in his hand. The bullets sparked like uncontrollable fireworks in the air as the gang leader hit the deck. Mac ran over and threw himself on his knees by Reuben. The Russian's breathing came in tight, tiny puffs as he stared at Mac.

'Mil . . . os,' he croaked. A line of blood oozed out of the corner of his mouth.

'Where's Bolshoi?'

'Bolshoi.' Reuben's eyes stared over Mac's shoulder.

Then Reuben's whole face exploded like a crushed tomato, spraying flesh and blood over Mac as a single shot was fired from behind.

Mac twisted round to find Popov with the AK in his hand. Suddenly he understood. There was no Popov, only Mister Bolshoi.

seventy-nine

Mac carefully placed his hands around the dead Russian's shoulders as Mister Bolshoi aimed the gun at him.

'What kind of training do they give you at the police academy?' Mister Bolshoi calmly scoffed. 'It must be pretty poor, because I can't believe you didn't figure out who I was.'

Mac's hands dug into Reuben's corpse just as the high energy sound of a helicopter appeared overhead, its spotlight beaming down on the boat. Sirens split the air in the distance.

'You're a dead man, Bolshoi.'

'I think that's my line to you, Mac.'

Bolshoi's finger hit the trigger as Mac twisted Reuben's body high and around to shield him. The AK's bullets tore into the Russian's body, making it jerk. Suddenly Bolshoi's gun jammed. Frantically he pressed against the trigger. Nothing.

'Drop your weapon,' a voice yelled from the dock.

Mac turned to find the youths who had pestered him on bikes earlier, except this time he realised they were cops. Their hoods were replaced with checked caps and they were wearing armbands indicating who they really were. That meant the cops had been there from the start and must have known the 'delivery' was coming in, but they'd let the battle rage. What the fuck was going on?

Mac's attention switched back to Bolshoi, who threw his gun to the deck and ran for the edge of the boat.

'Don't move or we'll—'

But Mac moved. Bang, a shot tore into the deck, but he carried on, changing the pattern of his run into a zigzag motion, which would make him a harder target to hit. Bolshoi disappeared like a silhouette into the water. Mac dived after him.

eighty

11 p.m.

Liquid black surrounded him. Pulled him down. His mind
flashed back.

The water.

Sea.

Stevie floating, his head submerged.

Mac dragging out his body.

Cuddling and crying as he held his son close to his heart . . .

Mac broke the surface. Gasping, he pulled in mammoth
blasts of air. Where the fuck was he? Where was Stevie? He
was cold, so cold. Then his mind clicked into place. Bolshoi.
Mac tore into the water, but soon realised that swimming fully
clothed, in the dark, in sub-zero temperatures, was no easy
matter. Inside his head he chanted:

One. Roll. Two.

One. Roll. Two.

He kept his body going to this rhythm and was soon chopping his way through the water. He knew Bolshoi would swim
to the other side. There was nowhere else for him to go.
Gunshots echoed behind him again, but it was unclear if this
was a deliberate attempt to kill him and Bolshoi, or merely the
frustration of the police as their targets escaped.

It was so cold that Mac felt the water was stripping away

his skin. But he kept going, from time to time seeing a head and arms in front of him, at other times nothing. But the murdering bastard was out here somewhere . . . Mac's gaze froze. Was that a flicker of something going towards the foot-bridge? No . . . Yes, there it was again, bobbing in the water. He couldn't be sure . . . He started power-swimming, arms chopping, legs going, the expression on his face filling with rage as it jerked from side to side. He got closer. Yeah, there he was in the black water all right. Bolshoi.

Without warning, a wave of weariness struck Mac. He tried to shrug it off, shake the dizziness smothering his eyes. His body still moved but it was like a weight dropped on top of it was pushing him down. He went under. Let out a soundless gasp as the water swallowed him up.

Come on. Come on. COME ON.

He fought the tiredness. Fought the water.

Come on. Come on. COME ON.

He made it to the surface in time to see Bolshoi reach the opposite side of the dock, slightly further down from the bridge. Mac pulled in a huge lungful of air and an immense feeling of power entered him. He went after Bolshoi like a man possessed. Bolshoi heaved himself up and out of the water. Off to his left.

The iron ladder out of the water was still wet from where Bolshoi had hauled himself out, but when Mac reached the top there was no sign of the Hamburg master criminal. But he couldn't have gone far. Even for a man as strong as him, that swim would have been an effort. He wouldn't have run in the direction of the police. Or along the dockside, where any fugitive would be exposed. It must have been straight ahead. Down a street that led away from the docks. Mac, soaking and freezing, began his pursuit.

But he didn't have to go far. On a side road, he saw two men struggling. One was Bolshoi and the other a man whose phone he was attempting to steal. The phone owner was soon punched to the ground and Bolshoi hurriedly typed in a number on the mobile. Mac reached for his gun but then remembered it had been tossed away on the deck of the yacht. But he still had the flick knife from Club Zee in his soaking pocket. Charged.

Bolshoi swung round but was too late. The knife penetrated the jacket and jammed into the flesh of Bolshoi's shoulder. But Mac was off balance and the strength in his arms had been drained like a battery. The Russian yelped slightly with pain and shock and pushed his attacker onto the ground, the knife skittering further down the road. Mac crawled over to the weapon. Reached it. Picked it up and stood up in one move. He lunged, but the older man was ready this time. Bolshoi grabbed his wrist, and that's when Mac saw the tattoo on Bolshoi's arm.

Red star, yellow border, with writing over and above it.

But Mac didn't have time to dig into its significance as Bolshoi turned, and then hauled Mac onto his injured shoulder. He threw Mac like a wrestler to the ground.

Mac let out a tiny shrill of pain as he landed on his back. He tried to get up, but his body didn't react. That same weight of weariness that had plunged him beneath the water was back again. But this time he couldn't move. Just couldn't do it.

He saw Bolshoi examine his shoulder wound and shrug as if it didn't matter. Then he walked over to the flick knife.

Get up. Get up. For pity's sake, get up.

But Mac's body was a dead weight with nothing more to give.

Bolshoi picked up the knife. Turned his attention with deadly intent to Mac. He used his foot to roll Mac onto his back and then pressed his foot on his neck.

'And we were getting on so well, you and I.'

Even talking was a strain now for Mac's inert body, 'Kill me now. Because if you don't, I'll chase you all over Europe until you're dead. Who did you get to kill Elena? Reuben? Calum? . . .'

Bolshoi leaned his weight on his foot, digging into Mac's windpipe. 'I take it you're talking about Calum Burns. I use his services from time to time, but not to kill people. That's not his field . . .' His voice came to a sudden halt. Started again, but this time the tone was much higher. 'Kill who? Who did you say has been killed?'

Mac said nothing. Bolshoi raised his foot and stamped once against Mac's chest. Mac hunched inwards with the startling pain.

'Kill who?'

'Elena. Elena's dead.'

The other man turned his head. Even in the dim streetlight, Bolshoi's face had taken on a strange expression, as if it was him who had been thrown and kicked. He turned back. 'Where's Katia?'

'I don't know . . . I don't know . . .'

Finally energy poured back into Mac's system. He reached for Bolshoi's foot as a burst of sirens screamed in the background. Distracted, both men turned. Bolshoi jumped away from Mac.

'Do you buy lottery tickets?' he abruptly asked Mac.

'Lottery tickets?'

'You should – you're a lucky guy.'

Bolshoi ran into the darkness. Mac tried to get up, but weariness pulled him back.

eighty-one

Mac finally managed to stand up and run. But there was no sign of the other man. Mac stopped. Leaned over, letting his palms slide against his thighs as he pulled in some much-needed air. Then he rose up and looked back over the water at Bolshoi's yacht. It had been sealed off with police yellow tape, black writing:

POLICE LINE DO NOT CROSS

No one appeared to be on the small yacht. The only way back was through the water. And going back was essential. But to think about going into the water meant accepting, in his current condition, that drowning was almost certain. So there was no thinking about it, and the whoosh of the dive, the cold water on his face, came almost as a surprise.

But re-crossing the dock was different from his first swim. The freezing water was like a bucket of water in a boxer's face. The damp clothes that clung to his body, draining it of heat, were set free again and, with no one to pursue, he kept up a slow but steady pace back to the yacht. The quayside was covered with police vehicles and ambulances. Bolshoi wouldn't be among them, but some indication of where he was going might be on his boat. Unless, of course, Bolshoi wasn't really the answer.

Mac couldn't shake the memory of his face in the streetlight as it turned at the news of Elena's death. Of course criminals were practised actors. They had to be, in their line of work. But there was a world of difference between a gangster, sitting in an interviewing room at a police station, denying everything with a wink of the eye at the law, and a crim standing in the street with his foot on a cop's neck and a knife in his hand, denying everything. And Mac knew the difference.

He choked, his head hanging too low in the water as his mind played over the previous hour's events. Jerking it back upwards, he spat out the oil-tainted filth in his mouth. But he was near now. Mac pushed his legs across the last few yards and held his hand against the side of the yacht. Working his way round the vessel, he came to the anchor chain. Above it was the smashed window Reuben had used to get inside. He searched for the chain attached to the anchor, but couldn't see it. Shit, he didn't think he had enough puff left in him to leap up to the window. He didn't have a choice . . . One . . . Two . . . Three . . . He leapt up . . . Missed. The bounce of the water caught his flagging body as he re-entered it.

He couldn't do this. Couldn't do this. Couldn't..

He jumped up again. This time one hand caught in the window frame. His arm muscles stretched in pain as his body swung to the side. He kicked his legs out. His other came up. He grabbed the window. Wiggling like a creature from the sea, he pulled himself up. And in. He landed on the cabin's floor, wet, breathing like crazy.

Finally, he looked around as he stood up. The bed was still there, of course, and the covers showed where Bolshoi had been sitting while he spun his stories of Andreas Schmidt and Andrei Popov. The guns. The magazines. Some kitchen utensils and expensive food with German labels. But not much else. Nothing that would throw any light on what Bolshoi had really been up to in London or what his connection had been with Elena's killing.

Mac picked up the charred photo that he'd left on the table by the bed. There was no point in putting it in his pocket to become soaked, so after a moment he returned it. And on the table next to it was a mobile phone. Mac sat on the bed, the ship rocking gently under him, and began to go through its various functions. He found calls from and to Bolshoi with Reuben's name, together with some from Calum, interspersed with dozens of others to persons unknown. And calls, lots of them, from and to Elena and Katia. But of course Bolshoi knew the two women, he'd admitted it himself.

The text inbox showed messages from Elena and Katia. He went to the last one from Elena and opened it up. But he never got to read it. So engrossed was he that he hadn't noticed a figure walking down the steps into the cabin. As Elena's message appeared on the phone's screen, he heard a voice say, 'I'll take that, Mac.'

Phil Delaney.

eighty-two

11:53 p.m.

Mac was sitting in the back of his superior's car in St Katharine Docks. The tension between him and Phil was as taut as the blanket he had wrapped around his shoulders to ward off the night cold.

'Have you found Bolshoi yet?' Mac snapped.

Phil lifted an eyebrow at his disrespectful tone. 'You were ordered to leave this investigation alone. I wouldn't worry about Bolshoi if I were you; you've got more important things to take care of. Like what you're going to say to DI Wray when she gets out of hospital and arrests you for the murder of that Russian girl.'

Mac twisted to face Phil, the blanket slipping back on one side. 'I didn't kill her – but Calum Burns – don't know what kind of game he's playing –' Mac remembered how the other man had saved his life recently. 'But he's connected to both Volk and Bolshoi. I saw Bolshoi's phone. He was in touch with Calum. What was that about? Yachting tips?' His voice became uncertain. 'What if he murdered Elena?'

'Don't talk crap, Mac. You killed the girl. And yes, I do remember Calum, but I don't see what he's got to do with this mess.'

'Don't you?' Mac stared at Phil, but his superior held his

gaze. 'Your security files say different,' Mac continued. 'You knew all along that Calum is deep in this.'

Phil reared into Mac's face, irritation twisting his features. 'Right, you need to listen to me carefully, because I've got a proposal to make and I need you to have a clear head.' He eased back slightly, away from Mac. 'I don't know what happened to that girl and, I'll be brutally honest, I don't care – I've got more important fish to fry. But Wray appears to have solid evidence against you. Add in whatever you've been up to today, including your wild escapade at The Fort, you're looking at a charge sheet long enough to put you behind bars for the rest of your natural life.'

'Yeah, but–'

But Phil wasn't in the mood to let him finish. 'You're one of my best men and I don't want to see it go that way for you. I can make all this go away, speak to the right people and your name won't even be mentioned in relation to this investigation. You'll remain a member of my squad, even though you blatantly disobeyed orders. But in return, I need you to do something very simple. Go. Home. Forget about Bolshoi, Calum, Reuben, arms deals, shootings – and everything else you've seen and heard today.'

Mac looked at him with contempt. 'You're no better than Calum, are you? You're just another cop for hire like him. You and the rest of them. Like your mates in the Home Office–'

Phil interrupted, 'Home Office? Who said anything about H.O?'

'But I saw it in the computer files . . .'

'Did you?' The other man's voice was hard. 'Like I said Mac, forget everything you saw today. Go. Home. This is my final offer. I can't help you otherwise.' Then he added, 'We're talking about the national interest here.'

Mac burst out laughing. 'National interest? You sound like

a bent MP. I'll say this for Calum – at least he doesn't pretend to be doing his thing for anything other than raw cash.'

But Phil wasn't listening. Instead he was focused on a car that had pulled up abruptly behind police lines. Someone jumped out, but in the dark Mac couldn't make out who it was. Whoever it was was determinedly heading their way.

'Oh great, that's all I need. Supercop . . .' Phil said through gritted teeth.

A splash of streetlight caught the newcomer.

Rio.

From what he could see of her face, she looked pissed, really pissed. He could just see the base of the bandages on her wrist, now mainly covered by her coat.

The first thing she did when she reached them was to wrench open the back door in typical don't-mess-me-around Rio style. 'Someone'd better tell me what the effing hell is going on here.'

Mac spoke, not giving her an answer to her question. 'Shouldn't you still be in hospital? When I found you–'

'So you're the man who called the ambulance,' she interrupted, her deep brown eyes slightly widening. Then her gaze tightened as she continued, 'Well, thanks for saving my life. Now Mac, I'm arresting you for the murder–'

'No.' The single word from Phil stopped her. 'You need to speak to your superior officer, because this case is now being run by my team, like I informed you earlier . . .'

That stubborn expression covered Rio's face. 'No, I'm taking him in.'

'I'm giving you a direct order as a higher-ranking officer to turn round. Exit this crime scene. Check yourself back into the hospital . . .'

'And what, Phil? Contact Detective Martin's parents to let them know that we're doing sweet FA to find their son's butcher while another killer is sitting pretty in your car?'

Phil? Since when did Rio call the head of The Research Unit Phil? Mac's gaze swung between the two of them.

'If anyone has to atone for his death, maybe you should look closer to home,' Phil threw back, his body jamming slightly forwards.

The air became charged as Rio battled with her emotions, her face almost crumbling. That got Mac sitting up straight. There was something familiar, almost intimate, about the way his superior and Rio were head-butting and bitching.

'You both sound like Mr and Mrs.' Only when it was out did Mac realise he'd said his thought aloud.

Immediately Rio and Phil snapped their intense gazes away from each other. What was going on here?

'That was meant to be a joke,' Mac let out slowly, as it finally dawned on him that there might be more going on between the two than he'd realised.

Rio slammed her gaze back onto Phil. 'Screw. You,' she spat at him. 'You don't give a toss that Mac obviously isn't well, that he isn't coping. That I was attacked by some mad person with a tattoo that was exactly the same as the victim's . . .'

Tattoo.

The only other person he knew, apart from Elena, who had that tat was Bolshoi. Blinding anger swept through Mac's bloodstream with renewed killer energy. Fuck Phil and his 'I'll look after you' routine.

As his superior and friend got deeper into their verbal clash, face to face, eyeball to eyeball, Mac slowly eased out of the other side of the car and slipped away.

eighty-three

Midnight

The new day began with Mac knowing he didn't have a back story on Bolshoi. Mac cursed his disadvantage as he found Club Zee's fake paramedic motorbike. He put the helmet on and started the engine. He wasn't sure where to begin the hunt for his man without some Intel on Bolshoi's associates and potential hangouts in London, but he had to start somewhere. Finding Bolshoi was a long shot, but he had no other options, and it was more than likely he was still on the streets somewhere. A strange man, in a strange city, unfamiliar with the streets, it was just possible he was out there. Mac refused to believe that he wasn't.

Mac took the bike back to where he'd fought his battle with the gangster and then slowly drove around the neighbouring roads, down to the riverfront and back again.

Nothing.

He mounted the pavement and drove down alleyways, across patches of grass and through the forecourts of flats, both social housing and expensive.

Nothing.

Frustrated, Mac brought the bike to a shuddering halt. He wasn't getting anywhere by just driving around; he needed to think.

Where would he hide in a situation like this if he were Bolshoi?

Think, think, think.

The last place the cops would be looking for him was near the yacht. He'd worked a case, years back, a people-trafficking ring, where the main man had escaped. Turned out that he'd been lying low for a day and a half in a neighbour's garden shed, waiting for the cops to leave his house. He would've got away with it as well, if the neighbour's bruiser of a dog hadn't started sniffing and snarling at the shed.

Feeling defeated, Mac knew there was no way he was going to find Bolshoi. And the cold was getting to him as well, making him shiver violently as it settled deep into his bones. Maybe he should listen to Phil and go home. Rest up and then plan how he was going to find Bolshoi tomorrow. He thought about Rio. How she'd almost died. She was the only real friend he had left in the world and he'd almost lost her. He'd seen the pain in her face when she'd talked about the death of Detective Martin . . . And what had he offered her? Fuck-all. Hadn't even said sorry, placed a comforting arm around her shoulder. He needed her to know that he would be there for her just like she'd been there for him after Stevie.

So he revved up the bike engine and headed back to where he'd left Rio and Phil. The night and shadows danced over him as he made his way there. He saw the headlights of a car coming his way. He dipped closer to the other side of the road as the car came into view. It must've been a dark colour because it blended in with the night. But he wasn't really paying attention to the vehicle; all he could think about was finally getting some peace as he placed his head on his pillow. Well, as much peace as he could, with Elena's murderer still out there. He drew up to a traffic stop the same time as the car. Red light. He stopped, so did the car. The beat of the engine throbbed through him as he turned his head slightly to the side. Towards the car. That's when he got a good look at it close up for the first time. Merc. Different from the gunmen's one earlier, which had had raised ridge lines on the bodywork; this one was simply plain, a dead ringer for Phil's, in which he'd been sitting not that long ago. He leaned forward slightly and saw the driver's face – Phil. He noticed his superior's mouth moving and realised that he was talking to someone in the back. Must be Rio, Mac decided, taking her back to the hospital. Good, that's where she belonged.

Mac moved his head slightly back to see if he could catch Rio's eye. Stupid, she isn't going to realise it's you with your helmet on. So he moved back as he started pulling the helmet off.

Saw who was in the back seat.

Not Rio.

Bolshoi.

So Phil had already picked him up. Suddenly another face came into view. Mac shook his head. No, he couldn't be seeing straight. No way could that be Calum, sitting next to the Russian. But it was. And there was Phil, driving in the front, like it was the most ordinary day of his life.

eighty-four

Mac gave his head one quick shake. Maybe the cocktail of drugs in his system was messing with his mind again. No, they were still there. And now Bolshoi was laughing at something that Calum had said. Laughing. Bitch. He wasn't allowed to laugh while Elena was dead. Mac's already chilled blood ran colder as he wondered if all three of them had been involved in Elena's death.

The Merc pulled away. Mac twisted the motorbike round. Cut the lights. Followed, keeping a distance between them. On the narrow roads and with traffic diverted because of the gun battle down by the river, they weren't hard to keep up with. He kept tabs on them for a couple of miles before they turned into a smart four-storey terrace in Victoria Park, still in East London. He knew the house. It was owned by the government and occasionally used by The Research Unit as a safe house for people they were 'looking after'. Why was Phil taking Bolshoi to a safe house?

Mac hung back and watched the three men exit the car. Go into the house. Less than a minute later, Mac stood outside, a dark figure wondering how to get in. He was way too tired to go all Spiderman up the side of the building. He felt in his pocket for his new best buddy – the flick knife. Opened it and, with great care, tucked it up his sleeve. It was a few steps down the garden path and then up the steps to the heavy wooden door with its jet knocker.

He banged twice against the door

No answer. No sounds. But was that a flicker of the downstairs curtain?

Bang. Bang.

No answer.

'Open the bloody door,' he yelled, kicking it with as much force as his leg muscles could handle.

The door opened. Calum, his Glock trained point-blank on Mac.

Before Mac could speak, Calum yelled, 'It's your psycho member of staff, Phil. Do you want me to shoot him?'

Mac bared his teeth and reared into Calum, making the nozzle of the gun press hard against his chest. 'Go on, fucking kill me, because I tell you, if you don't, I'm going to take you down.'

Calum's face steamed up with an anger to match Mac's. 'Don't think I wouldn't.' He pressed the barrel deeper into Mac's flesh.

The men glared at each other. With one move, Mac flicked the knife up and out. Had the blade touching the skin of Calum's neck, near that strange red, misshapen lipstick-style print, which – close up – now looked more like a burn.

'Back off, both of you,' Phil's voice boomed behind them.

But they didn't move. Neither could let go of the unfinished business between them.

'Now,' Phil insisted.

Calum was the first to move back. Mac swiftly turned to his superior and growled, 'If you don't tell me what's going on . . .'

'Calm down,' Phil ordered, weariness punctuating his tone. 'Come inside.'

Inside was a functional sitting room with basic furniture and heavy-duty curtains. But the only thing that Mac noticed was Bolshoi sitting in an armchair, smoking a cigar. Calum placed his gun on a side table and sat down. Mac eyed the gun but was distracted by Phil, who was obviously pissed at his presence.

'I don't care about this case,' Mac started breathlessly, never taking his gaze off Bolshoi, but directing his words at Phil. 'Don't care why you're hooked up to these other two like the three bent musketeers. All I want is the person who killed Elena. And I know one of you bastards isn't telling me the truth.'

Phil looked at Bolshoi. 'Do you know anything about this girl's murder?'

Bolshoi blew pungent smoke across the room before simply saying, 'No.' He took another puff before adding, 'Although I can take some educated guesses.'

Phil looked at Calum who sighed, 'I don't know why he thinks that I had anything to do with it. I don't know who killed her. If I'm such a murdering bastard, why didn't I shoot you for Reuben while I had the chance?'

'Who knows why you do what you do? You'd do anything for anyone if the cash was right.'

'But you weren't paying me, were you? Has it crossed that messed up mind of yours that I was trying to save a friend?'

Friend? Who the hell did Calum think he was kidding? He only ever did stuff if it worked to his advantage. Before he left this house, Mac vowed, he'd find out not only what Calum had been up to, but every other sordid detail of what these three men were doing together as well.

Calum's hand went to his back pocket, making Mac stiffen his body into a defensive pose. The other man pulled something out and handed it to Mac. His warrant card. Mac took it. If Calum was waiting for 'thank you' he was going to be waiting a hell of a long time.

Mac eyeballed the box of cigars sitting on the mantelpiece as he tucked his warrant card away. 'Are the smokes going free?'

Delaney looked at the box. 'Yes, I suppose so.'

Mac got up and walked over to the mantelpiece. Picked up the box and opened it, but it fell out of his fingers and onto the floor. He bent down and began picking up the scattered Havanas. When he found one under the side table, he took it with one hand, grabbed Calum's pistol with the other and swung round and pointed it at Bolshoi's head. 'I'll shoot him, so help me. I need answers. You've got some and I want to hear them. Otherwise your friend is going to get his head blown off.'

Calum tutted and rolled his eyes. 'It isn't loaded, Mac. I took the ammo out because I knew you'd pull this stunt.'

Mac pressed the trigger. Click. Click. He threw it to the floor.

Bolshoi was still puffing on his cigar and seemed relaxed. 'Delaney, why don't you put the poor man out of his misery and tell him what's been going on?'

Phil sighed. Spoke. 'For the last three months, Mister Bolshoi's been assisting Her Majesty's Government.'

eighty-five

12:20 a.m.

Mac sat on the edge of the seat, the gun back on the table, still stunned by what Phil had revealed. His superior looked at him with something like sympathy.

'I'm sorry, Mac, but we're playing big boys' games here and, with respect, you're not a big boy. I might have found you a role in the final phase of the operation but you weren't needed. Especially in view of your somewhat erratic behaviour over the past few days . . .'

'I can still do my job.'

'Not from Cambodia you can't – that's where you were going this morning, wasn't it? Instead of which, you and your old friend Rio nearly messed up a highly sensitive operation.'

'A dirty operation.'

'It was all authorised.'

That was no surprise to Mac, he'd seen clearance from the Home Office on Phil's files. But now he knew exactly what H.O. had been clearing. 'So let me guess,' Mac started, 'your jet-setting, murdering comrade here did a deal with you to round up the London end of the operation so you could stop that gang war everyone's been talking about. Am I getting warm? Although I can't see what was in it for him, or why the fireworks started down on the docks.'

Bolshoi sat amused as he smoked his cigar. He gestured at Mac with the cigar and said to Phil. 'He's good, your employee. I like him.'

Phil didn't get the joke. 'Don't worry about the managerial side of things. I've told you this is big boys' games.'

The Russian seemed to be enjoying himself, and ignored Phil's attempts to stop him explaining. 'I needed the London end of my operation wound up, Mac. Normally I would have to pay top dollar to get it done professionally but, as Mr Delaney here offered to round them all up for nothing – well, that's the kind of business I like.' He sighed. 'But in the end I had to kill most of them myself from the yacht. If you want a job done, you have to do it yourself, as usual. Your English police are no more efficient than in Germany or anywhere else.'

This was too much for Phil. 'We would have rounded the whole gang up as arranged if the operation hadn't been brought forward by Reuben Volk. Something that you, for some reason, forgot to advise us of.'

Bolshoi remained relaxed. 'I sent you a message. It's not my fault if your people don't communicate with one another. If I had staff that incompetent, I'd shoot them.'

Mac interrupted their verbal ping-pong. 'And what about him?' He couldn't bring himself to use Calum's name. 'Did the Home Office clear a deal with him as well?'

'Stop it, Mac,' Phil warned.

But now he was centre-stage, Mac was in no mood to give up the spotlight. 'Let's see, it would be money with our dirty ex-copper here, wouldn't it? Tenners are his morals these days. Or did you agree to turn a blind eye to his law-breaking in return for his help? Yes, it would be that. No paper trail then.' He stared at Calum with contempt. 'And after all you've said about the police . . . and here you are working for them.'

Calum shoved his chin up, his green gaze defiant. 'Perhaps, but I earned my side of the deal. I got tasered by Delaney after Reuben's boy's birthday party for my trouble.'

The three thieves were falling out. 'That was an honest mistake. I thought you were Mac . . .' But then Phil stopped, drew breath and raised his hands. 'OK, that's enough. I told you on the quayside to make yourself scarce, Mac, go home, say nothing and I'll make sure there's no comeback about your escapades today. If you don't, you'll be on your own . . .'

Mac said nothing. He wasn't surprised that Phil had hired the services of Bolshoi and Calum in his effort to put Reuben's gang out of business. Fuck, he didn't want to admit it, but he knew it had been the right thing to do. Bolshoi and Calum would have carried on with their thing anyway, while now at least a violent gun outfit had been wound up and a war avoided. He'd done it himself often enough. Traded information for favours; defended the bad against the worse. There was no black and white in this world; it was all smoke and mirrors. It wouldn't have surprised him to discover that everything he thought he knew so far was the exact opposite of the truth. Except for one thing. Elena was still dead. And he still didn't know who'd killed her.

The hunt was still on.

'Sure.'

'Sure?' Phil fixed him with a penetrating stare that only eased up when Mac's expression remained the same. 'Good. OK then. You head along.'

'On one condition. One of you three jokers knows something about Elena's murder. If you tell me what it is, I'll be about my business.'

Calum shrugged his shoulders. Phil rolled his eyes in despair. Bolshoi remained impassive. Mac caught Bolshoi's eye.

'Oh please,' the Russian said. 'You don't still think I had

anything to do with Elena's killing. You seem to have forgotten, your colleague Rio Wray was nearly killed this afternoon by an assailant at Katia's home. Of course at the time I was on my yacht, as Mr Delaney here will be happy to confirm.'

'He's right,' Phil quickly added. 'Rio was attacked by a guy with a tattoo. Some Red Army thing. I spoke to her before they shipped her back to Mission Hill Hospital.'

Mac jumped in. 'But Calum and I found texts on Elena's phone from you saying you were going to kill her . . .'

'I never sent her any texts,' Bolshoi countered. 'If I was trying to cover my tracks, it would be a stupid thing for me to leave incriminating messages on her phone.'

Mac knew he wasn't making sense but he still had one more ace up his sleeve. 'What I'm sure *Mister* Bolshoi hasn't shared with you is that he has the same tattoo.'

Both Phil and Calum fixed their stunned gazes onto the Russian.

'Come on,' Bolshoi slammed in. 'If I was the person at Katia's house, would I have let you see the tattoo earlier?'

'So who else has got one?' Mac shouted.

'Only three people I know of,' Bolshoi offered. 'Me, Elena and her father. They're dead, I'm not, so whatever this Rio Wray saw, I'm sure it couldn't have been that tattoo.'

'Well, happily Rio is safely tucked back up in the hospital, where I'm sure she'll soon be fully restored – her very dodgy memory included,' Phil added.

But Mac wasn't buying it. Rio was the best cop he knew, so no way would she get a detail like that wrong.

'The only person left who might know is Elena's sister, Katia–' Mac urgently threw in.

But Phil had obviously had enough. 'Mac,' he interrupted sternly. 'Piss. Off.'

Mac gave Bolshoi one last, see-you-in-hell look, then got

up. Held his hand over his trouser pocket and left the room without a word. When he was outside, he walked slowly down the street. He had nothing. He knew about Katia but not nearly enough to find her. He'd already been to her home, but hadn't had time to look over it properly. And now the police would have it under lockdown because of Detective Martin's murder, so it was going to be too hard to get into. And he still didn't know what, if any, connection she had to Elena's murder. Behind him he heard a front door slam and hurried footsteps. He turned to find Bolshoi catching him up.

The two men stood next to each other for a few moments before Mac asked, 'Shouldn't you be inside with your two buddies getting a DVD and a Hawaiian pizza?'

'I told Mr Delaney I was going outside for some air.' Then he added in a whisper, 'Have you got a plan?'

Mac wasn't sure that he had but said, 'You think I'm going to tell you? Think on . . .'

'I've already explained that I never sent Elena any of these –' Bolshoi waved the hand that held the cigar – 'texts. That I was a close associate of her father's in the army and promised him that I would look after her and her sister if he ever died. Did you know that he died right in front of me during an ambush in Afghanistan?' He took a deep breath. 'You were not the only person to love her. I loved her a lot longer than you did, Mr MacDonagh.'

The muscles in Mac's jaw bunched and pumped.

The older man continued: 'You need to start thinking with your head and not with your heart. You're a police officer. You're familiar with the art of framing someone? I've already told you, those texts were planted. I was framed. Someone wanted you to believe it was me. Surely you can see that?'

Perhaps he was right. The wiping of Elena's phone, except for incriminating texts, had been odd all along and Mac knew it. Something didn't add up, but he didn't know what it was.

'There is someone else with the tattoo,' Bolshoi whispered.

'Who?'

'I can only reveal what I know if you let me help you find Katia—'

'What makes you think my next move includes her?' Mac shot out.

'She's the only link left. I need to make sure she's safe.'

'Why?'

'Because she's the link to the tattoo and . . .' Bolshoi inhaled deeply 'And I'm Katia's father.'

eighty-six

It was a sight Mac had never expected to see – the hardened international criminal looking shame-faced.

Bolshoi averted his eyes but explained, 'I'm afraid it's a story of weakness; one I'm not proud of. I slept with Gregory's wife while I was on leave and he was still at the front. It was one of those moments of comfort, not love.' He shrugged. 'It just happened. Neither of the girls knew and Gregory came back on leave so he always thought she was his. But her mother and myself had tests done that proved she's my daughter. Luckily Elena and Katia look like their mother and look very similar to each other.'

'Who else knows about this?'

'No one. All families have secrets, Mr MacDonagh.'

Mac's mind reeled back to what the pole dancer had said about hearing Elena and another person arguing. Family business, she'd thought when she'd heard the word for 'father' in Russian. Maybe Elena had just found out about Katia being Bolshoi's daughter? But that still didn't leave a straight trail of explanation for Elena's murder.

Mac hesitated. Then turned to go, but Bolshoi called after him, 'Perhaps I can give you a word of warning?'

Mac kept walking.

'Your superior's not going to be very happy when he finds you've stolen his car.'

Mac stopped. Half turned back. 'What makes you think I'm taking Phil's car?'

'Drive away in that two-bit motorbike you arrived on or in a black Merc? I know which one I'd choose.'

He was right. Mac walked towards the Merc, the Russian following behind him. Mac reached the back of the car as the older man softly called out his name. Mac looked back as Bolshoi reached him. Then he held out a small black card. He leaned into Mac, shoving the card into his pocket as his other hand leaned against the bottom of his T-shirt, as if needing support.

'I like you, Mac,' Bolshoi said as he stepped back. 'I wouldn't like there to be any unpleasantness between us.'

'What sort of unpleasantness might there be?'

Bolshoi smiled as he twiddled the cigar, but said nothing. Mac left the dirt of family secrets and Bolshoi behind as he strode away and eased into the car. As soon as he got behind the wheel, he pulled the card from his pocket. Business card.

No writing, just a mobile number.

Mac pushed the card back into his pocket. He hot-wired the car. Set the sat nav. Mission Hill Hospital.

As Mac fired the engine, he didn't hear Bolshoi finally answer his question.

'I may have to kill you.'

eighty-seven

1 a.m.

The hospital was surprisingly busy for such an early hour of the morning. Mac hurried through the front entrance, overtaking a woman wearing a floppy hat. Took the stairs, instead of the lift, to the second floor. Entered the Maggie Lane Children's Ward. The corridors were painted a mellow yellow; there was an eerie calm that felt more like a school during class time than a medical facility. He approached the solitary nurse at the main desk.

'I'm looking for Milos Volk,' he said, keeping his tone soft so as not to unsettle the peace around him.

The nurse stared up at him, her gaze assessing. 'Visiting hours are over. Also, we've been told that no one is allowed to see him.'

Mac shoved his hand into his pocket and let his badge do the talking for him.

The nurse visibly relaxed as she said, 'He's in a room down on the corridor to the left.'

'Which room?'

'You'll know which one.'

He knew what she meant as soon as he turned the corner; there was a uniform stationed on a chair outside a room midway down the corridor. Seeing Mac, the policeman stood up. Mac flashed his badge again.

'I don't think there's much point seeing him now, sir, he's asleep.'

Mac ignored the advice and went into the room. A room that had one wall completely composed of a light, bright painting of floating astronauts in space. The wires coming out of the two astronauts were dead ringers for the tubes attached to a sleeping Milos on the bed. His small body was tucked under a blanket that resembled the pattern and design of one of those precious family quilts that were handed down from grandma to mum to daughter.

Mac approached the bed with a hesitation he didn't realise he felt. He stopped by the foot of the bed and pulled off the patient medical chart. The notes said there was nothing physically wrong with Milos, but that he was in aftershock from the trauma of the explosion. He'd been prescribed sedatives of some sort. He put the notes back and moved towards Reuben's son. Stared down at him. His baby skin was pale and worn, his lips just a touch dry. But at least he was alive. Without realising what he was doing, Mac's hand began to move. He let it settle, with the gentleness of a goodnight kiss, in the boy's hair. The strands were damp and clinging tightly to skull and skin. Mac's slim fingers stroked with a calm, slow ease. The hypnotic movement of his hand started to pull his mind back. Back to a time he didn't want to remember. But he couldn't stop the caress of his fingers, just like he couldn't stop the storm of memories that assaulted him . . .

They told him that he could touch him. But Mac's hands lay as lifeless at his sides as the body of his son on the makeshift bed he looked down on. The emergency room had been a hive of activity and manic noise only a few minutes ago; now it was still. Quiet. Just him and Stevie. He couldn't cry, couldn't speak, couldn't move. All he could do was stare at the child he'd called son for the last six years.

'Imagine he's sleeping.'

That's the advice he'd given to a young mum, when he was still a bog-standard detective, before she had to identify her four-year-old daughter who'd been killed by a speeding car. But he knew that Stevie wasn't sleeping. Stevie never, ever slept on his back. Always on his side, facing the window, knees tucked deep in his tummy. And his breathing. It was hard to hear unless Mac almost touched his ear to his son's partially opened mouth. Tiny puffs, grabbing oxygen . . . flowing out. Grabbing . . . Flowing.

He leaned forward, arms still rooted down, towards Stevie's motionless face. Kept going until his ear grazed the top of Stevie's frozen mouth. Listening. Waiting. For that sweet sound of air being drawn in and out. In and out. In and out.

Silence.

But he still couldn't touch him . . .

'Uncle Mac.'

The sound of Milos's weak voice snapped Mac back into the room. Mac's hand dropped from the child's head. The boy tried to speak again but no words came out. His throat convulsed as if he was fighting to catch his breath. So Mac poured some water from the jug on the mobile table into the pink plastic mug covered in polka dots that resembled Smarties.

Milos drank greedily, but Mac eased the cup back slightly and gently instructed, 'Easy, easy. Small sips.'

The child stared up at him with his big eyes and nodded as he sucked moisture into his body. Finally he slumped exhausted back against the pillow.

Mac placed the cup back and said, 'How you doing, kid?'

Milos rapidly blinked. 'I'm not well.'

Mac sat on the side of the bed. 'You're doing good, kid. You'll be buzzing about like a Spitfire before you know it.'

'I'll be all right when my dad comes.'

Mac felt the words oozing in his stomach. He took the boy's small hand and squeezed it.

Milos swallowed. 'Is it the day?'

'What day?'

'The day Daddy doesn't come back? He said that there might be a day when he has to go away, just like his dad did with him. He told me to be brave, to hold my head tall . . . No, up high, my head up high and no crying.' But there were already tears gathered in the bottom of his eyes. 'Uncle Mac, could you ring him up to find out if it's the day?'

What a shitty world it was when parents had to prepare their children for their death. Mac thought through the past day. Of course, it made sense that he'd been thinking only of himself, and that he'd forgotten there were other victims in the fallout from the day's events. He stared deep into the boy's eyes, which stared back up at him, tears sucked back. He was an adult, which meant he must have the answers, because that's what adults were for.

'I'll tell you what,' Mac finally said. 'I've got to go and see someone else. What about if I do that and then come back and talk to you a bit later?'

'Is someone else not well?'

'That's right.'

'OK then.'

Mac hesitated. Then leaned down and planted a light kiss on the boy's cheek. Whispered, 'Don't worry, son; everything's going to be all right. I'll make sure. I promise.'

Easy breath in, easy breath out. In . . . Out. Mac realised that Milos had fallen asleep. He pushed his head back as he gazed down at the child and knew that he owed it to him to tell him that it was *that* day; his daddy wasn't coming back. Mac eased to his feet and made his way to the door. Gently closed it behind him.

His fellow cop was back on his feet.

Mac asked him, 'Do you know which ward DI Rio Wray is on?'

eighty-eight

Another ward, another room. Mac found an impatient Rio sitting in a wheelchair.

'I might have guessed you'd turn up,' Rio threw at him. 'I'm not in the mood.'

He didn't realise she was holding anything until she slung her mobile on the bed in disgust, the bandages on her lower arm pulling tight.

'Tough,' Mac answered. Moving towards her. 'I need your help.'

She stared back at him, eyes blazing. 'I've just spoken to Jamie Martin's father so, whatever you want, I'm not in the mood.' Her voice hit a dead, weary note at the end. She wheeled the chair away from Mac, presenting him with her back.

He didn't need to see her face to witness what she was feeling. Loss, frustration, helpless grief. But he didn't leave her alone, he couldn't. She was the only one who might have the answers he needed about Katia. So he pulled up the spare chair in the room and plonked it in front of her. As soon as he sat down she tried to wheel away again, but he clamped his hands round the arms of the wheelchair.

He spoke evenly and quietly. 'I know this isn't the best time in the world but I need answers.'

Rio punched out a tiny, fun-free laugh. 'That's just what Mr Martin said – he wants answers. Why wasn't his son being protected—?'

'Look,' he cut in sternly. 'It wasn't your fault. Danger, and yeah sometimes death, comes with the job. It's not written in our job descriptions, but we all know it's there, big and bold, right at the top of page one.' He pulled his hands from the chair. 'I know the last thing you want to do is go back over it in your head, but I've got to ask some questions about what went down in that house.'

She tilted her head to the side, her knowing brown eyes roaming over his face with the heat of a laser. 'I thought Phil would've tucked you up for the night in your bedroom and locked the door.'

'Phil?' His gaze dug into her. She didn't look away. 'Are you and Delaney involved—'

'In a Serious Crime Unit tango?' she interrupted boldly. 'Yeah. He's a big boy and I'm a big girl.'

Mac raised an eyebrow. 'He's old enough—'

'To know where to put it.'

Mac matched her eye-for-eye as he switched the conversation back on track. 'The one thing I know about you, Rio, is you hate unsolved cases. And this case is still wide open. But it doesn't have to be like that. Tell me what I need to know and maybe I can close the file on this one for you.'

Rio slammed her head straight. 'Help me? After all the muck you've sprayed around town today, I should arrest you . . .'

'You don't still believe that I killed Elena?'

'All I know is that every time I turned a corner in this case, there's only one face that keeps staring back at me – yours.'

Mac leaned in closer to her. 'You just said that Detective Martin's dad wanted to know why his son was murdered? So what are you going to tell him: that you couldn't be bothered to go that extra mile to find out?'

Rio half hitched herself out of the chair. 'You're bang out of order . . .'

'No, what's out of order is that two people we both swore to keep safe are dead.'

Rio wobbled on unsteady legs. Their stares fought with each other. Then she fell back, making the chair swing slightly to the side. Loud voices came from somewhere outside, but neither of them took any notice, only interested in what sat between them in the room.

Rio twisted her lips and then pulled in a few tight breaths. 'It was Martin who found out that Elena Romanov had a kid sister.'

'How did he find the information?'

'A bit of digging at Europol, and he also had a contact – someone he was sweet on, at the Russian Embassy.'

Russian Embassy. Mac's mind ticked away at that. Someone else had mentioned the embassy today. Who? His thoughts clicked into place – Reuben. At his son's party, he'd said that the last time he'd seen Elena had been at some bash for Russian vets who'd served in the Afghan–Russian conflict. But what did that have to do with anything?

'Did his friend tell him anything else?'

Rio shook her head. 'Can you believe I didn't even know he was gay? I'm meant to be looking out for him, and when did I really take the time to get to know him?'

Mac knew she was hurting bad, but he also needed whatever information she had right now.

Rio must have realised what he was thinking and said, 'Her sister's name is Katia. Martin tracked down her address through the gym she used.' She gave him a funny look. 'I suppose that was you playing cops and robbers, minus the cops, at that gym earlier today?'

Mac had the grace to blush.

But Rio let it pass as she continued, 'When we arrived at the house there was a red Mini parked outside . . .'

'The only car outside when I got there was yours . . .'

'I've got a number plate, but don't get your hopes up – it was fake through and through. The motor will be a burned-out wreck by now . . . But if you still need the plate number . . .'

Rio's hand shook slightly as she fiddled in her pocket and pulled out her notebook and read out the digits and letters on the false number plate.

'And when we got inside . . .' Suddenly Rio squeezed her eyes tight and Mac knew she was back seeing the scene in her head. 'There was nothing unusual about downstairs, but upstairs, in one of the rooms, there was a packed rucksack. And passports with false names. I think Katia must've been getting ready to leave the country. I also found a map of the St Katharine Docks area, and that's how I knew where the action was going to be happening later on.'

The shouting from outside intensified.

'And whoever attacked you had a tattoo, the same one as Elena.'

Rio nodded. 'Yeah, the woman who attacked me—'

Mac sat bolt up straight. 'Hold up. I thought it was a man. How do you know it was a woman?'

'Believe me, a bloke wouldn't be caught dead wearing the perfume I smelt just before I was whacked on the head. It must've been the sister.'

Mac swore low and harsh. Shit, he should've figured out much sooner that the only other logical person to have the tattoo would be Katia. For fuck's sake, it was staring him in the face; it was a family thing – dad, his two daughters and bosom-buddy friend.

'What did you find out about Elena's family . . . ?'

But Mac never finished the sentence because the yelling and hysterically raised voices were now coming from outside the door.

'What the heck . . . ?' Rio said as she swivelled the chair to stare at the door.

Mac got up and opened it; what he found outside was a hospital running on chaos. Medical staff were shouting and waving their arms around. Mac caught the arm of a nurse who rushed by, pulling her back.

'What's going on?'

'There's an emergency situation down on the children's ward.'

An alarmed Rio asked what the emergency was. But Mac didn't wait for an answer. He merely whispered:

'Milos.'

eighty-nine

Milos, Stevie.

Milos, Stevie.

The names twisted and burned in Mac's brain as he flung open the door to the stairwell. Jumped the steps two ... now three at a time. Bashed the door to the children's ward. And hurtled into chaos. People, some in medical uniforms, some not, rushed this way and that along the corridor. A woman and man clutched a child in their arms as they hunched low against a wall. A large glass vase of deep red roses lay broken and leaking water on the floor. The place radiated fear and confusion. His heart punched high against his chest when he saw a crowd of people further along the corridor. That's when he realised where they were gathered – outside Milos's room.

The police guard was nowhere in sight. Mac started running. Almost there, something slammed into his side, shoving him hard against the wall. Quickly he flicked his head to see a nurse tottering towards him. She must have collided with him as she came round the corner. He snapped his arm out to grab her before she fell. When she gazed up at him, dazed, he realised it was the nurse he'd spoken to earlier about Milos.

He yanked her to him. 'Where's Milos?'

Her light brown eyes widened. Then she took a deep breath. 'It was a woman ... Oh God ... She shot him. The–'

Mac didn't wait for her to finish as he thrust her to the side and belted back down the corridor. *He can't be dead. He can't be dead. Not like Stevie.*

He reached the crowd of people. Urgently pushed his way through. Eyes frantically scanning the room. The bed was empty, with the blanket thrust back. His gaze swung to the side . . . his breathing hitched deep in his throat. Three people were on their knees around something he couldn't see. He didn't need anyone to tell him that they were looking down at Milos's body.

Sensing his presence, one of the people on the floor twisted and looked up at him. A man and, judging from the stethoscope in his hand, a doctor. The two other people also turned their attention to Mac, leaving enough space for him to see who they were attending to on the floor. Not a little boy's body, but that of a man. The cop who had been guarding Milos's room. So where the hell was the boy?

'Detective MacDonagh,' Mac threw out as he quickly joined them on his knees near the fallen policeman.

The cop's eyes were open, brimming with pain. Blood seeped from holes in his chest and shoulder. Mac realised that the nurse must have been referring to the cop when she'd uttered, 'He's been shot.'

'What happened?' Mac asked the policeman.

But before he could answer, the doctor broke in, 'For Christ's sake, man, he's seriously injured and needs immediate medical attention. He can't answer your questions.'

But Mac ignored him and asked, 'Where's the boy?'

The injured man swallowed hard. Then spoke in a pain-filled whisper. 'It was a woman . . .' He swallowed again. 'Said she was the boy's relative. I told her that no one was allowed to see him . . .' Swallow. His breathing became harsh. 'That's when she pulled the gun . . . She took him . . .' His voice twisted into a groan.

'Right, that's it,' the doctor ordered. 'No more questions.'

But Mac ploughed on. 'Who was she?'

'I don't care if you're a detective,' the doctor ground out. 'I'll call security to have you escorted from the hospital.'

Mac only got to his feet when the policeman's eyes closed. He stepped back. A woman? There was only one woman left in this murderous tale.

A woman running with a kid was going to be easy to spot. He rushed for the door again, but was stopped by the sound of the cop's voice behind him.

'She had a tattoo . . . Star . . . Red.'

Katia.

ninety

1:17 p.m.

Forty-seven seconds.

  Forty-eight seconds.

  Forty-nine seconds.

Time's running out. Mac chanted furiously in his head as he plunged down the stairs towards the hospital exit. No way was Katia still in the building. Her first priority would be to get Milos away from the hospital. And now Mac's first priority was to get to her before she escaped from the hospital grounds.

  Fifty-two seconds.

  Fifty-three seconds.

He made it to the exit door at the bottom of the stairwell. Punched it open. Hiked up his speed as he stormed down the corridor. The longer he remained in the building, the less chance he'd have of finding Katia and Milos.

  Fifty-six seconds.

  Fifty-seven seconds.

The automatic exit doors were in sight. The sharp, fluorescent lighting sliced into his eyes as he moved forwards. The sweat popped out of the pores on his back. He reached the doors. They hissed sideways.

  One minute.

The unkind, cold air struck Mac as he hit outside. He

scanned the car park. Dead night. Nothing unusual. Then he spotted three figures on the edge of the car park talking together. Quickly he made his way across. Three men. Two were security guards, the other was wearing a high-vis jacket. He caught the end of their urgent conversation – the man in the jacket was explaining to the guards that he'd seen a car.

Mac butted in. 'The car, was it a Mini?'

The man shivered as he gave his attention to Mac. 'Dunno. As I've already told the guys.' He lifted his chin towards the other men. 'It all happened so fast. It came bombing down the slipway . . .'

One of the security men punched in, his expression filled with suspicion as he stared at Mac. 'Who the heck are . . . ?'

Mac impatiently pulled out his badge. Carried on. 'Was it a red Mini?'

The man shrugged. 'Not sure. Could've been.'

'Where did it go?'

'Down the main road.' The man's voice picked up a speed of confidence. 'Then it took a side road about a hundred yards to the left . . . the woman was wearing this summer hat . . . Floppy brim.'

Floppy hat? He'd seen that somewhere recently. Mac's mind went into rewind. *Floppy hat.* His brain screeched to a halt as he remembered – the woman he'd overtaken as he'd rushed into the hospital. He couldn't believe that Katia had been right next to him and he'd let her get away. He felt like pounding a fist against the wall.

'Get all the images from the security camera ready for when the cops get here,' Mac shouted at the guards.

Then he ran to Phil's car. As he turned the ignition, he pumped the engine and then took off towards the exit gate. When they saw him coming, two more security guards stood in front of the gate with their hands raised. While he controlled the car with one hand, Mac desperately tried to find the police siren on the vehicle but failed. He leant heavily on the horn and it howled with a single note over the squealing wheels. But the two men in front of him didn't move, their hands stretched in a gesture meant to stop him. Mac pushed down harder on the accelerator. 'Sorry boys, I'm coming through . . .'

At the last moment, they scattered. Mac heard a crump and a scream as he went by. He flew out into the middle of the road and heard the horn from a car, which narrowly avoided hitting him. Turned the car ninety degrees and accelerated a hundred yards down to the side road that Katia was supposed to have taken. Drove a few yards down the road. It looked like a strange route for a kidnapping desperado to take. Quiet and suburban, it seemed to lead nowhere. Unless . . .

Mac pulled over. Jumped out of the car and began searching the front gardens. It didn't make a good escape route, but it was a good place to throw something away. As he went down the road looking over walls, he noticed a middle-aged woman, in a dressing gown, clipping roses and watching him with suspicion.

He ran over to her and shouted, 'Did you see a car come down this road about ten minutes ago? A red Mini?'

She took an unsteady step back. 'Who the hell are you?'

'I'm a police officer. Just tell me what I need to know, this is an emergency.'

'Yes, I did actually. I've already reported it to the police. Driven by some yob in a hoodie.'

So Katia had ditched the hat.

'He got out and changed the number plate. Threw it into one of my neighbour's gardens and drove off. I went and picked it up.'

'Get it – please. Hurry.'

The woman came back a few seconds later holding a number plate. It matched the vehicle registration that Rio had told him about.

'Was it a male or female?'

'Hard to tell. He or she was wearing a grey tracksuit with a hood. It could have been a girl, I suppose.'

'Was there a kid in the car?'

'I couldn't see one.'

'The car?'

'A red Mini.'

Mac kissed the shocked woman on the cheek and ran back to Phil's car.

He did a three-point turn, crashing into a parked car as he did so, and headed back down towards the main road, reviewing what he'd got as he did so. If he were in Katia's shoes, where would he be headed? Only one place – out of the country. Then he remembered what Rio had said about finding the false passports in Katia's home. She might have an assumed name, but how was she going to do it? He might not have figured that out yet, but what he knew for sure was that he wasn't going to let another little boy lose his life just like Stevie.

ninety-one

Airport? No, that wouldn't work for a kidnapper, Mac reasoned as he drove at a furious pace. Too many checks at an airport. He thought about a ferry. Quiet, unobtrusive, no one would notice an adult and a kid in a car going to France or Belgium. The boy would still need a passport. In fact, that was going to be her insurmountable problem. So why take the kid anyway? A kid she couldn't take anywhere? Mac thought of Bolshoi's yacht. If they were in cahoots, that might work. But the police had put the boat on lockdown. Plus, Bolshoi had claimed he was going looking for her. It didn't make . . .

Mac cursed as he became aware of the road and realised he was heading straight into the back of a stationary car positioned at the roundabout.

He slammed his foot on the brakes, but was going too fast. His body flew sideways as he smashed into the back of the car. The vehicle in front jerked forwards. Mac's head snapped back. Molten pain radiated on the left side of his neck. He tipped his mouth open. Took in large gulps of oxygen. Gritted his teeth as the pain shot into his shoulder as he eased his head straight. He saw a figure getting out of the car in front. Mountain of a man who looked like he had murder on his mind. He inspected the damage done to the rear end of his car and then turned his attention to Mac. Mac tried to restart Phil's car, but the only sound he heard was the rattle of an engine that was going nowhere.

The man reached Mac and hammered on the driver's window.

'I want a word with you,' the man demanded, spit flying with his rushed words.

Mac wasn't in the mood for more aggravation and he needed an out of this situation. So he did the one thing he knew he shouldn't be doing in public – pulled out his gun. Pain still pulsing in his shoulder and neck, he got out of the car and pushed the piece in the other driver's face. The man shuffled back, raising his hands in a defence position. 'No need for any—'

But Mac didn't allow him to finish. 'Change of plan – we're swapping cars.'

'OK. Take it easy, mate.'

'Keys?'

The man quickly shoved a hand in his trouser pocket and pulled out the car keys. Threw them. Mac snatched them from the air in a one-handed catch. Rushed over to the car and stopped dead. Inside was a woman moaning in the passenger seat.

'Get out,' Mac ordered.

Her eyes grew wide with horror when she saw the gun. 'I can't move. I think I've got whiplash.'

'Come on sweetheart . . .'

'Please . . .'

Mac waved the gun. She started crying but didn't move. Quickly he pushed the gun in the front of his trousers. Leaned down and placed an arm around her shoulders, the other under her legs. She screamed with the alarm call of a banshee. He took two steps back, then laid her gently on the road. The woman screamed again. Mac looked across at the man and yelled, 'Don't just stand there, you prat, call an ambulance. It's an emergency.'

Mac scrambled into the hijacked car and hit the road. He knew he was driving on a road to nowhere. He just couldn't figure out how Katia was going to get the hell outta Dodge. Abruptly the words he'd shouted at the terrified driver hit him.

'Don't just stand there, you prat, call an ambulance. It's an emergency.'

An emergency. An emergency.

His head spun with the possibility of what was beginning to form in his mind. He eased the car into a layby. An emergency. A sick child. That would be perfect for someone fleeing the country. A child who'd suffered injuries in an explosive criminal operation. Maybe in those kind of rushed medical situations, a kid didn't need a passport? Or maybe Katia was going to use one of the many false passports Rio had discovered at Katia's home.

He took out his phone and started checking for ambulance flights and other methods for getting an injured kid out of the country, but soon fell short. He didn't have the resources to find out where a woman and child fleeing the country would be able to get a flight under false names.

He leaned his head against the steering wheel. If he didn't find that info soon, Milos . . . Stevie's image crowded his mind. His son was smiling just before he blew out the candles on his birthday cake.

Mac inched his head up. He needed access to those resources now. He yanked out something from his pocket. Studied it. His gut burned. He didn't want to do this. Didn't want to do this. But who else did he know who had access to a web of resources to help him find Katia and Milos.

'It's Mac. I need your help. Meet me at—'

'I know where you'll be, Mac.'

The line went dead.

ninety-two

'How did you find me so quickly?' Mac asked the person who slid into the shadows of the front passenger seat of the car.

He'd been waiting in the car park of a service station on the M25 for no more than ten minutes.

The newcomer pulled out a smoke. Pressed a lighter. The mini-flame cast half of their face out of the shadows.

Mister Bolshoi.

He took two easy drags from his cigarette. Satisfied with the spots the nicotine hit in his body, he gave Mac an answer. 'I stuck a tracking device on the underside of your shirt earlier.'

Startled, Mac immediately raised up the hem of his T-shirt to find something that looked like a tiny black dot. Then Mac remembered how Bolshoi had leaned on him, clutching his T-shirt as he gave him his business card outside the safe house. He should have figured that out, but sheer tiredness had pushed him off centre.

'So, it seems we have a situation here,' the Russian continued.

'Let's lay out some ground rules first,' Mac said, his hand resting securely on the outline of the gun in his trousers.

'I don't make promises, not where the safety of my daughter is concerned.'

'I know what she's up to and I don't think even someone with your resources will work it out. So you need me. And I need you.'

Bolshoi hitched the side of his mouth into what could have been a smile or a sneer. 'When I suggested this temporary partnership an hour ago, you weren't interested – so what's changed?'

Mac tipped his head to the side. 'Just because I've figured out what she's up to doesn't mean I have the know-how to get there . . .'

'Ah, I see. You want me to use my connections to pave the way for you.'

Mac didn't like that he was having to ask this filth-ridden bastard for help but he didn't have much choice. 'Something like that,' he answered tightly.

Bolshoi wound down the window. Flicked the unfinished cigarette outside. 'OK. We can work together to find my daughter. When we catch up with her, I'll order her to tell you what she knows about her sister's killing. Then me and Katia go one way and you go wherever it is that undercover cops creep off to in the dark.'

'And what if she was the one who killed Elena?'

One of Bolshoi's hands curled into a fist against the car seat. 'I won't allow any harm to come to Katia. Surely you understand that?'

Mac thought carefully. He knew the risks he was running getting involved with this man who had his fingers on too many triggers.

'OK. Agreed.'

Bolshoi grunted approval, but added, 'Let me just repeat my warning of earlier – don't give me a reason to put you in the earth next to Elena.'

Mac explained his theory that Katia had kidnapped Milos as part of a plan to flee the country, but Bolshoi was unconvinced.

'Unlikely. A professional would know to keep it simple.

There's a thousand ways to swap from one country to another without being traced.'

'But your daughter isn't a professional, is she? Unless there's something about her you're not telling me?'

Mr Bolshoi pulled out his phone. 'No, she's not . . .' He punched in a number. Spoke. 'Calum . . . ?'

'Are you crazy?' Mac furiously whispered.

Bolshoi ignored him. 'I've got a job for you. I need some information. Reuben's son Milos was kidnapped from the hospital. Our mutual friend Mac thinks the *kidnapper* might be planning to leave the country using the boy as a cover. Can you make some phone calls and see what leads the police have got? If there's anything else in the mix? If they've got any other leads? Spread some money around if you have to . . .' Bolshoi listened and shrugged his shoulders. 'I'm sure Mr Delaney is upset with me. I never said I didn't have business of my own to sort out while I am here. He'll just have to remain, as you English say, "hopping mad".'

He cut the call and looked back at Mac. 'What's with the stony face, my friend? Still holding a grudge against my free-lance employee? Calum's a businessman; you can't expect a businessman to forgo lucrative work to help a former client out. That's not realistic, especially given the circumstances.'

'He's lower than the return on my pension,' Mac spat back. 'Only interested in who bids the highest for his services. He could've told me what was on Elena's phone and saved me a hell of a crap-load of trouble.'

'The simple answer to that is you should have put in a bid for his services. If you'd slipped him some cash this morning, he'd have told you all you needed to know.'

Mac didn't want to admit that Bolshoi was right, but knew he was. When he'd gone to see Calum, he'd worked on the 'friend in need' angle, assuming that would be enough for Calum to help him, rather than recognising the fact that his former friend had turned into a ruthless, money-for-hire operator.

'You shouldn't confuse business with friendship. That's a bad mistake. Men in our line of work shouldn't have friends.'

'I'm not in your line of work.'

Mr Bolshoi laughed at him. 'Deception. Wearing the mask of someone you're not. Believe me, we're in the same type of job.'

The two men waited. Mac wasn't happy doing nothing so he asked: 'If you were looking after Elena as a promise to her dead father, why did you make her one of Reuben's people?'

Bolshoi took out another cigarette. But didn't light up, just played with it between his fingers. 'She's like all young women these days, she wanted her own career. I thought arranging for her to take care of Reuben's comms would keep her out of trouble. That's a low-risk occupation and Reuben was given strict instructions to keep her in the background. But it seems I was wrong about that. She wasn't cut out for this kind of work, anyway. Too much like her father. Too much honour and morals and all that sort of nonsense. You know – the things that keep people poor. And now,' he sighed, 'she's dead.'

'You seem to be getting over it.'

Mister Bolshoi pulled a face. 'Death is my business and I don't get sentimental over business. Unless it's flesh and blood of course. Like Katia. That's different.'

'And does Katia have honour and morals and all that sort of nonsense?'

Bolshoi's phone went off.

He discarded the cigarette. Turned his attention to the phone. Listened. 'Thank you, Calum. Your fee will be paid in the usual way . . .' He sighed again. 'I'm sure that Delaney is, as you put it, tearing this town apart looking for us. No doubt the German surveillance teams will inform him when I'm back in

Hamburg. Or perhaps not, I'm getting bored with that city. Nothing interesting has happened there since The Beatles last played there.' He cut the call again and looked over at Mac. 'Your people have nothing to go on. And the tattoo on the kidnapper seems to match Katia's. Let's see if your theory about her is correct.'

Bolshoi's body tensed up as he used the phone again. 'I need you to do a global search on airline and airport databases in the UK. I want to know if a single woman in her twenties is travelling with a young boy tonight from one of the London airports. She could be going anywhere, but Eastern Europe is the most likely destination. The woman may be using the name Katia Romanov. Or she may not. See what you can find. And I need it quick – so move fast.'

As soon as Bolshoi turned to him, Mac said, 'Calum won't be able to find that type of information—'

Bolshoi cut over him. 'I'm sure he won't – that's why I was talking with my people in Hamburg.'

So they waited, the silence crawling and crowding around them. The phone went off.

'You're sure about that? That's disappointing . . . OK. Spread the search. Try ferries, coaches – any means someone could use to flee the country.' When he'd ended the call he whispered to himself, 'Silly bitch. What is she playing at? Why didn't she call me . . . ?'

Mac grabbed Bolshoi's lapel. 'You know what's going on here, don't you?' Bolshoi looked down at his fist with a malevolent stare. For an instant, Mac tightened his fists. Then let go.

Bolshoi straightened his jacket for the second time. 'I don't speculate. I'm a businessman who only deals in facts . . .'

Mac couldn't let go of his anger. 'You're a fucking killer, just like Reuben and whoever snuffed Elena's life out . . .'

The sound of the phone stopped his rant.

Bolshoi quickly answered. 'OK . . . That makes sense. Good work. I'm hoping to be back tomorrow, I haven't decided how.'

Bolshoi tapped the steering wheel with his phone. He took a receipt that had been left on the dashboard and made some notes on the back of it. 'Do you know London Metropolitan Airport?'

'Sure. It's only five miles away. Up the river from St Katharine Docks.'

'It seems that your theory might be right . . . Or wrong, we'll see, but it's the only lead we have. A woman booked an air ambulance to fly to Switzerland with a sick child tonight. It's flying in an hour's time. I suspect that's her.'

'An air ambulance? They cost a fortune . . .'

'She's got money – too much money, in fact. I have spoiled her a little.' Bolshoi was lost in thought. 'We need to get down there before she goes and I suggest we take my car.' He threw his car keys at Mac. "You drive."

ninety-three

2 a.m.

The car careered down the road. They went down main roads, honking traffic out of the way and shooting lights. London passed by in a fast mist of disjointed colours. The roads melted away and soon signs for the airport jutted out on the side of the roads. Above them, red and white lights flashed and turned as planes took off and landed. Mac brought the Bolshoi's car to a halt once they got past the barriers. Then slid his hands on his lap.

On the other side of a security fence, various planes were parked up or waiting their turn to taxi to the runway. Among them was a small red and white jet with a red cross on its tail. A trail of vapour was coming from its twin engines. Bolshoi took out the receipt from his top pocket that he'd written on earlier. He checked the number and name on the fuselage and then wrinkled the paper and threw it out of the window. 'That's it.'

The two men looked around on the other side of the fence for any sign of a woman and child. There was none. But they could see a pilot wandering around performing pre-flight checks. Mac leaned over the steering wheel, but slid his hands closer to the seat between his legs as he searched harder before saying, 'They must be inside the airport building, so we'd better go into the terminal.'

He felt a sudden coldness against his temple. Mac didn't

need to turn to know what that meant. But he did, anyway, to find Bolshoi holding a semi-automatic against his head. 'I'm sorry, my friend, but you aren't going anywhere. Your day-long vendetta is over.'

Bolshoi was cold, crisp and to the point. 'I haven't come down here to help you solve Elena's murder. I'm here to find out what's happening to Katia. Your presence will only be one of those boring complications, so I'm afraid it's goodbye.'

He shoved his hand into Mac's waistband and took his gun.

Mac had been ready for this. He had known Bolshoi wouldn't need him after they'd arrived. He sneered, 'I'm afraid it's not quite that simple, *my friend*. Don't you think I figured out that you could've tracked Katia down on your own through your contacts? The only reason you needed me along for the ride was to make sure you got me out of the way permanently.'

His hands between his legs, he slipped a finger into the pin of one of the grenades he'd stolen from the hit men earlier. Very carefully, he used the palm of his hand to show his explosive insurance policy to Bolshoi.

The Russian nodded. 'You'll be long dead before you can pull the pin.'

'Probably. But possibly not. You've seen plenty of men killed, haven't you? Strange things happen when shots get fired into people – and I only need a fraction of a second. Or perhaps my muscles will reflex in my death throes and the pin will get pulled anyway. Go on – I've been ready to die all day . . .'

Silence.

Bolshoi kept the gun in place.

Finally, 'I like you, Mac. It's too bad you haven't wised up like Calum and gone into business on your own. I could put some work your way . . .'

Mac turned his head slightly and smiled. Bolshoi smiled back. Without taking his eye or the pistol off Mac, he reached behind his back with one arm. Unlocked the door. 'I'm going to find Katia. You do as you please – but I'm warning you now, if you cross my path in the coming hour, I will kill you without hesitation.'

Bolshoi scrambled backwards and disappeared into the night.

ninety-four

Mac didn't follow at once. He knew the sorts of cars that high-end technicians supplied to people like Bolshoi. They always had high-quality concealed weapons in the dashboard or bodywork. He flipped various harmless buttons until, with a tug on the cigarette lighter, a hidden walnut panel opened near the gear stick and a drawer hummed as it ejected. Inside were two pistols. Mac inspected them and chose the high-capacity, low-recoil Glock. Checked the magazine. Fully loaded.

Running was going to bring him attention he didn't need, so Mac got out of the car and walked smartly across the car park to the doors of the terminal. He peered through the glass. Bolshoi wasn't hard to find. It was late in the day and there weren't many people around. The Russian was deep in conversation with a woman on the information desk. She was trying to explain something to her visitor, but didn't seem to be getting very far. The conversation seemed to heat up. But then Bolshoi seemed to cool everything down by backing off, raising his hands in what Mac was sure was an act of apology. He stopped for a few moments and then headed off in another direction. From his vantage point, Mac couldn't see where that was.

The automatic doors slid open and Mac took a few steps inside. He wasn't in the slightest doubt that, given the chance, Bolshoi would follow through with his threat and shoot him.

A quick glance around revealed no sign of his man. Slowly and carefully, keeping a constant eye on the doors and entry points, Mac walked over to the information desk. The woman on duty was all smiles when he showed his badge. But her smile cooled when he asked about the air ambulance.

'As I explained to a rather rude gentleman who raised the same issue a few moments ago, I have no information about private flights or a mother and son who may be travelling. I suggest you contact the company that's arranging the journey.'

Dead end. He looked in the direction that Bolshoi had gone, but there was no indication of the where or the why. There were doors with 'no admittance', 'staff only' and 'security clearance area'; there were toilets and a chapel. But no obvious places a Russian gangster might be pursuing his enquiries. Mac moved back outside, a little faster this time, and over to the security fence. The air ambulance was gently taxiing backwards and forwards, preparing to pick up its 'delivery'. But there was no sign that Bolshoi had got through any security cordons and was lying in wait for Katia.

Back in the terminal, he twisted round – they were here somewhere, but where? Where? A uniformed airport worker to the left caught the corner of his eye. He kept his gaze pinned on him as a solution started to form in his mind. Distract the worker, disable him, steal his uniform and attempt to get airside with it. Determined, he started forward. Only got half a metre to the left before he heard the voice behind him.

'Uncle Mac.'

Mac twisted round. In a chair that was far too big for him sat Milos.

'Milos, who brought you here?' Mac asked as he sat beside the child.

Milos's face was pasty, his shoulders slightly hunched as if he was in pain – which no doubt he was, Mac decided, remembering the last time he'd seen the boy, lying in a fretful sleep in a hospital bed.

The boy gazed up at him, his eyes red as if he'd been crying. 'Uncle Mac – do you know where my dad is? I don't want to go to Swissiland. I want my dad.'

Mac gently caught the boy's shoulders in his large hands. 'Did Auntie Katia bring you here?'

The child's voice dipped to a whisper. 'I'm not allowed to say.'

'Why not?'

'It's private. I'm not supposed to say anything to anybody.'

'Don't worry, I know Katia . . .'

'She's not called Katia, her name's Natasha . . .'

'Where's she gone?'

Milos looked confused, as if trying to find the right words. 'Some men from the airport wanted to talk to her. Her name came booming around the room.' Mac quickly figured he meant through the loudspeaker. 'But we weren't here – we were in the other room. She's gone with them. She says it won't take long. She told me not to talk to anybody.'

Mac patted his head. 'She won't mind you talking to me because she told me she'd changed her mind. You aren't going to Switzerland any more. All she wants is for you to have a good night's sleep.'

'Will I see my dad in the morning?'

The sonless father looked into the eyes of the fatherless son. Mac hated lying, but at the moment the one thing this child didn't need was the truth. 'I'm sure you will.'

Milos yawned and nodded, so Mac reached over to pick him up, but stopped when he saw a well-dressed woman walking towards them. His arms fell back as he tried to see her face. But he couldn't make out her features because her head was down. She got closer. Closer.

'Milos, if I tell you to hide under the chair, make sure you do it.'

Mac didn't check the boy's face to see if he understood his command because he only had time to see the woman. She got closer. So close . . . Raised her head. Middle-aged, twin-set-and-pearls membership stamped all over her.

'Excuse me, young man.' She addressed Mac in one of those clipped English accents where the speaker doesn't appear to be moving their lips. 'I left a bag there – have you seen it?'

At the shake of his head, she rolled her eyes. 'Fuck. I expect the bastards have taken it away and blown it up.'

With that she turned and stomped away.

'Do you want me to play hide-and-seek now, Uncle Mac?'

Mac didn't answer. He couldn't take Milos to safety as planned, not with the chance that Katia-Natasha might appear.

The boy yawned again. 'I'm tired. Can we go now . . . ?'

'Not . . .' But Mac never finished the sentence. He noticed the boy's eye was fixed on something behind them. He turned to find Bolshoi standing over them.

ninety-five

The Russian stood motionless, looking down at the man and boy. Walked round and took a seat next to Mac. 'Is this the kid?' When he got no answer he whispered, 'Katia can't be far away then.'

'Please, don't start anything now, we don't want Milos involved, do we?'

Bolshoi grunted and gestured at Reuben's son, who was confused and alarmed by Uncle Mac's new friend. 'He was involved from the day he was born. And please don't ask me to believe that this child's welfare will stop you doing what you have to do, any more than it will stop me doing what I have to do.'

Mac looked down at Milos and wondered if that was true. Bolshoi sneered at him because he knew he was right. 'Make sure . . .'

Bolshoi broke off and looked urgently over at the door to the administration block, from where a figure in a plain grey tracksuit and hood – pulled down like a mediaeval monk's – had emerged.

'Katia?' Bolshoi whispered as he jumped up.

He started power-walking to the figure that had stopped just as Mac shot up.

'Katia! It's me!' Bolshoi's voice grew louder as his feet picked up speed.

'Get under the seat,' Mac ordered Reuben's son.

'Katia. It's me . . .'

Katia tipped her chin higher just as Bolshoi shifted in Mac's eye line, masking his view of her face. Suddenly Bolshoi stumbled.

'Katia?'

With a sharp one-two move, the shape of Katia's body changed as her hand whipped out. Only when someone screamed did Mac realise what she held in her hand. A semi-automatic pistol. She pointed it at Bolshoi and pumped the trigger.

ninety-six

2:30 a.m.

The side of Bolshoi's head exploded and he toppled backwards as another volley hit him in the chest. Mac dropped down and rolled to the side as people scattered and screamed. He pulled his head up to see Katia running towards a departure gate.

As he shot to his feet he yelled at the woman with the lost bag, 'Make sure the kid under the chair is looked after.' Then he pulled out the Glock and set off after Elena's sister.

There would be no escape for her. With fences and waterways around the airport barring her escape, and plenty of armed security available, the killer was caught like a rat in a trap. After seeing the professional, almost gleeful, way Bolshoi had been cut down, Mac ran past a desk where someone was yelling, 'Gunfire in the hall . . . how the heck do I know . . . ?' The person ducked when they saw Mac and the gun.

'Armed police!' he shouted as he ran through the security area, jumping over metal detectors and scanning machines. Then along a glass corridor towards the departure gates. Out on the tarmac, waiting patiently, was the air ambulance. No sign of Katia. Mac pumped two rapid bullets into the glass that separated him from the plane. The glass shrieked as it shattered. He stepped outside onto the tarmac. Caught his breath in the cold wind and looked around.

'Identify yourself,' a voice screamed behind him.

Mac turned to find two Airport Special Unit cops pointing their sub-machines at him. 'My name's Calum Burns. Security detail. TY45 Section.' Mac knew the men wouldn't have the time to check. 'You need to get inside the terminal building now. There's a smartly dressed young Asian man shouting religious slogans and carrying a rucksack. I'll check out here.' But they hesitated. 'You need to go now; there are women and children inside.'

That got them motoring away from him. He didn't want anyone else chasing his quarry. Katia was all his. But where was she? What would he do in a similar situation? Not head back to the terminal building, that was for sure. There were plenty of places to hide: refuelling lorries, staircases, buses, stepways, and of course a number of planes parked up and left where they'd been abandoned when the airport went into lockdown.

He fixed his gaze on the air ambulance again. Lights off but the engines were still running. It was a hundred yards away, so Mac bent slightly and rushed over. As he came round the front wheel, he noticed a small staircase propped up against the fuselage. Ten steps maybe. He ran his gaze up the temporary staircase, but froze when something flashed out at the top. A hood. A shadowed face.

Katia.

Startled, she jerked her head back in. Mac stormed up the stairs, weapon at the ready. He caught a flash of paramedic greens and a hood as he reached the top. She tried to slam the passenger door in his face. He tried to force her back, but she increased the pressure. Mac shoved his gun into the small gap between the door and frame, but half an arm shot out, displaying a red star tattoo. Katia dug her fingers into his wrist, trying to twist his gun away. Mac felt the door start to give, so he pushed on it with brute strength. But then he almost fell through the door as the pressure on the other side let up completely.

He stumbled, pushing out his arm to stop himself falling, slamming the door open. His head came up as he saw Katia rushing forwards. Quickly he straightened up and rushed inside the plane. He saw Katia's figure run into the cockpit. He belted forward. But he was too late. The cockpit door slammed in his face. The lock turned.

Mac hammered on the solid metal with his fists. 'Katia. Open the fucking door or I'm going to shoot it off.' His fists beat in time to his screaming, 'Open the door, you murdering bitch.'

He stood back. Aimed the Glock at the lock. But he tumbled back as the plane shook. There was a noise out on the wings. A gentle plume of fumes was visible outside as the engines powered up. The plane juddered and lurched forward. He went back to the door.

'I'm warning you,' Mac picked up his yelling. 'I'll shoot the engines out and kill the pair of us. Suits me – at least you'll be dead.'

The aircraft veered shakily to the right and he fell to the side, clutching a piece of medical monitoring equipment. The plane began moving down one of the short runways in jerks and bumps, like a car being manoeuvred by a learner driver. Suddenly a window was blown out by a volley of bullets. Mac instinctively ducked.

'Hear that, Katia? They're shooting. You'll never make it.'

The plane dropped slightly to the left as the tyres on that side were shot out. It veered off course, close to the side of the disused former docks that bordered the runway. It slowed and pulled back to the right before sinking again as the tyres on that side were blown to tatters by gunfire. Through the shattered window, Mac could see parts of the wing being shot away. The bare metal of the wheel rims scattered sparks everywhere as they scraped along the runway. The engines became louder as the plane picked up speed, but the shooting stopped as they moved out of range. Mac went over to the window and leaned out into the cold air rushing by. He thought they were doing about 50 mph. Not enough to take off but enough to turn the plane into a fireball at the other end. He went back to the cockpit door.

'Katia – why did you kill Elena? Are you listening? Crash the fucking plane, but tell me why you killed your sister . . . ?'

The plane see-sawed as the ground became more uneven under its groaning, screeching and rubber-less wheels. The nose rose slightly and then fell back down. Mac rushed back to the window. They were out of runway and in front of them was the perimeter fence. Behind that several cops were standing and a police car was parked up. The engines howled and the crazed plane began to accelerate wildly. Mac ducked from the window as it crashed through the fence, sending the car spinning off and the policemen scattering in all directions. Mac crouched on the floor, head tucked into his body as the plane went into its death spiral. The nose wheel collapsed and the front scraped the concrete underneath. It spun round like a drunk and one wing broke off before it ground to a halt facing back the way it had come.

Mac coughed as the overwhelming tang of kerosene filled his nostrils and smoke filled the bodywork of the wrecked aircraft. Shots rang from the cockpit: that was enough to get Mac back on his feet. The cockpit door was bent and buckled but still solid. He pulled it a few more times before doubling back. The passenger door was hanging open. Mac jumped down and ran to the front of the plane. One of the windows had been shot out. He climbed on the nose and peered inside. Empty. When he turned and looked across the blasted, post-industrial landscape, he saw a figure running.

ninety-seven

ninety-seven

Mac knew that the plane was going to blow any moment, so he ran. But not quick enough. An almighty explosion ripped through the plane. An orange, red and billowing black fireball and twisted metal erupted into the air. Mac was lifted up and tossed in the air. He landed hard on a patch of grass. Lay winded for a while, his ears ringing. But he didn't have time to rest; if it was the last thing he ever did on this earth, he was going to hunt Katia down.

Slowly he rose, hearing voices and lights coming his way. He had to get out of here before they reached him. So he mustered up the power and took off. Just kept moving and moving. Finally, near a disused pumping station, he stopped. Bent down, resting his palms flat against his thighs, filling his lungs with strong lugs of oxygen. Then he raised his head, saw, in the distance, billowing red, orange and black from the burning plane. He did a three-sixty look around but could see no sign of his target.

'Shit, shit, shit.'

There was no way he was going to find her now. The plane had been a confined space, but now they were back in the open, she could be anywhere. But he wasn't giving up. Clicking his body onto autopilot, he jogged away from the pumping station and soon found himself going down a lane that was bordered by council blocks, betting and pawn shops towards a bridge. Crossing the bridge was a distinctive red, white and blue Docklands Light Railway train. He was surprised the trains were still running, but remembered that the new mayor of London was piloting a three-month overnight service to meet public demand.

If you're lost, follow railways, they always lead somewhere. Mac remembered the instructions from his undercover training.

He went under the bridge and turned left, following a road that bordered the railway. Abruptly stopped when he saw something on the ground. He reached for it. Green paramedic's top. He threw it back and started power-running. Reached the open-air Docklands Light Railway train station. He leap-frogged the gate that had no night staff to man it. Walked up the steps to the platform for trains into the city.

Passengers were gathered by the fence, curiously peering at the flames and smoke in the distant sky. All except one, a hooded figure sitting on her own at the dark, shadowy end of the platform. He moved towards her. At the same time the figure lifted her head. She watched as Mac drew closer and seemed to be becoming increasingly uncomfortable as he bore down on her.

Mac stood over her, slightly nervous that she'd made no attempt to flee and remembering she was armed.

'Had enough of running, Katia?'

'Sod off, you perv, or I'll call the cops.'

This wasn't Katia. A sound caught his attention, coming from the platform on the other side. He saw a hooded figure leaping up at a high wall, missing and slamming back down. A man jumped onto the track. The waiting passengers gasped as they watched him but he only had eyes for Katia. He scrambled up the platform as Katia sprang high against the wall again. This time her fingers gripped the edge. As Mac belted forwards, her legs began to frantically climb. He reached the bottom of the wall. Grabbed one of her legs. Dragged her down. She fell. Landed, her front hitting the wall.

'Nowhere left, Katia,' Mac threw high above the blast of cold wind. 'Just me and you.'

Finally she turned her face to him. Lifted her chin, clearing it of any shadows. Mac saw her face for the first time. Stumbled back.

'Elena?'

ninety-eight

2:40 a.m.

'Elena.' Stunned, he said her name again. This time it wasn't a question.

Even though the mingled platform light and shadows illuminated the grace of her nose, the breath beating out of her partially opened mouth, the blood rushing under and heating up the skin on her face, he still wouldn't believe what he was seeing. Any more than Bolshoi had done before he was gunned down, he now realised. His whole day flashed before him – the woman in the bath, the pursuit of Reuben, Sergei and Bolshoi, the car wash, Milos, Stevie . . .

'You set fire to your flat?' The words came out of him stuttering and confused, like he couldn't believe what he was asking her. 'You tried to kill me . . .'

He reached out to touch her, her bracelet dangling against his wrist. She flinched. Her movement broke the spell. The horror of what he'd been going through all day caught up with him. The power of the emotion overwhelmed him. He raised his hand and slapped her across the face. Her head snapped back. She held the pose, but only for a few seconds, then slowly moved her head dead centre, with defiance hot in her eyes.

'You set me up,' he said simply. 'Why? Was your life ever

really in danger? Was this fucked-up day all your idea to get me to take out Bolshoi?'

Elena twisted her lips together like she wasn't going to answer him. Then she unlocked her lips and spoke. 'You're an undercover cop. No matter how many people you killed, your people would always make sure you'd never go down for it. Bolshoi was the ultimate professional. I knew it would take a special professional to kill him.'

'How could you be so sure I would do it?'

'Because I left all the information you would need on my mobile phone. The texts that were signed Bolshoi but written by me. I left the simplest password on the phone for you to unlock it – 1,2,3,4. Once you had the information, you were meant to sit tight and just wait for Bolshoi to appear at eleven tonight. Of course I only realised later today that he was working with your government.'

So if Calum had given him the information from Elena's phone this morning, he'd probably have ended up killing Bolshoi. He hated to think he had something else to be thankful to Calum for, but he did.

'And I gave you a motive,' she carried on. 'I gave you a reason to live. And you needed one, didn't you? You felt helpless about what happened to your son. You weren't ever going to let yourself feel helpless again. So there was no way you were going to let anyone get away with killing me.'

'How did you find out I was a cop?'

'You were just too good to be true. I managed to get into your phone one night while you were sleeping . . .'

'Who was in the bath?' Then he remembered there was only one other person with a tattoo and he answered his own question before she could. 'Katia.'

Elena's breathing grew stronger.

'But the DNA?' he persisted.

She finally spoke. 'DNA that could only be traced back through our mother . . .' She drew in a ragged breath that left a streak of irritation across her face. 'I couldn't have made it any easier for you, Mac. How hard could it have been? I left those messages on my phone, you knew Bolshoi was coming to town. All you had to do was kill him to avenge my death for me . . .'

'But why? He was your guardian, protector, like a father to you . . .'

'He killed my father.' The fury of her words backhanded him across the face. 'He had to die . . .'

'So I was the instrument of your revenge?' The singed photograph he'd found in Elena's fireplace of the two men smiling flashed through his mind.

But it was like she didn't hear him, her voice continuing in a soft, faraway tone.

'My father was a captain who always turned down promotion because he wanted to be in the field with his comrades. His commanding officer was Major Andreas Ryatin . . .'

'Bolshoi?'

She gave a sharp nod. 'Their unit was ambushed and Andreas tried to save my father, but he was killed.' Her mouth twisted. 'I believed that for years – and then two nights ago at the reception at the embassy to celebrate with the other former comrades of my father, I found out different. The drink was flowing too freely and, just as I was ready to leave, one of the old timers grabbed me and wouldn't let go.'

Elena took another breath. 'He started cursing and saying how all of this was bullshit. How bad the war was, how messed-up everything was. That if the commanders-in-chief had really cared about the foot soldiers, what happened in the Valley of Death in August '88 would never have happened. I knew he was talking about my father so I let him speak. Can you understand what I felt when he told me that Major Ryatin was no hero, but had been treating the war as a business opportunity – stealing from the stores, organising desperate local girls into prostitution rings for scared soldiers; there were even rumours that he was doing deals with the enemy over guns and drugs. I told the vet to shut up, that he was wrong . . .'

The wind grew stronger around them, another sudden rush of noise in the distance gathering momentum.

Tears glittered in the bottom of Elena's eyes. 'But he wouldn't. That night in the valley, no one could find Ryatin, so my father, being the honourable man that he was, assumed command. It was turning into a bloodbath, so Father went looking for the major.' Her mouth twisted. 'And found him drunk, singing some peasant song about wine and women, hiding in a truck. They quarrelled and Ryatin shot him dead. Shot him like a dog. My father. They gave Bolshoi a fucking medal? For killing my father . . .'

'How could you have killed your sister . . . ?'

'But Katia wasn't my full blood, was she? After we left the embassy, we came back to my home and called our mother to find out if she knew about what Bolshoi had done.' She swallowed. 'She said she'd heard the rumours, but we shouldn't believe them. He was a *good* man. She was talking so much . . . you know, wildly . . .' Elena shook her head. 'It just came out that Katia was his daughter. How my mother had betrayed my wonderful father.'

Her nostrils flared. 'She said that she'd made a mistake.' The words wrenched from her with such passion that Mac thought she was going to double over in pain. 'Katia cried when she learned the truth, but I didn't care, she was still my little sister. I told her that we had to kill him, but she wouldn't do it. We quarrelled and she said she was going to call him . . .' She drew in another deep breath. 'I couldn't allow her to live because she knew what I was going to do. So I called you first to set up our meeting at the hotel. Then I told Katia that we needed to talk more, so I persuaded her to come to the hotel . . .'

'But you weren't on the hotel's security footage . . .'

"Because I used the fire exit round the back to get us in and picked the lock of the room. I had a change of clothing in my rucksack.' The tone of her words changed as if she felt genuine pain at murdering her sister. 'I gave her a drink laced with one of those date rape drugs . . . Dragged her to the bath. Put my clothes and bracelet on her and left my phone. Then I waited outside for you to come . . .'

"Knocked me out and killed her with my gun,' Mac finished.

Seeing the look of horror on Mac's face, Elena screamed, 'She was *his* daughter and she proved it morally when the crunch came . . .' She shoved out her arm, displaying the red star tattoo. '"To live with wolves you have to howl like a wolf."' She repeated the words proudly. 'She had a choice. To be my sister – or his daughter. She made her choice. And I made mine.'

'And what about all the other people you killed? The doctor? Sergei?'

Elena's face hardened. 'I took her to my doctor to confirm her pregnancy, so I needed to get rid of any evidence that I'd been one of his patients and the only way to make sure that happened was to shut up the doctor for good. And she might have told that maniac Sergei something. It wasn't me that marked him for death, but her.'

'How could you have killed her baby?'

Her answer was defiant. 'It was Bolshoi's blood, don't you understand? That baby would've become just another player. They were all players; they knew the risks. With the right kind of money, it was easy to hire the right type of men at such short notice to make sure the doctor and Sergei remained silent for ever. I was going to put them on Bolshoi's trail as well, but when I spoke to one of them I knew they'd fucked up, so I had to get rid of any traces of them as well.' She inhaled deeply. 'I could have killed you any time I liked . . .The fire at my home was just to keep you on your toes . . .'

'Don't kid yourself Elena. The fire was to keep me angry to find your "killer" You were just using me to carry out your dirty work . . .'

'You were doing the same thing Mac, just using me to carry out *your dirty work.* That's what undercover cops do – pretend to be someone they're not and wriggle and lie their way into another person's life.'

It was Mac's turn to sound bitter. 'If you're expecting me to get down on my knees and kiss your feet for keeping me alive?'

'Not me.' Her voice softened like the movement of the wind around them. 'Our baby.'

That shook him up. 'There is no baby. Katia was the one who was pregnant . . .'

'Are you sure about that? That's why Bolshoi had to die, so he couldn't hurt our baby as–'

'You're lying. You're a taker of life, not a giver . . .'

Suddenly the wind kicked up around them. A roaring sound gathered pace behind Mac. He half turned just as Elena's gaze intensified over his shoulder. A train coming in to the platform. Before Mac could react it had stopped and the doors opened. Mac instinctively went for the Glock, but he never made it because Elena started yelling and shrieking.

'Help! This man is attacking me. Help!'

Passengers streamed onto the platform.

'For God's sake, help me.'

Faces turned towards them, including a group of three young men. Elena backed up. And screamed. That galvanised the men into action. They moved towards Mac as Elena backed off some more.

'What's your game, pal?' one shouted at Mac.

'I'm a police—' But he didn't have time to finish the sentence before he caught a punch across the face. He toppled onto his back. They closed in around him to finish the job. He pulled out the Glock.

'Back the fuck way off,' he warned.

The men scattered. Mac jumped to his feet. Elena was gone. His gaze darted in the half-light.

Shit.

He couldn't see her. He looked right. Left. Looked . . . He found her, a running shadow heading for the footbridge that crossed to the other platform. The doors to the train closed as Mac ran the length of the platform. Heart pounding, he picked up pace as he leapt up the steps. Elena had reached the top. He sounded like a horse nearing the finishing line as he racked his speed to the next level. Mac reached the top as the Docklands train below began to shunt forwards. He didn't miss a beat as Elena climbed onto the parapet of the bridge. Elena braced herself. Let go.

'Bollocks,' Mac cursed as he leaned over to see her land on the roof of one of the carriages. Slipping and sliding, he was sure she was going to fall off. But Elena regained her balance and clung to the roof as the train picked up speed.

ninety-nine

The audience on the platforms below who'd been watching Elena's escape screamed, scattered and dived for cover as Mac began shooting wildly at anything that might possibly bring the departing train to a halt. He shot at junction boxes, signals and pylons until the magazine was empty. But the train rolled on.

He had one card left to play. Attached to his belt was the hand grenade that he'd threatened Bolshoi with earlier. He ran down to the now deserted platform. Pulled the pin and threw it onto the middle of the railway track. It rolled along the stones and came to rest. He watched, and only when it flashed did he remember that he was supposed to dive to the ground. The explosion threw him onto his back and sucked the air out of his lungs. The silent station reverberated to the sound of arcing electricity, falling stones and other debris. The track flashed and sparked in whites, blues and yellows with the hypnotic effect of a fireworks display.

When he recovered his wits, he looked down in the direction the train had gone. Fifty yards away, dark and silent, it had ground to a halt.

Like the train itself, his body and soul was at the end of the journey. He crawled on his hands and knees down the platform. Jumped up and ran the distance to where the train had stopped. The lights of the neighbouring towers lit up the roof of the train, but he could see no sign of Elena. He pressed on down the rails towards a bridge that carried the railway over a lock in the docks. Until he was tripped by a sack lying beside the tracks.

Only when the sack groaned with pain did Mac realise it was a body.

Elena.

He sat down and put his arm out to cradle her shoulder.

She stared back at him with an expression that reminded him of the woman he had once dared to dream of loving.

'I fell off,' she said hoarsely.

He used his shirt to wipe the cuts and scratches. Then began to fish around in his pocket for his phone.

She smiled at him in the half-light. 'You're not going to turn me in, are you?'

His thumb hovered over the phone, but he didn't press any buttons. 'Right now, you need an ambulance. We'll worry about the other things later.'

He called an ambulance. He realised how vulnerable he was, cradling this woman protectively. Because he knew how easily this other Elena could manipulate him. 'Can you get up?'

'I don't know. My ankle . . . Hurts.'

He pulled her to her feet anyway, ankle or no ankle. She slumped against him and he held her against his body.

'Help me escape, Mac. I haven't harmed anyone who didn't need harming. Even killing Katia – she was Bolshoi's daughter, as evil as he was. As for Reuben, Sergei and their gang, they would have all ended up dead anyway. I had to kill Bolshoi. It was no different to you setting out to kill the person who killed me. Remember what you said – anyone who harms me, you'll kill them. Help me get abroad and then we can meet again later. I was going to get in touch with you. I promise. I knew you wouldn't come to any harm. You're my Mac ... We could get a home in Europe. Me, you and the baby ...'

'Shut up, Elena ...'

But she wouldn't. 'Find somewhere quiet. I've got money. Loads of it from Katia. Bolshoi gave her lots of money, that's why she lived in that smart house. We could adopt Milos ...'

Mac pushed her away. She fell to the ground as her ankle gave away.

'And you were doing so well. Fancy reminding me of Milos ...'

He turned his back on her. Made one more phone call. 'Rio, listen. I've caught your killer. You might be a bit surprised at the perp, I'm afraid the DNA led you astray. I'm with her now. I'm taking her to hospital but it's nothing serious. When we're there, I'll call again and you can get some people sent over ... I'm not worried about Phil Delaney. He'll look after me.'

Mac rang off and turned back to Elena. But she was gone.

She was sitting on the parapet of the railway bridge, looking down at the cold inky water of the once busy but now ornamental docks.

Mac laughed at her. 'Going to throw yourself in? Go on then – you'll save everyone a lot of time.'

'I mean it. If you don't help me escape, I'm going in.'

'No, you're not. You kill other people – not yourself.'

He moved towards her but she raised herself on her hands and tilted forward. In spite of himself, he was worried. 'OK, take it easy. Don't do anything stupid.'

He backed off slightly and she sat back. Mac looked around. For the first time that day he was wondering where the authorities were. No police, no ambulance. But then he remembered the crashed plane and the gun and grenade-blasted station and decided they probably had other things to do. So he did what police officers are trained to do in these situations. He started to negotiate. 'Whatever you want I'll do, but come off the bridge first.'

'The only person who's coming off this bridge is you. Now.'

He raised his hands slowly and backed off. Retreated twenty or thirty yards back down the tracks. When it was safe to do so, he dropped down, using the embankment as cover, and checked back on the bridge. Elena was climbing off the parapet. She hobbled slowly across and disappeared on the other side. Mac took deep breaths and prepared to make one final effort. He crossed the bridge, ducking low, hugging the parapet, staying out of sight. But he couldn't resist taking a moment to look into the inky water forty feet below. He knew that water. He'd been swimming in it earlier and, with her wounded ankle, she wouldn't have lasted five minutes if she'd gone in. He shivered, as if the murk was closing over his own head. He felt a lightness; he seemed to be floating in the blackness. Faces from the past came in and out of focus. But were they real or were they in his mind?

He lurched forward again, shaking his head in a desperate effort to bring himself back. She'd be nearby and he had to be ready for her.

Something clubbed him once, twice, on the side of his head. His legs gave way, but an arm locked round his neck, preventing his fall. The world swam around even more as he was dragged backwards.

'You should have let me go into the water,' Elena hissed into his ear.

He tried to move but was too dazed. With a strength he didn't know she had, Elena hooked an arm under his thigh and half lifted and rolled him onto the parapet. She shoved him, making his head hang over the side.

Viewing the ripples of blackness below upside down was a scary sight. The dark, gently moving shapes and movement in the water seemed to form into a figure. Was that Stevie down there? His life ebbing away all over again?

When he felt her shove him again, he knew she wanted him to follow the fate of his son. Abruptly he found the strength from somewhere and seized her wrists; Elena sank her teeth into his fingers. He groaned, but didn't let go. Used her body weight to pull himself upwards. Snapped her across his lap. Now it was his turn to dangle her head down towards the water. But he pushed too hard and Elena tipped over the edge.

They did a strange dance as his hands slipped from her wrists and one of her hands snapped round his lower arm. She swung in the unforgiving, cold night breeze. Her bracelet on his wrist slipped down and the edge of the rabbit charm touched her skin.

'Just keep looking at me. Hold on . . .' Mac shouted.

'I never did tell you the end of the Russian nursery rhyme about the rabbit and the hunter and how it ended happily,' she said between quick puffs of breath as her face contorted with fear. 'Everyone thinks the rabbit is dead because the hunter shoots her. But when he gets her home, he realises she was never really dead at all, but alive.'

Then the rhythm of her body changed as it went slack, dragging against him like a dead weight. *What the fuck was she doing?* Her fingers started loosening.

'Elena?' he shot out.

A tiny smile hitched up one side of her mouth. 'Me living through my father, you living through your son . . .' Her smile died. 'Why couldn't we find our own paths to happiness?'

She let go of his arm. He closed his eyes as she disappeared into the bleak blackness of the water below.

one-hundred

One year later

'My boy was the best son a man could ever have. He liked a laugh, a beer, and all he wanted to do was help people . . .'

Mac and Rio sat next to each other as they listened to DC Martin's father talk to the packed congregation at the memorial service for his son. The police from The Fort had turned out in force, all decked out in their uniforms. Most of the top brass were in attendance as well. Mac could see Rio's hands trembling in her lap, but her face remained stony. Emotionless. He knew she was hurting, had been tearing up for the last twelve months, but he couldn't get her to talk about it. She'd refused to take time off, refused to see the in-house shrink. She'd been there for him two years back to shoulder some of his pain, but she wouldn't let him do the same now.

'To all of you who are parents,' Mr Martin carried on. 'To all of you who have sons. To all of you who have daughters – cherish them. Guide them. Lend them a hand to help them reach their dreams. We thank you all for taking the time to join us in remembering our beautiful boy.'

Abruptly Rio stood up and hustled past Mac, her legs banging against his knees. No one said anything as she rushed down the aisle and out of the church. Mac got up and followed her.

* * *

Mac found her by a tree on the other side of the road, smoking. She'd given up the vice a number of years ago, but had taken it back up soon after Jamie Martin's death.

'Cry,' he said softly when he reached her.

Rio flicked her eyes up at him. Then back down. She dropped the cigarette and ground her heel into it. 'Yeah, well, crying and praying to the Lord aren't going to bring him back.'

'Funny, I thought the same back in the clinic. I kept holding on and holding it in and then one day it just burst out. I couldn't stop.' He blew out a long pulse of air. 'That was the first step on my journey back. Sure, I've got a long way to go, but I'm getting back into my groove.'

His mind swam back to that fatal night at the dock. The police had dredged the water but no sign of Elena's body had been found. An unrecovered body meant it had likely been drawn downriver and swept out to sea. Case closed. Mac had spent four months inside Springfield Clinic, detoxifying both his body and mind. He still had flashbacks and that feeling of being held down in a locked box, but not as much any more. Healing took time, and he had all the time in the world.

He opened his mouth again, but Rio violently waved her hand, anticipating what he was going to say. 'And don't say it wasn't my fault . . .'

'You told him not to come in, to wait in the car . . .'

'But I should've dragged him by the scruff of his neck and dumped him in the car myself.'

The cold wind circled as spots of rain tumbled around them.

He took a step closer to her. 'Why don't you come back and talk to . . .'

She shook her head. 'His parents? I can't face them. Don't know what to say to them. Look, I'm out of here.' And before he could say anything else, she was gone.

Mac swore as he watched her figure growing smaller in the

distance. She never said it, but he wondered sometimes if she blamed him. If he hadn't gone loco over some woman who'd been tagging him along by his eager nuts, maybe Jamie Martin would still be alive? Maybe, maybe, maybe . . . ? No, he'd stopped living that type of life. He'd been back on the job for a couple of weeks now, this time as a suit in Phil's team. Surprisingly, he liked being tied to a desk. Strange, he never thought he would. Instead of going back to the church, he headed back to The Research Unit.

Mac was grateful that there was no one around back at base, just the quiet hum of the old-fashioned central heating system to keep him company. He sat at his desk and picked up the framed photo of Stevie he now kept there. Now when he gazed at his son's face, there was still guilt, but it was slowly fading. He wasn't sure if he'd ever get rid of it, but he felt a kind of peace he hadn't before, and maybe that was going to have to be enough.

As he placed the photo back, he noticed a padded envelope on the floor, near the corner of his office door. He must've not noticed it on his way in. Mac got up. Walked over. Picked it up.

His name was written on the front in large black letters. No name or address on the back. He peeled the envelope open. Peered inside. Small, rectangular piece of paper. Drew it out. A photo of a smiling baby. Confused, he kept staring at it. Why would someone send him a picture of a baby? Maybe it had been delivered to the wrong address; the wrong Mac. He turned the photo over. Writing. He read it, rocking his whole world.

'I named him after you. His name is John Mac . . .'

No, it couldn't be . . . Quickly, he flipped it back to the baby. That's when he saw them – the baby's eyes. His Stevie's blue, blue eyes. And a tiny bracelet round the baby's wrist with a small metal blob that Mac couldn't make out. He didn't need to see it to know it was a bunny-rabbit charm.

Mac staggered to the wall. Leaned against it. His legs gave way as he slid down.

acknowledgements

It's traditional for authors to thank their agents but in this particular case, without the help of Thomas Stofer and Amanda Preston at LBA, this book wouldn't have happened. Massive thanks to them, especially Thomas devising new plots as he cycled into work. And good luck Thomas in all your new adventures.

Another shining light in the Vendetta venture is the amazing and wonderful Kate Howard and her team at Hodder.

Special, special thanks to Lee Child for always being only an email away from giving advice and his ever precious time to read Vendetta.

And of course, to mine and Tony's long suffering and ever supportive families.

Blood Sister
Dreda Say Mitchell

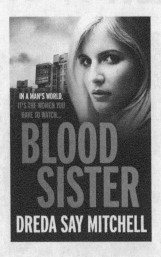

There are two ways out of Essex Lane Estate,
better known as The Devil. You make good,
or you turn bad.

Jen Miller is determined not to make the same
mistakes her mother did. She's waiting to find herself
a good job and a decent man.

Her younger sister Tiff is running errands for a
gangster and looking for any opportunity for fun
and profit. But she might just be in over her
head . . .

At least they can rely on each other.

Can't they?

HODDER

ENTER A WORLD

Four women.
One last job.

GEEZER GIRLS

GEEZER
GIRLS

DREDA SAY MITCHELL

'As good as it gets ... fiction's brightest new voice' *Lee Child*

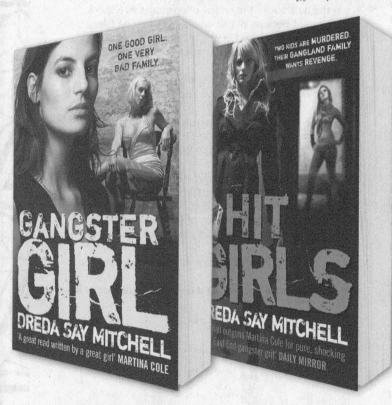